"If you try to fence me into their world I swear I'll jump in the Mersey. You knew when you married me that I was not . . . domesticated."

"I did, and I shudder to think what I would do if you were, my pet, but it would be pleasant to come home sometimes to find you gracing my fireside with a bit of embroidery in your hands."

She glanced sharply at him and then began to laugh when she saw the glimmer of humour in his eyes.

"You wouldn't like that at all, Ben Maddox. I don't know why you married me but I do know it wasn't for my domestic accomplishments."

"True, my love. You suit me as you are . . ."

By the same author in Coronet

The Mallow Years
Shining Threads
A Day Will Come
All the Dear Faces
There Is No Parting
The Woman from Browhead
Echo of Another Time
The Silence of Strangers
A World of Difference
Promises Lost
The Shadowed Hills
Strand of Dreams
Tomorrow's Memories
Not a Bird Will Sing
When Morning Comes
Beyond the Shining Water
Angel Meadow

About the author

Audrey Howard was born in Liverpool in 1929. Before she began to write she had a variety of jobs, among them hairdresser, model, shop assistant, cleaner and civil servant. In 1981 she wrote the first of her novels when she was out of work and living in Australia. There are now more than twenty, and her fourth, *The Juniper Bush*, won the Boots Romantic Novel of the Year Award in 1988. She now divides her time between her childhood home, St Anne's on Sea, Lancashire, and a home in the Yorkshire Dales.

RIVERS OF THE HEART

Audrey Howard

CORONET BOOKS
Hodder & Stoughton

Copyright © 2000 by Audrey Howard

The right of Audrey Howard to be identified as the Author
of the Work has been asserted by her in accordance with the
Copyright, Designs and Patents Act 1988.

First published in Great Britain in 2000 by
Hodder and Stoughton
First published in paperback in 2000 by
Hodder and Stoughton
A division of Hodder Headline

A Coronet Paperback

10 9 8 7 6 5 4 3 2 1

All rights reserved. No part of this publication may be
reproduced, stored in a retrieval system, or transmitted, in any
form or by any means without the prior written permission
of the publisher, nor be otherwise circulated in any form of
binding or cover other than that in which it is published and
without a similar condition being imposed on the subsequent
purchaser.

All characters in this publication are fictitious and any
resemblance to real persons, living or dead is purely
coincidental.

British Library Cataloguing in Publication Data

Howard, Audrey
Rivers of the heart
1. Love stories
I. Title
823.9′14[F]

ISBN 0 340 71812 9

Typeset by Palimpsest Book Production Limited,
Polmont, Stirlingshire
Printed and bound in Great Britain by
Mackays of Chatham plc, Chatham, Kent

Hodder and Stoughton
A division of Hodder Headline
338 Euston Road
London NW1 3BH

1

Irritably Kitty Hayes tapped the toe of her high-heeled satin dancing slipper on the well-polished wooden floor of the drawing-room which, for this special evening, had been transformed into a ballroom. Not a very large ballroom, to be sure, but with the furniture, except for the small chairs, cleared out, it was big enough to allow fifteen to twenty couples to swirl about in one another's arms in a dipping waltz, which the young among them were doing with great enthusiasm. A shifting andante of pale colours, white and ivory, cream, primrose and apple blossom, for the ladies were mostly unmarried, mixed with the traditional black and white of the gentlemen's evening dress.

One of the couples was Kitty's brother and sister, Freddy and Ciara. Kitty leaned forward, glaring at them in a most unladylike way, one elbow on her knee, her chin in her hand, her lips clamped tightly together, and the man who lounged indolently against the frame of the French windows, which stood open, narrowed his eyes. The smoke from his cigar was not the reason. Kitty did not see him, nor anyone but the couple on whom her whole attention was riveted; the man turned his head to see who it was she was looking at, surprised to find it was her own brother and sister. He turned again to see her slump back in her chair with a sudden impatient movement. The lady beside her, who had been conversing with another, turned and spoke to her sharply but over the sound of the music, the laughter, the chattering voices of the other guests he could not hear what she said.

"What is the matter with you, Kitty?" Nancy Hayes was asking her daughter, her manner implying she knew full well what the matter was but hoped somehow to avert it.

"Just look at them, Mother. It really is a disgrace."

"What is?"

"Freddy and Ciara. Surely they are aware that it is the height of bad manners to dance exclusively with another member of the family when we have guests. James Lambert particularly wanted to waltz with Ciara, you know he did, but she refused him, and Freddy should be performing his duties as host by dancing with—"

"As you should, Kitty, since it is your party as much as Freddy's. I have seen you refuse the last three gentlemen who asked you so you can hardly—"

"Boors, all of them." Kitty tossed her head disdainfully. "They can talk of nothing but how well I paint which is utter rubbish and how light I am on my feet and at the same time they do nothing but step all over them. I'd rather sit out and gossip with you and Aunt Jennet than—"

"Keep your voice down, Kitty, and behave yourself or you will upset your father. And it would please me if you would accept the next gentleman who asks for you, no matter who it is."

"Oh, Mother," Kitty wailed, causing a few heads to turn and a few faces to take on an expression that said Kitty Hayes was up to her tricks again. "It could be old man Baker . . ."

"*Kitty!*"

". . . or worse still Mr Pickup who must be ninety if he's a day."

"Then perhaps that will persuade you to accept a gentleman of your own generation when he asks."

Kitty subsided mutinously, sliding down in her chair and crossing her arms over her full breasts and her mother let out a relieved sigh of exasperation. Kitty was the biggest trial and tribulation in her mother's otherwise harmonious life and her one wish was to see her fall in love with some suitable gentleman, marry and leave home, thus giving Nancy Hayes and the rest of the household some welcome peace.

Her daughter had been well known as a "little madam", her old nanny's words, from the day, as an infant little more than a few months old, she had discovered how to manipulate those who had her in their care. As a young child she had been rebellious of all discipline, truculent when denied her own way, given to fits of red-faced temper when crossed, but as cherubic as an angel when she got the better of her opponent. To avoid the furious and wearing bouts of tantrums they had given in to her, which had been a mistake since she had grown up believing she had the God-given right to do as she pleased. She was afraid of nothing, even as a small child. She was proud and haughty and yet could be warm-hearted, generous, fun-loving and full of charm when she was in the mood, and those around her could not help but respond to her. A complex child and young girl and now, on this her twenty-third birthday, when her parents had hopes that she might have grown out of her stormy explosions of fire and fury, here she was acting like a spoiled child and all because Freddy and Ciara were dancing together more than she liked. Her mother agreed with her that it was not good manners for two members of the same family to dance even one dance together on an occasion such as this but short of tearing Ciara out of Freddy's arms, which was what Kitty longed to see happen, there was nothing their mother could do about it.

The man on the far side of the room straightened up. Looking about him for an ashtray he stubbed out his cigar and began to move round the edge of the dance floor. Several mamas sat up eagerly and their daughters began to simper and shyly cast down their eyes, thinking he was about to approach them, but he continued to saunter round the room, avoiding the whirling, laughing dancers until he reached the slumped figure of Kitty Hayes who was staring sullenly at her own feet.

He bowed gracefully to Nancy Hayes who smiled up at him. A warm smile which seemed to light a candle at the back of her golden-brown eyes and which, as her lips parted, revealed her even white teeth. Though he knew she was the mother of six children he could scarce believe it, amazed by her exquisite figure and loveliness. She was, without doubt, one of the most beautiful and serene women he had ever seen. Apart from a small, unusual scar on her cheek her features were perfect. He had met her only for the first time this evening, she and her family, but, by God, they were a good-looking lot and the young woman beside her, her eldest daughter, was surely the most stunning of them all.

"Aah, Mr Maddox," Mrs Hayes said, holding out her gloved hand over which he bent his head. "I hope you are enjoying yourself."

"Yes, indeed, Mrs Hayes. It was kind of you to invite me."

"You were a good friend to my son at school, so he tells me, so I was glad that you were in Manchester and able to come. It gave us an opportunity to meet you at last. We have heard so much of the heroic Maddox." Her smile deepened and so did his.

"Thank you, ma'am, but I did nothing."

She turned graciously to the lady on her right. "May I introduce my dearest friend, Miss Jennet Williams. She and I have known one another for . . . oh, how many years is it, Jennet? Well, more than I like to count. Jennet, Mr Maddox is a school friend of Freddy's. You have probably heard Freddy speak of him. They were at Deanhampton together but not in the same year."

He bowed again and took her friend's hand.

"Miss Williams."

"Mr Maddox."

"And this is my eldest daughter Kitty, Mr Maddox. Kitty, Mr Maddox is Freddy's—"

"Yes, I heard," Kitty muttered, her eyes still fixed on the laughing couple who were waltzing by. She did not even look up into the suddenly cold face of the man who had greeted her mother. It was an attractive face, lines already beginning to be chiselled about his mouth and eyes which were a deep brown surrounded by thick, dark lashes. His hair was a shade between chocolate and chestnut, smoothly brushed, his skin as dark as a gypsy's. He had a strong mouth with a curl of good humour at each corner, inclined to lift in a smile but not at this precise moment.

"Kitty!" Nancy Hayes's voice was as crisp as the ice that froze in the garden pond in January and Kitty, despite her determination to be as awkward as she could since she felt so miserable, looked up into the unsmiling face of the stranger.

"How d'you do," she snapped ungraciously, then turned away to stare moodily at the dancers.

"How do you do, Miss Hayes. As you do not appear to be taken for this waltz I wonder if I might . . ."

"Thank you, Mr . . . er . . . but I am not dancing at the moment." She did not even glance at him again and his face tightened ominously. The two ladies watched with bated breath.

"I can see that, Miss Hayes. That is why I am here. Now, if the ladies will excuse us . . ."

Bowing in the direction of the open-mouthed Mrs Hayes and Miss Williams, Ben Maddox took Kitty's hand, hauling her to her feet, not caring overmuch how roughly he did it, put his arms about her and whisked her into the centre of the circling dancers. She was so astounded her feet automatically performed the right steps, her left hand rested on his shoulder and her right hand fell into his left.

It did not last long, that confoundment. She knew she could not shame her mother and father, particularly her father, by creating a scene here among the guests, old friends who had known her grandparents, those who were in the social circle in which her parents moved and friends of hers and Freddy and her other brother and sisters, but, dammit, she'd not speak to this bastard nor remain with him for long. As soon as the music stopped she'd be off the floor and away back to Freddy, with whom she meant to have the next dance no matter what the conventions might be.

"Do you know, Miss Hayes, you are quite the rudest young woman I have ever come across," her partner told her conversationally, nodding at Freddy as he glided past with his sister, "and why your papa doesn't have you whipped and locked up with nothing but bread and water I can't imagine. I know I would if you were mine."

For an incredulous moment she was speechless, then, forgetting her intention not to engage in conversation with this overbearing bully who had dragged her on to the floor, Kitty glared into his face. Since she wore high heels and was already tall for a woman, her eyes, a brilliant ice-chipped blue, were on a level with his and though she had not meant to she could not help but notice his were the exact colour of the conkers with which she and Freddy and Alfie, who had once been their boot boy, used to do battle.

She decided she hated them, and him.

"Well, I'm not yours and I thank God for it," she hissed. "I wouldn't wish a more loathsome fate on my worst enemy, and I would be obliged if you would not hold me so tightly. I am only dancing with you to please my mother and because I was forced into it. Believe me, I would rather dance with any man in the room than with you, I can tell you, and there are some real halfwits present. I don't know who you are and—"

"Ben Maddox, Miss Hayes. I come from—"

"I don't give a damn where you come from, Mr Maddox. I'm only concerned with when you'll return there. I can't believe that Freddy could make a friend of a . . . of a vulgarian like you. I thought he had better taste."

All about them couples dipped and swayed but Kitty Hayes and Ben Maddox were, for the moment, totally unaware of them. One strong will clashed with another, both of them doing their best to master the other, to force the other to look away in confusion and doubt, but neither was prepared to back down. Kitty was trembling with outrage, since he had outwitted her in getting her on to the dance floor and though she would, if she had been alone with her family, simply have thrown him off and told him to go to hell in a handcart, a favourite expression of hers, even she could not do so with friends looking on. She was not overly concerned with her mother's feelings, for they had never got on, but she adored her father as much as she adored Freddy and on this, hers and Freddy's twenty-third birthday, she could not bring herself to hurt either of them. It cost her dearly to continue to glide round the floor with this overbearing man but she gritted her teeth and allowed him to steer her adroitly among the other couples.

He was a good dancer, light on his feet, keeping gracefully to the rhythm of the music, holding her at the proper distance from himself despite her recent complaint. He was tall with wide shoulders which were well muscled. She could feel them beneath the expensive cloth of his evening dress coat, rippling in a way that, to her surprise, tickled her fingertips, though she had no idea why. His waistcoat was white, figured silk, his trousers were straight and well fitting and he wore black patent leather button boots. He was, in fact, an exact replica of every other well-dressed and wealthy gentleman in the room.

"Have you nothing further to say, Miss Hayes?" he asked her, guiding her skilfully between the waltzing couples. "By the look on your face I would wager that you have. Please, don't disappoint me by holding it in. I would hate you to explode with frustration, which it seems to me might happen at any moment."

"Believe me, Mr Maddox, you wouldn't want to see me explode. I am told I have a quick temper."

"I can scarce believe it!" He lifted one eyebrow ironically.

"Even a violent one, which I admit to, and I also believe that my way, about everything to do with my life and how I live it, concerns only myself."

Her eyes glinted like blue diamonds as they glared into his. She was flushed and could barely speak through her tightly clenched teeth and Ben Maddox had a strange feeling that her rage was directed not just at himself.

"I can see that, Miss Hayes, but don't you think we dance well together? You appear to be enjoying this waltz so may I take that as a compliment?"

"No, you may not, damn you. I am here for one reason only and that is because my mother, and you, forced me into it."

"Are you saying that you would rather be dancing with someone else, Miss Hayes? I wonder who that could be?" He smiled coolly, the smile not reaching his eyes as his gaze drifted over her shoulder and came to rest on her brother and sister who had their heads close together as they drifted past.

"Anyone but you, sir, as I have already told you. Now, I believe the music is about to end so oblige me by returning me to my mother."

They had stopped dancing when the music did, directly opposite the open French windows, but again he was too quick for her. The breathless couples were turned away from them towards the musicians who were grouped in a corner at the end of the room. They were clapping and bowing before the gentlemen returned their partners to their chaperones. Everyone's attention was on the young ladies and gentlemen as they moved across the floor. The unmarried females were taking a peep at their dance cards to see who was to lead them on to the floor for the next dance and the gentlemen had begun to single out their new partners. The older ladies who gossiped round the room were busy studying deportment, manners, the gowns of their young charges and not one of them noticed as Ben Maddox, holding Kitty Hayes firmly about the waist, whisked her out on to the terrace, down the wide stone steps and into the darkness that lay across the lawn where the lights of the house could not reach.

Kitty Hayes was so unused to anyone, male or female, forcing her to do something against her will, she went with him before she realised what he was doing. She almost tripped on the elaborate ruffled hem of her evening gown and would have fallen had he not held her firmly.

"What the hell d'you think you're doing, you bastard," she mouthed furiously. "Let go of me at once." She longed to scream and stamp her foot as she had as a child but she was too conscious of the guests in her mother's drawing-room and, more importantly, how it would look to others when they discovered that, perhaps for the first time in her adult life, a man had got the better of Kitty Hayes.

"Not just yet," he drawled, his superior strength hurrying her across the lawn. "Aah, this will do," he murmured as they came to a small, open-fronted garden house at the edge of the grass just where the crowded trees began.

"My father will have you flogged for this," she panted as he placed her firmly on the wooden-slatted bench just inside the small building. "He'll have you thrown from the house. Believe me, no decent home will receive you when word of this gets out and I shall make it my business to see that it does. You may be Freddy's friend but—"

"Aah, Freddy!" There was a wealth of meaning in his voice. He stood back from her and at once she sprang up, ready to dart away, but something in his voice and the words he spoke made her hesitate.

"And what the hell's that supposed to mean?"

"Really, Miss Hayes, you have a foul mouth for such a young, well-bred lady."

"Never mind my mouth, or what comes out of it. What exactly did that reference to Freddy mean?" she challenged. Her strong chin jutted dangerously and her eyes flashed in the darkness. She seemed to bare her perfect white teeth, like an animal on the defensive and did her hands curve into claws? God, she was a magnificent creature but heaven help the poor sod who got landed with her. He liked his women spirited, even a bit quick-tempered since it made for a lively relationship, but this one would need a husband as strong-willed as herself but with the patience of a bloody saint. He had a strong will, too strong, his dead father used to say, but his patience was minuscule. Now why should that thought slip through his mind? he wondered for a fraction of a second, then the memory of how this girl – woman – had gazed yearningly at her brother, and also something her brother had said to him in confidence some years ago, took its place.

He and Freddy had met unexpectedly one day in Liverpool when Freddy had been staying there on some business for his father. Joshua Hayes owned the thriving Monarch Cotton Manufacturing Mill in Manchester and his son, though he had admitted that he did not care for it, had worked there since he had left Deanhampton at the age of eighteen. Ben was several years older than Freddy but he had taken a liking to the lad and had protected him from bullies when he first came to the public school. Freddy was handsome, slender, somewhat girlish, without the faintest idea how to stand up to the boys who baited him. He was gentle, having been brought up with four sisters, one of whom had led him about since he was a baby! His brother Sebastian was born just after Freddy began his schooling at Deanhampton so he had known no male siblings. He had been taught by a governess and was a clever lad, but he was sadly lacking in the gritty endurance that a boy needs to get through the rigours of boarding school. Had it not been for Ben, who had even then been big for his age, strong and handy with his fists, young Hayes would have fared ill. They could not exactly have been called friends, since there was too much of a difference in their ages and neither had met the other's family, but now and again, when Freddy was in Liverpool, or Ben came to Manchester on business, both being in the cotton trade, they would dine together, sometimes get drunk together.

It was on such an occasion that Freddy had divulged more perhaps than he should have of his family's background.

Expansive over a good cigar and a brandy after dining well at the Adelphi where Freddy was putting up for the night, it was Freddy who had set the ball rolling.

"Ever thought of getting married, old man?" he had asked, leaning back in his chair and blowing smoke into the already smoke-filled air of the gentlemen's games-room where they intended to round off the evening with a game of billiards.

Ben took a sip of his brandy, nearly choking on it.

"Good God, no, man. There's all the time in the world for that. After all, I'm only twenty-five. What about you?" It was said jokingly, since at the time Freddy had been no more than twenty-one.

Freddy sighed. "Fat chance of that at the moment."

"Bloody hell, old chap, don't tell me you have someone in mind? Not at your age."

"Oh, yes." It was said with great sadness but firm conviction.

"Great God in heaven, who is this paragon?" Ben held his cigar in one hand and brandy in the other, in his consternation not sure which to put to his lips.

"Well . . . I don't know whether I should . . ."

"Hell's teeth, Freddy, you can trust me. You should know that by now," and Freddy Hayes did. Ever since that first day at Deanhampton when a terrified eleven-year-old had been taken under the protective wing of fifteen-year-old Ben Maddox, he had trusted him with, if not his life, then his person.

"Yes, I do but . . . well, I suppose since it's no secret in Manchester there can be no harm in telling you the story."

"Jesus, Freddy, this is most intriguing," expecting to hear that young Freddy Hayes was madly in love with an actress or a shop girl or some other equally unsuitable young woman who could not possibly be welcomed into the Hayes' circle. He was unprepared for Freddy's answer.

"It's no laughing matter, Ben, so I'd be obliged if you'd take that sneer off your face."

"Hell's bells, Freddy, I'm sorry. I'd no idea . . ."

"No, and you'll be even more pole-axed when I tell

you who it is that I love. Who I've loved all my life, it seems."

"*All your life!*"

"Yes. Well, since I was five or six when she was brought to live with us."

"*Brought to . . . ?*"

"Yes."

"Who?"

"My sister."

"Your . . . *sister!*" Ben felt the blood drain from his face. He downed his brandy in one long swallow, realising in his horrified shock he had spoken out loud and several gentlemen were turning round to stare curiously.

"Oh, don't look like that, Ben. She's not really my sister. Not by blood I mean. Lord, I don't think there's enough time to explain it all to you so I'll try to condense it but . . . well . . ."

"For God's sake, lad, spit it out."

"Very well, but it's a strange tale. Kitty is the same age as myself. We were born on the same day, the same month and year. Ciara is six years younger. We are all three . . . illegitimate." His young face twisted with some feeling that hurt him.

"Great God in Heaven!"

"We all had separate mothers but the girls had the same father. My mother, my real mother was a . . . Dear God this is hard . . . she was a laundrymaid in my grandmother's house. My father seduced her . . . had an affair with her . . . whatever you like to call it before he knew my stepmother and my mother died giving birth to me so he adopted me. A lot of men wouldn't have bothered."

"Great God in Heaven!" Ben stammered again, too stunned to even signal to the waiter for another brandy which he desperately needed.

"It gets worse. My stepmother was . . . raped as a girl of fifteen and Kitty was the result. Five or six years later Ciara was brought to the nursery. Her dead mother was my stepmother's younger sister and her father was the same bastard who had sired Kitty so Kitty and Ciara are not only half sisters but cousins. Yes, you may well look dumbfounded. I told you it was a complex tale. My stepmother and father had married by then. Kitty and I were adopted legally and when Ciara came along, so was she so the whole affair was legalised and as far as possible, normalised."

"I don't know what to say, old man."

"What is there to say, Ben? It was all hushed up, covered up, accepted even, thanks to my grandmother, I believe, who loved us all. We mix with the best people in Manchester but it is very obvious that Kitty, at twenty-one years old, though the daughter of one of the wealthiest men in Manchester and very beautiful, has received not one proposal of marriage. God knows what is to happen to her, for if ever a girl needs a strong and – dare I say it – *lusty* husband, it is Kitty. Ciara is only fifteen but she will . . . she will not need to look for a husband, for I mean to marry her myself when she is a couple of years older."

"Dear God, does your family know?"

"No, not yet, but that isn't the problem."

"What is?"

Freddy sighed. "Kitty, she's the problem. She considers me her personal property. Has done since we were children. She's jealous of anyone who takes my attention from her, though she knows nothing of my intentions towards Ciara."

"Does Ciara?"

"Oh, yes." It was said simply with a small smile and a wealth of deep tenderness. "Ciara and I are . . . alike. We want the same things. We are the two halves of the same . . . Jesus, this sounds half-baked but it's true."

"You're a lucky man, Freddy."

Ben remembered this conversation as Kitty Hayes stood defiantly before him. She had been rejected by the eligible young men of Manchester but she didn't give a damn since she was in love with Freddy Hayes. She was waiting for him to declare himself and would, he was pretty certain, do it for him if he didn't look lively. Her heart was trusting, hopeful, but watching suspiciously as he whispered in her sister's ear; what would she do when the truth was revealed to her?

It was a warm night, the sky a clear purple-blue but for a drifting wisp of silver-edged cloud above the roof of the house. The moon hung over the western side of the city, earth shine reflected in its surface, and its light turned Kitty's face to a pearly white in which her eyes glinted without colour. Her gown was a marvel of blush-white satin, plain and sheath-like at the front with a deep square neckline which revealed the slightest swell of the top of her breasts. In the fashion of the day her waist had been gathered in to a mere twenty inches and her hips accentuated by a froth of ruffles which gathered at the back of the skirt in an enormous bustle. It seemed she did not care for the eccentric trimmings with which many ladies decorated their gowns. One could have collected from the persons of fine ladies a whole aviary of birds, flights of swallows and humming birds across the skirt being very popular, but Kitty's gown was simple and elegant.

"Well?" she was demanding. "What have you to say about Freddy? I know you and he were at school together so I suppose you are going to tell me some dreadful schoolboy escapade you got up to with him."

"Hardly. I am four years his senior."

"Then why have you dragged me out here?" she snapped. "You seem to be implying it is something to do with Freddy, but let me tell you before you start that Freddy is a decent, upright and honourable man and . . . and I . . ." She hesitated, obviously unwilling to reveal her true feelings for the man who had played the part of her brother all her life but longing to defend him to the death if necessary.

So how could he tell her what Freddy had told him, which was what he had intended? That Freddy was in love with the lovely Ciara. Why hadn't she seen it for herself? Surely anyone with eyes in their head could not fail to notice what lay between them, that almost visible aura with which two people in love seem to surround themselves. And if he'd seen it surely that meant their parents had too and had no objection to the match.

But it is said that love is blind and it seemed this extraordinary young woman had no sight at all when it came to Freddy Hayes. Or perhaps, with that bull-headed stubbornness that afflicts those who love, she was deliberately hiding it from herself, from her heart and quick, intelligent mind, hiding from herself the knowledge of what lay between her brother and sister. Could he tell her? Could he cut the blindfold and make her see the truth? The answer was, no, he couldn't. Not only because compassion had laid its hand on his own heart but because it was not his secret to disclose. Besides which, from what he'd seen of Kitty Hayes in the past couple of hours, he knew she would not believe him, or if she did, would take her desolate heart into the house and tear the place apart demanding an explanation from the two people involved. He had meant to warn her without exactly repeating what Freddy had told him but now, backing away, mentally if not physically, he knew he couldn't do it. It was nothing to do with him. He wasn't even a friend of the family, only an old school chum of the elder son of the house and, quite honestly, he had no wish to be involved.

So, he had to have a reason for bringing . . . *dragging* her out here. A reason she would understand. She would despise it too but at least her heart would be intact and perhaps she might feel a trifle flattered that a man should find her attractive.

Reaching out, he gripped her by the upper arms and pulled her to him, holding her tightly against his chest, his fingers digging cruelly into her soft flesh. His mouth found hers, parted her surprised lips, caressed and clung to them and after a startled moment and for a slow beat in time, hers responded. She leaned against him as though the strength had gone from her and he put his arms about her. Her mouth was sweet, warm, moist, then, with a horrified gasp, she broke away from him, wiping the back of her hand across her mouth, her whole manner conveying her disgust and fury.

"You beast," she hissed. "You filthy bastard. How dare you lay your hands on me . . ."

"Come, come, Miss Hayes," he managed to say smilingly, though he himself was shaken by the moment. "It was only a kiss. Surely you have been kissed before?"

She hadn't, at least not like that and she was as furious with herself for not only responding to it but *liking* it.

She resorted to the phrase that was taught to all well-brought-up young girls for situations such as this.

"Sir, you are no gentleman" – still violently scrubbing at her mouth – "and when I tell my brother he will give you the hiding of your life."

The idea of the pale and slender Freddy Hayes taking his fists to the big man who lounged before her did not strike her as being ludicrous. Casually he was reaching into his pocket for his cigars. Lighting one, he blew smoke into the warm, scented air.

"Then I'd best take my leave, Miss Hayes. May I say what a pleasure it was meeting you and as for the . . ."

The sentence was not finished, for she was striding away from him across the dewed lawn, contempt written in her straight back and imperious head. She was a lady insulted and if he knew what was good for him, her posture implied, he'd best not darken the doorstep of Riverside House again.

The scent of his cigar and his soft laughter followed her up the steps to the terrace.

2

The breakfast-room at Riverside House was quiet as the Hayes family addressed themselves to the good, wholesome breakfast Nancy Hayes thought suitable for growing children. It did not concern her that the two eldest were twenty-three years of age and well past the days when Nancy was responsible for their health and wellbeing; she believed in the precepts of her own long-dead mother who had always said that milk, cheese, fruit and vegetables built healthy bones and teeth. Not that Nancy Hayes and her two sisters ate such things on a permanent or even frequent basis, since their mother had been a whore and they had lived a hand-to-mouth existence throughout their childhood in Angel Meadow, one of the worst vice-ridden and deprived slum areas of Manchester. But her mam, who in her youth had once been friendly with a girl who had been skivvy in the kitchen of a doctor, had picked up from her, who had picked it up from the doctor's cook, the notion that these basic foods were the secret of good health. Nancy's own splendid teeth and skin, her glossy brown-gold curls, her straight limbs and fine figure attested to this fact and she had continued her mam's scarcely understood beliefs with her own children.

The room in which they ate faced south-east and the sunlight streamed through a row of tall windows, clear and bright, polishing the glowing mahogany of the long, oval table to a mirror shine in which the faces of the seven people who sat about it were reflected. Eight places were set with silver cutlery, knives, forks and tablespoons with ivory handles on white damask place mats edged with the finest Honiton lace. The cups and saucers, dessert bowls and side plates were of the best and most expensive English china ware decorated with love-birds perched on a bough. On the table was a silver sugar basin with sugar tongs, a sugar sifter and a cream jug, with a silver salt cellar and spoon placed beside it. All of the finest quality, of course. In the exact centre of the table was a vast silver fruit stand holding a richly chased cut-crystal bowl. The bowl was heaped with oranges, apricots, damsons, peaches, nectarines, plums, apples and a pineapple, most of them grown in Riverside's own orchards or hothouses.

Joshua Hayes replaced his knife and fork on his empty plate and leaned back, wiping his mouth on his napkin. He was still a handsome man despite his forty-seven years. Tall and rangy with smoky grey eyes which his two daughters and elder son had inherited, he was an engaging man, much respected in Manchester and much loved within his own family. His marriage had been a happy one and it showed in his warm, slow smile and his easy-going charm, his relaxed attitude towards others which said he was confident they would be friends. In business he was straight and tough and he was doing his best to teach his elder son to be the same.

A maidservant, on seeing her master had finished, moved forward from her place by the serving table and with an enquiring smile at him was given permission to remove his plate.

"Will you take another egg, sir?" she asked him. "Mrs Bright cooked plenty. Or perhaps a slice or two more of bacon?"

"No, thank you, Tilly. Just toast, I think, and I wouldn't mind some of Mrs Bright's lemon marmalade if there is some."

The maid looked askance at him, for Mrs Bright's excellent marmalade was always available and the master knew it, bless him. It was just his way of asking for things as if he didn't want to be a trouble to anyone. As if he could!

"Of course, sir, and perhaps another cup of coffee."

"Thank you, Tilly." Josh Hayes's smile reached the foot of the table where his wife was seated and she smiled back at him, a flush at her cheekbone, for it was no more than half an hour since they had made love in their big bed as they did on most days. A fulfilled and happy couple were Josh and his lovely wife who looked, so he told her, no older than the day he first saw her in the yard of his father's mill. A spinner she had been and the first words she had spoken to him had been in anger but he loved her then and he loved her now and the warmth of it had permeated their home and their lives for twenty years. Twenty years this coming September since they were married, and still "at it", as Ivy, the housemaid who "saw" to their bedroom, liked to inform the other serving girls when the men-servants were not about.

Mrs Hodges, the housekeeper, would go mad, her face red with indignation.

"Ivy Harrison, if I've told you once, my girl, I've told you a thousand times I will not have you discussing the master and mistress that way. What they do in their bedroom, or how often, is nothing to do with us, so think on. I won't tell you again."

It was an idle threat and Ivy knew it. She had been at Riverside House as long as the mistress, longer than Mrs Hodges, and considered herself to be that privileged being who, through her hard work and loyal service for over twenty years, was almost one of the family and could, within reason, say what she liked. Only inside the four walls, of course, and not in the family's hearing!

There were three large and handsome dogs lying in a tumbled heap in the one long shaft of sunlight which lay across the honey-coloured carpet. They were so big not one of them alone could have fitted into the patch of warmth but, in the mistaken belief that it fell solely on each of them, they hitched themselves together companionably. One was a black labrador, the second a golden retriever, the third a black and white English setter. All three had just had their daily brushing from Richie, one of the stable lads and their coats gleamed like satin.

Joshua sighed deeply as he buttered his toast and heaped it liberally with Mrs Bright's lemon marmalade. He glanced at the empty place next to him, shaking his head sadly, and at once every face in the room, even the animals, who seemed to sense his worry, turned to look at him with great sympathy.

"Where does that girl get to? Does anyone know where she is?" he asked, turning his greying head to each member of the family in turn, knowing he had no need to mention her name. He raised his eyebrows in Freddy's direction, for if anyone would know Kitty's whereabouts it was her brother.

"No, Father. I've only just got out of bed myself."

"Mmm," his father replied. "After last night and the way she danced I thought she might be up late. Has anyone been up to her room? Tilly?" turning to the maid.

"Yes, sir, I have. I took her a cup of tea about half an hour ago but she weren't there."

"Chester's not in the stable either, Father," Josh's younger son, his last child, piped up. "Me an' Anna and Marguerite went for a gallop as far as Singleton Brook but we didn't see her, did we?"

The boy turned to his sisters for confirmation and

they shook their heads vigorously. They were all three still in their riding outfits. The girls, Anna and Marguerite, sixteen and thirteen respectively, were dressed in fine blue box-cloth, a jacket bodice, a neat white cravat and a full, trained skirt. Sebastian, at almost twelve and a boarder at Deanhampton for nearly a year now but home for the summer, wore pale beige kid breeches, polished knee-length boots of rich brown leather and a riding jacket of tweed in a mixture of caramel and chocolate. He scorned a hat of any sort, though the girls wore neat black bowlers with a face net. They had discarded them at the table though they were allowed to wear their riding habits as it was Sunday.

"Did Charlie say in which direction she had gone?" their mother asked, not anxiously, since they had long ago given up worrying about Kitty who was a law unto herself.

"We didn't ask him, Mother."

"You don't think it's anything to do with that chap – what's-his-name, Freddy? – the one she danced with last night," Ciara said, turning innocently to Freddy and putting a hand on his arm, a gesture that was not lost on the rest of her family, or Tilly!

Freddy's face was a picture of consternation. "Ben Maddox! Whyever should you think that?"

"Well, I heard she danced with him for rather a long time and then Mariella told me she saw her go outside with him."

"Outside? Outside where?" Joshua frowned and

leaned forward in his chair and Tilly pricked up her ears. You could always rely on Miss Ciara to stir up a bit of mischief, doing it in such a way that made it plain that it was nothing to do with her. Especially where her older sister was concerned. Chalk and cheese they were, not exactly cat and dog, for Miss Ciara hadn't the fire that Miss Kitty had, but if they could get each other into trouble they would. From young children they had been the same, fighting over one thing or another, usually for Master Freddy's attention. Miss Ciara went about it in a subtle, some would say underhanded way but Miss Kitty was open and noisy, not caring who was made aware of her true feelings. She was always in trouble over something, getting a reputation for a hellion, while somehow Miss Ciara managed to hide her tracks and was thought of as sweet and biddable. Mind you, Miss Kitty *was* a hellion but she was at least honest about it, not pretending to be something she wasn't and you couldn't help but like her for it.

"Outside where?" Joshua repeated, fixing Ciara with his suddenly flinty grey eyes but Ciara was not about to take the blame for her sister's waywardness.

"I don't know, Father. It was Mariella who saw her go, not me."

"How long was she gone?" her mother asked her.

Ciara turned towards her, her face as innocent as an angel, her hand reaching for Freddy's under the tablecloth and at once he jumped to her defence.

"Mother, Ciara didn't see it so how can she know?"

"Shall I go and ask Charlie when she went, Mother?

I mean this morning?" asked Sebastian, since the fuss over Kitty and whatever she had got up to last night seemed irrelevant now.

"Would you, darling? Have you finished your breakfast?"

"I'll take a couple of slices of toast with me," he told her as he pushed his chair away from the table. At once the three dogs leaped to their feet, their tails on the move, their ears pricking, their eyes bright with anticipation.

The boy hurried from the room, the toast he had filched from the toast rack on the serving table already to his mouth. Tilly had spread it liberally with best butter and home-made blackberry jam, the way he liked it. The trouble was, so did them damned dogs and as Master Sebastian surreptitiously fed them under the table they now followed him, begging for a tit-bit. The boy banged the door behind himself and the three animals with a crash that made them all wince and they could hear his voice remonstrating with them as he made for the side door that led to the stables.

"Get *down*, Jess, you idiot, you'll have me over. No, I am not sharing my toast with you, you greedy beggars. Holly, I swear I'll shut you in the study . . . Stop it, Rex, get down I say."

"Did you ever hear such a commotion and all over one young woman," her mother sighed.

"Well, it's hardly her fault, my darling," her husband said mildly. "She doesn't know what an uproar—"

"Of course she does, Josh," his wife answered

crisply. "She always knows. Now then, get on with your meal, children. It will be time for church in an hour."

They all sighed in unison, even Tilly.

The young woman in question idled along the narrow lane, her feet dangling, the stirrups loose, the reins hanging about the neck of her lathered black gelding. She allowed the animal to go at his own pace, since, for a good half-hour, she had galloped him mercilessly across the fields and meadows to the north of Higher Broughton, risking not only her own life and limbs, but his, not caring what crops grew there or the fright she gave to grazing herds of cattle. She had flown like a bird over fence and hedge, her arms nearly pulled from their sockets, the thunder of the gelding's hooves assaulting her ears. She had lost the ribbon from her hair which she had plaited before leaving home and it had streamed out like a windblown flag behind her, the colour of a blackbird's wing but with highlights of bronze put there by the sun's rays. Several farm labourers had watched her go by, their mouths agape in astonishment, shouting after her to stop her headlong flight or she'd "tekk a tumble" but she hadn't, of course. She was too good a horsewoman for that and Chester was too fine a horse.

Now her hair hung down her back to where her buttocks rested in the saddle, heavy waves of dark silk which she tried uselessly to tuck behind her ears. Her eyes were unfocused, the vivid blue of them half lit between her narrowed eyelids. Though she didn't appear to react to it she was vaguely conscious of what lay about her as she followed the slight incline up to the top of Crablane Head. It was high summer, a clear day, the heat haze of the early morning burned off so that in every direction she could see the patchwork counterpane of fields and woods. The scattered roofs of Blackley shimmered to the south-east and a few tiny cottages and farms could just be made out in the west where the Radcliffe and Cheetham Hill branch line of the Lancashire and Yorkshire Railway wound through the dips and dells of the rolling farmland which lay between her and Cheetham Hill.

When the gelding reached the top of Crablane Head she pulled him to a halt and slid from his back. Fastening the reins loosely to a protrusion in a rocky outcrop so that he couldn't wander, she lowered herself to the grassy ground and leaned her back against the rock, staring out sightlessly into the distance. There was bracken below but up here heather grew, turning to a rich purple as the summer drew on and in the rough grass were tiny purple dog-violets, one of which she plucked and held carefully in her half-cupped hand. As though in a dream she lifted the hand with the flower to her lips, running her fingers along its softness and fullness, then sighed dramatically.

She had been kissed. For the first time in her life she had been kissed by a man and the sad thing was, that man had not been Freddy. She knew it had not been her fault. The devil, for that was what

Ben Maddox was, had taken her by surprise, taken a liberty and she had been livid about it, for hadn't she been saving that delight, that sweet moment all women dream about when the man they love kisses them for the first time, to be shared with Freddy. She had waited and waited since she was sixteen for him to acknowledge that what they felt for one another was more than the fondness shared by a brother and sister; to make good the promise they had made to one another as children.

"We'll be married when we're grown up," she had told him confidently. "Then we can always be together. That's what ladies and gentlemen do. You'll be my husband and I'll be your wife and we'll have a lot of children to play with. We will, won't we, Freddy?"

"If you say so, Kit," he answered amiably. He was seven years old at the time, as she was.

"Promise me."

"I promise."

And that to Kitty Hayes had been as binding an oath as the marriage vow itself. They would be married one day since no one, no woman could love a man as she loved Freddy, and she knew he returned her love. She had realised, at sixteen, that though she was ready, Freddy wasn't. That was the trouble when a man and a woman were the same age for it was a well-known fact that a female matures much earlier than a male. That was why men married at thirty and women at twenty or younger, but she couldn't wait until Freddy was thirty, could she? She was twenty-three, as he was, and was ready for marriage and that lout last night had only highlighted the fact. She should be Freddy's wife by now, safe from the attentions of such a low person, but what could she do except remind Freddy of their promise. Well, blast it, that's what she would do if he didn't get a move on. Swallow her pride and jump right in with it. She admitted to herself that she was stronger than he was, not physically, of course, but she had always known her will was more forceful than his, that she could chivvy, persuade, even bully him into giving in to her, so she must find a way to do it, and soon. Perhaps if she were to corner him and . . . well, kiss him like that dolt had kissed her last night it might jerk him out of the daydream he seemed to live in, moving from day to day, week to week, the months going by and she wasn't getting any younger. Something must be done to winkle him out of his complaisant belief that they could drift on like this for ever. Though she didn't care to contemplate it, in fact she jerked away from it now, she had wondered at times if it was her imagination that he was keeping out of her way.

She had nearly hammered on his door this morning and would have marched in and dragged him from his bed as she had on many an occasion but something, some image still lingering at the periphery of her vision from last night, she didn't know what, had stopped her. After she had left Ben . . . whatever his name was, smirking like the idiot she knew him to be she had longed to march into the drawing-room, grab Freddy by the arm and force him to go outside and give his so-called friend, if not a good hiding, then a piece of his mind, followed by an order to remove himself from the vicinity of decent people. She had been so furious she would have done it even if it caused an enormous rumpus but Freddy had been dancing with Jane Rivers who Kitty could not abide. Jane was the silliest, most tactless girl in their circle, the worst gossip who would have had the whole thing blown up into enormous proportions, spreading it not just about the room but the whole damn county of Lancashire. Kitty might be a hothead, impetuous and longing to see Ben what's-his-name thrown out ignominiously into the street by the men-servants but she did not want to have her name bandied about as a girl who had fainted because she had been kissed, which was probably what Jane would tell everyone. Kitty didn't give a damn what anyone called her – wild, unmanageable, outrageous, a trial to her poor mother and father, a tomboy who liked to gallop her gelding at breakneck speed all over the county and who sometimes swore like a stable boy – but she would have no one calling her faint-hearted, mocking her because a man had kissed her!

So she had pasted a false smile on her face and danced with every man who asked her; not Freddy since he always seemed to be cavorting about with someone else, but to anyone watching she was having a wonderful, wonderful birthday.

It was hot. She was wearing a riding habit of broad-cloth in a rich shade of burgundy, a tight-fitting bodice with a high neck and long sleeves, with a full skirt. Under the bodice she had on a thin, sleeveless camisole top and under the skirt a pair of trousers in the same material as the habit. She liked to ride astride and as a compromise and to prevent a storm at the dressmaker's in St Ann's Square, a business her mother had owned and run until the babies, starting with Anna, had come along, she had been allowed to have trousers made to be worn *with* the skirt. She would, if not allowed her own way, her mother and Aunt Jennet, who now ran the business, had been well aware, have simply bunched her skirt and petticoats about her waist and with her drawers in full view have ridden shamelessly about the neighbourhood of Broughton.

Now she removed her bodice and skirt, revelling in the feel of the sun on her bare arms and neck and the tops of her breasts, stretching out her trousered legs, crossing her booted feet at the ankle. Her breathing slowed, her head fell sideways and she slept.

Ben Maddox placed his hands on his hips, bent one leg, put his booted foot on a loose rock and sighed as he looked down at Kitty Hayes. He distinctly felt his heart move and soften, then something speared him in the centre of his chest, rising to catch him in the throat, threatening to choke him. What the bloody hell was wrong with him now? He had been overwhelmed after she had stalked off last night by the stunning realisation that this woman, if he didn't take care, could mean something to him and he didn't want it. He was not ready for it. She was a wildcat, there was no doubt about that, but he sensed something sweet in her, something worth pursuing, something untapped which she had allowed no one to see, not even the estimable but totally unsuitable Freddy Hayes. Freddy was not for her, of course, even if she thought he was, which it seemed she did. He was too faint-hearted, too good-natured, too malleable, and the tigress in Kitty Hayes would devour him, find him tasteless and spit him out.

So, what about you, Ben Maddox? he asked himself as he gazed down at the sleeping, shamelessly rumpled and semi-naked figure of the woman who sprawled on the springy grass of Crablane Head, where Freddy had directed him.

He had been lucky to catch the lad alone – which is how he always thought of Freddy, a lad – when he had called at Riverside House this morning. The family had gone to church, the elderly housemaid told him, all except Master Freddy who was in the study going over something or other which should have been seen to a week ago, the master had said. But that was Master Freddy all over, putting off until tomorrow what should have been done yesterday, or even last week, she rambled on in that familar way of old family retainers as she showed him to the study.

Ben was staying with the Lamberts in Cheetham Hill. He had been invited to spend the night with James and his wife, who had also been guests at the

Hayes birthday party, and when, this morning, he had expressed a desire for a ride James had loaned him a chestnut mare. He had packed his riding clothes just in case before he left home. The mare was sweet-natured and gentle, not used to wild gallops so he had cantered her the four or five miles from the Hayes home up to here, Crablane Head, where Freddy said he was pretty sure she would be.

"She likes it up there. We all do and often take a picnic, me and Kit, with Anna, Marguerite and Seb. Not Ciara though. She doesn't care for riding so I haven't been for . . . well . . ." His face showed a tremor of what might have been regret, for there was nothing, absolutely nothing Freddy Hayes liked more than riding. That his love didn't was a sad lack in his normally contented life and Ben could see where Kitty Hayes's advantage might lie. He was pretty sure she would have seen it too.

"But what d'you want Kit for, old man? Can't I give her a message? Why don't you sit down and I'll ring for coffee, or better yet, stay for lunch. Mother and Father would be delighted." It was clear Freddy would welcome anything that would interrupt the task his father had set him.

"Thanks, but no. I'm off back to Walton this afternoon but, well . . . I think I offended your sister last night and I wished to apologise." A lie, of course, and if you'd asked him for the truth he would have twisted and turned, even from himself, rather than reveal it.

"Offended Kitty! Good God, what did you do?"

"She said nothing to you?"

"Not a word. She danced the soles of her slippers through, laughed her head off, you know how she is, then went to bed as cheerful as a sparrow. Nobody's seen her since."

He would hardly have described the exotic Miss Hayes as a sparrow, but following Freddy's instructions and warding off his curious questions, he had ridden along drowsy, sun-filled lanes, between hedgerows that were a tangle of wild roses, bryony and honeysuckle. Climbing up the banks were foxgloves, purple and yellow vetch and pink clover blossom. Bees, heavy-laden with pollen, blundered from flower to flower, the sound hypnotising him and he felt the peace thread through his veins and stitch itself to his heart. Whatever came of it he knew this journey must be made.

Now he watched the slow rise and fall of Kitty's half-revealed breasts, as white as buttermilk and as round and ripe as melons. Her nipples, a rosy pink, showed clearly through the thin fabric of her camisole and he felt the first male stirring of desire in the pit of his belly. God, she was a glorious creature. Her midnight-dark hair lay about her head in a tangle of loose curls. Her lips, moist and carnation pink, were parted slightly. She had flung an arm above her head and in the curve of her armpit he could see a patch of sweat-dampened hair. Her trousers, clinging tightly to every line of her long, shapely legs, had parted from her camisole at the waist and a couple of inches of her white belly, dimpled by her neat navel, glimmered in the sunlight.

For perhaps five minutes he watched her, studying the long and lovely curves of her body, the flushed contours of her face, the thick crescent of her lashes and the fine line of her eyebrows which frowned as though even in sleep something or someone had displeased her. He longed to put out a hand, run a fingertip lightly along her jawline and down the slender column of her white throat. To continue downwards until his hand cupped her breast, to the flush of her nipples which he knew, without understanding how, would at once peak and harden to his touch. She would wake and stretch and yawn, showing her pink tongue, lift her arms to him, draw him down and devour him with the passion which would not do for Freddy Hayes but which he, Ben Maddox, would meet, and match. She would make a magnificent bed partner; he had sensed it last night with her instant response to his mouth on hers, but by God she'd fight him every step of the way until his will overcame hers, his strong, male body dominated hers and what a glory that would be.

Knowing the truth, he gave in to it. It would happen. He would make it happen but not here. She wasn't ready yet. Her wilful heart and mind were filled with romantic, nonsensical notions of Freddy Hayes who hadn't the faintest idea in his own youthful head and heart of the feelings this woman had for him. Freddy loved Ciara. He had told Ben so two years ago and the way they had danced and whispered together last night would have told anyone but the most blinkered how things were between them, making it obvious that the situation would very soon come to a head. What would happen to her then, the beautiful, bull-headed Kitty Hayes who, he was sure, every man in Manchester wanted but no man would care to marry?

He had left the mare peacefully cropping the grass a hundred yards away, not wishing to alarm Kitty by clattering up on the animal's back. He smiled as the thought struck him that it would take more than a man on horseback to alarm Miss Kitty Hayes, then he frowned. With his recently acquired feeling of – what would he call it? – ownership, perhaps, of the peacefully sleeping woman on the grass, since there was no doubt in his mind now that one day she would belong to him, he found he did not care to have her dashing alone about the countryside. And still less did he care for her lolling about up here, as near as dammit half naked. Well, perhaps not that, but certainly with parts of her body only her husband should see revealed to all and sundry who passed this way. He looked about him and his frown vanished. There wasn't a living creature in sight except Kitty's gelding and a hawk sweeping graceful circles in the hot blue sky. A lark sang out of sight, bees droned in the heather and the horse chomped lethargically on a mouthful of tough grass. There were no other sounds.

Carefully he stepped backwards, watching where he placed his feet, since he did not want her to wake and find him gawking at her like some half-baked schoolboy. His own emotions were well tamped down now and that was where they would stay until . . . until the devastation which must surely come exploded about Kitty Hayes. Her touching belief in her dreams of Freddy Hayes would evaporate like mist in a hot sun. He meant to cultivate Freddy Hayes. Make it his business to befriend the Hayes family, for when it happened he would be there!

3

"Did he find you, then?" Freddy asked casually at the dinner table that night and everyone stopped eating and looked at him, and then at Kitty, who raised her eyebrows enquiringly.

As at the breakfast table earlier in the day, the atmosphere was one of comfort and luxury, of fine silver and cut-crystal glasses. The table linen was laundered so superbly there was almost a sheen on the damask, highlighted by the candles which gave out a soft and pleasing glow not only to every highly polished surface of the room but to the faces of those who dined there. Joshua Hayes had had gas lamps fitted by brackets to the richly papered walls, not only here in the dining-room but in his own study and in the drawing-room but his wife preferred the flattering lambency of candlelight and the gas lamps were lit only rarely.

It was a tradition begun by Joshua's mother that the

family dress for dinner. She had come herself from a family who were loosely connected to the aristocracy, marrying beneath her when she wed the wealthy mill owner Edmund Hayes, but she had brought with her that well-bred way of life she had known from birth. Her own family had been reared in that same tradition.

The gentlemen were in the usual anonymous black and white uniform they had worn in the evening for the past two decades but the ladies, Anna still in a blush-white muslin, Ciara in rose pink, Kitty in a rich honey, both of silk, and their mother a midnight-blue velvet, were dressed in the very latest fashion. It had altered from the bell-like crinoline with its huge skirt to the sheath-like style now in vogue. The front of the dress was fitted superbly into the waist and over the bosom, trimmed with lace or plain, but the back was draped into what was known as a "waterfall", constructed of a series of short flounces over a bustle or "crinolette" from waist to hem. As the year had moved on the bustle had become larger and more pronounced until it jutted out so far Nancy complained it was possible to carry a good-sized tea-tray on it!

"Find me? Who?"

"I told him where you would most likely be though I couldn't be sure, of course. I must say I can't imagine what he did to displease you, since he's the best chap in the world and wouldn't knowingly cause offence to anyone, particularly a lady."

Freddy, seemingly unaware of the open-mouthed

interest his words had caused, continued to spoon thick, sweet custard on to the slice of apple pie Tilly had just placed before him.

"Are you talking to me?" Kitty asked him in astonishment. They each and every one, including the maidservants, turned their gaze back to her.

"Of course, since you're the one he was looking for. Did he find you?"

"What the devil are you talking about, Freddy? Dear God, sometimes I wonder if there's an ounce of sense in that head of yours." Despite the incontestable truth that she loved him more than anyone in the world sometimes Freddy exasperated her beyond measure.

"Come off it, Kit. You know who I'm talking about. Don't play the innocent with me. He asked for you and I could see no reason why I shouldn't—"

With a clatter that made them all jump Kitty flung her dessert spoon to her plate, then clapped her right hand to her forehead in a gesture of intense irritability.

"Freddy Hayes, if you don't stop drivelling on and tell me who—"

"Ben Maddox, that's who."

Kitty's mouth dropped open and her face lost every vestige of colour. She felt her heart begin to thud, a drumbeat of sound and movement which she was convinced the others would hear and see. A remembered sensation of how she had felt last night when the man whose name Freddy had just spoken had put his arms about her and his mouth on hers. It rippled through her body and along with all the other strange things she was experiencing, her mouth dried up.

She swallowed convulsively and Tilly and Ivy, who were at the serving table, exchanged meaningful glances, which asked a question: what on earth did this mean? They did not know the young man in question, nor was his name familiar but he was the first gentleman ever to come to the house and ask for Miss Kitty, so what were they to make of that? A damn shame, they had all thought so for years now, ever since the lass had been of marrying age, that she had been passed over. Even Miss Anna, only sixteen but pretty as a picture and the legitimate daughter of Mr and Mrs Hayes, was beginning to have admirers. But Miss Kitty's beginnings had been so . . . so unconventional, the young bachelors of Manchester couldn't be blamed for choosing a wife with a more traditional background. No one knew who her father had been, nor Miss Ciara's, though Ivy could remember, years ago, on the day the master's sister and brother were so tragically drowned, there had been a man here who had drowned with them in the floodwaters of the River Irwell and his eyes had been the same intense blue of Miss Kitty's and Miss Ciara's. Mind, it didn't really matter *who* Miss Ciara's pa was since she and Master Freddy were so obviously a match. They were well suited for one another since they had both been born on the wrong side of the blanket.

There was total silence about the table and Freddy

looked up from his apple pie, glancing from one to the other.

"What?" he said to no one in particular. "Now what have I said? Ben Maddox was here this morning asking to see you and when I told him where you might be he galloped off as though the devil himself was at his horse's tail. I invited him to take coffee, or even to stay for lunch but he said he had to be back in Liverpool this afternoon. So what's wrong with that?"

"Ben Maddox?" Kitty managed to croak.

"Yes."

"D'you mean to tell me Ben Maddox had the gall to come knocking on my door asking for me and you were imbecile enough to tell him where I might be?" Her voice rose and strengthened with each word.

"Well . . ."

"After what he did last night?"

"I know nothing of last night, Kit, and if I had—"

"I can't believe that you would be so stupid."

"Now look here—"

"No, you look here—"

Her father's voice, deceptively mild, cut through their wrangling. "Just what *did* happen last night, Kitty?"

Kitty did not appear to hear and if she did, chose to ignore her father's question. She seemed to have lost all sense of reasonableness, to be in the grip of a fury that was threatening to get away from her, her wild anger out of all proportion to what appeared to be a perfectly innocent occurrence.

"I can't believe this, Freddy Hayes. First of all you invite a total stranger to our home who turns out to be an out-and-out blackguard—"

"Hey, hold on, Kit. Are we talking about the same man here? Ben Maddox is a gentleman."

"He damn well isn't." The scorching memory of Ben's kiss still burned her lips and seared her heart which had always belonged to Freddy. "He's a low-down skunk who isn't fit to be in the company of decent people."

"God above, what in hell's name did he do to—?"

"He insulted me."

"Stop it, the pair of you," Josh Hayes thundered. "What the devil's going on here and what in God's name has Ben Maddox to do with it? Isn't he the chap you were at school with, Freddy?"

"Yes, Father."

"The one you invited?"

"That's the one."

"And am I to believe that this man while he was a guest in our home offered an insult to my daughter?" He turned to Kitty. "Now then, young lady, I'll have the truth out of you if you please. How did he insult you?"

Kitty could feel the pull of her explosive temper dragging her into further turmoil, but somehow she must not allow it to control her as it so often did. She spoke before thinking, acted without considering the consequences, which very often she didn't care about anyway, but this time she must be careful. She had been caught off guard by Freddy's revelation that Ben Maddox had been here today looking for her and in her horrified disbelief had almost revealed what had happened between them, which was the last thing she wanted Freddy to know. For some reason it was imperative that Freddy should remain ignorant of . . . of Ben Maddox's attack on her, which was how she saw it. Well, if you were kissed against your will did that not constitute an attack? She definitely thought so but somehow she must hide it. Freddy was a mild-mannered man but who knew what he might do if he learned that some other man had not only kissed her first, which was *his* privilege, but that he had done it against her will.

Her mother spoke, giving her a moment to clear her mind. "Mariella told Ciara that you went into the garden with this man, Kitty. May we know why?"

Kitty shot a venomous look at Ciara and the colour that had drained from her face flooded back. "I might have known you'd have something to say on the subject."

"It was Mariella—" Ciara began indignantly but Kitty cut her off.

"Perhaps it was but you made sure you repeated it to Mother and Father."

"I'm glad she did, Kitty. You know it is not con- sidered the correct thing for a young, unmarried woman to be alone with a young, unmarried man."

"Fiddlesticks, Mother."

"Don't speak to your mother like that, my girl. She

is only considering your reputation which will be completely in tatters if you continue in this imprudent way. How can you hope to make a suitable marriage—"

"I don't care about a suitable marriage, Father. I will marry only the man I love." Stealthily she looked at Freddy from under her long, downswept lashes and though Freddy, enjoying his apple pie, missed the glance, both her mother and father saw it and exchanged an anxious look. She had been like this since she was a child. Then she had remarked boldly that she and Freddy would marry when they were grown up but, believing that it was no more than a childish fancy, they had not protested. Now, still unmarried, still not even *asked* for, they were frighteningly aware that she still hoped for it.

"Don't be foolish, girl. Of course you . . . but, anyway, I will not be sidetracked. This is not getting us to the reason you are in such a tantrum over Ben Maddox, so what I would like to hear is what offence he is supposed to have committed."

"Oh, it was nothing, Father, merely something he said about . . . horses but I found it most offensive."

"Horses!"

"Yes, we . . . I know it's not good form and I shouldn't have gone outside with him but really, does it matter? It was hot and it seemed only practical to . . . Oh, dammit . . ."

"Kitty!" her mother warned.

"Well, we were discussing horses and he said he thought . . . thought a real lady would ride a gentle animal . . . one suitable for a lady and I told him to . . ." She smiled wickedly and shrugged. "Well, you know me, Father. I told him to . . . go somewhere rude."

"Kitty!"

"And he told me he thought I was the most ill-mannered young woman he had ever met," which was the only truth in the whole fabrication of lies.

"I'm not surprised. And that was it? That's what all this fuss was about?"

"Yes, Father." She glanced at Freddy again from under her lashes but he wasn't looking at her. Ciara was whispering something in his ear and he was smiling. Kitty thought she had done rather well with the supposed argument she and that Maddox man had got into, adroitly manoeuvring her parents away from the real reason for her anger. She felt she had covered her tracks most effectively, hiding the true cause of her aggravation from Freddy and, really, she thought he might show a little concern or even interest. He was smiling and nodding at whatever Ciara had said and for an instant it was as though a trickle of icy water ran down her spine.

Then Anna who, at sixteen, was now allowed to dine with her parents and the three older members of the family, spoke up. "And what sort of mount does Mr Maddox ride?"

"How the dickens should I know?"

"But if you were discussing horses and you, or so it seems, told him you rode a gelding, which he thought was improper, he must have mentioned what kind of animal he favoured."

"Dear God, what is this? The Spanish Inquisition?" She glared at her sister, then picked up her spoon and attacked her dessert as though not only had Ben Maddox deeply offended her, so had the food.

"So that is all there was to this uproar?" her father questioned grimly. "Some foolish nonsense about horses and yet you let us believe that the poor chap had offered you an insult of such magnitude Freddy and I might have to resort to horse-whipping. Really, Kitty, you must curb that temper of yours, and that tongue." It was said somewhat hopelessly since everybody, from her first nursemaid to her last governess, and, of course, her mother and himself, had been saying the same thing for twenty-odd years.

"I just thought he was far too opinionated. What I ride is nobody's business and certainly not his." She was beginning to believe the story she had made up.

Her father looked at her mother and shrugged his shoulders in resignation as though to ask what could be done with their wayward daughter and her mother shook her head.

The rest of the meal was eaten with nothing more than the most general conversation. The recently popular comic opera by Mr Gilbert and Mr Sullivan, *HMS Pinafore*, was to be staged in Manchester and Nancy was to get up a party to go and see it. She thought she might invite her sister Mary, she told them, and Mary's husband Philip, and perhaps Mariella, who was their eldest daughter. They could spend the night at Riverside House since they, like Ben Maddox, lived near Liverpool, though Nancy did not voice this last.

Should they like to go to the Free Trade Hall on Thursday night, Thursday night being Hallé night? Though the orchestra gave its famous concerts in winter, Nancy had heard that there was to be a special performance to commemorate its founder's death. The great Gustav Behrens was to conduct. Only Anna, who had inherited her mother's love of the arts, showed any interest.

The latest novel by Mrs Henry Wood, of whom Nancy Hayes was very fond, was discussed, at least by Nancy and Anna. The opening of Lewis's Market Street Store had caused great excitement and it was reported that thousands were coming by train and omnibus to purchase goods and services not available in surrounding towns. Had Joshua heard and would it make any difference to Kendal Milnes as far as sales were concerned? they asked one another. Kendal's, then known as Kendal Milnes and Faulkner, had been the first ever department store in Manchester and the general consensus of opinion was that it would not, since Kendal Milnes catered to a more élite class of person. Of course the more discerning and wealthy shoppers would still frequent the most fashionable shops around St Ann's Square, Exchange Street and along lower King Street. Next time they went to town, Nancy remarked to Anna, since Kitty was obviously not listening, they must take afternoon tea at Parker's in

St Ann's Square, or perhaps the recently opened Meng and Ecker's in St Ann's Passage which was reputed to be excellent. These days more and more ladies were, as well as the traditional "calling" which was carried out in their circle, meeting one another, in a smart and reputable café, of course, to drink a cup of China tea and eat dainty cakes not made by their own cooks!

Had Joshua heard that the Mortimors, Andrew and Josephine, were selling their old family home in Broughton where the Mortimors had lived for decades and had bought a smart villa in Alderley Edge? Yes, a great shame but then so many of the old families were moving further away from the city as it sprawled ever outwards. It seemed the sons and grandsons of the most successful entrepreneurs often had little taste for business. Sent by their fathers to public school, they had acquired the manners and expectations of "gentlemen". This was not spoken out loud but it had not gone unnoticed that Joshua Hayes cast an anxious look at his own son, who had been educated at one of the finest public schools in the country, and where his young brother had followed. The Hayes business was, after a few setbacks over the last two decades, the American Civil War and the cotton famine and a recession in trade in the seventies, thriving and growing and though Freddy obediently followed the orders his father gave him and was learning the trade from the spinning-room upwards, his father was not altogether convinced that his heart was in it. He had no drive, but then, he always comforted himself, neither had he at the same age. It was not until Freddy himself was born that Joshua had knuckled down to his own father's expectations.

"I thought we might spend a week or two in Lytham at the beginning of August, my love," Nancy proclaimed serenely to her husband in particular and her family in general. "The weather is so splendid at the moment it seems a shame to stay in town. You could travel on the Blackpool Club Train each day. You know how fast it is and I'm sure the sea air would do your chest good."

"Now, Nancy, there is absolutely nothing wrong with my chest."

"No, not now, in the middle of summer but you know how you cough in the winter. The doctor says it puts a great strain—"

"Doctor Croxley is nothing but a scaremonger and—"

"Darling, to please me," his wife pleaded.

Their four children continued to eat in silence as this exchange took place between their mother and father. They were used to it. For as long as they could remember their father had been prone to that dreadful affliction of the lungs which was the curse of those who worked in the factories and mills of Manchester. Factory smoke, engine fumes, breathed in day after day, year after year did great damage to the respiratory system, not only of the workers themselves but the factory and mill owner who breathed in the same lethal fumes.

"Well, I'll see," he promised. "As a matter of fact I

have a bit of business to attend to in St Anne's. There's a group of businessmen from Rossendale who formed a company a few years back with a view to developing the place. There's been a bit of a slump and they're looking for investors. I thought I might put a few bob in it. I'm pretty certain that in a few years the resort is going to overtake Lytham."

Kitty yawned, doing little to hide her boredom. She tried to catch Freddy's eye but he was cleaning up his plate as though he hadn't had a morsel to eat for weeks. She fidgeted in her chair, hoping he would look up at her and smile in that way that made her heart turn over but he sat back contentedly, then turned to listen politely to his father. What Joshua Hayes was saying was somewhat over his head and of little interest to him anyway but he had been brought up to be polite.

"I think we'll take our coffee in the drawing-room, shall we? Oh, and tell Cook that was a fine piece of beef, will you, Ivy, and that she surpassed herself, as always, with her apple pie," Joshua remarked as they rose from the table.

"I will, sir. She'll be pleased." Ivy sketched a curtsey, just a brief one since her old knees weren't as supple as once they'd been.

"In fact, I've a good mind to give her a further chance to shine. Sometimes I think she's wasted on these philistines of mine. How about asking Mr Maddox to dine with us, Freddy? Then we can perhaps clear up this . . ."

Kitty, who had been just about to leave the room, meaning to hang about in the hallway and catch Freddy as the others moved into the drawing-room, whirled about so fiercely her father, who was directly behind her, fell back in dismay.

"Father, you can't mean it. After all that has just been said about what a boor he is . . ."

"Rubbish, Kitty. This is another of your wild absurdities. To say he insulted you by giving his opinion on the correct mount for a lady is the—"

"Father, you can't mean it," she wailed.

As she watched from beside her chair which her son had just held back for her, her mother wondered if this child of hers would ever grow up. She was twenty-three years old and though she was not academically clever, since she had not been encouraged to be, she was intelligent, quick-thinking, sharp-witted even, except where Freddy Hayes was concerned, where she became as obtuse as a block of wood. From the moment they had met as crawling babies she had claimed him for her own and though it was very evident to every member of the household, with perhaps the exception of Sebastian who noticed nothing that was not to do with food or horses, that Freddy was fond of her *as a sister*, she lived for the moment she seemed convinced would come, the moment he would ask her to marry him. And if Nancy Hayes knew her daughter, she would not wait much longer. She would throw her pride, which was important to her, to the wind, and ask the question herself. Something had happened last night between the perfectly mannered and eminently suitable Mr Ben Maddox and her unmanageable daughter and whatever it was it had upset her to the extent she had made up this cock-and-bull story about her horse, of all things. Nancy had noticed the way Mr Maddox had taken her daughter on the floor last night. Who could help it, and the idle thought had occurred to her that here was a man whom Kitty could not get the better of. For some reason she heartily approved of her husband's intention to ask the young man to dine.

"I do mean it, Kitty. It seems to me the young man meant no offence and it also seems to me, knowing you as I do, you let him feel the length of your tongue which can be vituperative. I think you owe this—"

"I can't believe you mean—"

"I do mean it. I believe that the next time Mr Maddox is in Manchester we should invite him to dine. What d'you think, my love?" he asked his wife.

Kitty stood in the doorway, her eyes wide with horror, her hand to her mouth so that even Tilly, who was not as sharp as she might be, wondered what the devil was wrong with her. You'd think the master had suggested they have to dine that monster who'd taken a pot shot at their beloved Queen earlier in the year.

"Well, in that case don't expect me to attend," she spat out, whirling back to the hallway, her full bustle swinging quite alarmingly against the door frame. Even as she felt the anger rise in her again another small part of her brain was whispering the question, "Why,

why, why?" Why was she acting like this? And the simple truth was she didn't know. She didn't really have anything against this man who was Freddy's school-friend. He'd kissed her, certainly, but if she was totally honest he had not been unpleasant about it and even as the thought occurred to her she was suddenly aware that that was why she was so bloody mad. She *shouldn't* have liked it one bit. She should have been mortified that a man who wasn't Freddy . . . Oh, God, why had he come to disturb the even tenor of her life, her life which was spent waiting for Freddy to catch up with her? She was too confused; she must talk to Freddy, she must, before she went out of her mind. In fact this very night, if she could part him from the rest of the family, she would speak up, tell him . . . tell him how she felt and then, when it was all out in the open it wouldn't matter a damn if Ben Maddox came to dinner or not.

"Kitty," her father was saying grimly, "I will have no more of this nonsense. I don't very often put my foot down, which perhaps I should, but this time I will be obeyed. Mr Maddox will come to dinner and you will be at least polite to him. D'you understand?"

"Yes, Father," wanting to smile all of a sudden, because they were all staring at her with their mouths hanging open for when did Kitty Hayes give in so easily. It was written in their faces, even her father's, since he had expected more arguments, if not down-right disobedience.

"Very well." It was clear he didn't know what to

say next, the wind being taken out of his sails, so to speak. And when Kitty marched out into the hallway and up the stairs, regal as a young queen, he watched her go, his feelings uneasy, his face anxious until his wife put her hand on his arm and led him into the drawing-room.

She waited patiently by her bedroom door, the door itself opened the smallest crack so that when Freddy went past to his own room, just beyond hers, she would catch him. Anna had long since gone by but there was no sign of Ciara, which was strange, for she and Anna, being much of an age, usually came up together. Oh, where the devil was Freddy? It seemed to be hours since she came up, though when she squinted at the small enamelled clock on her mantelpiece she saw that only an hour had gone by. Perhaps he had been summoned to her father's study, which was often the case, to sort out some muddle he had got into at the mill. She knew that this morning he had been going over some papers so maybe he and Father were still at it. But what could Ciara be doing downstairs all this time?

Her bedroom window, which faced the extensive gardens at the front of the house, stood wide open, for the night still held the warmth of the day. She had pulled back the curtains, which Tilly had drawn, and a tiny breeze stirred the nets. She heard Jess bark, a deep, easily recognisable sound and the other two answered and she wondered who had taken them out, for by now they were all three usually tucked up in the stable block.

Leaving the door slightly ajar so that she would see and hear Freddy as he walked up the corridor, she moved to the window and peered out, lifting the nets so that they draped over her like a bride's veil. Putting her head right out of the window she was about to call Jess's name, for though she could barely see his blackness against the deep shadows of the lawn, Holly and Rex were clearly visible.

And so were two other figures. Walking up the slight incline of the lawn, their arms entwined, were Freddy and Ciara. They stopped for a moment, facing one another, and when they kissed the hammer blow to her heart brought her to her knees.

4

She wasn't certain whether she had dozed or whether she had slipped in and out of some kind of semi-conscious state. She was still on the floor, the moss-soft, velvet-smooth carpet of her bedroom floor. All about her she could see her familiar things, the things she had known since girlhood when she had come out of the nursery. It was almost dawn, she thought, the light of another day creeping round the edge of the drawn-back brocade curtains but in the shadows she could make out the muslin-draped canopy above her bed and the silk counterpane which one of the maids had turned back the night before. A low chair with a shell-shaped back inlaid with mother-of-pearl, the legs of which were close to her face, stood in its usual place by the window and the rest of the furniture, a rosewood chest of drawers, a wardrobe to match it, a dressing table backed by a silver-framed mirror with a stool in front of it, a comfortable armchair by the empty grate, were all in their usual places. There were the vague shapes of flowers in vases placed on small tables and the aromatic scent of potpourri made by her mother: dried flowers, herbs, spices blended with rich oils. All as well known and taken for granted as her own face in the mirror but for ever foreign to her now. She was no longer the same person who had entered this room last night and the things in the room no longer seemed to be hers. They belonged to the girl who had slipped, not only from the windowsill last night but from the life, the world, the existence she had known before.

Slowly, hand over hand, like some ancient crone who has taken a fall and attempts to regain her feet, she pulled herself, with the help of the chair, to a kneeling position and then upright, or as near to upright as she could manage. She leaned her hands on the windowsill, as she had done last night, and looked sightlessly out into the garden. It was raining. There was no one about, not at this early hour, whatever it might be. Nearly daylight but not quite with the grey wash of the low scudding clouds paler above the trees to the east. There was no sound but the tick of the clock on the mantelpiece and the slow dragging agony of the beating of her heart. She could hear it plainly and with a vague and vagrant thought she wished it would stop. For ever. She knew it would get worse. Just at this precise moment she was numb. Badly shocked and she'd heard that shock was a merciful thing, nature's way of protecting something that was broken, like her heart, she supposed. An oblivion that was empty but which would, she knew, fill up and overflow with the pain and she was aware that if she didn't remove herself from this house, this place where ... where ... dear sweet God ... Freddy and Ciara had kissed one another with the lingering tenderness of ... of ... lovers, she would do something, probably herself, some permanent damage.

Still dressed in the honey silk evening gown she had put on a hundred years ago when she was young and optimistic, she turned and blundered across her bedroom to the door, knocking over a small table on which a crystal bowl of blush-pink roses stood. Some deep primeval instinct told her to hide, to keep away from others of her kind, for she thought they might tear her to pieces in their sympathetic efforts to find out what was wrong and how they could put it right.

The house was still and silent, not even the young skivvy who was the first riser up yet. The kitchen was like a new pin, if she had been in a state to notice it, for Mrs Hodges and Mrs Bright, the housekeeper and the cook, were sticklers for cleanliness, tidiness and had instilled it into the other servants from the moment they were first employed. You just did not go to bed until every last pot and spoon had been washed and put in its proper place.

The back door was locked, for Mrs Hodges was also a stickler for security since there were some chancy characters hanging about in what had once been the most genteel neighbourhood on the outskirts of Manchester; that is until vast developments of estates of terraced cottages for the workers had been erected, almost up to the very gates of Riverside House.

She shivered but not with cold as she ran across the kitchen yard, through the archway and beyond the kitchen garden to the stable yard. It was almost full daylight now but it was murky with the drifting slant of thin rain and as she was about to open the stable door, some stray thought wisped like a strand of smoke into her blank mind. She must get away. She didn't know for how long. Probably just long enough to . . . to put her thoughts in order, if such a thing was possible, to organise some meaning into her life which stretched out barren before her, or at least to give her a chance to brace her weak and damaged heart to what it would suffer, to strengthen her frail body to the superhuman task it must take on. No one must know. *No one must know* and so, as if she were recovering from a devastating illness, she must go somewhere to be alone with it. And if she disappeared in her evening gown they would come looking for her. She must, somehow, change into her riding habit, saddle Chester, and . . . and . . . Oh, God, help me, give me strength; let me get away before . . . please . . .

The sound of Chester's hooves on the cobbles woke Charlie, the old groom who did not sleep as well as he once had done. Since his old woman had died he had lived in a cosy room above the tack-room, his bits and pieces about him, his brindle whippet to keep him company. Tizzy, he called her, for when she had been a pup, no more than a handful of shivering bones, she had been in one, a tizzy that is, all excited and nervous, and it had taken a lot of caring affection on his part to bring her up to scratch. Her bright eyes peered at him from the gloom where she lay on the foot of his bed and she pricked her ears when he spoke.

"Now, 'oo the bloody 'ell were that, my lass? I'll give yer three guesses. Eeh, she's a rare bird, that one, an' if some man don't snare 'er an' teach 'er ter sit on 'is 'and she'll 'ave no peace."

"Miss Kitty's not in her room, madam. Her riding things have gone and so has Chester, so Charlie told me ten minutes since. He said she went out right early. Woke him up, in fact."

"Dear Lord, what are we to do with that girl?" Josh Hayes beseeched his wife but she merely sighed, shook her head and reached for her cup of coffee.

Nancy Hayes had long since given up wondering what was to become of her daughter and if you were to ask Jennet Williams, who was Nancy's oldest friend and had been present at Kitty's birth, she might have told you that Kitty's mother, though she had always done her duty by the child, had left her upbringing to others. She had been too busy clawing her way out of the poverty and wretchedness she and her sisters had been born into. Even the love the child had received had come from others. From Jennet herself, from Nancy's sister Mary and from the old woman, dead these six years, who had looked after Kitty from the day of her birth. So was it any wonder that the child had grown up wild, unmanageable, strong-willed, self-absorbed, knowing with that sure instinct of a child that her mother had not welcomed her arrival.

"She was to come with me to the Wood Street Mission this morning. She didn't want to, of course, but I insisted. She can't spend her days doing nothing but riding that wild horse of hers. There's a tennis party tomorrow at the Lamberts but she's not been invited since it's beginning to be noticed that she's the oldest unmarried girl in the group. She's . . . I hate to say this, Josh, but she's become that object of pity, a spinster."

"Oh, no, dearest, not our Kitty." Her husband was distressed. "She's too lively, and such a beautiful girl. Surely someone will . . . will be willing to . . . overlook her beginnings. I've let it be known, God help me, that she'll have a good dowry when she marries."

"I know that, my darling, but I fear it is not doing any good. It's not just her past that is against her but her nature. What man will take on a wife who will not live by the rules of decent society? She is a burden to herself, really she is, and where the dickens she has gone this morning, and why, is anybody's guess."

Tilly, who was serving the master and mistress this morning, clattered a dish and at once, realising that they were discussing intimate family matters before a servant, they stopped talking. Not that Tilly would spread a murmur beyond the walls of Riverside House. She was a loyal, conscientious woman who had been with them for years, looking after Josh's parents when they were alive. She'd already served Master Freddy, who had been in great spirits this morning, whistling cheerfully and untying her apron strings as he used to as a boy.

"How are you this fine morning, Tilly?" he'd asked her.

"It's pouring with rain, Master Freddy," she'd protested, wondering what was up with him.

"So it is, Tilly, but who cares?"

"Well, Trudy, for one. She's the washing to get dry."

"Oh, the sun will be out before you know it. You tell her, and I'll have the lot this morning, Tilly. Porridge to start, then bacon, mushrooms, an egg and some fried tomatoes. I'm famished. Oh, and plenty of toast."

He had driven off to the warehouse in Moseley Street where he was to work this morning, still whistling, Richie had told her, and the girls, Miss Ciara and Miss Anna, and Miss Marguerite were not yet up. It was barely seven thirty and, as was usual, the master and mistress breakfasted alone.

"Well, I suppose I'll have to go to the mission by myself, unless one of the girls is willing to come. Not that they're concerned with the poor and I suppose you can't blame them since they've never known want, but some of those children are very bright and might make something of themselves." As she had!

"And I must be off too." Josh Hayes shook his head and sighed.

She followed him into the hallway, helping him on with his long box-coat, then stretching up to kiss him tenderly, a scene Tilly or Ivy witnessed every morning.

He sighed again. "I wonder where that girl has got to, and in this rain, too."

She rode for hours, first at a gallop, tearing into the slanting rain, then, as Chester tired, slowing down to a walk. She was wet through within an hour, right down to her chemise and drawers, for she had not thought to bring a waterproof ulster. She had no thought at all beyond the one that got her dressed, saddled her gelding, put her foot in the stirrup and got her away from Broughton. She had gone west, she didn't know why, making not for any of the familiar landmarks that Freddy would know, just in case they decided to look for her, striking across country through Pendlebury, crossing the railway lines that cobwebbed Lancashire, and the old Bridgewater Canal, plodding across field after field and avoiding the small villages in her path. She had no sense of where she was going, hunched down in the saddle, her head bowed, the rainwater dripping off the brim of her hat which something had told her to put on.

Whenever she hit a road passers-by stared at her in amazement. She was obviously a lady of quality so what the devil was she doing out in this weather when she had no need to be? Not like them who had to go to work, or to the nearest town or village to shop for their families' food. They wished they had the choice to stay indoors in this drenching downpour but then there was no accounting for the idiosyncrasies of the gentry.

She found herself on a narrow lane which was ankle-deep in mud, rutted, slippery and treacherous. To her left was a strip of woodland and not really knowing why, she turned in under the trees. It was an oak wood, dim and gloomy on this day of driving rain, the leaf canopy above her head dense, shutting off any glimpse of the sodden sky. Rain dripped, a rustling patter on the layer of shrubs, ivy, holly and bramble which did their best to block her way. There was no sign of life, animal or human, not even the sound of a bird, and when Chester stopped she slid from his back, again for no apparent reason. He had stopped so she dismounted. She felt an amazing sense of calm, not a tranquil calm that warms and soothes, but ice-cold, frozen, like the pond on a winter's day. Not that it mattered. Not that anything mattered now. She had lost Freddy. Ciara had stolen Freddy from her and she had not even noticed her doing it. He had been Kitty's ever since the day she herself had been brought to the nursery at Riverside House. They had belonged exclusively to one another for six years as children, then Ciara had been introduced into their world, hers and Freddy's and, without Kitty being aware of it, had taken the only man she would ever love.

The thoughts darted into her head, like minnows beneath the surface of water. She didn't want them but there seemed to be nothing she could do to stop them as life, slowly and agonisingly, crept back into her numbed brain.

She sank down on to a fallen tree-trunk, shaking uncontrollably. She wrapped her arms about herself, rocking backwards and forwards in the way women do when they have reached the boundary where bearable sorrow becomes unbearable. It was wet. About her feet grew fern and bracken, stiff, dripping with rainwater, and she stared down at it, raindrops running into her eyebrows and down to her lashes where they hung for a moment until she blinked them away. It was as though she wept but there were no tears in her, not yet, though in her desolation she knew they would come. Her mind was still clouded, and yet one image remained to torture her: that of Freddy and Ciara standing on the lawn in one another's arms. It was engraved in her mind, in her heart, in the very soul of her, but somehow she must gather her strength about her and though it tormented her until the day she died, which she supposed it would, she knew deep inside her where sense lay that she must go back. Face it! Face them! Somehow!

She sat for an hour, her mind set in the dark cast of grieving, just as though Freddy had died, which, to her, she supposed he had. Then, getting slowly to her feet she waded through the undergrowth to where Chester stood, tired and patient, in the shelter of a vast canopy of oak. She climbed on to his back, turning him towards the lane that had led into the wood, setting him on the way east where Manchester lay.

*   *   *

It had stopped raining so Bridget was just about to start "donkey-stoning" her front step, which she prided herself was the whitest in the row. Bridget had been taught all her housewifely skills, despite being unmarried, by Mrs Wilson, who had been Bridget's guide and mentor for over twelve years before Mrs Wilson died. Bridget had come to Grove Place, the home now of Miss Jennet Williams, when she was thirteen and her pa had begun to show an unhealthy interest in her growing woman's body. Her ma had soon put a stop to that by getting her this place with Mrs Wilson and she had been here ever since. That had been seventeen years ago and in those years Bridget had known a content, a happiness, a satisfaction she could have described to no one. She was a "do-er" was Bridget, not a talker, which didn't matter, for Mrs Wilson, who had been like a mam to Bridget, did all the talking that was needed.

She'd been here when Miss Kitty had been a babby. It was into Bridget's arms that the newborn infant who had become Miss Ciara had been placed when *her* mam had passed away. Mrs Wilson had been housekeeper to Miss Jennet and Miss Nancy, who was now Mrs Hayes, and Bridget had been her right-hand man, Mrs Wilson had been fond of saying. Bridget had loved Mrs Wilson. She loved them all, Miss Jennet, Mrs Hayes, Miss Mary who had become Mrs Meadows, the children who were dearer to her than her own numerous brothers and sisters, and her one aim in life was to serve them in any way she could.

She was on her knees, her bottom stuck in the air, swaying from side to side, moving in the same satisfying rhythm as the stiff bristled brush in her hand, when she heard the clatter of horses' hooves on the road beyond the gate. She took no notice since hundreds of horses, of all kinds, passed along Bury New Road every day of the week. She hummed a tuneless little song as she worked and when she heard the gate click her first thought was one of annoyance, since she wanted to get her steps done before Miss Jennet got home. She'd a tasty casserole in the oven and fresh vegetables waiting to be cooked and she thought she might make a rice pudding. Plain fare but nourishing, Mrs Wilson had told her. Both she and Mrs Wilson had known nothing of fancy dishes, not the sort she knew were prepared at Riverside House where Miss Nancy had moved on her marriage, but Miss Jennet ate *good* food, and though Bridget said it herself, well cooked.

Not getting up from her knees she turned to see who had come through her gate, nearly upsetting her bucket when she recognised the visitor. And not just a human visitor, but a bloody horse an' all, which was being led up the garden path as though it were to be brought into the house. Leading it was Miss Kitty for whom, she admitted it to no one, of course, Bridget had a soft spot.

Struggling to her feet, impeded by her bucket and her apron which she trod on as she stood up, she was about to smile, despite the horse, to welcome Miss Kitty and beg her to come inside, minding Bridget's newly donkey-stoned step, naturally, but taking one look at her, not just her face, which was gaunt, hollow, ill-looking, but the state of her sodden clothes, she was struck dumb. She dropped her donkey-stone, shoved the bucket aside with little care for her step and put out a hand. Miss Kitty let go of the reins with which she led the horse, who stood like some old nag between the shafts of a hansom, head down, coat all filthy, and put her hand in Bridget's.

They moved up the steps and into the bright, fragrant hallway of the house in Grove Place which had belonged to Kitty's mother, first rented, then when she married, bought for her by her husband, for the past twenty-two years. Bridget led the senseless young woman carefully by the hand up the hall and into an equally bright kitchen-cum-parlour where a small fire crackled, where two comfortable chairs stood before it, where a snowy cloth was laid on a round table set with one place. With the gentleness of a nurse caring for a sick, perhaps dying patient, Bridget led Kitty to one of the chairs and sat her in it, kneeling down before her.

"Chuck," she murmured softly, "yer wet through. Where yer bin? What's 'appened? Is there summat up at 'ome? Eeh, my lass, yer'd best gerrout o' them things or yer'll catch yer death. See, let Bridget 'elp yer . . ."

It was as though Bridget's words had turned a key, lifted a lever, opened a sluice gate through which, at last, Kitty's despair was released and she spoke the first words that had passed her lips since she had left the dining-room the previous evening. It was no more than a croak.

"Catch my death, is it? If only I could, Bridget. If only whoever's in charge of these things would strike me dead, let me sleep. Sleep for ever and never wake up."

Bridget was horrified. "Nay, Kitty Hayes, what a dreadful thing ter say. I'm ashamed o' yer, really I am, an' if yer ma—"

"Leave my ma out of this, Bridget. D'you think she gives a damn about me? D'you think she's *ever* given a damn about me?"

"Miss Kitty, yer know that's not true," which, of course, it was. "Yer mam's always looked after yer," which *was* true.

"It doesn't matter, anyway, what my mother thinks of me. I don't care. I only care about . . ."

"What, lass?"

"Freddy."

"Master Freddy, what's 'e got ter do wi' it, whatever it is?"

"Bridget . . . oh, Bridget, how am I to live?" She began to moan, rocking backwards and forwards as she had done in the wood and Bridget, appalled, put her arms about her, drawing her head down to her shoulder in an effort to calm her.

"I don't understand, chuck. Tell me what's 'appened."

"I always thought . . ."

"What, lass? Tell Bridget."

"Right from the start, when we were babies, d'you remember?"

"Aye."

"I loved him . . ."

"An' 'e loves you," not yet understanding.

"No, he doesn't."

"Give over."

Suddenly wrenching herself from Bridget's arms, knocking her back on to her bottom, Kitty stood up and began to throw herself about the room, crashing into the table, knocking over a chair that stood by it, banging her clenched fists on the wall in a fit of what seemed to Bridget close to madness. She trailed a cascade of water from her sodden skirt, spotting Bridget's clean tiled floor and marking the square of carpet that stood before the fire. As she whirled about, spots of rain flew from her soaked hair, hissing into the flames of the fire, and out in the garden Chester began to eat Bridget's prized dahlias.

With a muttered oath Bridget clawed her way up from the floor and caught Kitty by the forearms as she flung herself once more towards the fireplace. Kitty was strong but Bridget was stronger. She had worked, hard manual labour since she was six years old, doing many jobs that would have overcome a grown man and when, holding Kitty with one hand, she slapped her across the face with the other, she almost kocked her off her feet. At once, as though the lever had been moved in another direction, the sluice gate closed, the words, the weeping, were cut off and Kitty sagged, at the end of her resources, against Bridget's compassionate shoulder.

"Come on, lass, let's get yer upstairs and outer them clothes. There's nowt o' Miss Jennet's'll fit yer so yer'll 'ave ter mekk do wi' summat o' mine. Then we'll 'ave us a cup o' tea an' yer can tell me all about it."

"No," Kitty mumbled, hanging her head as though in deep shame. "No one must know."

"An' I'll tell no one, yer know that, my lass. Wharrever yer say, I don't care what it's about, it'll be safe wi' me. Now then, let's get yer warm, then we'll 'ave ter see about that animal in't garden."

Charlie was quite appalled when he saw the state of Chester.

"What the 'ell does she think she's doin', treatin' a thoroughbred animal, or any animal fer that matter, the way this poor old chap's bin treated. He's buggered, poor lad, an' will yer look at state of 'is coat. Where's she 'ad 'im, for God's sake? Honest, Richie, I'm surprised at Miss Kitty, really I am. I thought she were fond o't beast. What did she say?"

"Nay, Charlie, I never seed 'er. That Bridget wouldn't let me in th'ouse. Said she were asleep an' couldn't be disturbed an' I was ter tekk th'orse an' gerr off 'ome."

"Is that all? Nothin' about where she's bin? She set off before it was light this mornin' 'cos I 'eard 'er messen, gallopin' off as if summat were after 'er. D'yer know, I don't know why they purrup wi' it, Mr an' Mrs Hayes.

She wants a bloody good 'iding an' by God, she'd've gorrit if she'd bin mine. 'Appen she'd o' turned out a bit better."

"I dunno, I quite like 'er," Richie said mildly. "A woman wi' a bit o' spirit . . ."

Charlie snorted. "A bit o' spirit, is it. That lass'll drive a man mad, that's if she ever gets one ter tekk 'er on. Now then, tekk Chester an' give 'im a good wash an' rub down while I unsaddle Merlin. Good job Master Freddy went ter work in't carriage this mornin' or yer'd 'ave 'ad ter walk up ter Grove Place."

"Aye," said Richie, leading away the sadly woebegone figure of Chester who had never in all his life been treated as badly as he had been today.

Nancy Hayes and her husband were both away from home when the message came, brought by the lad who lived next door to Bridget, that Miss Hayes was at Grove Place and thought she might stay overnight. She would be glad if one of the stable lads would come and pick up Chester as there was nowhere to stable him at her Aunt Jennet's. The message made it all sound so ordinary, just the sort of thing Miss Kitty was used to doing, unconcerned with anyone's feelings but her own, that when her mother returned from the Wood Street Mission where she worked with underprivileged children she gave it no thought beyond reminding herself to tell Mrs Bright there would be one fewer for dinner.

"She did say could someone fetch her a change of

clothes, madam," Ivy added. "She got wet riding this morning."

"Very well, Ivy, see to it, will you. Send Dulcie or Cissie."

"Yes, madam."

It was dark when she woke. Not a solid darkness, for the bedroom door was ajar and a comforting glow came through the gap. She could see the unfamiliar shapes of furniture, a wardrobe, a dresser, a chair placed before an empty fireplace. Beside the bed was a small round table with a lacy cloth thrown over it and on the table was a vase of some sort of flowers and a book. The book looked like a Bible. She knew where she was and who had put her here in this soft, comforting feather bed; who had dressed her in her own voluminous and utterly modest nightgown; who had kissed her cheek and smoothed back her tangle of hair, promising to give it a good brush when she woke. She felt . . . well, she could only describe it as *smooth*, as though all the tortuous twists, the ragged edges, the crushed and shattered surfaces of her had been ironed out. Last night, before her Aunt Jennet had come home from her shop in St Ann's Square, she had ranted and railed, wept and even screamed so that those next door must have thought murder was being done, exposing to the appalled, compassionate Bridget all that was in her, all the engulfing love she had harboured for Freddy Hayes, which, to be honest, she knew had shocked Bridget since all the servants had always thought of them as brother and sister, which, of course, they weren't. What Kitty felt was a woman's love for a man and now that man had chosen someone else, and the grief in her was so wild it made her seem unbalanced. She had knocked several cups of tea from Bridget's hand and it was not until after a few sips of something Bridget had brewed and managed to get down her, that she had become calm.

And now here she was, empty but not as yet in pain. It felt good to snuggle down under the fat eiderdown which Bridget thought necessary for a good night's sleep. She knew she would soon have to leave this cocoon of unreality and face the life that was to be hers from now on, but just for the moment, until daybreak came, she would lie here and be nothing. Nobody. A form without a mind, without all the emotions, the feelings of the woman she must become. She thought perhaps she might sleep again, for God knew she would need all her strength to get through, not only the next few hours, the next few days, but the rest of her life and she knew she would get little rest for a while, if ever again. She had to play a part, you see, act out a charade that said that Kitty Hayes hadn't a care in the world beyond getting whatever *she* wanted out of life, which was certainly not Freddy Hayes. She couldn't yet think what she might do in the months and years to come, the years she had imagined she and Freddy spending together, but she knew, when she became herself again, when she became Kitty Hayes with the sharp mind, the quick brain, the clever, quick-witted way she had of getting the better of other, slower powers of reasoning, she would find something.

Her heart might be broken, but she was not.

She watched the dawn creep, the new day creep over Bridget's windowsill and spread itself over the achingly clean room. Over the sprigged wallpaper, the ticking clock on the narrow mantelshelf, the pictures on the wall of kittens in baskets and cows in fields, and when the first birds began to murmur she got out of bed and went to the window. She was rested. She was strengthened. She was in control of that dangerous impulse that wanted to weep and wail her loss. She didn't know how she was to do it, she only knew she would.

Her heart might be broken – God help her, it was – but Kitty Hayes was not.

5

She was sitting at the piano the next time he saw her. The graceful curve of her neck as she bent her head over the keys caught his breath and for a moment he froze in the doorway. Her fingers moved softly, gracefully, smoothly, each finger striking the keys with exactly the same force so that every note was clear. She was playing the old English love-song "Greensleeves". She seemed oblivious to the other people in the room, humming softly to herself, occasionally murmuring a few words here and there.

"Alas my love . . . Greensleeves was all my joy . . . was my delight . . . my heart of gold . . ."

The smartly dressed housemaid who had taken his hat and cape in the hallway and shown him to the drawing-room stepped back and Freddy rose to greet him from the sofa where he was seated with Ciara.

"Ben, old chap . . ." he began, holding out his hand, but Ben, fa ;t in the magic of Kitty Hayes as he had never seen her, held up his own hand in what, he supposed later, was an extremely curt manner, to silence him.

For a moment or two they stood side by side, watching the amazing but charming picture of Kitty Hayes in a mood of tranquillity which Ben, at least, did not know was in her. He had seen her up on Crablane Head, of course, but that was different, for she had been asleep.

There were several other guests in the room, beside the family, which included Anna, who at almost seventeen was considered old enough to be included in a formal dinner party, and they were all quite enraptured, silently paying homage to what was a talented performance.

Kitty was dressed in a shimmering colour which reminded Ben of the carpet of bluebells in May under the trees surrounding his home. The Hayes ladies were all superbly, expensively dressed and he supposed it was down to Mrs Hayes who had a natural good taste where clothes were concerned. He had heard somewhere that she had once had a dressmaking establishment of her own in the exclusive St Ann's Square district of Manchester, which explained it. She and her daughters were dressed in the sheath-like gowns that were the fashion of the day, with draped bustles, but where the other ladies were a glory of frills and flounces, bows, ornamentation of an extraordinary kind, stiff swathing about the hips, all in the brightest of colours, such as green, pink, vivid yellow, blue and carnation, the Hayes ladies wore simple, elegant gowns of subtle shades with nothing to mar their superb cut and style.

Kitty's fingers continued to ripple across the keys, and her eyes closed for a moment as though she were in a private world where no one else could enter, a place of calm and solitude and quiet joy, then she opened them and saw him in the doorway.

At once the soft expression on her face became hard and brittle and she smiled, a slow, wide smile of pure glee as though her devious mind were already up to some mischief, probably hurtful.

"Well, if it's not Freddy's friend, Mr Ben Maddox. You will all have heard of the heroic Mr Maddox, I'm sure," she said to the astonished company who all turned to look at the newcomer. "It's said that Freddy couldn't have got through his schooldays without the friendship of Mr Maddox, so we have a lot to thank him for, wouldn't you agree?"

He bowed in her direction, his face totally expressionless, then turned to her mother who had also risen to greet him.

"Mrs Hayes, this is a great pleasure. It was kind of you to invite me." With a smile, this time of genuine pleasure, he bowed over her hand, then looked up into her eyes and Nancy Hayes was struck by his great personal attraction, though he was not strictly a handsome man. There was a warmth about him, a sense of humour in his smile and yet his mouth was firm, hard even, with a twist to it that said he was not a man to be trifled with. She liked him. Her husband joined her, taking Ben's hand in his, engaging him in the polite conversation that was the custom in mixed company. Later, when the ladies withdrew, the gentlemen would get down to the interesting, totally male talk which the ladies did not care for: business, the state of the country, the state of the world, politics, serious matters, but for now it was nothing but pleasantries.

But Kitty had not finished with him. From the piano she called out his name again and the assembled company, especially members of the family, groaned inwardly, for it seemed the eldest daughter of the house was not, as had at first seemed possible as she played "Greensleeves" for them, to behave herself. The guests had heard her play before, of course, when she could be persuaded, and had often been astonished at her talent and the way her playing and the instrument she played on transformed her. It was a talent, a gift, and a benevolence to her governess who was often heard to say, to the other staff only, of course, that the only time her pupil was bearable was when she was at the piano. Like the other girls she had been taught by a good teacher and the hours she had spent with him and when she played for her own enjoyment were the only times there was peace in the house, at least when she was in it!

"Let me play you something, Mr Maddox," she begged him, her grin even broader. "What'll it be? How about this one?"

'I 'ad a tart in Birkenhead.
A true friend, if you know what I mean . . .'

"*Kitty!* That is enough," her father hissed furiously, his face turning an alarming shade of puce, for Kitty had continued in a shouted chorus with the words that soldiers, ribald, derisive, put to the songs they sing in wartime. Her hands crashed about the keys, still fluid but with the enthusiasm of a music-hall entertainer, which was where the song had come from and God only knew where Kitty Hayes had heard it. Her father strode across the room and with a crash and a careless unconcern for her hands, flung down the piano lid.

"Kitty, we have guests and I would be obliged if you would treat them with respect. One of your other pieces would be—"

"But, Father, I thought Mr Maddox might care for something a little more lively."

"Stop it."

"Very well, if you don't wish me to play, of course, I won't. I shall sit in the corner and be as quiet as a mouse. Perhaps Mr Maddox would like to join me."

"Certainly I would, Miss Hayes, but perhaps later." Ben Maddox smiled a cold but polite smile and turned on his heel, moving across the carpet to stand before Anna, while on Kitty's face an expression of disbelief made one or two of the company turn away, smiling. It was not often that their host's daughter got back as good as she gave. She didn't like it, you could see that, but instead of moving to the corner as she had threatened she strode with that long, mannish walk of hers to a tall, handsome young man who was doing his best to make polite conversation with a Mrs Underwood, an old friend of her mother's.

"Martin, come and play a duet with with me. I'm sure we can manage 'Chopsticks' or something and if we can't, I'll teach you. I've no doubt Mrs Underwood will excuse you," and, towing him across the room, she seated herself and the grinning young man, very close together several of the ladies noticed, on the piano stool, where they proceeded to hammer up and down the keys, at the same time shrieking with laughter.

But it seemed Mr Maddox had eyes for no one else as he spoke warmly to Kitty's sister.

"I don't believe we've been introduced," he said, smiling down at her, which was somewhat cruel, for she at once, in the way of inexperienced young girls, fell in love with him. "I'm not wrong in thinking you must be Anna. Freddy has spoken of you and you are so like your mother." He sat down beside her then turned to smile at the company as though to say there was no need for embarrassment. He was not embarrassed by Kitty Hayes's rudeness. Indeed he had scarcely noticed it, or her and at once they were easy again, turning to one another in the small talk that always preceded the walk into dinner. The outrageous and noisy peformance at the piano was ignored.

Nancy Hayes took her husband's hand and let out her breath on an anxious sigh as they both watched their eldest daughter. Kitty's eyes were bright with malice, though, as they looked up from the keyboard at Ben Maddox and her parents knew it was far from over. She had been, even more so than usual, a thorn in their side for weeks now. They didn't know what to do about it, that was the trouble. No matter what steps they took to curb her it made no difference. She was not a child – only in her ways – she was a woman of twenty-three and though still under her father's protection in her father's home, they could not control her nor prevent her from doing whatever she felt like doing. Really, it was making Joshua ill, Nancy was well aware, and with the winter to get through which would inevitably herald his old complaint, the one she was painfully aware had killed his father, Nancy felt she could stand little more of her daughter's tantrums.

They were walking from the drawing-room to the dining-room, each lady on the arm of a gentleman when she remembered, with despair, that she had seated Kitty directly across the table from Mr Maddox. Next to her was Martin Baker, the young man who had been drawn, not unwillingly, to be her partner at the piano, a young man not noted for his discretion or his judgement!

Her fears were justified. The pair of them whispered and giggled through every course, totally ignoring their partners to left and right, and when they were not engrossed with one another seemed bent on taunting Mr Maddox into making some impolite remark which she was sure he longed to do.

"Tell us about yourself, Mr Maddox," Kitty remarked sweetly. "I believe you come from Liverpool," making it sound as though Liverpool were made up of nothing but broken-down slums.

"I do, Miss Hayes." His eyes narrowed challengingly, a challenge she rose to with great fervour.

"I have never been there, have you, Martin?"

"I have not, Kitty. Tell, what is there to do there, Mr Maddox? Is there any . . . fun to be had?"

"It depends on what you call 'fun', Mr . . . I beg your pardon, I seem to have forgotten your name." He grinned wickedly and for some reason Joshua sat back and smiled. For a dreadful moment he had been afraid he was going to have to intervene to defend his guest but it seemed there was no need. He thought Mr Maddox was well able to deal with these two silly children, which was how he saw his daughter and young Martin Baker.

Josh Hayes was not to know that his daughter, despite the brilliant smile on her face and the whip of her vitriolic tongue, could feel the pain of her breaking heart as though someone had pierced it once again with a meat skewer. Though Freddy and Ciara were opposite one another at the table they rarely spoke to their partners but exchanged loaded glances and secret smiles. She could not help but remember that the last time she had seen the man opposite her had been the last time she had known happiness. The last evening when she had still held the sure belief that she and Freddy had a future together and the memory seemed to scratch something up from the depths of her being, something that wanted her to hurt Ben Maddox as she had been hurt. He had implied then that he knew something about Freddy that she wouldn't like and then had backed off. Now she realised that it had been something to do with Freddy's . . . Freddy's feelings for Ciara and hers for him and, by God, it was killing her but she'd not let this bastard see it, nor anyone.

"Well, parties, social life, that sort of thing," the arrogant Martin drawled.

"We have been known to give dinner parties somewhat like this."

"Really!" It sounded as if Kitty found that hard to believe.

"Oh, yes. You and your family must dine with me soon then I can prove that we are quite civilised." He did not include the sniggering Mr Baker in the invitation.

"We even have a theatre or two," he went on, "and I believe it is said that our art gallery, our libraries and museums are second to none."

"Well, we shall have to go over there and see for ourselves, won't we, Martin," as though she didn't believe a word of it.

"Indeed we must," the young man said, then whispered something in her ear which made her snort with laughter. She put her hand to her mouth, then lifted her head and the laughter died away.

Their glances clashed across the table and for a fraction of a second Kitty found herself marvelling at the colour of Ben Maddox's eyes. They were brown, that was for certain but such a warm, glowing brown,

an autumn colour like a horse chestnut at the turn of
the season, rich and glossy. They were surrounded
by thick lashes, long and dark and in them was an
enquiring look as though to ask her what she had
seen to arouse her interest. His mouth lifted at one
corner and he raised his eyebrows quizzically. Furious
with herself, she looked away hastily.

It was September, two months since the day – *the
day* – on which she would not allow herself to dwell.
Often in the night, when she could not escape it, when
she had seen it and wondered why she had been
blind to it before, what lay between Freddy and Ciara,
she would weep soundlessly, dragging her anguished
body from the bed, to the window, to the door, then
back again, turning like a trapped and wounded animal to escape the pain. She could not. Wherever she
twisted it followed her until, in desperation, she would
curl up in her bed, like a child in a womb, making
herself as small as possible as if that might diminish
the pain. It did not.

But the next day to those who saw her she was
as she had always been. And yet, though they did
not recognise it, to defend herself she had become
someone else. She had always been a difficult child.
She knew that because numerous nursemaids, nan-
nies and governesses had told her so. She had jibbed
against any sort of discipline and had, she was well
aware, been mutinous when it was applied. She had
disregarded orders, seeing no sense in so many of
them, like wearing a hat when out of doors, never

being seen without one's gloves, speaking only when spoken to. She preferred to run like a hoyden, ride her first pony as though she were a boy, climb trees, and shriek in sheer joy when she and Freddy raced away from the others. A hundred things. She had been bloody-minded; Charlie the groom had told her that when she rode her new pony until the poor thing was in a terrible lather, but everything she had done she had done innocently, not meaning to hurt, sorry when she did. She had this longing to be free, to be wild, to do exactly what she felt like doing, when she felt it. She had an overwhelming warmth in her, a passion, if you like, to be joyful, laughing, even as she rebelled against all restraints; but now her wildness had become something else altogether. There was an edge to her that was cutting. She was sharp, bitter, contemptuous, arrogant, not caring who she hurt with her wicked, acrimonious tongue. She reduced Anna to tears with her mockery, telling her she hadn't a thought in her head that hadn't been put there by her governess. She taunted Ciara with her irregular beginning until she ran to her mother, provoking Freddy into almost striking Kitty in his defence of the young girl he loved. She was rude, cruel even, ignoring every request her mother made to behave herself, and refusing to apologise when her father took her to task.

"Whatever has come over you, Kitty?" he despaired. "To tell Ciara she was the granddaughter of a . . . of a . . . I hardly like to say it."

"A whore, Father, is that the name you're looking

for? It's true, isn't it? My dear brother Freddy told me years ago where we had all come from, me and him and Ciara, I mean, though the others had more luck being born in wedlock."

"*Kitty!* Your mother is devastated."

"Really. No more than I was when I found out. Anyway, what does it matter? What is done is done and can't be undone. Now, if you'll excuse me, Father, I'm going riding," and she had simply walked out of the study, ignoring her father's thundering command to "Get back in here, my girl."

She kept out of the house as much as she could, riding through the glorious August days, going out often at daybreak when the white mist still curled about the dark trunks of the trees. She rode through meadows, stopping to talk to field workers, pleasant and polite with them since they had done nothing to hurt her. She even took off her jacket and, working in her thin chemise, gave them a hand with their harvesting, sitting in the shade of a hawthorn hedge and sharing their ale and bacon "butties", finding some small peace in their simple company.

Sometimes, when the mood took her, she dressed herself in a fashionable day dress of printed delaine in a soft shade of apple blossom with kid boots dyed to match. She wore a small bonnet tied beneath her chin with wide ribbons, decorated with blush-pink roses made from silk. She carried a dome-shaped parasol in white, trimmed with lace. A perfect lady who ordered out her mother's carriage, ignoring the protests of Brewer, the coachman, that Mrs Hayes might require it, bowling along Bury New Road, turning to smile and wave at Bridget should she be in the garden at Grove Place. She would instruct the coachman to put her off at the lower end of King Street where she would spend the afternoon running up an enormous bill on her mother's account, to the confoundment of the sales girls in each shop who were not used to young, unmarried ladies of the gentry going about without their mothers. Dainty boots, gloves, handkerchiefs, parasols, fans, a muff of sealskin, enamelled card cases. A feather boa and a bracelet of gold on which charms made in the shape of animals hung, and all thrown carelessly into a drawer when she got home or given to the maidservants.

She delighted in being controversial. She thought she might look into this new craze for cycling, she told them all languidly one evening at dinner, leaning her chin on her hands and her elbows on the table in a way she knew her mother abhorred. Had they heard of it? It was said that the most outrageous outfits might be purchased to wear on these wonderful machines. Bloomers, or knickerbockers or some such thing. She had been talking to some chap the other day . . . which chap? Oh, one she had met on the road to Blackley Top, she had added vaguely, who seemed to know a lot about them. A company in Coventry had produced a "safety" and was calling it a "bicyclette", which seemed appropriate, didn't Freddy think so, and what did he say to a day out to have a look at the things?

Total and horrified silence had followed and Kitty felt the delight flow through her. This was what she hoped to achieve with her high-flown behaviour. She wanted to bring them all to this state of amazed disgust. Well, perhaps not disgust but amazement and puzzlement and disbelief. She didn't reason why. She was desperately unhappy and some bitter thing inside her told her it was their fault and she desired nothing more than to shock them, to mortify them, to cause them hurt as she hurt.

"What on earth are you talking about?" Freddy managed at last, placing his knife and fork carefully on the edge of his plate.

"Well, I would have thought that was obvious, Freddy." Her voice was filled with scorn. "You have heard of the bicycle, surely. I believe young men are forming cycling clubs and getting out into the—"

"Yes, but not women. Not ladies."

"Oh, come now, Freddy." She smiled brilliantly. "You and I both know I am no lady, just as you are no gentleman."

This time a gasp echoed about the room while at the serving table Tilly and Ivy froze.

"Kitty, I must ask you to leave the room," her father barked. "I don't know, recently you seem bent on being as . . . as obnoxious as you possibly can be. You have always been . . ."

"Yes, Father?" Again that lovely, wild smile.

"Awkward, but you were never . . . never . . ."

"Yes, Father?"

"Will you leave the room. You are upsetting your mother."

"And we must never do that, must we?"

"*Kitty!* Do as I say. Ivy, see that Miss Kitty has a meal served to her in her room." It was as though a child had misbehaved at table and was being banished to the nursery.

Ivy came to with a start, clattering the lid of a silver serving dish against its base.

"Yes, sir," she quavered.

Kitty rose to her feet and sauntered from the room, turning at the door to give them her flashing smile.

"Let me know when you can spare the time to take the train to Coventry, Freddy, and don't worry if you can't, I'll go by myself. Oh, and Ivy, don't bother with a tray. I shall go and play for a while." And she dragged herself across the hall, into the drawing-room and sat down at the piano, the only pastime from which she gained any peace.

Now, weeks later, she was still in a state she couldn't describe but which she knew she could not stand for much longer. Though nothing had been said, no formal announcement, she knew that it was expected that Freddy and Ciara would marry soon and how . . . For God's sake how was she to stand living in the same house with them when that happened? Knowing that not only were they holding hands under the tablecloth, as they so often did, but would be man and wife with the right to disappear each night into their bedroom and do all the sweet and exciting things she had longed for herself. Like her mother, she despaired over the question of where she could go, what she could do to escape. She had considered going to live at the family house in Lytham but she knew her father would not allow it. Not a young, unmarried woman on her own, since servants didn't count. It was driving her mad and, as she was driven deeper into the madness, so she drove others the same way.

Most of the guests from the dinner party had gone, agreeing with one another the moment their carriages left the front steps of Riverside House that really, they had never, in all the years they had known her, seen Kitty Hayes behave so badly. It was quite disgraceful and how poor Nancy and Joshua were to deal with it they couldn't imagine. Heaven knew where she would finish up, the way she was behaving, and they certainly would never invite her to their homes again for fear she made a scene, or scenes, as she had done tonight. That poor Mr Maddox, what had he done to deserve the impertinent, nay *rude* way she had treated him? And that young man beside her, Martin Baker, was just as bad, though they decided it was she who had led him on.

The young man in question, along with several other young men, including Freddy Hayes and Ben Maddox, had stayed on, intent on a game of billiards, a challenge having been laid down by Martin Baker, who was much the worse for drink and hoped he could boast of it later, that he could beat Ben Maddox hands down.

"My pleasure," Ben had answered smoothly, drawing deeply on his cigar and narrowing his eyes against the smoke. "What wager did you have in mind."

"How about a fiver?" Martin, who played a lot of billiards, being a young man of leisure, smirked about the room at the other young sparks.

"Why don't we make it . . . a hundred? Guineas!" Ben drawled and the others gasped. It was at that moment that Kitty Hayes entered the room.

"What's this then?" she demanded, whirling about so that the bustle at the back of her gown bounced joyfully. She had retired to her room with her sisters and mother but a burst of laughter from downstairs, where it seemed the young men were having some fun, had drawn her from her furious pacing of her own room.

"Kitty, you shouldn't be here, you know that," Freddy began.

"Oh, fiddlesticks, Freddy. Where's the harm? You men have all the fun and I only want to watch. But I will have one of those cigars, Mr Maddox," she announced casually, strolling round the billiard table to where he leaned against the wooden fireplace.

The billiard-room was a gentlemen's room, a totally male preserve where smoking was not frowned upon and gentlemen could enjoy their port in their shirt sleeves, which they were doing now. The room had a high, vaulted ceiling and walls of carved wooden panelling. There was a full-sized billiard table, a cabinet scoreboard and bench seats on which the gentlemen might sprawl with their drinks. Over the table hung four large lamps, lit by gas. Billiards was a game played by most young gentlemen since it had been made popular, and acceptable, by the Queen's husband before his death. He had loved the game and it was said that the Queen, to please him, had installed a billiard table in every one of the royal residences. With the royal seal of approval the billiard-room had become an integral part of a wealthy gentleman's home.

"Certainly, Miss Hayes." Ben smiled, taking his case from his pocket and handing it to her. "Would you like me to light it for you?" His mouth twitched in what might have been the beginning of a smile.

"Please, if you would, and then I might have a game of billiards. I know how to play, you know. Freddy and I and the girls often have a game during a wet Sunday."

"Indeed, Miss Hayes?" He held out a match to her, watching the delightful way her rosy lips pursed round the end of the cigar, noting the soft swell of her full breast as she leaned forward.

"Thank you, Mr Maddox." As she drew in the smoke she made a great effort not to cough, watching him from under her long eyelashes in case he should smile but he kept his face in check, casually replacing his cigar case in his pocket.

"So, will you take me on, Mr Maddox?"

Again he almost exploded with laughter. Really, she was the most diverting woman he had ever known and despite the fact that she had done nothing but bait him all evening, he felt he could sweep her into his arms and kiss her until her supercilious face exploded into laughter, into passion, into all the things he meant to have from her when she had got over this ridiculous yearning she had for Freddy.

"I would be delighted, but first Mr Baker has offered to beat me so I'm afraid you must stand in line."

"Good for you, Martin," she declared, as though there were nothing she would like more than to see Ben Maddox brought to his knees. "And while I'm waiting I'll have a port. Fetch me one, Andrew, there's a good chap."

"Steady on, Kitty, d'you think you should drink?" the young man faltered, recoiling as she turned on him.

"What I drink is nothing to do with you, Andrew Mortimor. Now, shall we get on."

Ben was seriously distracted by the shrieks of laughter that Kitty's presence seemed to have sparked off. He could sense the horseplay at the end of the room and at one point he almost walked off and left Martin Baker to his own devices as some young bastard begged Freddy to fetch some champagne so that he might drink it out of Kitty's satin shoe.

The game ended and much to young Mr Baker's chagrin Ben pocketed the cheque for a hundred guineas he had won from him and at once turned to where Kitty, with the cigar firmly clamped between her flashing white teeth, attempted a spirited Highland reel while the men clapped and cheered her on. Freddy, his face creased with anxiety, was doing his feeble best to put a stop to it. As Ben, appearing to stroll but in reality almost at a run, reached the group he was just in time to see Miss Kitty Hayes's flushed, excited face drain of all colour and then become a bilious shade of green.

"Oops," said one of the young gentlemen.

"Oops, indeed," Ben murmured as he grasped her about the waist, lifted her into his arms and before anyone knew what he was about, raced with her through the open French windows and into the gardens where he held her head as she vomited her dinner into Mr Tinker's bed of prized dahlias. When she had done she straightened up and angrily accepted the handkerchief he held out to her.

"Well, I suppose you're satisfied now?" she snapped and was greatly put out when he began to laugh.

"Dear God, I might have known it would be my fault," he spluttered, taking his cigar case from his pocket and beginning to withdraw a cigar.

"Don't you dare light one of those things near me."

"Why, I thought you rather liked them, Miss Hayes."

"And I won't be laughed at."

"Of course not. I apologise, but may I remind you that it was you who asked *me* for one. I took it that you were accustomed to them." His teeth were a white slash in the darkness. Kitty looked at him for a moment, not sure what to make of this man who seemed to be quite unoffended by the sight of a woman being sick. Indeed she seemed to remember he had been very gentle and even murmured a word or two of comfort. For once lost for words she glanced off moodily into the pitch dark beyond the terrace.

"Would you care to walk, Miss Hayes? They do say it is the best thing for a hangover."

"I do not have a hangover, sir. How dare you?"

"Oh, I dare to say a lot of things to you, Miss Hayes. That's why you find me so fascinating."

"Fascinating! You! You're the most puffed-up, arrogant man I have ever met."

"But interesting, don't you think?"

"Don't flatter yourself, Mr Maddox. There isn't a man walking this earth who interests me."

"With the exception of Freddy Hayes!"

The silence was like a solid sheet of ice forming about them and she was frozen in it. In the light that spilled from the billiard-room window where high jinks were getting out of hand, he watched her face become shadowed, gaunt, white as marble and he thought he had gone too far. He knew he must shock her, hurt her even, but he didn't want to add to her desolation by cutting her to the bone. He saw her lips become a thin line and her eyes deaden and she swayed as though she would fall. He caught her, holding her cold body against his warm one, his arms strong about her shoulders, his cheek resting on her hair, feeling the violent trembling of her as shock took its hold, saying nothing, waiting, for what, he didn't know. How she would react, he supposed. Would she hit him, which seemed the most likely, or give him a mouthful of obscenities, of which he was certain, being the woman she was, she would know a few? But this clinging, this desolate weeping was totally unexpected. It seemed he had just caught her when she was at the lowest point of despair against which, having fought so hard, she had no defence.

At last she was quiet, leaning against him as though she found it not unpleasant, then she spoke.

"How did you know?"

"I saw it on the night of the party. Your face . . . everything you feel shows in it, whatever it might be. Anger, contempt, pleasure, and . . . and affection. Oh, I don't think anyone else would notice it," he added hastily, *only me who loves you*, "so don't worry that they all know. Your family, I mean."

"I don't know what I'm to do," she whispered sadly, her breath stirring against the curve of his chin.

"Well, there is one thing you could do which would not only give you a purpose in life but distract those who might have thought . . . well, I'm sure you'll know what I mean."

"No."

"It seems likely – I beg your pardon if this displeases you – that Freddy and your sister will announce their engagement fairly soon."

He felt her wince away from him but he held her more firmly and in her desolation she let him.

"So it seems to me there is only one solution," he continued.

"Oh, and what's that?" Her voice held little interest.

"That you become engaged before they do. That would certainly allay any suspicions, scotch any rumours. Don't you agree?"

"I don't understand. Get engaged? Who to?"

"Why, Miss Hayes, here you are in the most compromising position any young lady could be with a gentleman and you have to ask that."

She raised her head, understanding at last, and stared in horrified disbelief into his wryly smiling face, her mouth open, the tracks of her tears still shining on her cheeks. He began to laugh.

"Really Miss Hayes, it can't be as dreadful as that. I'm offering to deliver you from a barren future, to give you the perfect answer to your dilemma and you are staring at me as though I had suggested we commit murder. I'm asking you to marry me, Miss Hayes. By the way, may I call you Kitty? And please, do feel free to call me Ben."

6

They were married on a cool sunny day six weeks later in October. The path to the church was carpeted in leaves of crimson, gold, burnt orange, half green and brown so that when she and her father walked up to the church porch from the carriage their feet crunched and rustled among them. For a moment she was transported back to her childhood and she looked up at her father and smiled with delight. He smiled in return and she had the feeling she was back with Freddy running through the strip of autumn woodland that bordered Riverside House. And it was strange, she told herself with that level of her senses still functioning as the old Kitty Hayes had done, that she had never noticed before how alike they were, Father and Freddy. Then, as the small crowd of well-wishers, those who come to watch a wedding whether the participants are known to them or not, lined the path, oohing and aahing, her father was her father again and

Freddy was inside the church with his own bride-to-be.

Her train, which should have been held up by the bridesmaids she refused to have, saying it was enough of a circus as it was, collected leaves like a shrimping net and though she was unaware of it caused great annoyance to the parson's wife who had to sweep them up when the ceremony was over. Rose petals and confetti and rice were bad enough, she complained, but autumn leaves were just too much and would her husband please see that they were removed from the path before the next wedding!

It seemed a long walk beneath the curving avenue of trees where almost naked branches reached towards each other, intertwining their thin twig-tips. It was like floating – that was how she felt she moved in her unfamiliar wedding gown – under a delicate trellis with the pale autumn beauty of the sky above. A grey squirrel chattered overhead and though she watched its progress with a totally out-of-place awareness on this, her wedding day, it vanished like a streak of grey smoke down the trunk of the tree. Rooks were showing an interest in the rookery at the top of the trees, she noticed, squinting myopically through the delicate gauze of her veil. They streaked across the sky then swept confidently into the trees and settled down to preen.

She noticed all this in the last hour of her freedom as she held her father's arm. Her hand clung to the fine material of his morning coat in the crook of his elbow and he put his on hers, continuing to smile down at her lovingly. He could show his love openly now that their life together was ending and the sharp edges of the last months had been smoothed down, rounded, made safe by the man she was marrying. He was glad she was going, she knew that, and bore him no grudge, for she had made his life hell since she had learned that Freddy did not love her.

It was different with her mother who made no attempt to hide her vast relief that the daughter who had been nothing but a trial to her since the day she was born, an unwanted child she had not loved but by whom she had always done her duty, was at last to be taken off her hands. Her mother loved her father, or rather the man who had pretended to be Kitty's father, with a possessive, passionate love that saw no further than his needs, his health, his comfort, and in her eyes Kitty's behaviour had weakened his never strong constitution. The worry, the anger, the fretting over what mad thing she would do next had worn him down, brought on a recurrence of the chest complaint which did not usually afflict him until the winter months. The moment she had got Kitty off her hands, though she did not put it quite so baldly, she was to whisk him off to the good sea air at Lytham and if she had her way would keep him there until spring!

It was dark in the church porch after the pale brightness of the October morning and for several moments, as the music thundered and her father led her up the aisle, she could neither see nor hear. There was a man, two men who rose to their feet as she approached, one of whom moved forward, half turned so that he might watch her progress towards him. His face was serious, almost harsh and she was not to know that Ben Maddox was fighting to control the strong wash of emotion that swept through him at the sight of her. His love threatened to break out in the most embarrassing way, wanting to hold out joyous hands to her, to welcome her, to comfort her, for he knew she would be frightened, though she'd not show it, naturally. Not fearless Kitty Hayes, so soon to be Kitty Maddox.

Kitty moved blindly, clinging for a last moment to her father's arm, reluctant to stand beside this stranger, this handsome stranger, she supposed, for he looked well in his tailed morning suit. Through the gauze of her veil she could see the speculative narrowing of his eyes as though he were studying the bride he had bought and was wondering if he was getting value for money. To one side she caught a glimpse of her mother and beside her were Ciara, Anna, Marguerite, Sebastian . . . and Freddy. *Freddy!* He had broken her heart and yet he was smiling, approving, glad to see her go, like the rest of them, the troublesome woman who was now, or would be shortly, the responsibility of another man.

None of them loved her and she loved none of them, only Freddy and he was lost to her, finally, irrevocably; and as the thought struck at her despairing heart, ready to bring her to her knees, from somewhere came that fierce and durable strength which had got her through the last three months. It put a stiffener in her spine, lifted her head to an imperious angle, squared her drooping shoulders and guided her feet to the man who waited for her at the altar. Incredibly, she found herself smiling. Her heart and soul felt as though they were being smashed to pieces on the rocks of her misery but she smiled and the man who waited for her thought he had never seen anything so courageous as Kitty Hayes walking past the man she loved to a man she scarcely knew who was to be her husband.

The last six weeks had been got through with a speed and a chaos that blurred them into a mist except for small instances which were sharp and would always be remembered, beginning with the night Ben Maddox had asked her to marry him.

With that characteristic rashness with which she tackled everything in her life, from her first headlong gallop on her new pony to this next step in her life, she had rushed ahead of him into the billiard-room and clapped her hands, shouting for attention since the young men were playing one of those foolish games only they find amusing. Some were on the backs of others, piggy-back like children, while those who bore the burden whooped and raced round the billiard table before collapsing, laughing hysterically, in a welter of arms and legs. They sat up, still giggling, and stared drunkenly at Kitty.

"Freddy," she clamoured, "run upstairs and fetch Mother and Father, and the girls too. Tell them I have an announcement to make and then go to the wine cellar and bring up a bottle of champagne. Better make it two, or even three, and Andrew, you may drink a toast out of my slipper if you are still of a mind. Quickly, Freddy, before Mother and Father go to sleep, though I doubt it, the row you lot have been making. Oh, do hurry up," she babbled, then turned a brilliant face towards Ben, who was leaning, his tall figure the picture of amused indolence, against the frame of the French window. He smiled enquiringly at her, the pale smoke of the cigar between his parted lips wreathing about his head. It was as though he, like the others, was wondering what all the excitement was about.

"Shall I tell them, Mr Maddox, or will you?" she begged him and he wanted to tell her to stop it, to come here and lean against him, to give herself to his comforting arms, for there was a look of death in her eyes.

"By all means, Miss Hayes, whatever you prefer, but don't you think it might be better to leave all announcements until morning? It's late and your parents must be tired. It hardly seems fair to disturb them."

"Nonsense, Mr Maddox, I'm sure you want to get it settled, as I do," and he knew she was telling him that if she didn't get this over and done with before witnesses, by morning she might have lost her nerve. She didn't want to marry him. She was still raw with the pain of losing Freddy Hayes, a rawness that abraded her nerves and her spirit but this was her escape, this marriage, an escape from not only being forced to watch Freddy marry her own sister, but from sharing a life with them. An unmarried woman with no home nor income of her own, apart from what she was allowed by an indulgent father, must for ever remain in the family home, taking second place first to her mother, then, when her mother was gone, to her brother's wife.

Nancy and Joshua Hayes were not asleep; how could they be with the sound of young men at play resounding throughout the house. In fact Joshua was just about to do something about it when his son knocked softly at the door and, equally as softly, called out to them.

"Mother, Father, are you asleep?"

"Good God, what now," his father hissed and his wife patted his arm in an effort to calm him.

"Father," Freddy said in a louder voice, bringing Ciara to her bedroom door further along the hall, pulling on her wrapper.

"What is it, Freddy? What the devil . . . ?"

"It's Kitty. She—"

"Sweet Jesus, will that girl never give us any peace?"

"Can you come down, Father, and Mother, too? In fact she wants us all. She says . . ."

Joshua Hayes's voice had an unaccustomed viciousness in it as he fumbled his way out of bed and into his dressing-gown.

"Hell's teeth, Nancy, if this is one of your daughter's mad fancies then I swear I'll take a strap to her."

Never mind the strap which was an idle threat, Nancy knew, it was a measure of her husband's rage that he should use the phrase "your daughter" which told her how close he was to breaking point, how close Kitty's behaviour was driving him to despair. Not once in all their years had he referred to the girl as anything but "our daughter"!

They were all astonished and, as the shock wore off, positively enraptured, when Kitty, lit up like a firecracker about to explode, broke the news to them, though they found they were somewhat disconcerted by Mr Maddox's manner, which seemed to them to be one of amusement rather than of the amorous. Despite this no one said anything such as "But you hardly know one another," or "Don't you think it might be wise to wait a while?" or any of the doubts which any other parents, concerned parents, might voice. It was not that they were unconcerned, just that they could not believe their ordeal was over and that peace was to be restored to their lives. That this headstrong daughter of theirs was at last to be married to a decent chap, or so it seemed by all accounts and one, if appearances were anything to go by, who would lick Kitty Hayes into shape. The shape a young, married woman should be, which was . . . well, not submissive, for would the girl ever be that, but self-controlled, observing the rules of their society, considerate of her husband's wishes, tamed, if such a thing were possible and if it was not, no longer anything to do with them.

They drank champagne and toasted the bride- and bridegroom-to-be and even the servants, wondering what all the commotion was about and creeping down to see, were drawn into the wild celebrations, sipping champagne and lifting their glasses to the woman they had all been driven demented by. She danced, there was no other word for it, about the by now crowded billiard-room, brilliant and volatile as a shooting star, as a wild party, surely going further than such an occasion demanded, both Mrs Bright and Mrs Hodges agreed, carried on into the early hours. But then could you blame the master and mistress for being so elated at the thought of getting rid of her, poor lass, when it had seemed she was to remain a spinster for the rest of her days. They also noticed, and commented on afterwards, that not once did Miss Kitty and Mr Maddox address a word to one another, let alone exchange the looks a couple just betrothed might exchange!

It was the same for the six weeks preceding the wedding. They were invited everywhere, for didn't all their friends want to get a look at this man who was to take on the formidable Kitty Hayes. Parties in their honour, balls and soirées, the last of the tennis parties, so that their time was taken up on a mad round of pleasure, every evening spent drinking champagne, smiling endlessly, while Kitty spent every day being stitched into the crêpe-de-chines, the gauzes, the taffetas and silks that would equip her to be a wife. Poor Chester languished in his stable as his mistress was dragged to St Ann's Square where her Aunt Jennet oversaw the making of her trousseau, for it seemed she was to go to Paris for her honeymoon and the needs of her wardrobe would be enormous; to the bootmaker's, to the milliner's until she protested, for what was wrong with the extensive wardrobe of clothes she already possessed? Her protestations were mild though, for she existed in a glass bubble from which she could see all that went on in a kind of mist and where what they said was loud enough to be heard but the words indistinct.

The family travelled by train to Liverpool and thence by carriage to Mr Maddox's home at Walton-on-the-Hill, a splendid house by the name of Meadow View of which, when she was married, she would be mistress. She was introduced to the curious but welcoming servants who bobbed their curtseys or respectfully bent their heads, though not one face, or even one name was retained in her memory. She was told by Mr Maddox that she was at liberty to change the furnishings or the decorations of the room that was to be theirs when they married and even this made no dent in the hard shell of the refuge that mercifully seemed to have been erected about her.

They dined, she and her family, in the company of Mr Maddox with whom her father had had long discussions about Mr Maddox's ability to support her, to give her all the material things Joshua Hayes's daughter was entitled to. It seemed he could. The meal was superb, the servants unobtrusively efficient, pleasing her mother, and the bedrooms which they were allotted comfortable, even luxurious. Kitty scarcely noticed as she grieved quietly for Freddy Hayes. During those weeks it was as though she were not there, mercifully armoured against everything that was happening to her, quiet and biddable so that the servants gloated that already her forthcoming marriage had changed her from the maddening, self-willed and rebellious young woman she had been into a more appropriate wife for a successful businessman like Mr Maddox. Though they were glad of it for her sake and that of her husband, several of them thought it was a shame that she seemed to have had the stuffing knocked out of her so drastically. A bugger she might have been but, by God, she was always diverting!

On her wedding day she came out into the daylight on her husband's arm, her face blank and untenanted, her eyes unseeing, to the congratulatory cheers of the sightseers who wondered at the sober expressions on the faces of the bride and groom. It had clouded over while the marriage ceremony took place and a peevish wind had got up, flinging a thin handful of rain into the guests' faces, which was not an auspicious beginning on this important day, but even so it would have been nice to see a smile or two exchanged by the happy couple.

There were lace-covered tables festooned with flowers from Mr Tinker's hothouse, rosebuds of white and pale pink tied with white satin ribbons and draped with lacy fern. There was champagne and, to keep it informal, a buffet of cold meats, game pies, sausage rolls made by Mrs Bright and her bevy of handmaidens, the pastry of which melted away on the tongue. There was galantine of chicken served in aspic, patties and salads of salmon, crab and lobster and a plenitude of light, frothy concoctions, creams, custards, jellies, ices, fresh fruit, sweetmeats, light sponge cakes and biscuits, with, naturally, a wedding cake of giant proportions but such a marvel of ingenuity the general opinion was that it would be a shame to cut it. Mrs Bright preened when the word was passed on to her, for it had taken many hours of delicate work to achieve.

The new Mrs Maddox wore a going-away outfit the colour of sherry with a sheen on it like silk. It was, as were all her clothes, of superb quality and cut, fitting like a glove to her breast and waist, draped in a simple bustle adorned with one large self-coloured bow at the back. Her hat was small and under the narrow brim were stitched rosebuds of cream silk. Her new husband handed her into the carriage which was to take them to the railway station in Manchester where they would board a train to Liverpool. They were to spend two nights at Meadow View, since there was a bit of business he needed to attend to, and on the following day catch a train to London and the boat-train to Paris.

They waved her off, all the people who had been a familiar part of her life for as long as she could remember: Aunt Jennet who had been the first "mother" Kitty had known; Mrs Underwood, her mother's friend from her days in business; Bridget, looking bewildered in such grand company, ready to cry, since she was the only one among them who knew the real condition of Kitty's heart; the servants, mingled with the guests on the carriage drive since Miss Kitty belonged to them as well, from Mrs Hodges right down to Eddy, the latest in a long line of boot boys. Mr Tinker pressed a small bunch of violets into Kitty's hand and Freddy stood with his arm openly about Ciara, grinning and waving, as relieved as the rest to have their problem, herself, so neatly disposed of.

"Well then," said her new husband, reaching into the waistcoat pocket of *his* going-away outfit and bringing out his cigar case, "now we can relax. May I offer you a cigar?" He grinned at her sudden gleam of surprise. "As I remember you stated a liking for them once. In fact I do believe it was the humble cigar that brought us together." He raised one eyebrow wryly and selected a cigar from the case, lit it and unconcernedly blew smoke into the close confines of the carriage, its hood up against the drizzle.

"I don't think I would," she said coldly, ignoring his attempt at a joke. "In fact I would be obliged if you would not smoke. I feel somewhat nauseous after all that rich food."

"I'm sorry, my dear. I'll lower the window," which he did but his cigar remained lit.

"Did you hear me? I don't want you to smoke."

"Yes, I heard you but then I enjoy a cigar and I'm afraid you will just have to get used to it. There are, in fact, several things to which you must become accustomed."

"Indeed?" She looked at her most imperious.

"Yes, and this is one of them since I am inclined to be an affectionate man." Before she knew what he was about he had transferred the cigar to his right hand, put his left arm about her shoulders and, turning her face to his, began to kiss her. For several moments she was so confounded, so infuriated, she made no attempt to stop him. His lips smoothed hers, moving gently, warmly, his mouth open a fraction so that she could taste and smell the brandy he had drunk, the cigar he was smoking and the underlying sweetness of his breath. In the six weeks since she had promised to become his wife he had made no attempt to kiss her, to embrace her, even to hold her hand. She had thought nothing of it. It meant nothing to her. He might have been one of the company who entertained them, a guest, someone quite apart from Kitty Hayes, who happened to be in the same room as herself. He was a perfect gentleman, considerate, courteous, even casual, and the strange tension, the well-hidden energy of a sexually aroused male, the need in him experienced by all men to make this particular woman solely *his* went by her like the smoke from his cigars.

Now she came to life. Bringing up her hand she aimed it at his head, slapping at him ineffectually, spitting and spluttering like an infuriated cat, her face crimson with indignation, and inside Ben Maddox something sprang into jubilant life. Thank God, it said, she is not totally frozen, numb, insensate, the submissive wife she seemed about to become. He did not want her to accept his embraces with a sigh, enduring what he did to her with the tame compliance of a dove. She was an eagle, a tigress, fierce, ready to fight. He wanted her to fight, to match him in strength, for only that way could he at last find in her the equal he knew was there, the equal he meant to bring to magic life. But first he must break her in, show her that whatever she might say, or do, she was his wife, he was her husband and what they did together could be pleasing to them both.

"Take your hands off me at once. How dare you . . ." But he merely held her face with fingers which were like steel, continuing to move his lips on hers, parting them, his tongue invading her mouth, touching hers, but he had seriously misjudged his wife. When her teeth clamped down, fastening on the end of his tongue, biting and drawing blood, he withdrew hastily with a smothered oath.

She smiled then, a triumphant smile that told him she had won, or thought she had. It was as though, having rebuffed him so savagely, he would now realise that she was not interested in his coarse games and he'd do well to leave her alone. She knew, surely, what marriage entailed? Her own father and mother shared a bedroom so what in God's name did she think would happen tonight? They were man and wife and if she didn't allow him to kiss her now, did she really believe that that was the end of it?

He watched as she arched her back, sitting up straighter than ever, then turned away to stare coolly out of the window at the houses along Bury New Road. Short of struggling with her, overpowering her, which he knew he could, he was forced to sit back in the carriage, favouring his throbbing tongue, thankful that it had not been some other part of his anatomy that she had attacked. He had thought of her as an eagle, a tigress but, by God, she was a bloody vixen and if it took him the rest of his days he would have her nestling up to him like a kitten, eager for his hands and mouth on her, eager to be fondled, to be . . .

He turned away from her and almost laughed out loud at the very thought.

They did not speak for the remainder of the journey. When, as a gentleman should, he attempted to take her arm as they crossed the road to the station forecourt, she pulled away from him, and again, short of creating a scene which he knew would not concern *her*, he had no choice but to walk behind her gracefully swaying, straight-backed figure.

It was dark when the carriage, come to meet them at Lime Street Station, drew up at the open front door to the house. Light streamed from every window and from the doorway where a buxom figure awaited them.

"Good evening, Mrs Maddox," his housekeeper, Mrs Ullett said respectfully as her new mistress strode over the threshold, but Kitty merely gave her a startled look then turned to speak to one of the maids who sketched hasty curtseys behind Mrs Ullett.

"Take my things up to my room, if you please. I would like a bath if it could be arranged," as though who knew what primitive conditions thrived here. "I shall dine in my room."

Mrs Ullett, looking astounded, turning to her master for confirmation.

"Show Mrs Maddox to her room, Tansy," he said mildly to the bobbing parlourmaid. "One of the men will bring up the luggage. And there is a connecting bathroom, Kitty. But I would prefer it if we dined down here. I'm sure Mrs Ullett has gone to a great deal of trouble to prepare a splendid meal to welcome you to your new home so we mustn't disappoint her."

Kitty felt like the princess in the story book who is awakened by a kiss from the prince, though she couldn't quite cast Mr Maddox in that role. But the principle was the same. She had been sleeping for six weeks now, barely aware of what went on around her, not caring, glad to be apart from it, from all that went on around her, but now, with that one horrible kiss in the carriage, she had come to her senses. She was herself again and though her heart was still broken and her love still hid there in the ruins, she was herself again. Ready to take on the world and certainly this man who thought he could take liberties with Kitty Hayes. She was married to him, she understood that. She was expected to be a wife and, presumably, one day, a mother, or so they would think, but when did what others thought ever matter to her? She had got away from Freddy and Ciara. She was in a strange and unfamiliar place but she was strong and would make a new life for herself. She'd need a good horse, preferably Chester if she could persuade her father to part with him and a decent piano and if this tall, brooding man who was telling her what *he* thought she should do didn't like it, then he could go to the devil.

"Nevertheless I will eat in my room, Mrs . . . Ullett, is it? Has the fire been lit?"

"Yes, madam."

The housekeeper kept her face blank though the three maids were goggle-eyed.

Ben Maddox smiled amiably, nodding at Mrs Ullett as he advanced across the wide hallway towards his wife. She watched him come, her eyebrows raised and was totally unprepared when he took her arm in a grip which cut down to the bone.

"We will be down shortly, Mrs Ullett, my wife and I. Shall we say seven thirty, which will give Mrs Maddox time to bathe and change," and anything else I might have in mind for her, Mrs Ullett, who was a worldly woman, thought. "We will dine then," and without further ado he began to lead, or perhaps it was *drag* the new Mrs Maddox up the stairs.

"This way, my darling," he told her mildly while she struggled and fought and railed against him every step of the way. They watched her, all four women, their mouths agape, then listened as Mr and Mrs Maddox disappeared along the landing in the direction of their bedroom.

He flung her inside so harshly she almost fell, then shut and locked the door behind him. It was not the way he wanted it, not this. Not this battle, this scratching, biting attempt by each one to dominate the other. He had imagined, knowing, of course, that it would not happen, a slow drifting of their senses, their bodies, smiling, anticipating, kisses, soft, dreaming, an initiation into the art of love, taught by him and received by her, joyously, tenderly, moving towards a climax that would please them both. He loved her. He had loved no other woman in his life. He wanted to take her face between his hands and kiss her closed eyes, her closed mouth, lightly to begin with, offering her his love, his heart and then, as her mouth opened, following it naturally with his body's need, *her* body's need, blending their minds and souls and bodies in love.

But this was to be rape, pure and simple, and it was breaking his heart, but what other way could he make her understand that they were husband and wife, that from this night on they would share a bed, share their bodies, be the lovers he dreamed of?

"Don't you touch me," she whispered, backing away from him, looking round her for a handy weapon with which to lay open his head.

"I mean to do more than touch you, my darling, so you'd best get out of those clothes and do try and smile while you're at it."

He began to remove his own clothing and when he stood before her totally naked she stared in horror, her face as white as the lacy, turned-down sheets on the bed.

"Kitty?" His voice was soft and so were his eyes but she did not see them since she was too busy staring at another part of his anatomy which, though she had known it was there, having brothers of her own, was such an appalling size and colour she wanted to scream.

She did scream and the servants heard her but then she was the master's wife and it was nothing to do with them what he did to her, for he had a right. When they came down an hour later, he seating her gently at the table, the maids kept their eyes averted. She was elegantly dressed, except for her hair which was brushed back into a curly knot and tied with a bright ribbon at the back of her head. She looked flushed, bright-eyed, you might say, Mrs Ullett whispered later to Mrs Pembroke, who was Meadow View's cook, and had it not been for the look of pure, cold hatred she directed at the master and her refusal to answer a word of the pleasant conversation he kept up, you could have sworn she had just been well and truly broken in, and, what's more, enjoyed it!

7

Though he should have been on his way to his office by
now to deal with the small emergency that had cropped
up on the day of his wedding, Ben lay in the bed which
he had last night shared with his bride and watched her
as she swirled about the bedroom. It was obvious that
she was in a state of high tension, her blue eyes almost
a purple-black with outrage as they snapped about the
room, her jaw clenched with that wilful arrogance he
was to know so well. His naked brown shoulders
rested indolently against the pile of white lace-ruffled
pillows and the bedclothes were carelessly rumpled
and pushed down to reveal his flat belly and almost
the dark mat of hair that hid his genitals.

His own eyes were slitted against the cigar smoke
which wreathed about his head and he gave the appearance of a man completely at ease with his world, a man
with the day stretching peacefully ahead of him, a man
discussing with his wife nothing of more importance

than the weather. But if Kitty had known him better she would have seen that it would not take a great deal for her words to turn him to black anger.

"Do you seriously expect me to get on a train," she was saying, "and go to . . . to Paris, or wherever it is you fancy travelling to, after what you did to me last night? I can hardly bear to be in the same house with you, never mind the same room, even though there are servants about, and to contemplate being *alone* with you for . . . for days on end fills me with horror. I insist that you get out of my bed and take that horrid cigar with you. It is imperative that I have a room of my own and should you force yourself on me again I will . . . I will . . ."

It was clear she had no idea what recourse an unwilling wife had against an amorous husband, if she had any at all, which, by the way this man smiled, she doubted.

"God," she stormed, whirling on her heel, "I must have been out of my mind to think that I could . . . could manage this . . . this charade, this pretence."

"Believe me, it's no pretence, my darling," he said lazily. "You are my wife, not only in the eyes of the law but after last night, in every other way as well. You might even be pregnant. Had you thought of that?"

Ben Maddox watched as his wife shuddered. Though his eyes were unreadable, at least to Kitty, on his face was a pleasant, good-humoured smile as if her words and actions left him totally unmoved but inside he felt a shrivelling pang of disappointment which bewildered him. What else, for God's sake, had he hoped for? After dining last night he had brought her upstairs, stripped her and himself naked, fighting her every step of the way until they were both panting with the exertion and they had shared the first night of their marriage, in their marriage bed, against her will. She would keep getting out of it, stark naked, which was how he would like her to be, he told her coolly, stalking about the bedroom as though looking for a way out. A caged beast, newly caught, could not have been more wild than she was, pacing from the window to the door, her tall, glorious body a lustrous shade of burned honey and polished amber in the wavering blur of the flickering candles and the flames of the fire. The triangle of dark hair at the base of her belly was a stark shadow, enticing and yet forbidden, and her breasts were rich as cream tipped in rose, big and full and exuberant as she strode about the room. She was rigid with fury as she searched for the key to the locked door and some garment to put on, for even she, in her madness, could not quite bring herself to leave the bedroom undressed. Her buttocks were round and tight and deeply divided and he knew it would not be long before, no matter how she clawed and scratched, he would have her again. She was as magnificent as he had thought she would be, but by all that was holy it was like mating with a lioness. And yet there had been a moment in that second frenzied union when he had felt her hands, instead of clawing at him, hesitate and then cling to his shoulders for a second as though to steady herself in the havoc that washed at them both before he climaxed.

She had slept a little then, held tight to his side by his

powerfully determined arms and it was only when he himself fell asleep that she had escaped him. He had captured her again, fighting her, dragging her back to the bed, turning her into a spitting cat for the third time, driving himself deep inside her and he had felt her hips rise to meet his. He was not even sure whether it was an involuntary movement of denial or desire or his own imagination, but he had thanked God for her spirit which told him she would never willingly let him subjugate her. Her heart might remain untouched as it grieved for Freddy Hayes but her body would soon know that it belonged to Ben Maddox.

This morning she was dressed for riding. All her clothes had been brought over from Riverside House several days ago and had been neatly pressed and carefully hung away by the young girl who had been appointed to "maid" her. Emma, answering her new mistress's clamouring ring, had run pell-mell up the stairs, breathing hard and flushed of face, to attend to the important task of fitting Mrs Maddox into her riding habit, of arranging her hair into a suitable style – at least *she* thought it was suitable, neat and proper for the wearing of a bowler hat – and of pulling on her high boots.

To Emma's blushing embarrassment the master lay in the bed during the whole performance, eyes narrowed in what appeared to be appreciation, calmly smoking his cigar.

"Are you to remain while my maid helps me to dress?" Kitty asked him icily.

"I believe I might. It is most entertaining. In fact, my pet, so far I have found marriage itself to be most entertaining. I think we shall do very well together. You must admit that I have not bored you and I might say the same about you. You were . . . quite delicious and if you care to get rid of your maid and come over here I'm sure . . ."

"How disgusting you are," she spat at him.

"So you told me several times last night but wait until you get used to me and what we do together. You will find—"

"I will never get used to you and I have no intention of trying."

His smile broadened into a grin. He was assured, totally certain in his arrogant masculinity that he would have his way no matter how painful she might find it.

"I'm afraid you have no choice, my darling. We are bound together by ties that can never be broken. And might I remind you" – his voice became cool and the smile slipped from his face – "you wanted to get away from Riverside House for reasons we will not go into here. A bargain was made and I expect you to keep your part of it. As I shall."

"You can go to hell."

Emma gasped and wished a hole would appear in the rich carpet and swallow her up. She longed for nothing more than to run from this room where her master and mistress seemed to be doing their best to do one another some damage and what would she do if it came to that and she was in the middle of it? She shouldn't be here. It was neither right nor proper for a gentleman to remain in the bedroom as his wife dressed and for two pins she'd ask to be released from this task with which she'd been so delighted, this promotion, for that was what it was, and the wonderful wage of fifteen pounds a year that went with it and go back to being housemaid.

"Really, my darling, I would be obliged if you would not swear like that. It is not becoming in a lady."

"Haven't you heard, Ben Maddox, that I am no lady, and neither was my mother."

"Well, you might be right about yourself but your mother is one of the finest ladies I have ever met."

Kitty snorted, sweeping Emma aside as she reached for her riding gloves.

"He just lay there," Emma told the fascinated maids who clustered about her when she returned to the kitchen, "the pair of them arguin', almost at each other's throats at one time an' me in the middle. I never felt so embarrassed in me life. 'Fetch me veil, Emma,' she'd say, 'and see if you can find me riding crop, and ask Mrs What's-er-name to make up another bedroom for me. I don't care what it's like as long as my husband isn't in it.' And really, I didn't know where to put meself."

"Did she look . . . well, knocked about?"

"Knocked about?"

"After all that noise she made last night."

"Not that I noticed but she hates the ruddy sight of him. She said so to his face."

"Then why did she marry him?"

"Gawd knows."

Up in the bedroom Kitty turned to look at herself in the mirror and for the first time addressed a voluntary remark to her husband.

"I presume there is a suitable mount for me in your stable?"

"I presume there is. Tim will know. As long as it's not Marcus."

"And who is Marcus?"

"He's my stallion and too strong for a woman."

For the first time since they had faced one another at the dining table last night she looked directly at him and smiled.

"Is that so?"

Slowly he sat up in the bed, then threw back the covers and stood up. He was still naked and his strong amber body, muscular, savage even and very determined, gleamed in the shaft of golden autumn sunlight that streamed through the curtains. Though he could not really be described as handsome in the classical sense, he had an agreeable, humorous face, but his male body was quite magnificent. Long, graceful bones and flat muscles that flowed smoothly from the curve of his chest to the slight concavities of his belly and thigh. He was large, powerful, dark, and for a moment Kitty felt her insides lurch, she didn't know why, and her mouth became dry and in the pit of her stomach flared a tiny spark of something, again she didn't know what, or why, then he spoke and the mood was gone. His face betrayed his irritation with himself, for he knew the challenge he had so carelessly, inadvertently flung down was one she could not ignore.

"Yes, that is so and on thinking it over I would be obliged if you would stay away from the stables today. There must be things to prepare for our journey tomorrow."

That was when she told him there would be no journey tomorrow.

He leaned indolently against the fireplace, his arms crossed, his nudity apparently not a concern and Kitty, knowing the feel of his body against hers, her body remembering his, felt a great need to study him, to sweep her eyes from the crown of his tumbled dark hair to his slim, graceful feet. She knew she loved Freddy and always would but this man was . . . what? Compelling? Yes, that was a good word. Resolute? Look how he had got her to marry him! Complex, for would she ever know what he was thinking unless he told her? Proud, insolent even. A fighter for what he wanted, for what he believed in and he believed that he would master her, subjugate her, turn her into the woman, the wife he wanted, the wife he thought she should be.

She smiled, feeling a tiny spurt of excitement, wondering what he would do now.

He watched her intently and her previous assessment was proving to be right, for she had no idea what was in his mind.

"Very well," he said at last. "I certainly have no desire to accompany a woman on a journey she has no desire to make. A pity, for Paris is a beautiful city, but there it is."

She frowned. "You've . . . been there before?"

"Oh, yes, many times."

"With . . . a woman."

He grinned audaciously and began to move slowly towards her and, ignorant as she was, she knew exactly what was in his mind.

"Of course."

For some strange reason she felt quite annoyed. She turned away from him, tossing her head in a way that had worked wonders on those at home. They knew it spelled trouble but something told her that it would not have the same effect on this man.

"Well, there you are then. If you've already been and I have no wish to go you might as well save your money. Now, I shall get down to the stables and see what sort of horseflesh you have there. I don't mean to have some gentle hack, if that's what you have in mind."

"No, my dear, that is not what I have in mind. If we are not to have a honeymoon in Paris, we might as well have it here. Now then, shall we see if I can remove that fetching outfit Emma took so much trouble to get you into . . ."

She backed away from him in alarm, holding her hands towards him, palms outwards, beginning to shake her head. She was sore and bruised in certain parts of her body and in her heart she wanted to weep, for this was what she had dreamed of with Freddy, but at the same time that small electrifying pulse, which surged just at that part of her that ached the most, flared in the most amazing way.

"You leave me alone, you beast, you bully. I'm going riding."

"No, darling, you're not."

"I swear I'll scream the bloody place down."

"Must you swear?"

"I'll say more than that if you lay another finger on me, you dirty bastard."

"Like you did last night, you mean, and who came running? Jesus, you're beautiful . . . come, let me . . ."

"No . . . no . . . no . . ."

"It's no good fighting, my darling."

"I'm not your bloody darling." She was thrashing out wildly, flapping her hands in what she knew was the most ridiculous way and when he forced her back on to the bed, holding those flapping, suddenly feeble hands above her head, she did not even turn her face away as his mouth came down on hers.

He left her at noon and when he had gone she stretched languidly, her flesh warm and soft, feeling as a cat would feel, she imagined, when it has just been stroked and smoothed and caressed, which she had. His lips and hands had taken hold of her again – Dear Lord, was it the fourth or fifth time since they had exchanged their wedding vows less than twenty-four hours ago? – and she had moaned, helpless, wordless, his captive as he brought her body to life, to a storm of passion she had not even imagined could exist, showing her, not only how to please him, but herself.

She hated him. She would always hate him. Freddy Hayes, despite his rejection of her, would always have her heart, she knew that, so why was it that the man who was her husband seemed to have the power to . . . to make her forget Freddy in the most disconcerting way. Disconcerting! What a silly word that was. What a futile word that was. It was more than disconcerting, it was appalling. She felt as though she had been unfaithful, and in such a short time, to the man she loved. She had known, of course, that she would be forced to submit at some time to Ben Maddox's demands since he was her husband and she had made up her mind that she would do so as she really had no choice.

But, dear God, she had not expected to enjoy it! She had not expected her body instantly . . . well, almost instantly, to respond to his in such an overwhelming way. She felt ashamed of herself. He had done things to her that should have disgusted her and instead she had clung to him, her treacherous woman's body glorying in it. Her heart, which was Freddy's, had fluttered, then thundered inside her ribcage and some exploding thing had raged through her and she had heard Ben laugh triumphantly.

"I knew you were made for it the first time I saw you," he told her, then, with an incredible tenderness, had held her closely, possessively against him, kissing her, pushing her disordered hair back from her sweaty forehead before leaping from the bed and telling her he would be home for dinner.

Idly, as she stretched and yawned, she wondered what it was he did in Liverpool. Something to do with cotton, Freddy had said. She dimly remembered her father telling them – not that she was interested – that each Tuesday and Friday at the Royal Exchange there could be as many as six thousand men engaged in myriad discussions and deals, which was where Freddy had met up again with his old school chum, Ben Maddox. Was he a broker, was that the word? Not that she was concerned with anything her new husband did as long as he did not interfere with what *she* did!

Which brought her back to her first intention of riding out and exploring this countryside that lay about her husband's house. Set in Walton-on-the-Hill, it was, which made no difference to her, for as long as she was far away from Freddy and . . . and . . . Ciara she could be on the moon for all she cared. And if her husband thought she was calmly to remain in this house and do . . . well, whatever wives were supposed to do, then he could think again. There was a perfectly good housekeeper, a cook, a bevy of maids from what she'd seen last night and they could do what was necessary to run this house, as they had been doing before she came. She wasn't awfully sure how she would spend her time. All she knew was that it would not be with him.

So, the first thing to do was find a suitable mount until she could get Chester over here and go for a good gallop somewhere. Was there a beach, a long beach on which to lose herself in the joy of riding a decent animal? It didn't seem impossible, since Liverpool was close to the sea. She wasn't sure how far Walton-on-the-Hill was from the city but that would be her first objective, finding out where exactly everything was.

She sprang from the bed, wondering at how well she felt, which was quite amazing after what she had suffered at the hands of that devil last night and then again today. She felt alive, bursting with energy and the only way to work it off was to get down to the stables, saddle up and escape from this place, even if only for a few hours.

For several minutes she wandered about downstairs, peering into rooms which she recognised as luxurious, warm with fires in most grates, splendid carpets, rich curtains and gleaming with polish on mahogany and walnut and rosewood. It was all very pleasant but where in damnation were the kitchens which would, she hoped, lead her out into the stable yard? There was no one about since, she presumed, they thought her still to be lolling in her bed after what she had been through. For some reason she found herself smiling and it was with this expression on her face that she opened a door and stepped into the biggest kitchen she had ever seen.

It seemed to be teeming with people, coming and going and swirling about the enormous central table. A girl was chopping vegetables on a side table, keeping up a cheerful conversation with another who was plucking a chicken. A woman in an enormous apron was stirring something in a pan and at the back door an older woman was speaking to a man who held a basket of fruit on his arm.

It was the girl plucking the chicken who first spotted her. Her mouth fell open and the maid chopping vegetables beside her turned to look in the direction she was staring. She, in her turn, was goggle-eyed with amazement, her eyes wandering the length of her mistress's long body, her mouth a round O, the vegetable knife falling with a clatter to the flagged floor. This in turn caused the woman at the back door to look about her. She put her hand to her mouth and the man to whom she spoke could clearly be seen to mouth, "Bluddy 'ell!"

Kitty was wearing breeches, the ones she put on beneath the skirt of her riding habit. But she was not prepared to ring for Emma, wait while she was fitted into the thing, have her hair dressed and her bowler clamped to her head, so she had simply slipped into the breeches, pulled on her riding boots, slung a tweed riding jacket, filched from Sebastian's wardrobe since he was as tall as she was, over a silk shirt and raced down the stairs. She had tied back her abundant black curls with a scarlet ribbon and they hung down her back to her waist.

"Madam?" quavered the cook from her position on the back step where she was examining the fruit, Wilf, the head gardener, had just brought over from the glasshouse. She didn't know where to put herself, really she didn't, she said later, what with Wilf's eyes out on stalks as they contemplated the new mistress's long, shapely legs which might, what with the colour of the breeches being *buff,* have been naked from the waist down. And there she was, grinning like a cat that's just had a saucer of cream, which she had, in a manner of speaking, since the master was a full-blooded gentleman who would take care to please a woman, at least in Cook's opinion.

"Ah, there you are," the new Mrs Maddox said. And where else would they be? Mrs Pembroke demanded of Mrs Ullett when madam had gone. "I'm looking for the stables so if you would be good enough to give me directions." She raised her eyebrows and on her face was an expression that said, "and at once please".

The gardener whipped off his old cap and touched his finger to his forehead as he thrust the basket of fruit at Mrs Pembroke.

"I'll tekk yer, madam, if yer'll follow me."

He would dearly have liked to have been following *her* what with that little bum all a-rolling and a-bouncing, but he led the way through the kitchen yard and into the stable yard where John, the second groom, was peacefully grooming a tall chestnut mare, and Tim, the head lad, was just about to unsaddle an equally tall black stallion.

At once the stallion began to fidget and paw the ground, casting a menacing eye in the direction of the newcomers, and the groom made a grab for his bridle and spoke to him in a soft and loving voice.

"Whoa, my lad, whoa, Marcus, theer's a good horse. Theer's nowt ter be scared of," then turned and in his consternation at the sight of a beautiful woman in trousers who could only be the master's new wife, allowed the animal to drag him halfway across the yard.

"Bloody 'ell," he bellowed, digging his heels into the cobbles and again the stallion, whose coat rippled like black satin, took offence, beginning to snort, to roll his eyes and nod his head.

"What a magnificent animal," Kitty said softly, and before a word of warning could be said she advanced on the ebony beast with her hand outstretched.

"No, ma'am, no. He's a wild thing an' only t'master an' messen can . . ."

"Hello, old lad . . . hello," Kitty went on softly, completely ignoring the groom, even going so far as to reach out for the stallion's bridle and the horse backed further away until its rump was touching the wall of the tack-room.

"Please, ma'am," pleaded the groom, doing his best to get a hold of the rearing animal. "I'm just gonner unsaddle 'im. He's highly strung an'll bite yer 'and as soon as look at yer. He needs a good gallop burr I can do nowt wi' 'im terday. So, if yer please, ma'am, stand back while—"

"Don't unsaddle him . . . er . . ."

"Tim, ma'am."

"Give him to me, Tim. I need a good gallop myself."

"Sweet Jesus, ma'am!" Tim was appalled and terrified, for if the master was to come home and find his new wife interfering with this animal, which had cost the bloody earth, it'd be Tim's job on the line.

"It's all right, Tim. Just give me a leg up."

"Eeh, ma'am, it'd be more than me life's worth. He's a right bugger, the 'orse, ma'am, I mean, if yer'll pardon me."

"Nonsense. He just needs to know who's his master, or mistress in this case. He knows I'm not afraid of him." And before the very eyes not only of Tim and John but half the servants at Meadow View who peeped from windows and doorways, the mistress reached out and patted the stallion's arched and quivering neck. She smoothed her gloved hand down his nose then bent to blow gently into his distended nostrils and at once the horse quietened. There was total silence in the yard except for the restless hooves of the chestnut mare who had also been disturbed by the commotion.

"A leg up, if you please, Tim," Kitty told the groom quietly but firmly.

"Oh, please, Mrs Maddox," calling her for the first time by her new name.

"I said, a leg up, and at once." And bowing his head and back to the inevitable, the groom linked his hands to receive the well-polished boot of his new mistress. She was up in a flash, her feet feeling for the stirrups and with no idea where she was going except it was through the arched gateway and away from this place, she put her heels to the stallion's sides and was gone in a blur, her eyes a radiant blue in her poppy-cheeked face, her grin wide and triumphant.

The silence that swamped the stable yard after she

had gone was one she was to create many times, then Tim spoke in a hollow, despairing voice.

"Well, lad, did yer ever see owt like that fer I never did. I can only feel sorry for't master."

8

He was waiting in the stable yard when she returned, leaning in a patch of sunlight with his back against the tack-room wall, both hands pushed deep in his trouser pockets, balled into fists by the look of it, as though he were doing his level best not to use them on her. He had the inevitable cigar clamped between his teeth, giving the impression that he was smiling, which he was not. There was no one else about, for if the servants had wished to witness the thrilling sight of their master punishing their new mistress – that's if she came back in one piece, which seemed unlikely – they were to be disappointed. He had sent them about their business with a brusque word and a foul look which meant he would not be disobeyed, if they had dreamed of doing so.

He had known as soon as he entered the house, as eager as a moonstruck schoolboy, he had to admit, for a glimpse of his love, that something was wrong.

There was an air of barely controlled excitement and yet anxiety about Tansy, the housemaid, as she took his Inverness cape and tall top hat in the wide hallway. Everything was as it should be. The rich carpet of Saxe blue was well swept, the fire crackled cheerily in the well-polished grate, casting dancing reflections on the brass poker and coal scuttle. He knew if he cared to glance into any of the rooms, upstairs and down, he would find order, symmetry, nothing out of place, harmony. Four generations of Maddox wives had made it so, each one keeping up the tradition of her predecessor, and he had time to wonder, but without much hope, if the one Ben Maddox had brought home would follow in their footsteps.

There was the usual smell of beeswax and the potpourri his own mother had introduced into the house on her marriage to his father, instructing the housemaids on how to make it, which they still did, one passing the accomplishment on to the next, but there was also a feeling of unease. Something that cast down the eyes and hid the glance of the housemaid so that she could not meet his gaze, which told him at once it must be to do with Kitty.

"Where is the mistress, Tansy?" he asked pleasantly enough, for surely, in the short space of time he had been out she could not have done anything too drastic? He had left her in bed and, he admitted to himself as he hurried through his business to the bewilderment of his clerk, he hoped to find her still there.

"She . . . she went out, sir." Tansy's voice was no more than a mumble.

"Out?" his voice sharpening. "Out where?"

"Oh, sir, I don't know. She didn't say." Tansy was clearly distressed.

"Did she take the carriage?" Images of her strolling along the arcades in Bold Street was what sprang into his mind, purchasing glossy and expensive furs, sparkling diamonds, fine gold bangles set with emeralds, expensive ivory knick-knacks of great value, spending his money of which, he reminded himself, he had an enormous amount.

His great-grandfather had started it all in the middle of the last century, becoming what was known as a "Merchant Prince" before he was thirty years old and he himself was the fourth generation to carry on the business, though now he dealt only in cotton. This house had been in the family since 1760, a small, ivy-covered Georgian mansion to the north-east of Liverpool, bounded by ten acres of mature gardens and woodland and he loved every inch of it. On the ground floor there was a drawing-room, richly carpeted in shades of sand and rose and apple green with apple-green curtains in velvet to match, and crammed with the treasures generations of Maddox wives had collected. Spindle-legged chairs of gilt, rosewood tables and sewing baskets, gilt- and silver-framed pictures and cameos, and, later, photographs on the wall. An elegant white marble Adam fireplace graced one wall, above which was a magnificent gilt-framed mirror. It had been an elegant age when the house was built and furnished, and the decor of this room reflected it. There was a piano which had stood in the bay window for as long as he could remember but he had had it removed and replaced it with a Bechstein grand piano in rosewood with an elaborate fretted music stand and heavy, octagonal turned legs. A beautiful piece of furniture and, he had hoped, having heard her play, a source of pleasure for his wife.

There was a library, the walls lined with books, ancient and modern, most of which he had read. As the drawing-room was a female room, the library was masculine with a splendid mahogany desk, an enormous fireplace stuffed with logs ready to be lit, a globe of the world, prints his ancestors had thought worth hanging on any available wall space, snuff bottles and boxes in silver and jade, a chess set of ivory laid out in readiness for a game – perhaps with Kitty? – deep leather chairs the colour of ox blood and a pair of chair steps to reach the highest shelves.

The dining-room in which he and Kitty had dined last night, much against her will, had a large oval table made from the finest walnut, with a dozen chairs to match covered with rich blue velvet, the colour of the plain carpet. It was simply furnished, elegant as the Regency and Georgian periods were with none of the heavy Victorian pieces that were now the vogue.

Apart from the addition of two modern bathrooms, the upstairs was the same. The bedroom he shared with Kitty had been the one his father and mother had slept in. It had a comfortable but exquisitely hung four-poster bed, which was not a thing with four posts as the name implied but had the silk curtains hanging from what looked like an imperial crown attached to the ceiling. There was a dressing table and tallboy of satinwood, silver-backed hairbrushes and silver-topped scent bottles, crystal lamps and pale-blue velvet chairs, potpourri vases and vinaigrettes of frosted silver and delicate watercolours on the walls. A lovely room filled with lovely things which he hoped would please his new wife. It seemed, by her absence, that it meant nothing to her.

He was an only son, an only child, his parents dying within a year of one another, his mother, he suspected, of a broken heart when his father went. He had been brought up in an atmosphere devoted parents create. Parents who love not only one another, but their child and he hoped to do the same in his marriage. He would have his work cut out, he told himself wryly when he brought Kitty Hayes back to his ancestral home. But he had loved her from the moment he saw her and, quite simply, he had no choice.

"No, sir," Tansy muttered, almost squirming in her desperation, and he was not to know that she had begged Elspeth, who was head housemaid, to receive the master's hat and coat as he came through the front door. She knew, they *all* knew what would happen when he learned that not only had his bride gone casually out for a ride, but had taken his prized stallion and was dressed in *trousers*. They were all shocked and

Mrs Ullett had been ready to give each and every one of them the rounds of the kitchen, she was in such a state, as though she expected to get the blame.

"What will he say?" she kept moaning and not one of them could convince her that it was not her fault. She couldn't be expected to keep Mrs Maddox in order, could she? they told her. But it made no difference, they were all in a ferment and when the sound of the carriage, *his* carriage and not the one he had bought especially for his bride which stood in the coach house, was heard on the gravel path it was all they could do not to burst into tears.

"Where is she then, Tansy?" he demanded in a dangerously quiet voice.

"She . . . the mistress went . . . riding, sir."

He turned towards the kitchen door, ready to stride out to the stable yard and greet his wife when she came back but something halted him and he spoke quietly as he turned to ask her the next question.

"Which animal did she take, Tansy?" knowing the answer before Tansy could sniffle it to him.

"Well . . . I wasn't . . ."

"Which animal?" His voice was a snarl now and Tansy backed away from him.

"Y . . . yours, sir," she stammered.

She'd had a wonderful time. The stallion had nearly pulled her arms from their sockets at first, tearing along the lane that led away from the front gates at such a pace, every cart and waggon, every man and woman on foot, every horseman drew hastily to one side, some of them almost going into the flower-filled ditches on either side. They stared after her, not sure whether she was a lass or a lad, the breeches shocking them if she was the former and it seemed she was. Her full breasts bounced joyfully and her mane of dark hair flew out behind her, her ribbon flying up and away like a red kite. Surely that was Mr Maddox's stallion, they asked one another, but how could it be for no one could ride the thing but him and his groom.

It was a fine day, cold but sunny and she went west, for that was where the shore lay. She leaped hedges plentiful with ripe blackberries, and dry-stone walls, leaving behind her an open-mouthed stream of country folk, ditchers and farm labourers, cowherds and the herds themselves, across stubbled fields and meadows still thick with blue speedwell and pink campion.

She galloped for two or three miles, crossing the Liverpool, Crosby and Southport Railway line, then slowed Marcus, who cantered obediently to her touch, along a wide road announcing itself to be Castle Street and there it was.

The river!

She had not expected to be so moved. The autumn sunlight, the sun lower now in the pale blue of the sky, lay in a wide golden swathe across the sliding waters, a swathe through which ships swam, sailing ships with wings on them, or so it seemed, skimming like birds not *in* the water, but slightly above it. There were coastal schooners and brigs running before the wind, three-masted barques and the glory of a tall clipper ship moving towards its berth further upriver. She didn't know the names of the craft, or of what sort they were, but she was enchanted with their movement, their grace and elegance. Even the sturdy steamships, ploughing a furrow through the golden river trailed by streamers of black smoke, filled her with delight.

Marcus stood quietly. To her right leading northwards was a low line of villas sitting comfortably among the sandhills and before them was the sandy beach, winding like a pale golden ribbon, curving out a little and then inwards again until it disappeared round a wide curve.

A working man sweeping the roadway leaned on his brush and stared at her, his expression revealing his astonishment and at the same time his masculine appreciation of her startling outfit.

"Where is this place?" she asked him peremptorily.

It took him a minute to find his voice.

"Yer wha'?"

"What is this place called?" sweeping her arm in a vague circle.

"Well, miss, yer just come through Bootle and that there's t'River Mersey."

"Bootle."

"Right, queen." He gaped some more, evidently wondering who the hell she was and what she was doing in such a get-up.

There were bathing-machines pulled by great patient horses in a row above the waterline and, amazingly, considering the time of the year, people splashing in the clear waters of the river. There were ladies walking and others driving smart little gigs pulled by ponies. There was a tang in the air, the smell of salt and what she thought might be tar, and above her head the endless crying of seabirds. There were children running with kites, dogs barking and Marcus began to fidget, taking offence at the crowds, the noise, even the flashing waters of the river.

"Right, boy, let's get away from this lot," she whispered in his ear as she led him down to the sands, then, turning him to the right, going northwards, put him to the gallop, his long, strong stride eating up the miles. At last she came to a wide stretch of sandhills and undulating beach where a sign said simply, "Rabbit Warrens", which sounded somewhat ominous, a danger to the expensive legs of Ben Maddox's thoroughbred stallion. There was a vessel in the mouth of the river from which lights flashed, even on this clear and sunny day, evidently to guide ships entering the estuary, and with a sigh of disappointment mingled with a strange content she turned Marcus's head and began the long ride back.

Even the sight of her new husband waiting for her, for what else was he doing in the stable yard, failed to spoil the wonderful afternoon she had spent. She was sore, damned sore, she realised now, as she jumped down from the back of the tall horse, contemptuously waving away his offer of assistance. The part of her that he had assaulted so many times had been ignored while she was in the saddle, but now it began to throb and her thoughts turned to a hot bath, a tray brought up to her room and a decent night's sleep, but one look at her husband's face told her there was little chance of that.

"He might have killed you," were the first words he said as Tim, who had been hovering in the stable doorway awaiting his master's command, came scuttling out to take the weary stallion.

"As you can see, he did not," she answered loftily. "Anyway, would you have cared?" She turned away from him, unconcerned, it seemed, with anything he might have to say. Her long hair, which the ride had flung into a tangled pennant of glossy waves, flew out round her head. She was flushed. Her eyes had the luminous quality, blue and dazzling, of a woman momentarily content and with no wish to have it spoiled by the foolish babbling of this man. It maddened him and fascinated him and made him desire her all at the same time, but he controlled his urge to drag her into his arms and spoke in a voice suspended with icicles.

"Well, having gone to the trouble and expense of marrying you, and that cancelled honeymoon left me out of pocket, I would like some return on my investment. The carriage in the coach house – I take it you've seen it? No, of course you haven't – wasn't cheap and there are other . . . things I spent money on so—"

"I take it that is your only concern, then? Money and the avoidance of wasting it."

"What else? And naturally the satisfaction I expect to gain from our . . . physical encounters. And of course I was worried about my horse. He is a valuable animal, and I expressly forbade you to go near him, did I not?"

"I believe you did," she answered casually, dismissing him as contemptuously as she might dismiss a servant, beginning to walk towards the archway that led into the kitchen yard.

Throwing away his still lit and dangerous cigar towards a pile of hay in the corner of the yard, he caught her arms and swung her round to face him, his eyes glaring into hers, unconcerned by what he knew were the curious prying gazes of many of his servants. They would not have missed this for anything.

"Well, as you have just seen," she managed to drawl, unconcerned herself her manner told him, "he is not damaged and neither am I. Or not yet. We spent a very pleasant time together, though why he has the reputation for being rebellious is a mystery to me." It was as though she were telling him he was not really the man he made himself out to be since she, who was only a woman, had had no trouble with this supposedly wild stallion of his.

"Nevertheless you will not ride him again. I have told Tim that he is not to saddle him unless I tell him to and if you should try to get round him I will sack him."

"Goodness, aren't you the fierce one. But I might as well make it clear from the start that I do not take orders from you, or a stable lad and I would find it no problem to saddle Marcus myself. Should I, that is, feel a need to take him out."

"I don't think so, my pet. If you go against me on this

I shall confine you to your room until you learn some sense."

"Don't be ridiculous, man. This is not the Dark Ages."

"Don't be too sure, Kitty. Providing you meet me half-way in this . . . arrangement we have between us . . ."

"Our marriage, you mean?"

"I do, then I am prepared to allow you a certain amount of . . . freedom."

She did her best to tear herself away from his grasp, unafraid of him or his threats and certainly not of saddling Marcus and taking him out when her husband was away from home. You couldn't help but admire her, really you couldn't, Tim whispered to John and Harrison, the coachman, who were all ears in the depths of the stables, as was young Artie, the stable lad who thought he'd never had such an exciting day in his life. Not that he'd seen the mistress when she climbed on the back of the master's wicked beast, since he'd had his nose in a pile of horse muck he was clearing from the back stable and had missed it, but he could see her now as he peeped over the sill of the tack-room window.

"Yer gotter 'and it to 'er," Tim went on in a low voice as he unsaddled Marcus, "she knows 'orses." He shook his head. "I never thought I'd see t' day any woman'd climb on tha' bugger's back."

It appeared Ben Maddox thought the same but his judgement was tempered not with admiration but with fear.

"I expect to be obeyed," he hissed, "especially when it comes to a dangerous animal like Marcus. He—"

"Is a wonderful horse and I found him easy to manage."

"Did you indeed? And what would have happened if he had taken it into his head to bolt?"

"Which he did not." She tried to pry her arm loose from the iron grip of his fingers but his fear for her and his anger with her made him cruel and the bruises he inflicted were to last for several weeks.

"As luck would have it."

"It was nothing to do with luck. I am a good horse-woman. I have been riding for many years. The trick is not to let them see you are frightened of them."

"Really." He began to back her up towards the wall that was pierced by the arch and when he had her there was overcome by a desire to crush her in his arms and kiss her until she begged for mercy, for forgiveness, for anything he cared to give her. To beg *her* to let him love her, take care of her, pet her and pamper her but he knew she would see it only as a form of weakness and would take every advantage of it because she did not love him.

"I think you'd better let me go," she told him, cool as a cucumber. She was surprised, he could see that, by the intensity of his emotions and slowly, inch by inch getting a grip on himself, he eased his hands away from her arms and stepped back. He was breathing hard and her curious stare and raised eyebrows, since she evidently thought he was making too much of it, brought him to his senses.

"Yes, go and change into something more suitable."

His voice was cold. He felt unbalanced by the strength of his emotions. His eyes ran up and down her magnificent body which in her breeches was revealed for all to see. Her jacket was open and pressed against the fine silk of her shirt were the hard peaks of her nipples. "I'm sure every man you met on your travels must have been fascinated to see so much female flesh on display and, more to the point, they would know who you are, for my stallion is a familiar sight. It will be all over the city before the day is out that Ben Maddox's new wife does not know how to comport herself."

"Rubbish, and anyway, who cares?"

"I do and I would be obliged if you would accept that you have certain obligations in this partnership."

"I see. That is how you view it, is it? First an arrangement then a partnership?" Kitty's blue eyes flashed with the dangerous radiance of a fireball, and she thrust her jaw forward.

"Of course, don't you, and if not, what is it then?" he snarled. "You wished to get away from Freddy Hayes and his . . . his feelings for your sister and I . . ."

"Yes?" she pressed ominously.

"I needed a wife. Now then, shall we go indoors and get you out of those ridiculous clothes. In fact . . ." His wide, strong mouth began to smile, the movement crinkling his dark skin at the eye corner. It turned into an audacious grin, his temper replaced by something else. "It would be a decided pleasure to get you out of those clothes and . . ."

"Dear God, do you think of nothing else?" But inside

her that treacherous spark ignited and she felt the warmth of it spread upwards to her breasts and into her face which flushed a rosy pink.

"Not at the moment, my pet. But then I am a new bridegroom and it is expected that I should be . . . eager, wouldn't you say?"

He made love to her before dinner, after dinner, at some point during the night and the next morning just as the birds began their dawn chorus.

"You really are the most obliging bed partner," he murmured into the back of her neck, drawing aside the tumbled fall of her hair. His tongue licked her skin and his lips smoothed and nibbled and she felt the annoying warmth creep over her again. It was the same every time he touched her. She had given no thought to him since he had left her bed earlier in the day, but the moment he put his hands on her in their bedroom, and even as they drank a glass of sherry before dinner in the drawing-room, where a maid might come in at any moment, he had laid a strong hand on her bare shoulder, a churning sensation in her stomach like wings in water, a mounting heat swept through her and her body began to stir. She had watched the look of triumph, which she hated as much as she detested him, come over her husband's face and had vowed she would not let it happen again. She would steel herself to pretend indifference. She had no choice but to allow him access to her body and to take pleasure in it but she would never again allow him to please her. Never.

She would keep her independence. Whenever, in the future, she felt that perfidious stirring at the pit of her stomach she would order it away with the sheer force of her own strong will. She would clench her teeth and her muscles and strangle it at birth. Dear God, what was wrong with her, what had happened to her in a mere twenty-four hours? Sweet heaven, it had been her belief, gleaned from she knew not where, that women were not as men were in the matter of lust. That was what she felt, she knew it. Lust, for she did not love Ben Maddox so what else could it be?

In the days and nights that followed she fought him, and herself, vigorous in her determination to deny him what he wanted, nay *demanded*. Her heart still ached and yearned for Freddy, not just in the incomplete way of a woman longing for her man – which Freddy wasn't, of course! – but the life they had led together, as brother and sister, since they were young children. She had loved him, still did, in a hundred ways, and all of them were now denied her. Soon she would have to see him again, for it would not be long before her family and Ben's friends, of whom he seemed to have a great many, business acquaintances mostly, he told her, would be demanding the hospitality a newly wedded couple were expected to extend.

So far she had done nothing but ride out on Chester who Richie, the stable lad from Riverside House, brought over for her, refusing icily to be accompanied by one of Ben's grooms and he had allowed it, drawing back from confrontation in the hope that as the weeks moved on she would settle, would become interested in the running of the house. There was a huge kitchen at the back of the house, splendidly modern, where Mrs Ullett and Mrs Pembroke waited for her to show an interest but she never went there except to pass through on her way to the stable. She went out every day. The strip of sand beside the Mersey was her favourite ride. She found that she loved the fresh smell of the sea, the sight of the dancing craft on the waters, whether they be the silky gold of a sunny day or the storm-tossed grey waves as the winter drew near. Chester, who was not accustomed to his surroundings since he had been ridden on narrow country lanes, rough uphill slopes, grassy tops, meadows and shallow valleys, showed a jittering of temper and nerves, jibbing at the tossing waters, the blowing sand, a scrap of paper, the waving couch grass on the sandhills, but he began to settle down, forming a great attachment for the small cob who pulled the lawnmower and who frolicked round the paddock with him.

Sometimes Ben rode with her, always politely asking her permission of course, just as if an hour since, the passion they had shared in bed, which he did not ask permission to rouse in her, had not taken place at all. They must have made a quite frightening sight, herself on Chester who, like Marcus, was as black as the devil, tearing along the sands to Formby Point. They would stop, not speaking much, for she was still stiff in his company, and on a clear day climb the high point of the sand-dunes to stare out across the waters to the smudge on the horizon that was the Isle of Man, the tinted shore of Anglesey and the blue-grey peaks of the Snowdon range. She wore her riding habit, of course, when he was with her but when she went out alone she put on her buff-coloured breeches, her cream silk waistcoat, her cream shirt with the cravat, her tweed jacket, a new one a smart dressmaker in Bold Street had made for her, her high polished brown boots and, tying back her hair, or not, as she pleased, she rode out exploring this new world of hers.

It did not last long, the uneasy truce they had formed. Just until after Christmas when she told him she was pregnant.

9

She was looking down at her plate, pushing a portion of Mrs Pembroke's delicious salmon mousse around its perimeter with her fork and so did not see his face light up with unconcealed joy when she told him she was to have his child.

It was January and they had been married exactly three months. In that time she had been persuaded to act as hostess – just as though she weren't really mistress of the house, Mrs Ullett muttered to Mrs Pembroke, but some casual acquaintance who had obliged by stepping in – at several dinner parties, though she professed to despise the rules of society and had no interest in entertaining it, she told her husband. On Boxing Day she had accompanied Ben to Riverside House to join in the family festivities and to mark the occasion of Freddy and Ciara's engagement.

"I'm not going and that's that," she had said stormily to Ben when the invitation had come just before

Christmas. Her mother and father, who were spending the winter in the clean and bracing air of Lytham to protect her father against further onslaughts on his damaged lungs, were to come home for a few days with, naturally, Ciara, Anna, Marguerite and Sebastian. The girls, as was proper since they could not be left unchaperoned at Riverside House, had accompanied their parents to the coast and would return there with them after the Christmas festivities and Sebastian would then go back to school. When they were married, of course, Ciara would remain with her husband and be, to all intents and purposes, mistress of Riverside House, a position Kitty knew she coveted. There would be several close friends at the celebration and, as Ben said mildly enough, it would look very strange if Kitty did not attend.

"I don't care. I'm not going."

He lifted his broad shoulders in a shrug. "I take it you're still in love with Freddy then? It's funny, but among all your faults, and you must agree there are many, I did not think cowardice was one." He spoke with seeming indifference, none of the emotions that churned inside him showing in the casual way he lit his cigar, turning to throw the match into the fire. He might have been remarking on the state of the weather.

At once she leaped to her own defence. "How dare you call me a coward, and no, I am not in love with Freddy." Which was a lie since she could not bear to face the moment when Freddy would put an engagement ring on Ciara's finger, and how she would manage to be in the church when they married was a horror she could barely contemplate. "And anyway, what would you care if I was? I am here, aren't I, at your table and in your bed. You have made it very clear what my purpose and function are in your life and, if I may say so, I have fulfilled my obligation admirably. I behaved myself at your dinner table when Mr Armstrong and his boring wife were invited and I have done my best to . . . to be the wife you wanted, though I know I have not succeeded. What else you require of me I don't know."

"My pet, I am not complaining, far from it." He smiled disarmingly, his teeth white and even in the warm amber of his face and Kitty watched his mouth as it curled upwards at each corner. Now and again she found herself somewhat disconcerted by the rush of feeling, she didn't know of what sort, that assaulted her when her husband's chestnut-brown eyes, though showing no emotion she could recognise, narrowed as they looked at her. "You have performed your duties" – his grin deepened – "particularly in one department, most obligingly. Of course, I must admit I would like it if you did not ride out so much."

"And what would I do with myself if I gave that up?" She was sitting at her dressing table wearing nothing more than the wisp of silk and lace in a shade of pale honey with satin ribbons to match that he had bought her to replace the modest velvet wrapper that had come with her from Riverside House, one satin slipper hanging on the end of her toe, the other lying carelessly on the floor.

In the weeks since their marriage she had become accustomed to drifting round their bedroom almost naked, Emma whispered to the others, her face red with embarrassment. Emma could not get over it, the way the mistress was before the master, and the way the master seemed to like it, which she supposed a man would, but really, it was unnerving when you were a spectator and though she liked the extra in her wages, she sometimes wished she was just a plain parlourmaid again.

Kitty turned to face him as she asked the question, a serious question since she could think of nothing to fill her days if she had not the sands at Bootle to gallop, the lanes and meadows about Walton to explore, the woodlands and bridle paths which led up the rising slopes on which Meadow View was built.

"Other wives seem to find plenty to fill their days."

"Oh, in their kitchens and stillrooms and pantries, you mean. Counting their linen and reprimanding their maids and when that is done, waiting for their husbands by the fireside doing fine embroidery."

"They seem to find it satisfying." His voice was calm. He was not really concentrating on the words he spoke, which came automatically they had been said so often, for the thrust of her breasts, rosy-peaked, the long graceful line of her back, the fall of her midnight hair which she was brushing vigorously, having sent Emma away, captured his attention. God, she was glorious. It was said that a woman fulfilled in love, or perhaps not love, but in her female senses, physically and emotionally, glowed and bloomed and became beautiful. Kitty had been beautiful when he married her but now she was more . . . well, not exactly *softer*, but there was a look about her, drifting, dreaming, sometimes, which he liked to think was the look of a woman well satisfied.

"Well, I don't and if you try to fence me into their world I swear I'll jump in the Mersey. You knew when you married me that I was not . . . domesticated."

"I did, and I shudder to think what I would do if you were, my pet, but it would be pleasant to come home sometimes to find you gracing my fireside with a bit of embroidery in your hands."

She glanced sharply at him and then began to laugh when she saw the glimmer of humour in his eyes.

"You wouldn't like that at all, Ben Maddox. I don't know why you married me but I do know it wasn't for my domestic accomplishments."

"True, my love. You suit me as you are."

"Really?"

"Really and truly. I couldn't manage it if you turned into Mrs Armstrong."

"There's no chance of that, Ben Maddox."

The day at Riverside had been a trying one for both of them. He wanted to protect her against the hurt of seeing the man she loved – no, he had begun to convince himself that Freddy Hayes was the man she *believed* she loved – fussing over his future wife who, it seemed to him, was already showing that quality a woman reveals when she is the dominant one in a partnership. Her gentle, plaintive voice begged him to fetch her this or that, to close the door for she felt a draught, to hold her embroidery silks while she decided on a colour. Freddy was still sweet-natured, eager to please and to be led, soft-hearted; God help him and Kitty if they had ever become the couple Kitty had wanted. She would have swallowed him whole, then, when she had ingested him and found him too bland for her taste, would have spat him out.

So when she told him of her pregnant state, rocking him on his heels, though why he should be surprised by it since they made love at least once a day, he found himself stunned, since he had not noticed her missing courses, stunned but exhilarated.

After the first mad rush of jubilation his next thought was for the servants, the two housemaids who were waiting at the graceful little satinwood sideboard, Elspeth to carve a succulent leg of lamb and Tansy to serve. To Kitty, though she had been their mistress for three months, they were no more than faceless beings whose hands passed her this or that, whose presence, when she met it on the staircase, or the hallway, was as important as a chair or a clock and therefore not acknowledged since one did not speak to either. As far as she was concerned, she and Ben were alone in the dining-room and the passing of such stupendous news, since she supposed all men wanted a son, could be spoken of without a thought for a servant's feelings, if they had any.

"Elspeth, Tansy, perhaps you could leave the next course for a moment or two. We'll ring if . . ."

They scuttled from the room, their faces bright and

flushed with their own joy, for would it not be wonderful to have a child in the house? And perhaps the mistress would settle down to what was surely her duty as the master's wife and the mother of the master's child. She had made no bones about her total disinterest in anything to do with the household arrangements at Meadow View. Some mornings she would call out her own, brand-new brougham, the one her husband had bought her for the unprecedented sum of one hundred and twenty guineas, or so Harrison the coachman told them in the kitchen, obviously longing to tell her as well. He believed she needed to be informed of such things, since she treated everything, except horseflesh, with complete disdain, or as if money grew on trees. She would only laugh if he did. She didn't seem to care about anything, that was the trouble.

She went into Liverpool and browsed around the shops, buying whatever caught her eye, keeping him hanging about for hours blocking the narrow streets to the consternation of the police constable on duty there who would have liked to give Harrison, and *her*, a piece of his mind. She ordered new gowns by the score, trinkets wrapped in pretty paper, jewelled combs which she gave to Emma, scent bottles and mother-of-pearl boxes which were thrown carelessly to the back of a drawer, embroidered gloves which she knew she would never wear, coming home with scarcely room in her carriage for all her parcels.

She made no attempt to speak with Mrs Ullett or Mrs Pembroke on the running of the house and had not these two ladies been accustomed to dealing with every aspect of the household since old Mrs Maddox died, her son would have fared ill, for there is nothing like an indifferent mistress to lower the standards.

So perhaps she would give up all this mad galloping about the countryside – well, she would have to, wouldn't she? – and the house would be a normal house, a family house, a home, instead of the luxurious hotel Mrs Maddox seemed to consider it to be. She had come on her wedding day and with no explanation not even gone on the honeymoon journey they all knew the master had planned, moved in with her often supercilious, sometimes humorous, frequently stormy ways, whatever mood she was in, and was still a stranger to them after all this time. She was haughty, disdainful, "stuck-up" they had heard Mrs Ullett call her, treating them all as though they didn't exist, and yet could laugh and share a joke with a stable lad or the laundry-maid as she hung out the washing as though they were the best of friends. You never knew which way to jump! Bloody unpredictable, Wilf called her, as one day she stalked past him as though he were one of his own rose bushes and the next begged him to tell her what the name was of that thing over there, the thing over there turning out to be a chrysanthemum. Could you believe that anyone wouldn't know a bloody chrysanthemum when they saw it? Everyone was familiar with the sight of a chrysanthemum, surely, but then what could you expect of a woman who thought more of her bloody horse than she did of her husband!

Even Emma, who was now and again summoned to sew up a hem or press a skirt, barely got to know her, for she had said scathingly that she was not a child and could be trusted to dress herself and Emma was only to come up when she was summoned. No, she didn't want tea in bed since the early morning was the best time of the day for riding. She didn't require her hair to be dressed, for she liked it simple; easy, she meant, to manage herself. Her hair, which was beautiful, and plentiful, they all agreed, was tied up in a curly knot on top of her head more often than not, fastened with bright ribbons, or simply left flowing down her back in a dark, tempestuous waterfall. She looked like none of the ladies who were visitors to Meadow View, those who still tried to do their duty by calling on her, and urging her to call on them, which she didn't do, since they had heard her and the master going ding-dong over it! She actually looked quite glorious, again they all agreed, needing none of the aids to beauty many ladies were forced to resort to and her husband didn't seem to mind. Elspeth had told them in the kitchen that she had heard the master speak of a need for more entertaining but now it looked as though there'd be none for a while.

They were bursting with excitement, an excitement with no malice in it, and certainly it would be kept within the four walls, they told one another as they hurried up the narrow hallway to the kitchen. They were filled with a sense of their own importance as they broke the news to the others, preening and swelling with pride as though it had all come about because of their cleverness! Mrs Ullett said this called for a small port each, though no doubt the master would be coming in to tell them and she wouldn't be surprised if it were not champagne all round! The only one not there was the laundry-maid who might have told them, had she not been a young woman who believed in minding her own business and certainly was not one for gossip, that she had missed the mistress's "clouts" for two months now.

In the dining-room there was silence and Ben felt his heart thud quite painfully, since he wanted to say the right words. Should he let her see how delighted he was? Should he commiserate with her, for it was evident from her mutinous expression and her refusal to meet his eyes that she was not exactly overjoyed herself.

He played safe. "When?" he asked carefully.

"God, I don't know. Not for months, I suppose. I have . . . have not . . . well . . ."

"Menstruated? Is that the word you're seeking?"

Her head shot up and she looked at him in astonishment. "Is it? I've never heard it before. We called it . . . the curse at home."

If it hurt him to hear her call Riverside House "home" he did not show it.

"I prefer to call things, whatever they might be, by their correct names and that is the correct medical term for . . . the curse."

He knew he sounded pompous but he smiled amiably and she felt herself smiling back. Sometimes she found that this man who was her husband had a curious fascination for her. His ideas were very modern and she knew there were not many wives who had the freedom she had. Apart from her refusal to return the calls of the carriage ladies, which irritated him, he allowed her to do as she liked as long as she was at his table in the evening, dressed in one of the beautiful and expensive gowns he encouraged her to buy, and in his bed at night dressed in nothing at all. They met as equals there, for his lips and hands had the power to make her sigh and stretch and glow until the sweet, curling filament which began at the centre of her spread and spread and her hands clung to his dark head as it travelled down her body and her voice lifted rapturously into the silken canopy of the bed. She knew she pleased him and he pleased her and she supposed that was a sign of equality, but in every other way they were strangers.

When they dined together he treated her as he would treat another man, she supposed, talking to her of things that were happening in the city, in the country as a whole, on the world's stage, which no one had done before, expecting her to be interested for she was an intelligent woman. The opening of parliament and the Queen's speech in which she said that trade had improved, which was a good thing, and the condition of Ireland, which was not; the attack on the Queen as she was driving from Windsor station to the castle; the opening of the Vyrnwy Water Works to supply clean water to the city of Liverpool which was welcome and would certainly help to do away with many of the diseases linked to dirty water. He asked her opinion on the music of Mozart and Chopin, on the books of Trollope and Tolstoy and when she owned up to little knowledge of the latter, led her into his library and, taking down from the shelves a beautifully bound leather book, put *Anna Karenina* into her hands, wondering as he did so whether she would read it. There were several plays on at the moment in Liverpool that he thought might interest her: did she like the theatre and would she care to visit the Philharmonic Hall if he could get a couple of seats for a concert there? She evinced little interest, throwing the book to rest among the clutter on her dressing table as though to tell him that his interests were not hers, but several days later, a wet day, and cold, he had come across her reading it by her drawing-room fire. He had said nothing and neither had she.

The only time she had shown signs of genuine delight was when she was introduced to her piano. Her pleasure in such a magnificent instrument had been genuine. She had turned to him and for a wonderful moment he had thought she was about to embrace him, a completely spontaneous embrace, an embrace from her heart which had up to now been closed to him. Had her arms begun to lift before she remembered their circumstances? Had her eyes had something in them that he would have liked to call, if not love, then affection? Had she swayed towards him or was it just his hopeful imagination?

"Oh, Ben . . . Ben," she said, or rather whispered; that was all before her sense of who she was and, more to the point, of who *he* was, returned to her. She had sat down and reverently lifting the lid run her fingers lightly up and down the keys, playing something he thought might be Beethoven, perhaps his Moonlight Sonata. He had sat down behind and to the side of her where he could watch her without her being aware of it, his eyes lingering on the graceful curve of her neck, the tendrils of her dark hair against her creamy skin, the movement of her hands and wrists, of her satin-shod feet on the pedals.

For half an hour she played, totally oblivious to him, and to the servants who, opening the green baize door that led into the kitchen, crept silently along the passageway and hovered just out of sight by the foot of the stairs. It was a moment of enchantment, a beginning, he had hoped, of something other than the lukewarm acceptance she brought to their marriage.

And now this! A child! Dear God, he had longed for it, not just for the child itself but for the anchorage that the child, itself needing an anchorage, would give her. The hope that motherhood would settle her down, bring her peace, perhaps happiness in a maternal love for something that was entirely her own.

He made his first mistake.

"So, I see I shall have to give Chester some exercise, along with Marcus. Mind you, John or Tim could probably manage."

"Forgive me, I'm not sure I take your meaning." She

pushed away her plate and straightened her back. Her head lifted and a long strand of hair, which was carelessly fastened up with a bright yellow ribbon to match her gown, fell across her shoulder.

"My darling, you can hardly expect to ride when you are with child, so it seems only natural that Chester should be—"

"Not ride? *Not ride!* You mean I am to sit about all day, as you have been begging me to do ever since you married me, and slowly go out of my mind. The only thing that keeps me sane is the time I spend in the saddle."

He felt the ice-cold anger settle in his chest, then spread to every part of his body and yet it was as though his thoughts were so hot and maddened they would set fire to his mind. His voice was coated with the frost from the rest of his body and he had to steady himself lest she see the way his hand trembled. She was out of her mind! She was expecting a child, his child, God alone knowing how far along she was, perhaps three months, and she still expected to get up on that bloody horse of hers and gallop madly about the countryside as though it didn't matter. He knew he should have been more diplomatic. Let her decide for herself how foolish that would be, make her own decision for the safety of the child but anyone, man or woman, could surely see that a woman who is pregnant would be most unwise to ride a horse. He thought, believed – or were his aspirations clouding his usually sharp mind? – that they were becoming . . . he hardly dare say the word *closer* but when they were alone of an evening, dining on Mrs Pembroke's excellent filleted sole with her own rich and creamy sauce, her fillet of veal *à la béchamel*, her strawberry tart and glacé ice-cream, accompanied by a glass or two of Chablis, she was relaxed, interested, he thought, in what he had to say, giving an opinion herself now and then, laughing, for he did his best to amuse her.

So was it all to be swept away, the small, careful steps they had taken, almost without her being aware of it? That hesitant toe in the door he felt he had achieved. The joy of how she responded to him in their bed was something he had hoped for, almost expected, since he had been aware from the first time they met that she had a passionate nature and needed only the right man – himself – to set it alight, but the progress that had most pleased him had been a sense of budding *friendship*. Was that the right word? God, he had hoped so. Was this – their first child, her pregnancy, her loss of freedom, for that was how she would see it – to cause a rift that would be enormous, hazardous, impossible to bridge?

He squared his broad shoulders and prepared to do battle.

"Have you seen a doctor?" He tried to put some warmth in his voice, not wanting to antagonise her further.

"No, I don't know one in Liverpool and, besides, what could he tell me other than what I already know?"

"Nevertheless you must be put in the care of a good man. I'll make some enquiries and get the best—"

"For heaven's sake, Ben, anyone would think I was ill. I have never felt so well in my life and had I not told you you would not have guessed, would you? I haven't put on any weight."

But she had. Her breasts were rich and full, heavy with what was to come, but he had thought it to be the blooming of a woman who is totally and completely satisfied in a physical way by the man in her bed. Her figure was still taut and trim, her stomach flat and yet now, now that he knew, he remembered the sweet curve of it beneath his hands.

"That may be, my darling, but you must see a doctor, and a nurse must be found for when the—"

"Dear sweet Jesus, at the most I am two months pregnant." Her face was scarlet with indignation and she slammed her glass down on to the polished tabletop. "There are months to be got through and if you think I am to be treated like a bloody invalid until the child comes, then you can think again, Ben Maddox. I shall continue my life just as it is."

"No, you will not. I was hoping that you would have the sense, and the natural wish to safeguard the child within you; your child and *my* child, don't forget, and I will not have its safety jeopardised by your madness. You will walk in the grounds and you may take carriage exercise. Perhaps you might even return some of those calls the ladies have made on you."

"Go to the devil and take the ladies with you." Kitty's eyes flashed blue fire and she thrust a pugnacious jaw in his direction. Her hand was still round the stem of the wineglass and for a moment he thought she might throw it at him. "I will not be confined to this—"

"Oh, yes, you will, lady. The servants will do exactly as I order them, particularly the grooms, so if you think you can sneak off on that horse of yours, then think again. I will protect you and the child, even if it's against your will and it will be more than their job's worth to allow you to go out. So think on."

"No, *you* think on, my dear husband. I will not, *will not* be imprisoned in this house."

"Yes, Kitty, you will, believe me, you will." Ben's voice was soft, mild even but there was a core of iron in it which told her to beware. His face was like granite, his mouth a mere slit, and his eyes were almost black in his fury. "This child will be born, whole, healthy and at the proper time which the doctor will reveal when he examines you. And if I think it's needed I will hire the nurse *tomorrow* and, by God, I'll make sure she keeps you handcuffed to her, if necessary. Do I make myself clear? Give me your promise that you will . . . behave until the baby is born and I will forget the nurse until nearer the time. I mean it, Kitty. I want this child and so will you when—"

"Go to hell."

"Then I'm to employ the nurse then? The minder?"

She gritted her teeth and her face was a mask of scarlet fury. The muscles in her neck strained with the obscene words she longed to fling at him but there was something in her husband's expression that told her he meant every word he said. That she would be wise not to do so. She was not a conventional woman and she was ready to rail against the restrictions he was placing on her. She was not placid, or submissive and the command to be so lit a fire inside her which almost consumed her. So far she had found him pleasant, amusing, tolerant and as long as she did not have to see Freddy and Ciara she thought she could manage her new life.

"Well," he asked her, "what is is to be, my pet?"

"I am not your bloody pet and I never will be. I will have this child since it seems I have no option but, believe me, your life and the lives of the servants in this house will be hell for the next few months. This is the first and, believe me, the last. I am not a brood mare and I refuse to be . . . Oh, go to hell!"

She stood up abruptly and her chair fell with a crash to the floor. Whirling about, she strode from the room, banging the door behind her.

Ben Maddox slumped slowly in his chair. He put his elbows on the table and placed his head in his hands, his breath easing out in a long and weary sigh. He did not doubt for a minute that what she had spat out at him would come about. They were all in for a rough ride!

10

She was sitting listlessly on the velvet sofa in her warm, luxurious drawing-room, idly flicking through the pages of the *Queen*, a smart magazine for ladies which one of her callers had left her to help her to get through her "long wait", as she delicately put it, when she heard the door open behind her. She did not look round. It was almost six and, she supposed, the time when her husband usually came home. In fact it seemed to her it might be earlier than he usually came home but as it was of little interest to her when, or even if, he came home, she did not wonder at it. She continued to read, or pretend to read, what the magazine had to say about the change in fashions, the growing size of the bustle, the increasingly elaborate design of the tea gown with a cap to match; the tennis dress with, incredibly, a skirt of gold-coloured sateen with a pale blue tunic and a large bustle, plus a side pocket in which to insert the tennis racquet when partaking of refreshment. Ye Gods, what next! Of more interest was the shorter and narrower train of the riding skirt but as she would not be riding for months and months it was again of no particular interest to her.

During the past month, probably due to the amount of time she sat about doing absolutely nothing, she said bitterly to anyone who would listen, she had put on an alarming amount of weight, her stomach suddenly curving out to what seemed to her, who was used to her own slenderness, enormous proportions, though her husband asked her what did she expect when she was four months pregnant, and anyway it suited her, the silly fool insisted. She had sensed the servants looking at her, watching her grow into this hideous shape, this distorted image of herself until she thought she would go mad, not just with boredom, but with . . . well, she hardly liked to call it embarrassment since she cared little what any of them thought, but it drove her crazy, as did their solicitude.

"Watch yer step on that there damp grass, Mrs Maddox," Wilf warned her, rushing to take her arm, that's if she had allowed it.

"I'm perfectly aware that the grass is wet, thank you, er . . ."

"Wilf, ma'am." Wilf still did his best to escort her across the lawn where his two lads, George and Joey, stood by should they be needed.

"Dear Lord, there is no need to hang about like that. I am simply taking a walk in the grounds."

"Where to, Mrs Maddox, so that we'll know . . ."

"That's none of your business. Did my husband put you up to this?"

"Well, ma'am . . ."

"Get out of my way and don't you dare follow me."

"No, ma'am." But just the same he instructed Joey to keep an eye out for her and if she'd not returned in half an hour to come running for him. The master had told them, most insistent he was, that she was to be protected, from herself, Wilf supposed, for she had a wild, restless look about her with none of the placid, breeding manner most women acquired when they were carrying a bairn.

It was the same wherever she went.

"Now, Mrs Maddox, what you doin' runnin' up them stairs carrying that book? It looks right heavy to me. See, give it here . . ." This from some trim housemaid Kitty could not even remember having seen before.

"No, I will not give it here, you impertinent girl. And what do you mean by hanging about on the stairs?"

"Nay, ma'am, I'm just doin' a birra dustin'," the girl said, not at all abashed, for she was only following Mr Maddox's orders.

If she went to the stable yard or the paddock, at once it seemed the place was thronging with grooms and coachmen, begging her to take care since the yard had just been hosed down, and when there was a particularly heavy hoar frost early in February made it their business almost to carry her down the slope at the side of the apple orchard that led to the paddock.

"Please, Mrs Maddox, that rail's right slippy," one

said when she made to climb on it. "Will yer not get down?"

"No, I will not and if you don't all go away and leave me in peace I shall climb over it and run with the horses. In fact I might even get up on Marcus's back and take off. Tell my husband that."

"Mr Maddox ses—"

"Damn Mr Maddox," she hissed at him and the groom fell back, shocked.

She didn't know how she was to get through it, for as the days grew longer and the feeling of the coming spring was in the air, as daffodils and primroses began to raise their lovely heads in the woods about the house, she became increasingly restless, even considering taking the train to Lytham to visit her mother and father but Ben wouldn't hear of it.

"I want you near Doctor Drysdale, Kitty. You know what he said. This is your first child and at your age—"

"Sweet Jesus, I'm not yet twenty-four."

"I know, but most women have had several children by the time they reach your age and—"

"You make me feel a hundred and seven and you know he said I was as fit as a flea. I'm strong and healthy and the chances of anything going wrong are absolutely nil. And I'm sure there are doctors by the score in Lytham. My mother—"

"Nevertheless I would prefer it if you remained at home until the child is born."

"You're suffocating me, Ben, you know that, don't you?"

"Rubbish. I'm looking after you, and the child, as any husband should."

"Looking after me! Yes, like a prisoner in gaol."

Even the servants began to worry about the way the master kept the mistress on such a tight leash. It was chafing her, that leash, and if he wasn't careful, she might slip it.

"She's a young woman with nowt wrong with her and should be allowed a bit more freedom. Not to go dashing about like she used to but without all of us spyin' on her night and day. I know the master said ter watch out for her but really, yer can't help but be sorry fer the lass," Mrs Ullett declared, filled with misgivings at the sight of Mrs Maddox storming through the kitchen without a word for the cat. The look on her face told them all that someone had said something to her, probably that Tim who had told them through gritted teeth that if the master wanted a gaoler for her then he'd best employ one, for he was nowt but a simple groom!

There was one aspect of her life that was beginning to fill her with a strange and quite incredible astonishment and relief. It was to do with Freddy. Whenever thoughts of him drifted into her mind she found that she could more and more easily dispel them. Well, perhaps not exactly dispel them but fragment them. She had only to remember the fatuous expression on his face on Boxing Day as he fetched and carried for Ciara, the stoop of his lean body as he bent his head to his bride-to-be, the slight look of apprehension about him as though he were just becoming aware of what a martinet Ciara really was, sweet-mannered but a martinet just the same. He appeared to have aged in the last few months, ever since his father had been taken to Lytham by his mother, which meant that he was now in complete control of the family business which she knew worried her father, for he had confided as much to Ben. Freddy was not a man prepared for the cut and thrust of business, despite his thorough apprenticeship under Josh Hayes's tutelage. He was not a man with a strong character. He was endearing, loveable, and she knew that she would always love him, for it was a habit – was that the word? – that she would never grow out of. From childhood they had been inseparable and she missed him quite desperately at times because he had been not only brother, but friend, a confidant; and who had she to talk to now? Since her husband had shown her exactly what she was capable of in a man's bed, for he had awakened something in her she had never felt before, indeed had not even known existed, she had stopped dwelling on the image of Freddy as a lover, so she supposed she had Ben to thank for that, but her marriage to Ben and her parting from Freddy had left an empty space inside her which she could find nothing to fill.

She continued to study the pages of the magazine casually. She had her stockinged feet tucked up beneath her as she leaned against a pile of velvet cushions when something was dropped into her lap. For a second or two she recoiled, then a squirming tangle of limbs and sharp claws, a cold nose, a wriggling tail, an eager tongue overwhelmed her and without thought she was a child again and she cried out in delight. It was a puppy and the smell of it, the feel of it enchanted her and she turned a laughing face to her husband, squealing and hugging the furry body as its puppy teeth made free with her flesh.

"Oh, Ben, I never thought . . . Dear God, those teeth. Where did you get her?"

"Him, and does it matter as long as he suits?"

He leaned over her shoulder well out of reach of the puppy and placed a kiss on her upturned lips and for the first time in weeks she did not turn her head away. She held the puppy with both hands round its writhing little body, studying it from every angle and her rapturous expression, the warmth in her smile made him believe that perhaps the coldness between them was over.

From then on the puppy went everywhere with her, though not into the bedroom where she demanded he should have his basket.

"Oh, no, I'm not having the thing piddling all over our good carpet which cost the earth when my mother was alive. In the kitchen by the fire."

"But, Ben, he's only a baby and will cry."

"Then let him. He has to learn his place, as we all do." She was so taken up with her new acquisition she scarcely noticed what he was saying.

Somehow she found it made a difference to have the small animal following the hem of her dress wherever she went. She was not quite so lonely. He fell over his own feet in his effort to keep up with her and picked himself up, cheerful as a sparrow, when she rushed to help him. She took him into the bit of woodland, still bare after the winter months, watching him as he tumbled about on his still uncertain legs, his baby nose to the ground, then, suddenly missing her, sat down and began to cry in a woebegone fashion. She picked him up and cradled him then set off to walk along the track that led to the side gate cut in the high wall surrounding Meadow View.

It was a clear, sunny day as she sauntered with him along Moor Lane and into Walton village where they had become used to seeing her, but only perched on the top of that tall horse she rode. She idled along the main street and glanced in shop windows and when she came to a shop that seemed to sell everything from dog collars to shotguns, went inside and bought the puppy a ball.

"A fine little feller yer have there, Mrs Maddox," the shopkeeper told her and she felt as proud as though she had given birth to him herself.

"Of course, he's a pedigree," the man continued.

"Is he?" She looked down at the puppy in surprise.

"Oh, aye, a good dog that. Probably from old man Smithers up by Rakes Farm. His bitch 'ad a litter a few weeks back an' he don't let just anyone have one."

"Doesn't he?"

"Oh, no. Not a decent huntin' dog like that 'un. Beagles he breeds. I bet yer husband paid a bit for the likes of him. They're good dogs, right friendly an' affectionate, so I heard tell."

"Well, thank you, Mr . . . er . . ."

"Armitage, Mrs Maddox, Alf Armitage at your service. If ever yer want owt in the way of hunting gear, tack, that sort o' thing, just call on Alf Armitage. I've a fine selection o' guns. Martini-Henry sporting rifles an' such."

"Thank you, Mr Armitage, but I don't shoot."

"'Appen yer husband . . . ?"

"I really have no idea," she said as she swept out of his shop.

"I shall call him Henry," she told her husband after dinner that night, holding the sleeping puppy on her lap.

"Why?"

"I don't know. Perhaps because he's a hunting hound and I was told today by one of the shopkeepers in the village that there is a hunting gun called a . . . something Henry."

"A Martini-Henry."

"That's it. Do you shoot, Ben?"

"No, I do not. The practice of certain English gentlemen of popping away at anything that runs or flies is something I find barbaric. That's why I don't care for hunting either, though the Burton Hunt isn't far from here and I have been invited to join them several times."

"Really. I have never hunted."

"Good, and I hope you never will."

"I might if—"

"No, Kitty, you will not. The thought of men, and

women too, on horseback, chasing some innocent creature with a pack of hounds, like the one you have there, perhaps; then, when they have cornered it, tearing it to bits is something that quite simply appals me."

They were dining by candlelight, giving orders for the new gas lamps to remain unlit, as they did most evenings. She leaned forward to study this husband of hers who somehow or other never ceased to surprise her. He was a strong, virile man, what she believed was known as a "real man", but he was complex, many-layered; she hesitated to use the word "sensitive", for it made him seem less of a man, but that's what he was. He did his best, she knew that, to be sensitive to her needs as she carried his child and she often found herself wondering why. She supposed it was not his fault that her soul yearned to be free, not just of him but of all the pettyfogging restrictions that hemmed in all the women she knew. Her mind longed to be allowed to decide what was best for *her*. For Kitty Hayes, or she supposed she should say Kitty Maddox. Nevertheless he seemed bent on persuading her into this mould which was the ideal of motherhood, the ideal of all the women in their social circle, and sometimes she thought she would run mad with it if she continued to allow him this power over her. As soon as this baby was born she meant to see a big change in her life.

He was leaning back in his chair, the inevitable after-dinner cigar clamped between his white teeth, a smile lifting the corners of his strong mouth. He

looked pleased about something and she supposed
he had reason to be, for he had a wife who was not
only performing her duty as a wife should by becoming
obligingly pregnant right after the wedding ceremony
but would perhaps give him the son all men longed
for. His eyes gleamed that rich, chestnut brown which
was decidedly attractive; she knew that, for she had
seen the way other women looked at him, but there
was that certain tilt to his eyebrows, a certain drooping
of his long brown eyelashes that were very familiar to
her. Soon he would hold out his hand and take hers,
ready to lead her away from the table and up the stairs
to their bedroom where his body would challenge hers,
nailing her to the bed in that long, shuddering path to
glory which she knew now meant that though her heart
was untouched, her purring, sighing, stretching body
was aware, if her heart was not, that it belonged solely
to Ben Maddox.

She almost told him so and was quite appalled by it, so
instead she said the first thing that came into her head.

"Do you know what he did today?"

"Who?"

"Henry, of course."

"No, what?" He had had the feeling that she was going
to say something quite different, something important
and felt a wave of disappointment when she didn't,
but at the same time he knew a feeling of exultancy
at the change in her since the pup had been thrown
into her lap. He had had no idea that the simple gift
of a puppy, which he had thought might make up for

the loss of Chester, at least for now, would have such an effect on her. She had moped for days, weeks, trailing down to the stables, so Tim told him when asked, to pet the animal, to feed him apples and sugar, to watch him trail round the paddock at the heels of the lawnmower pony, and to complain bitterly when Tim took him out for a canter.

"He chased after a ball."

"He's going to be a champion, I can see that."

"Don't mock."

"I'm not, my darling. I'm just happy that you find such joy in him. I know how you've missed riding and you've been a good girl."

"Don't treat me as though I were a child, Ben. A good girl indeed! I'm in this pickle because of you."

The moment of sweetness, of companionship was ended.

"Oh, no, madam, it takes two people to make a child and you were never reluctant when it came to accepting my . . . advances. In fact I seem to remember you made one or two yourself." Which was true.

"I must have been out of my mind."

"Probably, but just the same you are having a child. The doctor thinks it will be August."

"Dear Lord, what will I look like by August?" she moaned. "And then there is the . . . the . . . wedding."

"Aah, the wedding."

It had not been mentioned since Boxing Day when Ciara, her arm possessively through that of her fiancé, had announced that it would take place in May. A big affair, of course, with all their old friends and even some new ones that they had made at Lytham. It was to be a wedding day like no other, for Ciara Hayes, like Kitty, had come from dubious parentage and was determined to show everyone that though her mother and father – whoever he was – her *real* mother and father, that is, were not of the social class from which they came, she had been brought up to be a lady, and was to marry a gentleman. Her sisters, Anna and Marguerite, were to be bridesmaids but she intended having four others to float down the aisle behind her, friends who were not exactly friends, since Ciara had few of those, but girls from the same background as herself, not as pretty as she was, of course, to show off her own attractions. She planned as splendid a wedding gown as was ever to be seen in Manchester of satin and Honiton lace, white roses heavily massed at the altar of St John's Church, baskets of white petals on which she, as Mrs Frederick Hayes, would place her satin-shod feet as she left. There would be pealing church bells and a carriage lined with white satin drawn by four thoroughbred white horses and a wedding cake that would make Kitty's look like some-thing purchased at Smithfield Market. There was to be a marquee on the lawn at Riverside House, champagne flowing in a perpetual stream into fluted cut-crystal glasses and every gentleman who was anybody and his wife, including certain members of the gentry from Manchester, Liverpool, Preston and even from across the Pennines on the Yorkshire side, would be there. And when it was all over Ciara, dressed in pale-blue silk embellished with white swansdown, would go with her new husband on a lengthy honeymoon to Italy. She had it all planned down to the last satin-covered button, a hundred of them, down the back of her wedding gown, every minute detail of the day which would be solely hers though her father had been heard to say he'd like to know who was to run the business while her husband, his son, was dashing about Europe.

"I do hope you're not going to make the coming infant an excuse not to go, my pet," Ben said, lifting his dark eyebrows questioningly. "Because if you were thinking of it, then you can put the idea right out of your beautiful head. I would not like to think, and I would not be pleased if others took it into their heads to think, that Ben Maddox's wife had a reason not to see her brother wed. You may be many things but I don't believe you are faint-hearted, Kitty."

At once she flared up, rearing away from the dinner table and the two maidservants sighed and exchanged glances, for was this to be one of those evenings where the master and mistress bickered their way from the dinner table to the drawing-room and then up the stairs to their bedroom? It didn't take much to ignite that temper Mrs Maddox had and you could tell at once that she had a "cob" on her by the way she held her head and even tossed it a time or two.

"I'm afraid of nothing, Ben Maddox, and don't you dare say I am. It's just that Ciara is going to be queening it over all the other girls and if she thinks—"

"She certainly won't queen it over you, my darling.

She's a pretty girl but even six months pregnant you'll put her to shame. Get that Miss Whatsit in Bold Street to make you a stunning gown, you know, one of those that are cunningly draped to hide—"

"Don't, for Christ's sake."

"*Kitty!*"

"Well, you make me feel like a prize sow that must be disguised."

"Don't be ridiculous." Ben's voice was cold. "There are just certain things . . . conventions to be considered. I know a woman is supposed to hide from the gaze of others when she is known to be in an interesting condition but I don't mean for you to be one of them. Go and buy the most expensive gown you can find and then when the time comes you will put Ciara in the shade. There really is no need to bring your life to a halt, you know, just because you are to have a child."

"Really." Her own voice was just as icy and he sighed.

"Really."

There was no one in the yard but twelve-year-old Artie. He had Chester on a leading rein, walking him carefully round and round the wide stable yard as he had been told to do by Tim who was to take him out for a canter. He needed the exercise, Tim said and when he'd ridden Chester he would probably go for a bit of a gallop on Marcus, but until he came back from the paddock where he and John had just taken Marcus and Flame, the pretty little chestnut mare which the master had bought for the mistress before the wedding, Artie was to keep Chester from becoming too restive. The gelding had been saddled and it just needed Tim to climb up on to his back and Artie could get on with his task of cleaning out the stables. He did hope Tim would not be too long, for Chester was being particularly flighty, shying at the stable cat and her kittens which were larking about in a patch of sunlight by the stable door. There was a tangle of reins which, meaning to sort out, Tim had hung on a nail to the side of the tack-room door and every time Chester passed it he did a little dance to show he was not at all pleased, in fact he was definitely offended. Artie did hope Tim would not be long.

He was so busy coaxing Chester to behave himself he did not at first notice Mrs Maddox standing in the archway that led into the kitchen yard where the laundry-maid was hanging out the week's bedding. The flapping white sheets caught Chester's eye and he pranced sideways and it was then that Artie saw his mistress.

"Good-morning," she said to him mildly enough, her eyes on the horse, but it made Artie nervous which did not help with Chester since he sensed it.

"He looks a bit of a handful for you, lad," Mrs Maddox said to him. "Where are the others?"

"Tekkin' Marcus an' Flame down t't paddock, ma'am, if yer please."

"So why are you left in charge of Chester? Are you to ride him?" She was regarding the horse as though he were something she had never seen before, on her face a strange look which Artie found he didn't like, though he could not have said why.

"Eeh, no, ma'am, not me. 'E's too much fer me. Tim's just comin' up from't paddock an' 'e's gonner tekk 'im out."

"Is he indeed?"

"Aye, that 'e is, ma'am." Artie felt very nervous now and again the horse jinked to the side. There was something in the way Mrs Maddox just stood there, her head on one side as if she were considering what to do next and when, having decided, she moved slowly towards him he felt his heart fall into his stomach, for without another word being said he knew exactly what Mrs Maddox was going to do.

"Take him to the mounting block . . . er . . ."

"Artie, ma'am, an' I'd best stop 'ere 'til Tim comes, if yer please."

"No, I don't please, Artie. Kindly lead the horse to the mounting block and then help me up."

"Eeh, no, please, ma'am, don't mekk me do that. The master'd kill me."

"The master won't know, Artie, and I'd be obliged if you would do as you're told."

"Please, Mrs Maddox." Twelve he might be but Artie was ready to cry like a child.

"A few weeks ago I could have got on the damned thing's back without help but would you look at me now. Really it is most infuriating." It seemed Mrs Maddox was talking to herself. She had on a riding skirt which poor Artie noticed was fastened at the waist with several safety pins, but not her riding breeches which, he supposed, coming from a family of ten and seeing his mam in the same condition, would no longer accommodate Mrs Maddox's thickening waist. Not that his mam wore riding breeches; in fact she had on the same shapeless garment winter and summer, pregnant or not, but Artie knew the look.

"He did say life was not to come to a halt." Again Mrs Maddox was talking to herself, or so it seemed, and Artie could make neither head nor tail of it as his mistress climbed awkwardly on to the wide back of the fretful gelding. Artie knew Mrs Maddox had not been out riding for weeks now and for a moment she seemed unsure, allowing the horse to circle, to be skittish, tossing his head and stamping his well-shod hooves on the cobbles. From the archway the laundry-maid watched with her hand to her mouth, her eyes wide and frightened, a clean white sheet falling from her other hand on to the path.

"Oh, dear God," she moaned. "Oh, dear God, save us," as, with a great clatter, Mrs Maddox steered the great black horse through the far gateway leading round to the front of the house and the gravelled drive which would take her out into Moor Lane and then only God knew where!

11

She meant just to canter gently along Moss Lane, no jumping hedges or walls or anything like that, of course, and make her way through the village, along Bootle Lane and to the seashore, but Chester had other ideas. He had already been spooked by the stable cat and her kittens, by the flapping sheets on the line, by the nervousness of the young stable boy, besides which he was fresh, longing to stretch his pedigreed legs and simply go! With that instinct that animals possess he sensed the difference in his young mistress, the slight hesitancy, her inclination to be cautious which was not like her. He was used to her enthusiastic shout to "Go, boy, go," and so, even without her permission, he did just that.

It took all her strength to hold him in, to force him to a canter through Walton village where folk stopped to stare, since it was general knowledge that Mrs Maddox, wife of Ben Maddox who was well known since his family had lived in the district for over a hundred years, was to have a child. What was she doing on top of that mad horse of hers in her condition? It seemed the lady in question had quickened soon after her marriage in October and here it was March. Was Mr Maddox quite out of his mind to allow it? they asked one another as they watched her go by with the beast barely under her control. She was a magnificent horsewoman, or so it was said, but she looked none too skilful in her attempts to what seemed to them to be preventing the great black thing from bolting.

She turned Chester in a great swerving curve round the corner into Bootle Lane, giving him his head a little since the lane was quiet and fairly straight and it might calm him down to have a bit of a run. Her arms ached and felt as though they were being wrenched from her shoulder sockets and, though she hated to admit it, she found herself wishing she had listened to her husband. Of course, the doctor had not thought it necessary to advise her against riding, for what sane woman, a woman who is to have a child, would even dream of climbing on the back of a horse.

It had been a whim, a spontaneous impulse that had made her do it. She had brooded and brooded over what Ben had said about life not coming to a halt, turning away from him in their bed when he reached for her. He had sighed but had left her alone, turning his own back on her for the first time and she had found she did not care for it. Great God above, what was wrong with her that she could not sleep without his arms about her, for she found herself tossing and turning, so restless that he had quietly got out of bed and with a murmur that she would sleep more peacefully without him, meaning, of course, she thought bitterly, that *he* would sleep more peacefully without *her*, had gone to his dressing-room where a bed was always kept made up. Not that, so far, he had ever slept in it. She had lain on her back, one arm across her eyes and, incredibly, had even shed a tear or two, and the hell of it was she didn't know why. Just lately she had found she cried for absolutely nothing, or what would have seemed nothing to her in the old days. A rainy day, the sight of Henry making a fuss of the boot boy, the afternoon when Mrs Martha Cheers, who was her new dressmaker, told her she had put on five inches round her waist and that the day had come for concealment! Just the sight of her neglected riding boots standing forlornly in her shoe cupboard was enough to set her off.

She had been just about to drift downstairs, to do what she had no idea, for the day stretched emptily before her, but from the big window that lit the turn in the staircase she had noticed Chester being led round and round the stable yard by the boy. She had stopped and leaned disconsolately against the window, to watch as the gelding shied and pranced, resting her forehead on the cold glass, ready to cry again if the truth be known but even as she stood there, contemptuous of the lad's attempt to calm the horse, into her head had popped the most wonderful and exciting idea, and with it flooded the absolute certainty that this was meant to be. That she had passed the window at exactly the moment she was supposed to in order to see Chester and, what's more, to go down and investigate what the dickens was going on. Why was he being led round the yard? Where was that termagant of a groom who looked at her so disapprovingly as though he would like nothing better than to order her from his premises?

It was a beautiful day, a bright spring day with a warm breeze which lifted the newly budding leaves on the beech trees, making them dance a lively jig. There was a translucent quality to the light which gave the trees the appearance of being a bright new green. Through the partially opened window she could smell the delicious scent of growing things, grass and plants pushing through the rich soil towards the promise of spring, and she drew in a deep appreciative breath. She could hear the skylarks singing on the crest of the blue sky and along the borders which edged the path a ribbon of golden primroses led from the archway and round the yard. It was on such a day that she and Chester had ridden out together in the past and the bubble of happiness which was ready to explode inside her asked why they could not do it today. A sedate ride, she admitted that, for something warned her she must be careful, but a ride nevertheless. She would take no risks, she promised herself as she hurried back upstairs and with a reckless speed threw on her riding habit. She had several moments of despair when she found she couldn't fasten the damn skirt but a few safety pins soon took care of that and though it was a bit of an effort to bend down, she managed to pull on her glossy riding boots, greeting them as though they were old friends with a smile of pure glee.

Taking the side passage that led to the side door and then round the house to the stables, since she knew she would have had a hard time getting past the over-protective servants in the kitchen, she had come to the yard. And Chester.

It was just as she remembered, with the exception of the swimmers. The bathing-machines, despite the time of year, were drawn up in a neat line near the water's edge. The beach was crowded, since the good weather had brought out the ladies in their fashionable gowns, bustles and all, their wide feathered hats and their pretty parasols of silk and lace to keep away the dangerous rays of sunshine which could play havoc with a pale complexion. There were ladies and gentlemen on horseback, jogging along comfortably in one direction or another, and ladies in dog carts pulled by ponies. Donkeys with panniers on either side carried small children along the water's edge, led by a young boy, and the sky seemed filled with kites of every shape and colour.

The only intrusion on the lively scene was the presence of the new northern docks, opened only last year and named Alexandra by the Princess of Wales. The dock, with its vast array of shipping, encroached almost up to the road leading from the village of Bootle down to the seashore. One day, perhaps, she would walk in that direction, along the marine parade towards the Pier

Head and see the ships which brought cargoes from every corner of the world, for it promised to be not only interesting but exciting, or so Ben had told her.

For a moment the thought of Ben disturbed her, for she knew he would be vastly displeased when he heard where she had been today. There was no doubt he would be told and even now she was pretty sure a hue and cry would be out after her. The moment that overbearing oaf of a groom got back and was told by the lad that Mrs Maddox had ridden off on Chester – poor lad, he had nearly been in tears – he would have them all out looking for her.

They stood, she and Chester, studying with a great deal of satisfaction the familiar scene spread out before them, then, as though excited by the bustle, the noise, the sheer joy of being out, for she was sure the groom took Chester no further than the end of the lane, or perhaps remembering other days when he had been allowed to go like the wind along the shore, he was off, taking charge of her, racing like a mad thing in the direction they usually took. The sun was in Kitty's eyes, the wind was in her face, she could feel the movement of the gelding between her thighs, hear the sound of the sea and the seabirds, the shouts of the people walking at their leisure on the sand who took exception to the mad horsewoman on the great black devil of a horse ready to run them down. It all acted as a spur to the horse who had sensed from the first that this creature on his back had really no control of him, not as she used to. She couldn't stop him. She did her best to rein him in.

She did her best to make him swerve, knowing what was ahead of them but he had the mastery of her. The sign was a mere blur as she flashed past it but she knew what it said, for hadn't she turned back at least a dozen times when she came to it.

Rabbit warrens!

A thousand voices sang in her ears as she went down. She thought she heard a shout and then the crack of splintering bone followed by the appalling scream from her gelding. It was the last thing she heard as she fell into a black pit, an empty, echoing black pit in which she called out for Ben Maddox, though he didn't come.

"Well, this hair o' yours is comin' on a real treat, madam." It was Mrs Ullett who had instructed Emma to call her mistress "madam". "It's growin' right fast. I might be able ter put it into some sort of a bun in a week or two."

"Will you?" Emma's mistress asked without much interest.

Mrs Maddox was sitting at her dressing table while Emma, who at first couldn't get over the loss of it, tried to make a bit of an arrangement out of her short hair. The doctor had it cut off, almost cropped it, which Emma had thought a bit drastic but then, it was sapping her strength, or so *he* said, and there was nothing any of them could say about that, could they? Now she was doing her best with what was left, brushing it and pinning it and attaching a pretty jewelled comb among the curls but it was just too vigorous and the comb kept falling out. Her hair had a mind of its own, a bit like her, really, or how she used to be, refusing to be tamed. It had regained all its vitality, standing out about her head in a glossy halo of curls and falling over her forehead almost to her eyebrows, but apart from washing it in the mixture of rosemary and borax that Mrs Ullett had recommended and giving it a good brush there wasn't a lot Emma could do.

"Mind you," Emma murmured out loud, absorbed with what she was doing, "it looks right fetching as it is. It's that thick and such a lovely colour there's many a lady'd be glad to have it, even so short. But don't you worry, ma'am, it'll grow back as good as new."

"Will it?" her mistress said listlessly.

"Oh, aye, don't you worry yerself."

"I'm not, Emma," and Emma could see she meant it. She not only didn't worry, she didn't care and she'd been like that for a long time. Too long, in Emma's opinion.

They had brought her home in a stranger's carriage. It seemed Chester had been put out of his agony with a merciful shot from the gun brought by a groom from one of the villas along the seafront. She had been unconscious even then when they dragged her from beneath the quivering, suffering horse and had not come to as she lay bleeding all over the stranger's expensively upholstered carriage. When it drew up at the front door, Tansy flung it open, and had screamed, fetching Mrs Ullett and Mrs Pembroke hot foot from the kitchen, followed by several assorted maids who peered, speechless with shock at the sight of their mistress drooping in the arms of a burly, unknown coachman. The gentleman who stood beside him had been distraught, and not just because the upholstery of his smart carriage was ruined!

The housemaids had broken into frightened sobs. Every man and boy in the place, including Mr Maddox, was out looking for the mistress, since Tom had thought it wise to send for his master from his offices in Water Street. Mrs Ullett, who had not kept her job at Meadow View by being indecisive, had calmed them all down before sending Tansy, who was the youngest and therefore the fastest runner, to fetch Doctor Drysdale.

It was weeks now since that dreadful day. The doctor, or so the nurse he had employed had told them on the quiet, had thought that Mrs Maddox was beyond help. The bairn gone, of course, and the mistress all smashed up, but she had pulled through, at least physically, though anyone could see she was not herself yet. Not really right in the head. Concussion, the doctor had called it, but Emma was of the private opinion that there was more to it than that. She was so *quiet*. Mrs Ullett was not the only one to say sadly that they'd rather have the outspoken little madam she had once been than this impassive creature who drifted through the days like a mere shadow of her former self. She did nothing. She allowed Emma to do her hair and dress her, which was a far cry from the haughty young woman who had told her in no uncertain terms that she could dress herself, thank you very much and Emma could take herself off to whatever she had been doing before her mistress became Mrs Maddox. Ever since the . . .

accident, which was how they all described it, for what other word could you use, it seemed as though all the stuffing had been knocked out of her. Naturally, with a broken arm, cracked ribs and a conk on the head, as Emma put it, there was no way the mistress could dress herself or brush her hair, but she was healed now and there was no reason why, if she'd wanted it, she could not see to herself as once she had done. But Mrs Maddox seemed to have lost interest at the moment. She was no longer concerned, it appeared, in defying all the rules and social conventions as once she had done and so Emma was kept busy looking after her. And not only that but sitting with her, being a *companion* to her, as Mrs Ullett remarked.

Once the doctor was satisfied that his patient was on the road to recovery the nurse had been dismissed, leaving Emma in charge and she was enjoying it immensely. She had even taken to reading to her mistress from the books that lined the shelves in the master's library. Thank goodness she had been a good pupil at the local board school to which her mam had sent her, learning to write a good clear hand and to read fluently, though she wasn't much good at adding up. She had finished her education at the age of twelve as was customary, but she had kept up her "studies" at the free library in the old Town Hall building in King Street. Mind you, some of the books she pulled from the shelves of Mr Maddox's library were a bit heavy going but Mrs Maddox didn't seem to mind. She sat passively by her fireside, Henry on her lap, her hand smoothing his velvet coat as Emma floundered through something called *The Brothers Karamazov* by a chap with a funny name which she couldn't pronounce. It was spelled Dostoevsky.

"Perhaps we'd be better gettin' somethin' else, madam," she'd blurted out one wet afternoon. "This Russian chap's heavy weather. Happen another by that there Charles Dickens'd be more the thing."

And the mistress had answered with her usual, "Just as you like, Emma," her pensive gaze fixed on the flickering flames of the small fire.

Though she would not have said it last year when Mr Maddox had brought his self-willed and headstrong young bride back to Meadow View, Emma was pleased with her promotion from parlourmaid to lady's-maid. She had learned a lot in the last few months. Even though Mrs Maddox did not require it, or possibly was not aware that Emma carried out these duties, Emma had become familiar, under Mrs Ullett's tutelage, who had herself once been a lady's-maid to a baronet's wife, so she should know, with what was required of her. She was a bright, cheerful girl and a quick learner. Her own mother had been a seamstress and so Emma had from a young age been handy with a needle. Mrs Ullett had taught her how to look after Mrs Maddox's clothes, the way in which she should brush her bonnets and keep her shoes and boots in pristine order whether they be kid, satin or varnished leather. How to dress her hair, copying from the latest fashion magazines, which she practised on the other maids when they were all off duty. She had a working knowledge of the cosmetics that a toilet table needs. She was knowledgeable in the care of tweeds and other woollen materials and had learned the best way to clean delicate materials was with a thin cloth. Silk dresses, for instance, must never be brushed but rubbed with a piece of merino. She learned the art of ironing the mistress's lace frilled petticoats carefully, and mending stockings. How to wash hairbrushes, and in what solution, which was soda and hot water. How to clean combs and even how to make up a mixture to promote the growth of hair, which, naturally, was not required in Mrs Maddox's case. She wore a smart black dress and a starched muslin apron and cap and could dip as smooth a curtsey as any young lady in society. Oh, she knew a lot of things now, did Emma, but apart from helping her mistress to dress in the morning in anything Emma cared to put out, there was little for her to do, apart from the reading, to keep her mistress from brooding, which was what she appeared to do all the time, so that when the question was asked she nearly died with shock.

"Have you ever been in love, Emma?"

Emma felt the silver-backed hairbrush with which she was smoothing back Mrs Maddox's hair slip from her hand and fall with a small thud to the carpet. At once the little dog pounced on it, growling and worrying it as though it were a hairy rat and for a moment Emma was preoccupied with rescuing it.

She straightened up and stared, open-mouthed, at the reflection in the mirror on the dressing table, meeting the enquiring gaze of her mistress. Mrs Maddox looked just as she always did, or as she had looked for the past couple of months, her face devoid of expression, calm, tranquil, a word Emma would never have thought to use about the turbulent Mrs Maddox, but there was a glimmer of something in her eyes that startled her. Was she speaking of Mr Maddox, perhaps, was that it? The master came to see the mistress every day. He stood politely at the foot of the bed or leaned against the door frame, looking as he always did, freshly shaven, his hair smoothly brushed, his shirt well laundered, for life in the house went on as normal despite what had happened to its mistress. His boots were well polished and he looked the epitome of an English businessman just about to order his carriage and take himself off to his place of business, which he probably was, Emma thought. Just the same as always, and yet *not.*

It was in his eyes that the depth of his suffering was revealed. The deep, warm brown was gone, that lovely chestnut glow that lit up his face when he smiled at his wife, which he did no longer. His eyes were dead, flat, without expression like those of a snake Emma had seen in a book on the library shelves. His cheeks were gaunt now, hollowed out and though he had regained some of his healthy colour his face was stern, tight-clenched as though he were holding something in that he would dearly love to let out.

"I'm not sure I know what you mean, madam," Emma quavered, for though they had been thrown together for hours at a time lately they had not exchanged more than word or two: "Will you take cream in your coffee, madam?" "Can I get you a footstool, madam?" "Shall I brush your hair, Mrs Maddox?" for sometimes Mrs Maddox suffered from the most ferocious headaches and brushing her hair soothed her.

Her mistress sighed and her eyes slid away towards the window where a slight breeze lifted the muslin curtain. It was May and the weather was fine, sunny, mild. Next week was the wedding of Mrs Maddox's brother and her . . . well, it was sometimes said that the bride was the cousin of Mrs Maddox and at other times that they were half-sisters which was very perplexing. Mr and Mrs Maddox were to go to the wedding and Mrs Maddox's dressmaker, Mrs Martha Cheers, had been several times fitting her into the most beautiful gown Emma had ever seen, a gown of pale gold silk trimmed with coffee-coloured velvet ribbons. She had a bonnet to match, small and with barely no brim but with an enormous gold silk rose pinned to the crown. Though she was still thin, her glorious full-breasted figure not yet returned to her, she looked quite lovely, fragile, Emma had thought sadly, but lovely.

"Surely you know what it means to be in love, Emma?" her mistress persisted, which was curious in itself, for nowadays she soon lost interest in any conversation that might start between them. Emma sat for hours on end in one of the low, comfortable chairs in her mistress's upstairs boudoir, she on one side of the fire, Mrs Maddox on the other. When she was not reading

Emma would sew, mending a hem or a stocking, though truth to tell not much needed mending in Mrs Maddox's wardrobe since she did nothing to damage her clothing. Mrs Maddox did nothing much of anything at the moment, though now and again she got down on the floor and threw the ball for her little dog who never left her side now, even sleeping in his bed beside hers. She took short walks with Emma through the garden, the dog prancing at her heels, his excited barks fetching the gardeners hurrying across to her.

Wilf or George or Joey would ask her respectfully how she did and if there was any particular kind of flower they could bring in for her and she usually answered vaguely, wondering who they were, Emma could tell that. She knew *who* they were, of course, but not their names. Mind you, she hadn't known their names before the accident when she had full grasp of her wits so was it any wonder she didn't know them now? Emma knew they were concerned. All the servants were. They would discuss her among themselves like a lot of old women, even the lads, dwelling on the state of her health, which seemed to be improving, the slenderness of her swaying figure, which would soon be put right if Mrs Pembroke had her way what with egg custards, the delicate but nourishing beef broth, on the surface of which not a particle of fat or grease was allowed to float, the egg-nogs and the rice-milk she prepared to tempt her appetite but which at the moment didn't seem to be making much difference. She was recovering but she needed building up, Mrs Pembroke told them over and over again because if she didn't shape there'd be no more— Here she pulled herself up sharply but they all knew what she meant. If the mistress didn't pull herself together there'd be no more bairns which was really what was needed to get her back – and the master – to their old selves or she'd be a semi-invalid for the rest of her days.

Emma pulled a face and for the first time in weeks Mrs Maddox actually smiled.

"Go on, Emma, tell the truth?"

"Eeh, Mrs Maddox, what a question. Do you mean am I walking out with a lad?"

"Do I? Are you walking out with a lad, Emma?"

"No, not me, madam. I'm not interested in getting wed. I like me new job here with you and I'd be a fool to get involved."

"Why is that, Emma?" Mrs Maddox turned on the dressing table stool and leaned forward, her elbow on her knee, her pale face half smiling with interest.

Emma bridled, smoothing down the good stuff of her skirt and adjusting her cap proudly. "I come from a big family, madam."

"How big?"

Eeh, what was wrong with her, or was it that something was right with her at last that she should be showing an interest in Emma's life? Well, whatever it was Emma liked it.

"I'm the middle one of thirteen. Well, it was thirteen

at last count. Me mam an' dad never give over, yer see, or at least me dad doesn't."

"Give over?"

Emma sniffed disapprovingly. "Aye, they're always at it an' it's me mam I'm sorry for. It's always the woman what pays, madam," she added primly. "Men have all the fun an' the women pay fer it and that won't do for me, I can tell you. I'm right happy here at Meadow View and Mrs Ullett says if I go on this road I'll make summat . . . something of meself."

"So, you mean never to fall in love?" the mistress asked softly.

"No, madam, I don't."

"Sometimes it can't be avoided, Emma, but you're absolutely right about the woman paying."

"Beg pardon, madam?"

"Oh, nothing, Emma."

She suddenly swung round and studied her own reflection in the mirror, grimacing at the mop of short curls that swirled round her head. She pushed a hand through them then whirled again, filled suddenly with energy, an energy that had been missing for weeks.

"Right, Emma, I think it's time I had a look at that little mare in the paddock. I don't promise to like her but if I don't I'm sure something can be done about it."

She stood up and strode across to the door that led into her bedroom. Flinging it open, the dog barking at her heels, she moved to the wardrobe.

"Now then, where is my riding habit? I hope you've

kept it in good repair, Emma, because I've a feeling it's going to be well used."

With these words Emma understood that the quiet times she and Mrs Maddox had spent together were over.

12

If Ben Maddox was surprised to see his wife at the dinner table that night, beyond a slight lift to his eyebrows, he made no show of it.

Emma had dressed her mistress with special care, the pair of them deliberating on which gown to choose as though, even if the words weren't said out loud, they were aware that she must look her best.

"God, I'm so *thin*," Kitty moaned as she twisted about to look at herself in the full-length cheval glass which had been moved closer to the window so that she and Emma could get a clearer picture of what wanted doing. Distracted for a moment from her intention of flinging on her riding habit and going at once to the stables before she lost her nerve – or her strength, which seemed to be very capricious these days – she had begun to rifle through the wardrobe that held her evening gowns. She was astonished to see that they were all hanging like soldiers at attention on the parade-ground, symmetrically placed on their hangers, even the colours kept in a certain order, not a ruffle out of place, not a ribbon loose, not a hem undone.

"Well, you've been busy, my girl," she said, pushing the gowns along the rail.

"I had time on me hands, madam, when you were . . . poorly." Emma was somewhat put out, for what else was a lady's-maid supposed to do but look after her lady and her lady's wardrobe.

"Well, I'm not poorly now, Emma," insisted Mrs Maddox, though the words were said with a certain amount of bravado, "so you'll no longer have time on your hands. Before I put on my riding things, which I presume are all in the same grand condition . . ."

"Of course, madam." Emma almost tossed her head.

"There's no need to carry it too far, Emma, though I must admit that you've done well. Now then, which of these gowns shall you alter for me while I'm at the stables? That's if my riding habit fits me."

"If it doesn't I'll soon make it."

"Good for you, and not a word to . . . to anyone."

"Right, madam."

The dress she chose was a poppy-coloured silk mousseline, a stunning thing with a deep décolletage and scooped-out back with tiny puff sleeves and a vast poppy stitched on the bustle. Emma was inclined to think that Mrs Maddox might be better in something a little less . . . dramatic, since she was still very pale and the scarlet did seem to drain her of colour but Mrs Maddox was adamant. A seam here to be taken in, the sleeves lifted a fraction and the waist nipped in and it would look grand. It was as though Mrs Maddox had been at the brandy bottle she was so excited and Emma wasn't sure whether she liked it or not. Only a couple of hours ago she'd been drooping by the fire, as limp as a wrung-out rag and now here she was dashing about the bedroom trying on this gown and that and finally finishing up in her riding habit which Emma had to take in as Mrs Maddox stood before the glass.

Emma had a moment to warn them in the kitchen that Mrs Maddox was on the way.

"I think I'll have tea and toast before I go out, Emma, if you'll run down and fetch it, and send someone to tell that groom . . . I can't remember his name . . ."

"Tim, madam."

"That's the one. The one who likes to think he owns the stable and every animal in it. Tell him to saddle up the mare. Dear God, I can't recall her name, either." For a second her face clouded and putting her hand to her forehead she leaned back against the wardrobe, looking as though she might fall but as Emma rushed towards her she waved her away.

"No, I'm all right, Emma; it's just . . . I remember poor Chester and what I did to him. He was a good horse, Emma, and I killed him."

Emma almost said it out loud before she remembered that Mrs Maddox, for all her brave display, was not yet right, not really. And what about that babby, she wanted to say. You killed that babby with your wild and thoughtless ways, never mind the bloody horse, but she kept her lip buttoned. She and Mrs Maddox might have become . . . closer in the last few weeks – in fact, Emma felt quite sorry for her and would go as far as to say she had become fond of her – but it did not give her the right to speak up.

They were flabbergasted in the kitchen when they heard the news.

"Nay, she's never comin' down after all this time. I know we've not seen her, except fer Elspeth when she goes up to clean, but from what you've told us she's still as weak as a kitten." Mrs Ullett sank down in her chair at the side of the kitchen range and Mrs Pembroke did the same in hers. The maids looked at one another, their eyes wide, an excited air about them, for if it was true were their peaceful days over?

"She wants tea an' toast, so better look sharp, Cook," Emma said briskly.

"Does she indeed, and she'll have it but don't you take that tone with me, my girl. Mrs Maddox's personal maid you might be but in my kitchen you watch your tongue."

"Sorry, Cook," Emma said grudgingly. "Oh, an' someone's to go an' tell Tim ter saddle the chestnut."

Mrs Ullett put a horrified hand to her mouth. "Never," she whispered. "The master'll have a fit if he finds out."

"She'll probably tell him herself," Emma couldn't help adding cheekily. "She's comin' down ter dinner ternight."

They bobbed their curtseys and, doing their best to

keep the amazement from their faces, murmured their good-mornings which she answered cheerfully as she swept through the kitchen. She had allowed Emma to dress her in the correct and stylish riding costume that she had despised a few months ago. The skirt was narrow with vents about two inches deep at the sides of the basque and the train was short. She wore a high neck cravat and a tall shiny top hat which looked as though it had little chance of remaining fixed to her bouncing curls. The anticipation had put a flush of pink in her pale cheeks but she was still thin and where had that lovely bosom of hers gone, they asked one another in whispers after she had vanished through the kitchen door.

The mare was nowhere in sight, and neither was the groom, only the lad who was at his usual task of mucking out the stables.

He nearly skidded in a pile of manure when she addressed him.

"Where is the mare?" She looked about her as though expecting the animal to clatter out from behind the tack-room, and the boy did the same he was so bewildered.

"Please . . . ?" he managed to say.

"I gave orders that the mare was to be saddled."

"D'yer mean Flame?" His nose was running and he wiped it on the sleeve of his jacket. For some reason she felt her stomach turn over but she held her head high and told herself not to be such a fool.

"Is she a chestnut?"

"Aye, that be 'er."

"Then that is the mount I want. Where is she?"

Remembering the last time he had encountered this haughty woman and the consequences, a sly look came over his face, though God knew it was nowt to do with him.

"Well . . ."

"Oh, for heaven's sake," Kitty snarled and turning on her heel marched through the archway that led from the yard and down to the paddock.

"Fetch her saddle," she shouted over her shoulder, "and be quick about it."

Bloody hell, her accident had taken none of her dash and fire, Artie thought, his excitement gaining on him, for it promised to be an entertaining morning. He knew that Tim and John, the two grooms, were down in the paddock exercising the horses and neither of them had mentioned to him, not that they would, that Mrs Maddox was to ride this morning. He had seen one of the kitchen-maids running across the yard in the direction of the paddocks a while back but again, it was nowt to do with him. He did as he was told and kept his head down, did Artie, for was he not just a humble stable lad who spent his days cleaning out the bloody mess the horses made. Not just the two in the paddock but those that pulled Mr Maddox's carriage and the other two who had done nothing since they were brought to pull the mistress's new vehicle but eat their bloody heads off.

Grabbing what was needed from the tack-room and staggering under the weight as he was not yet full grown, Artie followed as fast as he could in the mistress's footsteps since he didn't want to miss anything.

He was just in time to see Tim, the leading reins in his hands becoming tangled about him, for though he stopped to stare at the mistress, the chestnut mare didn't, almost fall head-first in the rich grass.

"You there," the mistress called, not at all amused, despite the fact that John was in as much of a comical predicament as Tim and was being dragged round the perimeter of the field by a fractious Marcus who took offence at the slightest thing and who had bolted. The carriage horses, which had been peacefully grazing beside the lawnmower cob in the far corner of the field, took to their heels in fright and for several minutes chaos reigned.

When order had been restored Tim still looked quite pole-axed. True, the little kitchen-maid had gabbled something about the mistress and the mare but he hadn't taken it seriously. Who would? The mistress was confined to her room and had been for weeks but here she was with that same look on her face, the one that said she'd not stand to be kept waiting and why the hell wasn't the mare ready for her as she ordered? Bugger it, how was he to know that the message had been genuine? The kitchen-maid had been tongue-tied, not used to passing messages on to grooms, so, thinking it to be some foolish mistake, he had continued to exercise the mare while John dealt with Marcus in the hope that it might get some of his energy down to a manageable level. It was a bloody shame. Mr Maddox rarely rode the animal now and Marcus was too good a horse to spend his days in no more exciting a pursuit than cropping the grass with the others.

"Madam," Tim stammered, furious with her and with himself for letting her get him into such a state. "We wasn't expecting . . ."

"I sent a message down to you half an hour ago. I would like to ride . . . Flame, is it? I believe she is a . . . placid animal and can do me no harm. I realise that it is out of the question to go out on Marcus," gazing longingly at the spirited animal who was still fretfully tossing his head and stamping his feet.

"*Madam!*" Tim was appalled. Had she not learned her lesson in March when she got up on that magnificent gelding of hers and rode him to his death? She'd lost her child and been at death's door herself, or so it was rumoured, and yet here she was, only eight or nine weeks later, looking a shadow of her former self, true, since he remembered her as a woman of what might be described as "generous proportions" with womanly breasts and hips and a waist he could have spanned with his two hands.

Dear God, what was he about, allowing thoughts of his master's wife and her sadly lost figure to enter his head? Dwelling on how she had been weeks ago when it was nothing to do with him. But the horses were and though the master had not exactly told him in so many words that the mistress was not to ride, considering she was incapable of it, presumably, he was stony-faced in his determination not to allow it.

"Mrs Maddox, ma'am, d'yer not think it might be wise

ter wait another few weeks," he began ingratiatingly, but the furious indignation on Mrs Maddox's face dried up the words in his mouth.

"How dare you presume to tell me when I am fit to ride," she proclaimed in a voice that left him in no doubt as to who was in charge here, and it wasn't him. He might be employed to look after Ben Maddox's horses but he was certainly not empowered to tell Ben Maddox's wife when she might or might not have her horse saddled, to get up into the saddle and gallop off.

She did not gallop. She did not even canter or trot. She merely sat on the little mare's satin-smooth back, the sunlight glinting her beautiful coat to polished chestnut, and walked slowly along the path at the side of the paddock, on to the gravel path and round the house to the drive. They watched her go, gently moving with the horse between the rows of newly planted summer bedding plants until she reached the gate.

"Will yer not let me come wi' yer, madam?" Tim shouted after her hopefully, but she merely waved her hand in refusal as she walked the mare through the open gates, turning left into Moor Lane. Primroses were still thick in the banks and the hedges were sweetly green and in the orchards on either side of the lane apple trees were in blossom. The oak trees which lined the lane at intervals were showing the first sign of their golden-bronze foliage and from the woodland she distinctly heard the call of the first cuckoo. It was wonderful to be out of the sickly atmosphere of the invalid's room in which she had lain for so many weeks. Wonderful to see the high arch of the May sky above her head, to watch the new lambs skipping and tumbling beside their staid mothers and feel the newborn springtime as it turned softly towards summer.

As they had done before the good folk of Walton stopped to stare at her as she and the mare walked daintily through the village. Several of the men raised their caps or bowlers, smiling, for though she had been seriously ill she seemed to have regained her looks and men will ever smile at a pretty woman. The women too nodded, for the poor lady had lost her child and though it was said it had been her own fault it must have been a sorrow to her.

"Good morning, Mrs Maddox," Mr Armitage called out from his shop doorway. "It's grand ter see yer up an' about again."

She bowed cordially at each and every one of them, pleased in a strange way that *they* seemed pleased, even concerned about her. She had never known the regard of others, for all her life she had done nothing to warrant it. They had loved her in a way, she supposed, in the way family members love other family members even if they don't like them much, but she had always been part of a group, lumped in with her brothers and sisters, disapproved of by her parents' friends, by the servants at Riverside since she was so uncaring of their feelings and caused them so much trouble; but now, here, she felt a small wash of sympathy emanate from them to her, just as though she were now part of this community and deserving of their interest.

That was all she did. When she reached the end of the village street she turned Flame round and walked her gently back the way they had come, lifting her hand now and again to return the agreeable waves she received. She had never quite felt like this before and she wondered what it was, but whatever it turned out to be she thought she was going to like it. The air she dragged deep into her lungs was unbelievably sweet and she felt almost her old self again. It had been wonderful to get out of the house, out of that warm room upstairs where she had languished for so many weeks and tonight . . . well, tonight, who was to say what would happen when . . .

She began to smile.

Tim was unable to believe his eyes when she rode peaceably into the stable yard, the mare not even in a decent sweat and herself as immaculate as when she rode out. Even her bloody hat was still intact. He ran to help her dismount, his approval plain on his homely, weather-beaten face.

"Good ride, Mrs Maddox?" he asked.

"Yes, thank you, Tim. She's a nice animal. Very gentle."

"Aye, that she is, ma'am. Just the mount for a lady."

"Probably you're right, Tim, though not for me."

Well, what could you make of that? his astonished expression asked. He lifted his cap and scratched his head, then turned to John to see if he had any thoughts on the matter, but it seemed he hadn't. My, she was a rare one was Mrs Maddox.

* * *

Her husband got to his feet as she swept into the drawing-room, swirling the full skirt of her poppy-red gown about her. Though Emma had had doubts about the colour she had been wrong, for it seemed to reflect in her face, giving it a flush that was very flattering. Her loss of weight gave her a fragility, a vulnerability that most men would find attractive, for it would make themselves seem more virile, but it appeared to have no effect on Ben Maddox. In fact his dark eyes looked somewhere over her smooth white shoulder as if he really could not bear to contemplate her. Her dark hair tumbled about her head in a crop of glossy curls and behind her ear Emma had fastened a knot of poppy-red satin ribbons. She looked vivid, full of life, but he seemed to wince as if it were too much for him.

He had a glass of sherry in one hand and had been swirling the amber liquid round and round in the glass as he stared broodingly into the fire. In his other hand he had a cigar. He threw the cigar into the heart of the fire as he turned slowly towards her. She made a smiling gesture to show she did not mind him smoking, even here in what was her drawing-room but he did not appear to notice.

"Aah, it's true then," he said impassively, his eyes still retaining their total disinterest, even blankness, as though she were a stranger who had somehow got past the housemaid and invaded his privacy.

"What is?" She felt a great need to go to him and raise her face for his kiss as she would have done weeks ago but she restrained herself. She must not be too precipitate. They had been virtual strangers ever since the accident, she too ill at first even to realise he was in the room, and later too intent on remaining in what seemed now to be no more than a blowing mist in which she had spent her days. She had not looked for forgiveness after what she had done. She had hoped, perhaps, for some sign that time was to ease his loss, but he had always slipped away from her before she could register what it was she wanted to say. She didn't even know what that was now, and, suprisingly, she never considered it to be *her* loss, too. The child had never been real to her, just a burden she was forced to carry round against her will, a fetter that kept her chained to the house, to domesticity, cutting her off from all the things she loved the best. The only thing she had left had been her piano and she meant to play on it this very evening. She had even chosen a piece: Beethoven's Piano Concerto No. 4 in G Major, Opus 58, to give it its full title. It had a simple and unaffected beauty that she had always loved and she . . . well, she didn't know what she hoped for, she only knew that the past couple of months must be put behind them if they were to find . . . what they had lost. She wasn't awfully sure she could put a name to what they had lost, for it had been no more than an unopened bud on a branch waiting to unfurl. She only knew that now it seemed to her to have been worth while. And of course, the wedding was next week and she wanted to walk into that church on her husband's arm and show the world

– and Freddy and Ciara – that Kitty Maddox was doing very well, thank you.

"Tansy said you were to dine. You are feeling better then?"

"Yes, I am, thank you. I have even been for a ride. On Flame, I might add and never broke into anything beyond a walk." She smiled, a slow, wide smile that once would have delighted him.

"So I heard."

She was surprised that he hadn't more to say on the subject since he had once been voluble in his determination to slow her down. Still, she supposed now that she was well again, or at least on the way to it he would not mind if she had a gentle canter on the placid mare.

"You . . . do not mind?" she ventured.

"Not at all."

"Good."

There was a strange silence while she searched about in her mind for something to add, but he had turned away to the small side table where the decanters were placed.

"May I get you a sherry?" he asked her, just as though she were an unexpected guest who must be shown some civility.

"Thank you." He was careful not to touch her hand as he passed it to her.

"Won't you sit down? I believe dinner is almost ready."

"Thank you."

He sat down when she did and resumed his contemplation of the flickering fire while again she cast about for something, *anything* with which to break the echoing silence. What was wrong with him? Why was he not chatting to her as he used to? Making her laugh as he used to? Telling her stories of what had happened to him during his working day? What deals he had made, which men he had got the better of, not dishonestly but because he was cleverer than them. He had been an amusing companion, entertaining, making her laugh, arguing with her, fighting with her, she supposed, and her own natural need to be free. But he had never bored her, never dominated her with anything but good humour. Oh, yes, his attitude had said he would be obeyed but he had never been mean-tempered. He had been generous, indulgent when she did as she was told, which she admitted now had not been very often but there had been a certain – dear God, what was the word? – amity that she remembered she had liked. And, of course, their absolute equality in the intimate side of their marriage had never ceased to delight and amaze her, for it had been so surprising.

Now he seemed to be unaware of her presence, sipping his sherry and coming to almost with a start when Tansy came to tell them that dinner was ready.

Their places had been set together, he at the head of the table, she beside him as they had been before the accident, so that they might talk and laugh without the length of the table between them. The candlelight gleamed on the shining surface and cast iridescent shimmers off the crystal glasses. It showed her her own reflection in the silver. Everything was as it had always been, a warm comfort, luxury even. Her husband looked just the same, somewhat thinner, she thought, now that she had a good look at him, but still attractive and she was ready to resume the pleasant relationship that had, hardly with her knowing it, grown between them before the accident.

It was then that the first slivers of disquiet began to feather themselves down the length of her spine. The back of her neck felt cold and she noticed, quite incredibly, that though she was warm in herself there were what they had called "goose-bumps" when they were children on her arms.

They drank Mrs Pembroke's delicious consommé followed by salmon mayonnaise. There was a light and mouthwatering soufflé, then braised beef done in rich red wine with tiny potatoes and peas fresh from the garden. There was meringue topped with whipped cream and strawberries, for Wilf had been told Mrs Maddox was to dine downstairs for the first time and had produced his finest. Mrs Pembroke, indeed all of them, had gone out of their way to make this a memorable meal, for they wanted nothing more than for the master and mistress to . . . to get together and be as they were before. In other words to start another baby as soon as possible, for in that way the healing process would begin.

But no matter what she said, no matter what topic of conversation she forced herself to babble, he did nothing but answer politely, unsmilingly, and her heart began to beat to some dread rhythm which caught her breath in her throat so that the words dried up and they ate in silence.

They rose to go into the drawing-room for coffee, sitting down opposite each other and again he seemed to drift into a reverie from which she was totally excluded and she could stand it no longer. She had been most patient, she told herself. It was many weeks since they had dined together and after all, they . . . he . . . had suffered a great loss, she supposed, but they must put that behind them. They were man and wife and though she wanted no more children she was more than ready to . . . to resume the rather pleasant relationship that had developed between them in the first months of their marriage. He had, almost without her knowing it, pushed Freddy to the outer perimeters of her mind, his quick, wry wit sharpening her own, his often ribald humour making her shout with laughter at times. In their bed he had often whispered audacious suggestions and though she had pretended to be shocked, it had been – what? – quite delightful. She recognised that he was a skilled and accomplished lover, having had experience of women, she supposed, from his youth, and she knew now that she wanted it back.

"Am I to keep up this stilted monologue for much longer or are you to take part?" she asked him, doing her best to smile, to keep it light, treating the matter as though he were preoccupied with some business thing. As though he would come to with a start, begin to smile and apologise, but he did none of these things.

He stood up, placing his coffee cup on the table beside him and she looked up at him, smiling enquiringly, letting him see that though she was not used to compromise, to making concessions she was willing to meet him halfway, *more* than halfway, since she knew she had been the wrongdoer, in building up again the strange but rather pleasant rapport they had known before the accident.

For the first time he looked directly at her and she felt the need to recoil from the expression in his eyes. They were as hard as agate. There was nothing in them of the lively warmth, the good humour, the rich chestnut brown which had once lit up his face. They were mud-coloured, narrowed with what looked like venom and his mouth snarled in a cruel twist.

"You arrogant, heartless bitch," he said and his face was quite blank, only his eyes alive now with some dreadful emotion he could no longer keep hidden. "Do you seriously believe that after what you did we can take up where we left off? To satisfy your own whim, of which you had so many, you deliberately climbed up on that horse, disregarding not only your own safety but that of the child you carried. You killed our child, you killed your horse and you almost killed yourself and here you are tricked up like a whore hoping, it seems, to lure me back into your bed again. Well, my dear, you can go to hell, to the hell in which I have dwelled these past weeks, and I hope you roast there for all eternity. Now, I am going out so I will bid you goodnight."

Emma was waiting for her, sleepy but determined to do her duty and it seemed easier to let her undress her and brush her short hair, nodding at her chatter until she went away, puzzled, she knew, by her silence.

She heard the sound of horse's hooves on the gravel as her husband left to wherever it was he was going and why should she think, her heart quite astonishingly anguished, that it was to another woman?

13

The wedding went well and if the guests wondered at the manner in which Mr and Mrs Ben Maddox treated one another it was not spoken of out loud, at least in front of the family. She looked quite lovely if somewhat frailer than they remembered her, but then she had suffered a miscarriage so it was to be expected. He was cool, aloof, not just with her but with everyone, scowling, lounging in the hallway discussing some business matter, they supposed, with Philip Meadows who was in some way related to the Hayes family by marriage and was a cotton importer. The unexpectedly delicate loveliness of Kitty Hayes, Kitty Maddox they supposed they should call her, quite took the attention away from the bride, whose day it was, and it was apparent that Mrs Freddy Hayes was none too pleased about it, giving her new husband a whispered ticking off when he accidentally stepped on her veil, jerking her head back in a most undignified manner.

The cream of society was there, even a minor baronet whose son had gone to school with Freddy and who Ciara had assiduously cultivated. A gathering of great power and prestige, men of position and wealth from Manchester and Liverpool and even from as far away as Yorkshire. The bride, as brides do, looked quite glorious, but nevertheless it was on the headstrong and frailly beautiful Mrs Ben Maddox that the guests' gaze was inclined to linger, since they remembered how wilful she could be, and how entertaining. She and her husband barely exchanged one word, both turning coolly to whoever was beside them, she smiling brilliantly, he more sombre but civil enough.

Kitty found that if she looked everyone directly in the eye and smiled as though she hadn't a care in the world, and that included her brother as he came out of the church with his wife on his arm, she could get through it all. She had hoped, of course, to have her husband's arm to cling to, his protection round her, for he had known how she felt about Freddy, but it had disappeared now, that barrier of security he had erected about her, in the icy chill of what appeared to be his total indifference. He neither cared how she felt, nor even if she still felt anything for the man who had married her sister today. He was keeping up some sort of appearance, for the sake of business, she supposed, since he had dealings with many of the gentlemen here today. There was a terrible numbness inside her, an absence of sensation which she supposed was merciful and which she was at a loss to understand since she knew it was nothing to do with Freddy. When, after the reception, as the guests began to wander about the sunlit garden, taking a stroll, champagne glasses in hand, between the formal gardens which soon would be a smother of roses, she let herself be led down the sloping lawns towards the river.

She thought she would be alone but a young man stood there, handsome and dark as a gypsy yet with something about him she thought was familiar. He was dressed as all the other gentlemen in an impeccably tailored frock coat of the darkest grey with well-fitting trousers to match, a white silk waistcoat over his white pleated shirt, a high, turned-down collar and a neat bow tie. His shoes were of black patent leather. He was staring sightlessly into the placidly moving waters of the river on which floated drifts of debris, leaves and small twigs, eddying towards the bank and then out into the main stream again. He seemed to be fascinated by something, his thoughts far away, and as she approached on the smooth grass he did not appear to hear her.

"I hope you're not intending to jump," she said flippantly and was considerably startled when he whirled about and stared at her with what looked like outrage on his face.

"I beg your pardon?" She might have said something abusive the way he acted, his face cold, disapproving, and she stepped back, her hands, one of them holding a half-empty champagne glass, before her placatingly. She had drunk rather a lot of champagne, since no

one seemed to care what she did, certainly not her
husband whose responsibility she was, and certainly
not her father who had passed that responsibility on last
October. She felt pleasantly light-headed, bubbling and
fizzing like the wine, inclined to drift from a straight line
of walking, thinking, despite the hard knot of something
in her chest that she did not recognise, how delightful it
was that at last, after all these years, she appeared to be
able to do exactly as she pleased.

For a second or two the young man frowned, his
eyes still cold, then he smiled and it was like watching the sun come out from behind a cloud. His eyes
were an incredibly beautiful blue, somewhere between
sapphire and azure, with long, absurdly long black
lashes surrounding them. His hair was a tumble of
uncombed curls, as though he were in the habit of
running his hand through them, dark as night, and
glossy with good health. His face was sun-browned
and she had the pleasing thought that he might, like
herself, be a keen rider, or at least liked to spend his
time outdoors. He was tall, taller than she was, and
lean. When he smiled it was an engaging smile which
revealed gleaming white teeth.

"You looked very beautiful in the church."

She was astounded but she managed a rueful laugh.
"Did I? You'd better not let my sister hear you say that.
She was the bride, by the way."

"I know, but I didn't notice." He moved towards
her, stepping away from the river's edge where he
had been . . . well, she almost said *hovering*. "You

were standing in a shaft of sunlight and looked quite angelic."

She exploded into laughter, spluttering over the champagne glass. "Ye gods, my family would be vastly amused to hear you say that. And my husband."

"Is he the stern one?"

The laughter left her and she felt a breath of cold air waft over her. "Yes, that'd be Ben."

"Is he always so . . . aloof?"

"I couldn't say. I hardly know him."

It was his turn to look surprised. "That's an odd thing to say about your husband."

She shrugged and took another sip of her champagne, staring out across the river and the poppy-starred fields beyond.

"Perhaps. Anyway, who are you? Friend of the bride or the groom? I don't think we've met before."

He lounged gracefully beside her, his hands in his pockets, his eyes fixed once more on the swirling river. He seemed to be considering what to say next and she turned enquiringly towards him, putting up her hand to shade her eyes from the sunlight.

Behind them from somewhere up the slope came the sound of laughter and a female voice proclaimed that she wasn't about to spoil her shoes in the long grass and if he wanted to get to the river Martin would just have to carry her. Kitty recognised the rather high-pitched voice of Martin Baker, he who had so irritated Ben on the night of the dinner party when he had asked her to marry him, mingling with that of her cousin, Mariella

Meadows, who was one of the six bridesmaids Ciara had insisted upon.

"My name is Michael, Michael . . . Northwood." He turned his disarming smile on her and she wondered why she had the idea that he was not telling the complete truth. Perhaps because of the hesitation after his given name, but then why should a guest at Freddy's wedding lie to her about his name?

"I'm not familiar with the name, not that that matters. I don't know half the people who are guests. Were you and Freddy at Deanhampton together?"

"No . . . oh, no. I was educated at . . . Harrow." Again the slight hesitation.

"Really! How very superior."

"Not really. My . . . stepfather insisted I go there. No, I'm a friend of Jimmy Oliver. D'you know him?"

"I think I've heard Freddy mention him. Where does he live?"

"Now that I can't remember. I'm not a native of these parts, you see. Some place between here and Liverpool. St Helens is close by, I believe. Jimmy's father has coal mines and is rather rich. He has an estate there and I must say I'm rather partial to rich gentlemen with estates. You know the kind of thing, grouse moors and rivers specially stocked with trout." He grinned wickedly and though she was somewhat taken aback, not having met such honesty before, she could not help grinning back. "Anyway, I'm staying with him for a week or two. Doing a bit of shooting, you know, and your brother, on hearing I was there, asked Jimmy to bring me along. Very decent of him, I thought."

"I suppose so."

She sipped her champagne, finding herself totally at ease with this astonishing young man and without really seeing it stared at the glinting, sliding waters of the river. The sun on it, striking sparkling rays, dazzled her eyes and she narrowed them. Her golden gown was wet round the hem of the skirt, for there had been a heavy dew the night before and her satin slippers, dyed to match her gown, would be ruined but she couldn't find the energy to care. Her bonnet with its extravagant golden rose was in the house, thrown carelessly down somewhere and her hair which, like Michael Northwood, she had pushed her hands through, stood about her head in a swirl of disordered curls, bouncing as she walked. She knew everyone was looking at her, for she had not been seen since her own wedding seven months ago and she found she liked the murmur, as she had always done, of disapproval that hummed among her parents' guests. She hasn't settled down then, she knew they were saying. She's still the reckless young woman she had always been which meant that even that strong, brooding husband of hers had not tamed her.

"I am to be in Liverpool next week. Some business to attend to so perhaps, with your permission, might I call on you?" the young man next to her asked politely.

She turned to look at him, realising as he bent towards her that he was actually younger than she had first thought. In his early twenties, had been her first impression. A handsome, elegant young gentleman with the polished, sophisticated good manners that his education at one of England's foremost public schools had given him, but on closer inspection she could see that he was not yet twenty. Nevertheless his self-confidence was without flaw and his belief in his own attractions quite matchless.

"And then, I wonder," he went on, pulling at his lip as though hesitating. "Well, Jimmy and some of his friends are keen on racing and so Jimmy has got up a party to try our luck at Aintree. Do you like horse-racing, Mrs Maddox?"

"Do you know, I have no idea. I have never been. I love horses, though."

"Then you'd enjoy a visit to Aintree, which is a steeplechase course. You have surely heard of the Grand National? Of course that is run in March but there is the Craven Meeting, a three-day event which takes place next week. Perhaps you and . . . your husband might care to join us?" He smiled engagingly, telling her quite plainly that her husband could go to the devil for all he cared and again she was startled by the sudden feeling that washed over her that she knew this man from somewhere. And yet she had never met him before in her life. She would have remembered. He was so exceptional in his assuredness, so striking, tall and handsome with those electrifying blue eyes that seemed to say once you had met him you would never forget Michael Northwood.

She shook off the feeling and smiled. At last, here was a way that promised to alleviate the boredom, the loneliness, the wondering as she got out of bed each day how she was to fill it. Ben didn't seem to give a damn what she did. In the past week he had left the house immediately dinner was over and only God – and probably the servants – knew what time he came in. She had scarcely seen him, except at dinner when he answered her determined attempts to make some sort of conversation in monosyllables which she was sure was merely to give the maids something less to gossip about. It would be common knowledge that though she had now recovered from the dreadful happenings of the past months she and Ben were still occupying separate rooms. She had no women friends and, if the truth were told, wanted none.

The ladies who had determinedly come to call in the early days of her marriage had gradually stopped coming, since she did not return their calls and as Ben no longer cared to fashion some sort of social life as a married couple, what could she turn to? Her two joys were riding and playing the piano. She spent her evenings doing the latter and her days the former but now, here was a young man who came from somewhere that was very obviously not in Lancashire, which, naturally, being who she was, fascinated her, inviting her to go to Aintree, a venue which sounded exactly the sort of thing she would adore. Horses she loved and in fact meant to purchase a decent mount, one more like Chester, from the allowance her husband paid into her own personal account at a bank in Liverpool. Flame was all well and good for the moment but she was too docile to suit Kitty's taste and here was the very man, and perhaps his friend, Jimmy Oliver, who might be able to steer her in the right direction, which meant towards a good horse.

"I would be delighted, Mr Northwood. To have you call, I mean, and as for the steeplechase" – she glanced at him from beneath her lashes, a flirtatious look she was well aware – "we shall have to see. As for my husband I doubt whether you could winkle him away from his business during the week so you would have to make do with just . . . myself."

"That would be no hardship, believe me, and please, will you not call me Michael."

"Michael, then, and I am Kitty."

"I know."

"You seem to know more about me than I know about you, Michael. Where are you from?"

"Oh, here and there."

"Here and there?" She gurgled with laughter, deciding that she had not been so entertained, nor intrigued since . . . since before the accident. "And what do you do *here and there?*"

"This and that." He grinned disarmingly. He was looking into her eyes but something suddenly caught his attention over her shoulder and at once he stiffened. His face became expressionless but something in his eyes, so warm and friendly a blue a moment ago, turned cold. Looking back at her he bowed with old-fashioned charm and announced hurriedly that he thought that old Jimmy was signalling to him and he'd best be off.

"Very well, Michael Northwood, don't keep old Jimmy waiting or he might not invite you again."

Again she was startled by the look on his face. It was as though she had touched a raw nerve which spasmed his cheek in a nervous twitch and thinned his lips, binding them together in a white line.

"What does that mean?" he demanded harshly.

"Why, nothing at all, Michael. What on earth should it mean? It was intended as a joke."

It took several seconds and a great deal of willpower on his part but she saw him relax and his warm smile was put on again, lighting up his face and his eyes so that she thought she must have imagined the moment of ill humour.

"Well, I'd best be off so good-day to you, Kitty Maddox. I'll call on you soon," he murmured, then, turning on his heel, hurried away, going not in the direction of the house where the guests were gathered but off to the side where the kitchen gardens lay, darting among the trees until he was out of sight.

"Who was that, darling?" a voice asked behind her. It was her mother, her arm through that of her father.

"A friend of Jimmy Oliver's, Mother. Freddy apparently invited him when he learned he was staying with Jimmy."

"Do we know him?" Her mother looked very beautiful, elegantly dressed in a pale pearl-grey silk which was very suitable for the mother of the bride, *and the groom,* which several of the guests had already remarked on today, but her gaze was puzzled, anxious somehow as she looked in the direction the young man had taken. "But why did he rush off like that when he saw us coming?"

"Did he rush off? I didn't notice."

"Oh, yes, the moment he spied us coming towards you he picked up his heels and ran."

"Well, I'm sure I don't know."

"Did he tell you his name?"

"Yes, Michael Northwood."

"Michael . . ." Nancy Hayes's voice quivered and her husband looked down at her anxiously. She seemed to tremble and Kitty wondered what there was about the name which appeared to have upset her.

"Come along, my love," her father said to her softly, "or we shall miss the send-off."

Kitty began to walk with her parents up the slight slope that led to the house where Freddy and Ciara were just about to set off on their wedding journey. The carriage was at the door, surrounded by wedding guests and for the first time that day Kitty felt herself falter. Ciara had changed from her breathtaking bridal gown into a going-away outfit of the palest blue trimmed with cream ruffles, on her head a dashing bonnet with a cream feather curling round the brim. Freddy looked very stern, as though what lay before him must be treated with the utmost seriousness, but as he handed his wife into the carriage his face softened, his mouth curving into a tender smile, the sort of smile Kitty would have given the earth for several months ago. Ciara whispered something in his ear and the smile turned to laughter and that last sore spot inside Kitty throbbed and broke into quivering life. They loved one another. They had something she had never had and would never know now. She had learned, with Ben's help, to ease Freddy out of her thoughts, perhaps a pretence that she was over him, or what she had felt had been nothing but infatuation. Or just the strong affection a sister feels for a beloved brother. It was, she realised sadly, far from the truth.

She turned on her heel, ready to go indoors and escape from the cries of "Good luck" and "God bless you" that eddied about the drive and almost bumped into her own husband who lounged against the frame of the open front door, a glass of champagne in one hand and a cigar in the other. He raised enigmatic eyebrows as his eyes met hers and his lips curled in what might have been a smile, but wasn't.

She rode out on the mare the next day, and the one after that, roaming far and wide, further than she had ridden before. She found that if she kept to the very edge of the tide at Formby Point where the sand was wet and firm she could avoid the sandhills and rabbit warrens that had brought her down in March, going beyond Ainsdale, a small hamlet north of Formby, beyond Birkdale to the outskirts of Southport itself.

But Flame, who was sweet-natured and obedient, though with no fire in her despite her name, was not as strong as Chester. Kitty was forced to rest her before setting back, which made her all the more determined to have a mount of her own, of her own choosing, which would take her just where she wanted to go without tiring.

Each day Tim had smiled with approval, and a certain amount of self-satisfaction, she was inclined to think, as he helped her into the saddle and at the end of the ride out of it again.

"Nice ride, Mrs Maddox?" he would ask, patting the mare's nose, while out in the paddock Marcus tossed his head and whinnied, then broke into a mad gallop up and down the white painted fence nearest to the stables.

"He needs a good ride," she said shortly, ignoring the hand Tim put out to her. "Poor lad, it's not fair to keep him in the bloody paddock all day."

Tim was shocked at her language but it was not his place to remonstrate with her but, by God, if she was his wife she'd know who was master, like the horses.

"I've not the time ter be tekkin' 'im out, Mrs Maddox, an' John can't 'andle 'im." Tim's voice was short.

"No, but I can."

He watched her stride away towards the kitchen door, the short train of her riding habit just touching the cobbles. She was dressed as a lady should be and he wondered sourly how long it would be before she began to rebel again. She'd had a nasty shock losing Chester, never mind the baby, the former of more importance to her than the latter, in his opinion, and so she was keeping her wildness in check, but it'd not be long before she broke out again, you could be sure of that. She wasn't one to give in meekly to her husband's wishes, though from the whispers that came from the house it didn't seem as if the master had any, at least where she was concerned. She had her eye on Marcus, he could tell that and when he could catch him he meant to tell the master. That'd put a stop to her little game. That stallion was not a fit mount for a woman, even her who, he admitted, was a superb horsewoman. No, Flame was a lady's mount, bought last year by the master for his wife and Tim'd have nothing to do with saddling Marcus for her, if that was what she had in mind. He'd best get that straight with Mr Maddox right away then there'd be no bloody argument.

"I had a word with Tim today, or rather he had one with me. It seems you have taken into your head to ride Marcus—"

She exploded so furiously Tansy dropped the maraschino jelly she had been just about to serve, which spread over the carpet in a wave and before you could say, "Get out of it, you little devil," Henry was there, yapping and lapping and almost choking in his delight but neither the master nor the mistress took any notice.

"That bloody man should be sacked," the mistress roared, throwing her napkin to the table with such force it knocked over a vase of early roses Tansy had set in the centre.

"Mind your language, woman. Not every female has

your insensibility of tongue and I'm sure the housemaids—"

"Bugger the housemaids, I'm talking about that clod
in the stables who has the temerity not only to tell me
what horse I may ride and what I may not, but runs to
his master every time I do something, or say something
of which he does not approve."

It was clear Tansy and Elspeth wished the ground
would open up and swallow them whole, what remained
of the maraschino jelly, dog and all. Should they stay
where they were, cowering against the wall doing their
best to look invisible; should they make a run for it,
taking the blasted animal; or should they try to clear up
the mess on the table, from where water was beginning
to drip on the carpet?

"He has my full aproval and I have given him instructions never to allow you to ride Marcus. He is to refuse to
saddle him for you and if you give me any more trouble I
shall forbid you the stables. Your wilfulness has already
lost . . ."

For a second Ben Maddox faltered. Her eyes blazed
into his, just as they had done when they first met. She
was thin now, no longer the voluptuous young woman
who had lit such desire in him he had been prepared to
overlook her forceful character, her rebellious nature,
her determination to have her own way no matter who
was trampled underfoot in the process, and look where
it had led. To the death of his child and the death of his
marriage and he had only himself to blame. But she'd
not defy him again, not over this. He was doing his

best not to care what she did, and for the most part his indifference was genuine, for she had mortally wounded something inside him when she went against not only the most basic instinct of a breeding woman, which was to defend her unborn child, but against him, against society, against everything that was sane and sensible. Now it seemed she had recovered whatever it was that drove her and she was about to start again, upsetting his grooms and endangering not only herself but his stallion.

"So, I am to jog about on that spiritless creature for the rest of my days, am I? Like some child on a cob."

"My dear, you act like a child so don't be surprised if you are treated as one."

"What is wrong in having a decent mount?"

"Nothing, if you know how to treat it, but you, unfortunately, don't."

"You pompous prick."

"Dear Lord, you would try the patience of a saint. Have you no shame?"

"You drive me to it, and I will not—"

"You will do exactly as I say, my dear, is that clear? You may ride the chestnut mare whenever and wherever you choose, within reason, but if I hear of you—"

"Oh, go to hell. You make me sick with your mealy-mouthed spoutings. You don't give a damn."

"About you? You're right, but that stallion cost me a lot of money and I will not have him spoiled. Now, I think I will forgo the pleasure of taking coffee with you and go out. This house has been peaceful for weeks but suddenly it is in uproar again and I find I don't like it."

She wept in Emma's arms that night and she didn't really know why. She didn't love him. He had proved to be nothing more than a tyrant, a bully who thought he could make Kitty Hayes dance to his tune. She hated him, she told Emma, who had heard all about it in the kitchen, and if he thought she was to take the slightest notice of what he said then he was sadly mistaken. Emma was to look out her tweed jacket and kid breeches and see if a stitch or two was needed because she'd lost a bit of weight since last she wore them. Yes, right now this minute, and what the hell she was crying about, she didn't know, but Emma was to hear this. She'd not cry over him again. Never!

14

She was just coming down the stairs when the doorbell rang.

"Damn and blast it," she said to Tansy, who hurried to open it. "Who the devil is calling at this hour? I'm not in, Tansy, to whoever it is." She began to hurry up the hall towards the passage that led out at the side of the house to the stables.

Tansy noticed with some displeasure that her mistress was dressed in her outlandish riding outfit again, the one the master had, if not forbidden, then of which he disapproved. What lady wears riding breeches of buff-coloured kid that cling so tightly to her legs she looks as if she were naked? And her cream silk shirt and waistcoat were not much better. The waistcoat was not yet buttoned up and you could see the shape of her . . . well, of her nipples through the fine material of her shirt. She had discarded her sober top hat along with her riding habit, becoming once again the independent, unique young woman the master had brought home as his wife last year. Last night's argument, if you could decribe the explosion of anger on both their parts with such a mild word, seemed to have had no effect on her. Just the opposite by the look of her. She was off somewhere, that was obvious and it was God help Tim since it seemed to Tansy that Mrs Maddox wouldn't be satisfied until she'd saddled that wild black horse of the master's and galloped off on him. And it also appeared evident to her that the master should realise by now that the mistress would do whatever he forbade her to do. She would go against him just for sheer devilment.

The young man who stood on the step smiled, a smile that went at once to the head of the parlourmaid. Her voice seemed to die away in her throat as she stared, mesmerised at what she believed was truly the most beautiful male she had ever seen in her life. He was dressed for riding, though Tansy was not familiar with it, in a hunting costume. A well-fitting single-breasted frock coat in a shade of rich navy blue with two pockets. The collar and turned-back cuffs were of vivid scarlet. His breeches were beige, with leather facings inside the knee, buttoned at the side to ensure a neat fit and his spurred riding boots came almost to his knee, black leather with a turned-down cuff of brown. He carried a top hat and a crop.

"Good morning. Is Mrs Maddox at home?" this vision said to her and so hypnotised was Tansy she just stood there, her hand to her throat, all her strict training by Mrs Ullett gone to the devil. If Mrs Maddox hadn't suddenly reappeared, having recognised the young man's voice, or so it would seem, striding down the hall, beaming such a broad smile you'd have thought the Prince of Wales had come to call, Tansy told them in the kitchen later, she would have gone on goggling at him until the cows came home!

"Michael. This is a lovely surprise. I've never been so glad to see anyone in my life. Do come in."

Kitty was enchanted, her face flushed and excited. She did not notice Michael Northwood's appreciative inspection of her unconventional outfit. She was only concerned with the enormous and unalloyed delight she felt at the sight of him. She had been just about to pit her wits against Tim's in the hope that she could bully him into saddling up Marcus and then, hopefully, take off beyond Formby Point for an exhilarating gallop as far as Southport. Now, here was the perfect companion, not only to join her in the ride, but as a back-up in ordering Tim to her wishes. She had found that men took more notice of other men when it came to disagreements. Not that she would have meekly given in and taken Flame had Tim argued, which she knew he would, but with Michael along it would make wearing down her husband's groom that much easier.

Michael's smile widened. He stood to one side and for the first time she noticed the two young gentlemen, dressed just like him, who lounged on the gravel driveway, grinning engagingly and holding the reins of three tall horses. One animal had a coat the colour and gloss of a newly shed chestnut, while the other two were pure grey, but all three had the lines that told of blood and breeding. They were hunters, large, bold, alert, their beautiful brushed tails swishing to keep off the midges. Beside them, sprawled on the gravel, were four dogs, handsome as the men, smooth-coated in colours of white, black and tan. Their tongues hung out of their mouths and they panted slightly but their tails moved lazily, showing their willingness to be friendly. The men were very much alike, obviously brothers, good-looking and self-confident and very sure of their welcome.

"I've brought these two along. I hope you don't mind, Kitty. We thought we'd ride over and . . . but first, let me introduce Jimmy Oliver who is a friend of Freddy's, as you know. You probably saw him on Saturday at the wedding and this is his brother, Tam Oliver, who would not rest until he had seen the beautiful Mrs Kitty Maddox, about whom, my dear Kitty, Jimmy and I could not stop eulogising, could we, Jimmy? Now then, Tam, is she not the loveliest—"

"Oh, shut up, Michael," the one called Tam said lazily, tossing the reins to his brother and coming up the steps to take her hand. "I don't need you to describe her to me. I can see for myself. And may I say that for once you did not exaggerate, old fellow." He bowed over her hand, his warm lips lightly brushing her skin, his eyes looking up into hers as he did so. He seemed reluctant to let go of her hand and she felt a little shiver run through her. She was not quite sure whether it was pleasure or disquiet. "But let me apologise, Mrs Maddox, for descending on you like this."

"No, I'm delighted, really I am. Won't you come in."

"Well, the animals . . ." Tam let go of her hand and nodded in the direction of his brother who stood good-naturedly at the bottom of the steps.

"I'm waiting my turn to kiss the hand of the beautiful Mrs Maddox, so do hurry up, Tam," he drawled. His teeth shone white and even in his brown face and Kitty felt herself become rather breathless at the sight not only of such good-looking horseflesh, such handsome dogs, but such engaging gentlemen.

"Of course." She turned to the wide-eyed Tansy, her hair swirling about her head, her jacket swirling about her shoulders, failing to notice the meaningful look the three men exchanged. "Run to the stables, Tansy, and tell one of the men to come and see to these horses, and as you go through the kitchen order some coffee and fetch it to the drawing-room."

"Oh, we haven't come to indulge in a drawing-room call, Mrs Maddox," Tam drawled, his eyes, which she noticed were the exact soft blue-grey of a woodpigeon's feathers, smiling into hers. "We had hoped to entice you out on a ride and if I'm not mistaken" – his gaze swept over her from head to foot – "that seems to be where you are headed."

"I am if I can persuade my husband's groom to saddle up the only decent mount in the place."

"I'm sure there'll be no trouble in that direction, Mrs Maddox," Jimmy drawled. "Just show us the way."

By this time the fascinated parlourmaid had scurried off to send a groom round to the front of the house and when John arrived, open-mouthed and slightly out of breath, for he had been told to look sharp, and took the three horses from the swaggering young lordling who did not reply to his polite "Good-morning", they all three went inside with Mrs Maddox. No one seemed to object when the four foxhounds rose to their feet and padded after their masters. Who the hell were they, the gentlemen, not the dogs? John wanted to know, asking the question of the phlegmatic Tim who was rubbing down Marcus, whistling through his teeth as he did so, as though he expected the head groom to rhyme off their names.

They seemed to fill the wide hallway, their size, their noisy privileged voices, their superb self-command diminishing the place to a mere nothing, since it seemed they must be used to grander halls than this. The dogs' claws scratched the polished surround as they sniffed in the corners. The vicious spurs on the gentlemen's boots cut into Ben Maddox's expensive deep-pile carpet and Tansy eyed them with disapproval, wondering what the master would say when he saw the damage. They threw their hats and crops carelessly in her direction then strode into the drawing-room as though they owned the place, she told them in the kitchen, drinking their coffee as if they were doing her a favour, chatting and laughing with Mrs Maddox who'd never, since she'd come to Meadow View, looked livelier. She heard them say that they were to be off to Aintree the next day, quite a party of them, and they'd be devastated if Mrs Maddox couldn't join them. She must bring her husband, they told her politely, if he cared to come, but if he didn't there would be other ladies in the party, including the older one's wife, who could act as chaperone.

"I'd love to come. I *will* come but I'm afraid the possibility of persuading my husband to join us is very remote."

"What a shame," the older one was heard to say, grinning like a bloody Cheshire cat, and you could see he didn't give a damn whether Mr Maddox came or not and she was sorry if Mrs Ullett didn't like her language but she couldn't help it. She had a bad feeling about these young gentlemen.

They all strode out into the stable yard, tall and imperious, their heads erect just like her, their voices loud and carrying as they studied the black stallion which was doing his usual stuff, jinking and blowing through his nostrils, jerking his head away from Tim's hand so that Tim was ready to curse and swear and wished he could have ordered the lot of them out of his stable yard. The four dogs, apparently used to horses and stable yards, stayed well clear, standing quietly by the wall as they waited for a command.

"Is this the animal you're going to ride?" Tam asked Kitty, looking with what was an experienced eye at the lovely lines of the stallion.

Tim, struggling with the animal, looked at her in amazement.

"Yes, I believe he comes from Ireland, Mr Oliver. Is that not so, Tim?"

"Yes, madam, but I think it's time 'e were put in't paddock," Tim said firmly, beginning to lead the stallion away. "'E's none too fond o' company."

"Just a moment, my good man," Tam said loftily. "I believe Mrs Maddox intends to take the animal out today so if you will fetch his tack we'll saddle him up."

Tim shook his head stubbornly. He didn't know who they were, these three arrogant-looking bastards who were telling him, in his own yard, what to do with *his* master's horse, but he wasn't having it.

"I'm sorry, sir," Tim said politely enough, "but the master give strict orders that—"

"That's enough, Tim," she interrupted, looking at him in that way she had, a faraway look as if she were gazing beyond him at something far more interesting. That's what many of the gentry did, trying to intimidate you, but Tim wasn't easily intimidated and he had had his orders directly from the master. He was not, under any circumstances, to allow the mistress to ride Marcus.

"I have decided to ride out on Marcus today," she continued coldly, "and—"

"But, Mrs Maddox, the master said most particular—"

"That is enough, Tim. Now stand away."

"Yes, stand away, there's a good chap," Jimmy drawled, raising astonished eyebrows, for none of their grooms would dare to defy an order from them. "Let go of his bridle and fetch his tack, there's a good fellow."

"Mr Maddox—"

"Is not here and Mrs Maddox is. She wishes to ride this animal and I don't think it will do you much good if you continue to hinder her."

The trouble was, Tim didn't know who these sods were. They could be friends of Mr Maddox. They certainly had good horseflesh themselves and it was apparent they knew how to handle an animal. Marcus was standing as good as gold while the younger chap stroked his nose and murmured in his twitching ear.

Admitting defeat, Tim threw the numnah over Marcus's back then placed the saddle on top of it. When all was ready Kitty stepped forward and, looking expectantly at the groom, waited until he linked his hands for her foot.

Marcus didn't wait for the three men to mount up and follow him. He took off like an arrow from a bow, true and straight towards the fence and the paddock where the other horses were milling about restlessly. Kitty didn't try to guide him, or check him, but let him go. He jumped the fence with six inches to spare, landing with a bone-shattering thud on the other side. The horses scattered, racing away to the far corner of the paddock as, one after the other the three hunters, accompanied by the dogs who ran with their bellies flat to the ground, followed in hot pursuit. The men on their backs shouted to one another, their excitement intense, for here was a woman they could admire, a woman who seemed to be afraid of nothing, a woman who was . . . Great God alive, her outfit was enough to place her way above the ordinary, run-of-the-mill women who peopled their lives. It appeared she was prepared to . . . well, who knew what she was prepared to do? It was anybody's guess but, by God, it'd be damn fine fun finding out.

Michael was a splendid fellow to have found her and they would make it worth his while by inviting him to spend the summer at Brook Hall and perhaps even into the hunting and shooting season. He'd be grateful for that, since he spent his days moving from one country-house party to the next, a professional guest, so to speak, but welcomed by hostesses, for it was always handy to have a spare man. "Lap-dogs" they were called, who must be prepared to earn their keep by amusing the ladies – in any way the lady chose as long as it was discreet! If they could play whist or poker, so much the better and a "turn" after dinner was well applauded. Michael might be young but he was a gentleman who knew the rules, highly entertaining and a good sport. He was a splendid shot, a bold man across country and a chap with an eye for a ball in the cricket matches and tennis parties that were got up during the summer months.

She didn't think she'd enjoyed a day so much for years. In fact she couldn't remember *ever* having so much fun. Though it was May, almost June, the fine spell of mild, sunny weather was over for the moment. Crumpled skirts of clouds threatened rain and as the four of them thundered along the smooth sweep of sand beyond Formby Point, shouting at one another into the teeth of the wind, Kitty felt the troubled thoughts that she had brooded over rise to the surface of her mind and fly away like birds released from a cage. She felt as light as air herself, braced on Marcus's strong back, her heart beating to the rhythm of his pounding hooves. The others were behind her, their dogs keeping up courageously and it was perhaps a good job that the weather had turned, for the beach was deserted. Out to sea were white caps as far as the eye could see and the four of them were drenched with spray. When they clattered into the yard at Meadow View even Tim was grudgingly inclined to admit, not to her, but to John, that the gallop had done Marcus the world of good, which didn't mean he wasn't going to make a full report to Mr Maddox when he got home!

They were to pick her up tomorrow morning, the three young men told her, bowing gallantly in admiration of her horsemanship. The ladies were to travel in the Olivers' carriage, for it was recognised that they must look their most elegant for this important race meeting. Aintree Racecourse was admitted by all sporting gentlemen to be one of the best in the kingdom. There was a grandstand surrounded by sloping lawns and flowerbeds where, it being a popular and fashionable outing to which the gentry of the vicinity as well as the élite of the sporting world flocked, the height of fashion was demanded of all spectators. They knew, they said, as they kissed her hand in farewell that she would look her best!

She looked her best that evening after her wonderful

day. Her mirror told her so, for it showed in her vivid face. Her hair, as usual, would do nothing Emma tried to make it do, the jewelled combs slipping out the moment Mrs Maddox moved her head and, as her mistress said, she couldn't be expected to sit staring directly in front of her all evening. She was expecting fireworks, of course, they all were, the servants holding their breath and cowering at every sudden sound from the front of the house, and Tansy and Elspeth almost in tears over the prospect of serving dinner to Mr and Mrs Maddox, for they would be caught in the crossfire.

They didn't have to wait for dinner. The door to her bedroom crashed back so savagely Emma squeaked and dropped her mistress's jewel box, spilling all the bright baubles across the carpet. At once the dog, still a puppy at a year old and quite undisciplined, like *her*, leaped on them and began to toss a valuable emerald bracelet about as though it were a bone.

"Get out," the master snarled at Emma, "and take the bloody dog with you."

Kitty was so astounded she watched with her mouth open as her maid, with Henry scooped up under her arm, scuttled from the room.

"And close the door after you," Ben Maddox thundered. Emma was only too happy to do so, to put something solid between her and the master's violence, though God help her poor mistress who couldn't, or wouldn't, take heed of her husband.

"What the hell d'you think you're doing, ordering

my maid about like that," Kitty said icily. "She hasn't finished doing my hair yet and someone—"

"Sod your hair, lady. I'm here to get an explanation from you, a reasonable explanation as to why you thought you had the right to go against my express wishes in the matter of my horse. Tim tells me—"

"Oh, Tim, of course. Why can't that man learn to keep his mouth shut and mind his own business?"

"It is his business when three men who are not known to him march into my yard and start giving orders on the subject of my animals. A bloody valuable animal, I might add."

"I thought it might come down to that. His value. Well, he is not in the least damaged. In fact the run did him good."

"Is that so? The run did him good. And perhaps you are right but that is not the point. That is my horse, not yours, and certainly not the three young lords' who turned up on *my* doorstep and persuaded *my* wife to disregard totally my express wishes that she should keep away from him. There is a perfectly decent animal—"

"Oh, for God's sake, don't drag that up again. I am not used to jogging along on a placid rocking horse. Chester was—"

"You killed Chester, madam, which surely proves that you are not worthy of a decent horse. You rode him into a highly dangerous area, an area well signposted but, as with all your escapades, you chose to ignore the sign."

"How dare you criticise me. You get up on that stallion's back once in a blue moon so that the poor animal gets very little exercise and yet you pretend to value him."

"What I do is my own affair."

"And what I do is your affair as well, I suppose."

"Yes, it is, and so I am forbidding you the stables and even the mare. You will stay in this house or, if I am satisfied that you are behaving as a wife should, you may take the carriage and . . . do whatever proper ladies do."

"Go to hell!"

"And I would be obliged if you would not allow men I do not know into my home in future. I have no idea—"

"I see, it's all right for your friends to visit you but not mine, is that it?"

For a moment he looked bewildered. "Your friends? I didn't know you had any. Who the devil were they?"

"Michael Northwood and Jimmy Oliver were guests at my brother's wedding so they are perfectly respectable. I am to go to Aintree with them tomorrow."

"Are you indeed? Well, we will see about that." His eyes glared into hers, not with that cold, snake-like expression she had seen before but hot and burning, and for a moment she wondered what it was that was consuming him. Surely not just pique because she had disobeyed him yet again and forced Tim to saddle up Marcus.

"What's that supposed to mean?"

"It means, madam, that though I know nothing about

this Michael Northwood, the Oliver boys, for that is what they are despite their age, still boys, are well known for the way they racket about the countryside and I won't have my wife associating with them."

"They were perfect gentlemen."

"No, they are not. They are wild and dangerous."

"That sounds interesting. At least I won't be bored as I have been for the past seven or eight months."

The violent colour of his rage drained from his face, leaving it the pasty grey of unbaked dough and his eyes glittered. With a muttered oath he raised his hand. He wanted to hit her. He wanted to hurt her as she had just hurt him. He wanted to wipe that sneering smile off her face and the only way he could do it was with violence. But with a great effort, his large frame trembling with the tension of it, he stepped back, moving carefully towards the closed door. He must get away before she saw what was in him, what was still buried deep inside where he had built a little shelter in which to keep it. A poor thing that might collapse at any time and he must guard it against her cruelty but she wouldn't let him.

"You want to hit me, don't you?" she hissed venomously. "You can think of no other way to subdue me but with brute force, can you? But you haven't even the courage to do that. Look at you, backing away, slinking away, beaten by—"

They heard his roar of rage down in the dining-room where Tansy and Elspeth were putting the finishing touches to the table. They had no idea whether the master and mistress would actually be sitting down to eat the poached turbot, the veal cutlets and apricot flan drenched in whipped cream Cook had prepared for them, but they had to act as though there were nothing untoward happening just the same.

In the kitchen Mrs Pembroke put her arms round Clarrie, the young kitchen-maid, who had begun to cry and the rest huddled together as though for protection. Mrs Ullett put her hand to her mouth and shook her head in despair and Emma sank to the bench beside the kitchen table and put her head down with her arms wrapped about it as though to deafen the sounds from upstairs.

He struck her across the face, the crack of it surprising both of them but it did not make him stop. She fell across the bed, but even as her back hit the pretty bedspread she surged up again, her hands curved into claws, her nails going for his eyes. They found one of his cheeks and gouged four scratches from which blood began to bead.

Both of them were panting, growling even, like two dogs in the bloodlust of a fight but it was not a fight that the pair of them were intent on. He struggled to get a grip on her wrists, bending her savagely back across the bed and though she spat in his face and used a word she had picked up in the stables, he began to smile, a mad smile, a devilish smile and she smiled back.

"You're not capable of it," she taunted him, not knowing exactly what she meant by it.

"Really . . ." Then his mouth came down on hers and began to bite. Snapping and snarling they worried one another's mouths, their bodies nailed together and when his lips slipped down to her throat she arched it so that he could get better access to it. Holding her hands high above her head with one hand, he put the other in the neck of her gown and tore it down to her waist and his mouth travelled down to her exposed breasts where it proceeded to nip and worry her nipples and it was then that she began to moan. Her back arched and hips ground into his. Her gown was torn from her and flung to the far side of the room in a snarl of animal need and when his own clothing was removed she scarcely noticed its going since his hands and mouth had her captured, pinned to the bed in an unbearable rapture that she knew she could not do without.

"Ben . . . Ben," she cried out as he entered her, her nails making matching grooves down his back but he didn't even flinch. For what seemed an eternity they moved together, the turmoil growing until it exploded inside them at one and the same time and he fell like a fallen log across her.

For several minutes they lay, their sweated bodies locked together. She was just about to put a tender hand on his hair, to smile and whisper something, she didn't know what yet, something appropriate to let him know that it was all right, that she was glad, when he reared up and without a glance at her, his face unreadable, reached for his clothes, hurried himself into them and without another word left the room, banging the door shut behind him.

They heard him in the kitchen then there was silence

for a while. The next thing was his footsteps on the stairs, the sound of the front door crashing open and the clatter of his feet on the stone steps to the drive. His smart little curricle which he drove himself and which was standing at the front, as always, could be heard thundering away down the drive, then there was silence once more.

15

She didn't know how long she lay on the crumpled bed before a light tapping on her door brought her creeping out of the black cavern in which she cowered. She was hurt, not just her face where Ben had struck her, nor her aching body, which, in the right circumstances would have been a *pleasurable* ache, but deep inside her. Her mind was in a state of shock, she supposed, and not just that but a state of wretchedness, for she had believed for the space of a few minutes that Ben . . . that she and Ben were to thaw the distant chill that had existed between them since the accident. There was a weight on her spirits that threatened to overwhelm her and fasten her in the blackness of the cavern in which she had curled ever since Ben flung himself out of the room and she didn't know, at this precise moment, how she was ever to lift it.

"Madam . . . ?" a voice whispered hesitantly from the doorway and soft footsteps brushed across the carpet.

Lamps still stood about the room, one on the dressing table, its reflection in the mirror, another on the chest of drawers and a third on the table beside the bed. The summer fire which was always lit unless there was a heatwave had died down but a glow from the flickering coals coloured the white draperies about the bed.

She was turned away from the door, lying on her side in a foetal position, naked as Ben had left her and she sensed Emma's embarrassment, for it was she. Henry ran round the bed until he was looking into her face. He whimpered softly in his throat. If he got the chance he was through the bedroom door in a trice and he had followed Emma, but with that instinct that animals have he did not jump up on the bed as he usually would but rested his black nose on the bed, his tongue gently touching her hand.

She put out a vague hand and rested it on his head, getting comfort from the touch of his silky coat. She turned then, looking up into Emma's concerned face, watching the change in her expression from anxious sympathy to horror, and it was perhaps this, the overflowing kindness and compassion that one human being can show another that finished her off. She put her hands to her face and began to weep.

"Oh, lass . . . lass. Come here, see, Emma's got yer." Her maid gathered her into her arms, holding her as tenderly as a mother would a child, her cheek to her rumpled hair and Kitty wept as she had never wept before. She wept for her lost dreams which had begun many years ago with a fair-haired young boy whom she had loved, and ended with a man, who, for a brief moment, held the promise of fulfilling them. He had brutalised her . . . and she had been a willing partner. She knew about passion, since he had taught her. He had taken her against her will before, on her wedding night, but afterwards he had held her in his arms and kissed her hair and murmured soothing wordless noises and though she had done her best to escape him there had been a curious assuagement. But this was different. He had taken her violently, as on the first occasion, but there had been no tenderness afterwards, no closeness, merely a hurried retreat as though he had coupled with a whore whose fee he did not wish to pay. She would never forgive him. It was finished now.

Slipping a soft blanket about her mistress, for the sake of warmth rather than decency, for Mrs Maddox had begun to shiver, Emma continued to rock her and croon to her. Not that it was cold but something dreadful had gone on here and for the moment the touch of a sympathetic woman was what she needed. Emma came from a large and loving family and had soon learned the relief of comforting arms at the right time. It didn't take a genius to see that Mr Maddox had punched Mrs Maddox in the face and Emma was shocked. She couldn't believe it of him, really she couldn't, he was such a . . . a kind gentleman. Strong, oh yes, arrogant at times and woe betide you if he wasn't served as he wished to be served, but he was fair and just and they'd all liked him. So what had happened here, what had provoked him into striking out at her mistress as he had done? They had very obviously . . . been together as husband and wife, or why else would her mistress be unclothed? Dear God in heaven, it was a mystery and a worry, for what was to happen next? The whole house had been set on its ear since the young mistress had been brought here, with rows and arguments and the mistress defying the master at every turn. Look at the to-do about the horse! And it went on and on. Perhaps this latest was about the three high-nosed young gentlemen who had called yesterday and, so Tim said, forced him to saddle up Marcus for the mistress to ride. Lord, he'd been mad about that, had Tim, and who could blame him. Her rebellious mistress was responsible for it and you couldn't blame the master for seeing red, but just the same, to hit her as he had done was not right. Dear Lord, would they ever again know the peaceful existence that had prevailed last year or were they to tiptoe round the place wondering when the next storm would strike?

For what seemed a long time they rocked together but at last Emma could sense a difference in her mistress just as though she had done her sorrowing and was ready to put the misery of it behind her. She could see a certain relaxing in her tight curled body, an inclination to sigh and even to smile a little.

"Well, this is a fine mess, isn't it, Emma?" she said shakily, trying to sit up. "I look like a prize-fighter. One who has lost. What am I to do? How am I to explain?" She bowed her head as though in shame, then lifted it in that old imperious manner of hers, looking Emma directly in the eye and Emma felt a surge of admiration for this tempestuous woman she served.

"Eeh, lass," was all she could think of to say as the light fell fully on her mistress's ravaged face. "It's true you're gonner have a right shiner in the morning. We'll have to put our heads together and see what we can find ter put on it."

She wasn't going to discuss how Mrs Maddox had come by the bruises, not unless Mrs Maddox confided in her. No, best deal with how to heal them rather than how they came about.

"But first let me get yer bed ter rights. Why don't yer sit by't fire while I strip it off and put clean sheets on. Yer could have a bath if yer fancy it. Clarrie and Elspeth'd carry up the hip-bath and then yer could be cosy by't fire. Then I'll bathe yer face and fetch some stuff me mam used to put on the lads' faces when they'd bin in a fight. Tincture of arnica, it's called. She give me a bottle when I came here. Yer should have seen them sometimes; me brothers, I mean. They were right little ruffians and'd fight anybody, even each other, and come home with a . . . Oh, I'm sorry, madam, I wasn't meaning yer'd bin in a fight or owt like that but . . ." Emma was red-faced with embarrassment but her mistress only laughed harshly and told her not to be silly, for surely that was exactly what she had been in. A fight! A savage fight in which she'd come off worse, though she seemed to remember marking her husband's face which would be very apparent when he went down to breakfast tomorrow.

She honestly didn't know how she would have got through the night without Emma. Emma bathed her tenderly and even washed her hair, then, after applying the tincture to the area surrounding her eye and her cheek, tucked her tenderly up in her clean bed and then went to fetch her a tray daintily set with tea things.

"Have one with me, Emma," she said as the maid fussed round the room, putting away the detritus of her ministrations.

Emma looked shocked. "Eeh, no, madam, I couldn't."

"Why not?"

"It wouldn't be proper."

"Emma, are we agreed that you are trying to make me feel better, that you have, in fact, done so?"

"I suppose so, madam."

"Then I shall feel better still if a friend sat beside me and drank a cup of tea with me. Go and get another cup but don't be long. I should be glad of the . . . company."

They were agog in the kitchen. Elspeth and Clarrie, though they had staggered upstairs with the old hip-bath which had not been used since the modern bath-room had been put in, and with a dozen cans of hot water, had not got a good look at the mistress, for she had been swathed in blankets, her face turned away from them. They knew there was something wrong, for hadn't they heard the raised voices and, later, the master flinging himself from the house as though a tiger were tied to his coat tails. Emma was as close as a clam, talking vaguely of a "little accident" which meant nothing to them and now here she was asking for another cup and saucer because the mistress wanted her to drink a cup of tea with her. What next! And she was to spend the night upstairs, she told Mrs Ullett, as if defying the housekeeper to try and stop her, since the mistress had asked her to.

"Don't you be getting above yourself, my girl, that's all I've got to say," Mrs Ullett remarked coldly, knowing she could do nothing about it if the mistress had ordered it, but Emma had the feeling that she'd not heard the last of it.

Mrs Maddox drank her tea, then, saying she would never sleep, begged Emma to tell her about her life before she started work at Meadow View, about her brothers and sisters, her childhood which had been so different from the privileged one she had known. What her father did, and her mother, who had taught Emma to sew so beautifully. Where did she come from, since Emma's life, except where it concerned her own, was a mystery to her. It didn't seem to occur to her that Emma was a working girl whose day started at six and often didn't end until ten or even later and that at the end of the day, like the other maids, she wanted nothing more than to get to her bed and well-earned sleep!

So Emma talked about anything that came into her head, most of it a lot of nonsense about her own childhood, and watched her mistress carefully and when she drooped on her pillow, then slept, settled herself in the deep armchair by the fire and fell asleep herself.

Neither of them heard the door open quietly, only the dog who lifted his head but made no sound, as Ben Maddox crept across the carpet and studied his wife's bruised and vulnerable face where it lay on the pillow. For several minutes he stood silently beside her bed, once putting his hand to his eyes as though he couldn't bear the sight of what he'd done to her. He left the room just as quietly and the dog lowered his nose to his paws and sighed.

She'd had a nasty fall, she told the ladies in the carriage, smiling charmingly as they were introduced, even though her eye and cheek where Ben had hit her were excruciating. Yes, last evening which was a nuisance in view of this outing today. A new evening gown, with a slightly longer train than she was accustomed to and her heel had caught in it. She was coming down the stairs but with great good luck she had managed to catch the banister before she went too far but it had given her a nasty crack on the cheek and the result was as they saw. Her maid had devised some cosmetic which hid the worst but she had been forced to wear this small veil attached to her hat.

"Good heavens, Mrs Maddox, one shudders to think what it must have looked like before your maid's ministrations. You poor thing, do get into the carriage before you faint."

Tam and Michael, with Jimmy hovering at the back of them, all three of their faces registering their horror, for it was no banister that had given her the shiner under the veil, solicitously handed her into the carriage containing the two ladies, both of whom were very pretty and very well dressed. They fussed and fretted over her, tucking her under a light woollen carriage rug, turning to glare at Tim and John who were holding the horses' heads, just as though it were their fault that they had a master who had put their mistress into such a pitiful condition.

"Mrs Maddox, we are devastated, really we are," Tam was saying, his blue-grey eyes gazing into hers with such concern she began to feel alarmed, for surely one of these pretty women must be his wife. "See, move up a bit, Vannie, and make room for Mrs Maddox. This is my wife, by the way, Mrs Maddox," he confirmed, "and the other lady is my sister, Grace. The chaps and I have decided to ride over rather than take two carriages so I'm sure you'll be very comfortable. Won't she, Vannie?"

"Oh, indeed. We shall guard her with our very lives, won't we, Grace?"

"My word, yes. Now do tell us if you are quite comfortable, Mrs Maddox. My brothers would never forgive us if we did not cosset you as you deserve. We have heard nothing but 'Mrs Maddox' ever since they met you, and, despite your rather unfortunate . . . accident, I can see why."

"Please, Miss Oliver, I wish you would call me Kitty. I know we have only just met but . . . I would rather you did. And please, you must stop fussing. I'm as right as rain and looking forward so much to our day out. It is most kind of you to pick me up like this. Have you come over from St Helens this morning?"

"Oh, dear me, no, Kitty, and please call me Grace and this is Vannie. Vanessa. We are staying for a few days at the Adelphi with the rest of the sporting crowd. And Meadow View – is that right? – is not at all out of our way. It is no more than a mile or two to Aintree. I'm surprised you didn't know that."

"I must admit I have never been to a racing event but I have a passion for horses."

"Then you are going to the right place. And there might be more than horses to look at. There is a definite chance that the Prince of Wales is to be there. Very popular with royalty, is Aintree. We have been told that the royal train has been parked at Aughton overnight."

As she spoke, or rather drawled, Vannie looked at her from beneath drooping eyelids, just as though she might fall asleep at any moment, but there was an alertness about her, an interested gleam in her vivid green eyes. Though she could not be said to be a classic beauty her colouring was quite superb, her hair a rich, russet red and her eyes a shade between emerald and sea green. She wore a gown of emerald-green silk, much flounced about the hem and down the back of her bustle which Kitty noticed when they descended from the carriage. Her hat was large-brimmed with a swirl of cream roses on the crown and she carried a parasol so long it could be used as a walking stick. Her sister-in-law was similarly attired but in a pale blue-grey which suited her cream and roses complexion and the froth of fair curls which spilled at the side of her head over her ears.

The men were in formal dress, black frock coat, black striped trousers and a dashing top hat.

"Really? How exciting. I must say I am looking forward enormously to the races. Are there to be many? How many horses run in each race? Oh, you have no idea how thrilled I am to be here."

The two women, both sophisticated and evidently well used to the life the country set lived, exchanged amused glances.

"I think we might have, Kitty, and it quite does my jaded palate good to see such enthusiasm. Now then, are you to put a guinea or two on a race?"

Kitty felt herself go hot. She had a few shillings in her reticule but certainly not the guinea or two Vannie spoke of. It had not even occurred to her that there would be bets laid, which was ridiculous when you considered it, for they were going to one of the foremost steeplechase races in the country. What a fool she was, and how she hated looking a fool, but there was nothing to be done about it except pretend it didn't matter one way or the other.

But her face must have given her away, for they all laughed and for a moment she felt a surge of resentment that they seemed to find her so amusing. Certainly she was not used to their sort of people. Oh, she had mixed with the rich and influential all her life but they had been industrialists, mill owners, ironmasters and brewmasters. Men who had made their money as her father had, as *his* father had and who could probably buy out the Olivers ten times over. Michael had told her that the elder Oliver, father to Tam, Jimmy and Grace, a man with a knighthood, had made his money in coal but he had not added that it was only because coal had been found on his land, land that had been in his family for generations. *He* had not dug it out. He had had no hand in it except the hand which he had held out to grasp the vast fortune it brought him. The people she knew were not landed gentlemen as these people were. Not gentry, not willowy young dandies and languid ladies who strolled about her with that air of breeding and superiority which, though it didn't undermine her own confidence, irritated her. There was a gulf between them that had nothing to do with money but as they seemed to find her company pleasing, especially the gentlemen, and as she was enjoying theirs, she shrugged it off with her usual unconcern for anything other than her own pleasure.

"Now, my dear, I can see by your face that you did not think to bring some betting money with you and you mustn't give it a thought," Vannie told her, taking her arm in a friendly fashion. "Tam will let you have whatever you want, won't you, darling, and you can pay him back . . . whenever you can," his wife added carelessly, giving him a look that he seemed to understand though Kitty didn't.

Having left the carriage among the other grand carriages, the group began to saunter, exchanging greetings with dozens of people on the way, towards a handsome building which Tam told her was the grand-stand. There were several minor stands, he added with a shrug, all of which would be filled with lesser folk than them, or so he seemed to imply, and beneath which were drinking and refreshment booths. But inside the grandstand was a spacious dining-room in which they would take luncheon later and a handsome saloon the length of the building with many tall windows. A wide gallery ran outside it which would give them a splendid view over the racecourse and above that was the roof made up of upper and lower balconies from where there was a magnificent panoramic view of the surrounding countryside. He would take her up later, he told her, his manner hinting at something she found confusing, his eyes lingering on the night-black curls escaping from her pretty bonnet; on the pale, petal smoothness of her skin, which, despite the angry bruising, was still exquisite; on her remarkable eyes which, in her excitement, were a true aquamarine under narrow and delicately arched brows. Her figure, which had once been described as statuesque, was slender but curving and it was apparent he found her very much to his liking.

On the way to the grandstand, spreading out in every direction, she was fascinated with the raggle-taggle mêlée of tipsters, fortune-tellers and pedlars. Bookmakers with Gladstone bags, florid faces and cigars, blackboards on which were chalked columns of figures, half-empty pint glasses of ale and the incessantly signalling "tic-tac" men dancing frenzied attendance on them. Ostlers, grooms and stable lads were everywhere, for the steeplechase attracted many riders who brought their own servants to look after their valuable mounts. The onset of the railway had facilitated the easy movement of horses in "dandy-boxes" from one race to another and Aintree was a great favourite, not only with the privileged set, and with royalty, but with the common man who loved horse-racing as much as they did.

In front of the stand was a spacious, sloping lawn railed round for the convenience and accommodation of the frequenters of the grandstand, men of rank whose pedigree and wealth entitled them to be admitted there. It was filled from railing to railing with hundreds of aristocratic racegoers, a positive flower garden of elegantly gowned ladies holding dainty parasols above their patrician heads, the gentlemen no less aristocratic in their top hats and frock coats.

The horses for the next race were being paraded as the Olivers, with Michael and Kitty included in their charmed circle, arrived. Erected to the left of the enclosure was a board on which was printed a list of the names of the horses, their numbers and riders.

"Now then, Kitty, study the horses and if you fancy one, look its number up on the board and it will tell you its name. If the odds are good you can then put a bet on it."

"How do I do that?" Kitty asked breathlessly, her exhilaration almost overwhelming her.

"I'll show you, my sweet. There are a lot of things that I would be delighted to show you. So, which takes your fancy?"

They leaned on the railing and Kitty held her breath, for parading before her were the most beautiful and yet strong horses she had ever seen. There was one, a tall roan with a somewhat wild and rolling eye, which reminded her of Chester and when she glanced at the board she saw that his name was Dictator. She liked that too and as she turned to Tam to tell him he was her choice she became conscious of the group beside her. Surrounded by a circle of top-hatted gentlemen and what seemed to be a dozen beautiful women was a portly gentleman with a small beard and a gleaming eye which seemed to be focused on her with great appreciation.

She was confounded when both Vannie and Grace dropped low curtseys and all three of her male companions removed their hats and bowed. Tam's hand was on her arm, doing his best to pull her down, or so it seemed, but she was anxious to have him place a bet on Dictator, not at all concerned with a tubby little gentleman whom she did not know. She turned, ready to brush off Tam's hand but it seemed everyone about them was bobbing and curtseying and the words that Vannie had spoken earlier came back to her.

The Prince of Wales!

At once, as though she had been doing it all her life, she dropped into a perfect graceful curtsey, but something in her, some small spark which nothing, not even her husband's treatment of her and the black eye she knew was not really hidden beneath the small veil, made her glance up from beneath her lashes, a twinkling glance which turned into a mischievous smile. A smile of pure devilment. A smile that Kitty Hayes might have flashed when she knew she was doing something she really shouldn't be doing.

His Royal Highness was looking at her with the speculative interest that every gentleman, and lady, in his entourage knew well, and there were conjectures behind gloved hands on the identity of the lovely young lady with the obvious and colourful black eye!

The Prince of Wales bowed and put out a hand to Kitty Hayes, for that was who she was at that precise moment, then, with a small nod of his head and an answering twinkle in his eyes, gave her an almost indistinguishable wink as he helped her up.

"And who do you fancy, my dear?" he asked her, no doubt at all who *he* fancied.

"Why, Dictator, of course. There isn't a horse to touch him." Then added hastily, "Your Royal Highness."

"And how much are you to put on him, Miss . . . ?"

"Kitty Maddox, sir, and I think probably five guineas."

There was a gasp from Tam and from all about the party a concentrated sigh seemed to whisper.

"He is as good as that, Miss Maddox?" His Royal Highness asked her, raising his bushy eyebrows.

"Oh, yes. If you've a spare guinea or two take my advice and put it on him."

"I think I will, Miss Maddox. Now I must move on. There are certain people I must meet . . ." though his expression said there was nothing he would have liked more than to remain with the attractive and lively young woman with the black eye. He was about to move on when he stopped and turned, then, leaning forward, spoke into her ear so that no one else could hear him.

"Won't you tell me how you got that black eye, Kitty?"

"I walked into a tree, sir, or that is the tale I'm spreading about."

They all watched, astounded, as the future King of England raised Kitty Maddox's hand to his lips and kissed it, then walked away shaking with delighted laughter.

They couldn't get over it, they told one another, absolutely tickled to death that their new protégé had made such a big hit on her first day out with them, and with no less a person than the Prince of Wales himself. And on top of that, the bloody horse she had picked won and they all went home with more money in their pockets than when they had arrived. They had champagne, bottles of it, and a splendid luncheon and who should bow and raise his glass to her but Bertie himself and their party was quite the toast of the day, thanks to darling Kitty.

It was dark when they dropped her off at her front door, for they had persuaded her to return to the Adelphi with them for a spot of supper. She had been impressed with the grandeur of Liverpool's most luxurious hotel but she didn't let them see it, for Kitty Maddox was beginning to realise her own potential to charm, a characteristic that had been kept in strict check before her marriage. She had had no idea she could be so admired nor why. She was witty, they told her, and when that eye cleared up would be the toast of Lancashire, which she took with a pinch of salt, for witty she might be, but she was also a realist. Life had taught her that. She was to come the following weekend to Brook Hall, bringing her husband, naturally, if she wished, they said politely, for they were to have a party, tennis, cricket, a spot of fishing. Did she play whist? No, then they would soon teach her.

The ladies kissed her cheek as they saw her into the carriage at the front of the hotel, telling her that she would be in safe hands with Tam who was to escort her home, and when he did the same in the carriage, only on the mouth, she hit him! Life had taught her how to do that as well!

16

Emma was considerably startled the next morning when she answered the impatient ringing of the bell to find her mistress out of bed and pacing the floor of her bedroom.

"Right, Emma, I need some new clothes, a couple of evening gowns, afternoon gowns, a tennis outfit: oh, you know, all the things one would wear at a country-house party. I wonder if there'll be shooting? Is it the right time of the year, d'you suppose? Really, I don't know how these people keep up with their social calendar; it is so extensive and must start and finish at exactly the correct time of the year. Does one wear a special outfit to shoot in? And I think a new pair of breeches and a jacket, some silk shirts and . . . well, whatever Mrs Cheers advises. She dresses the gentry and will know the ropes. You'll have to come with me, of course. To Brook Hall, I mean. I've become used to you, Emma, and I'm not sure I could manage . . ."

"Mrs Maddox, please, you've had nothing to eat," Emma pleaded. "Before we go gallivanting off . . ."

"Gallivanting, Emma! This is not a gallivant, believe me. It is most important."

"Well, perhaps it is, but won't you let me fetch you up some breakfast on a tray? A poached egg, happen, and some toast, and then we'll—"

"Oh, Emma, we haven't time. I must get to Mrs Cheers at the earliest opportunity. She must have everything ready by Friday and today is Wednesday. Hurry, my girl, help me into something . . . what, I don't know. What's the weather like? And run down and tell Harrison I shall need the carriage in half an hour."

So it was true then, all that stuff she was ranting on about last night. She had come in like some giant firework, fizzing and crackling all over the place, begging Emma to believe it when she said she'd met the Prince of Wales and that he'd kissed her hand. Her Majesty's son had kissed her hand! Like a kettle on the boil she was, to use one of Cook's sayings, and there'd be tears before bedtime, to use another! Emma didn't know what to believe, really she didn't, she'd confided to the maids in the kitchen, who were positively agog with the wonder of it. Mrs Maddox wasn't the sort of person to make up something like that, was she, but sometimes Emma wondered if that fall she'd had from her horse, and then the blow she'd suffered to her face the other night, might have affected her . . . her . . . senses. She was so excited, so worked up, so brilliant and beautiful, even with the plum-coloured bruising to her face and eye. It had taken all Emma's tact and, in the end, her stern admonition that if she didn't get to sleep she'd be going nowhere tomorrow, before she'd got her mistress into bed. What a wonderful day she'd had, she babbled, and what wonderful people they were, the Olivers, so entertaining, so far and above the dull people with whom she'd mixed all her adult life. So fashionable, so expensively dressed and if she was to hold her own, which she fully intended to do, then she must have a new wardrobe.

"Is the master to go with you, madam?" Emma was foolish enough to ask, for surely it was not proper for a married woman to go gadding off for a whole weekend without her husband, and with folk she'd met only a few days ago.

"No, he is not, Emma, and I would be obliged if you would not speak of him in my presence. He and I . . ." Her breath seemed to catch in her throat and she gulped, then whirled away as though to hide the expression on her face. "Now then, get out something for me to wear."

Mrs Cheers was well named. Nothing showed in her face but pleasure as Mrs Maddox and the handsome young woman who accompanied her entered her sumptuous shop. Shop was too basic a word for her establishment, for Mrs Cheers was an accomplished dressmaker with the cleverest and most talented seamstresses and milliners in her employ. She was a gifted designer, having worked in her youth as an apprentice to a famous French couturier, and could dress any woman who came to her, whatever her age or size, so that from then on heads turned in admiration wherever her client went. She had among her clients the great, the wealthy, a sprinkling of aristocracy, wives of merchant bankers, merchant princes, of the millocracy, of all the prominent gentlemen of Liverpool and its surrounding districts and here was one who was the wife of one of the wealthiest. She had bought more than a few gowns from her in the past and Mrs Cheers welcomed her warmly.

Kitty was seated at one of Mrs Cheers's small glass-topped gilt tables in a spindle-legged gilt chair, behind which Emma took up her position. There were fashion books lying about on the uncluttered surfaces of other small tables, with shawls of the finest cashmere, embroidered gloves, cut-crystal scent bottles and other expensive little trifles, all set off by a great deal of apple-green velvet drapery. There were original water-colours on the wall and out-of-season flowers arranged in splendid vases. None of her awe showed in her face, for though Emma had never been in such surroundings before she had learned many things from her mistress and one of them was to reveal none of her alarm or even admiration in the face of the extraordinary. Coffee was offered to Mrs Maddox and Emma waited impassively, her eyes glowing. Emma was an attractive young woman and had not been short of admirers in the past. She knew she had only to say the word and John, the second groom, would come a-courting, but Emma had her sights set higher than a second groom, though what those sights were to be had not yet been revealed to her. She had a good, buxom figure, like her mother, a smooth country complexion, rosy and apple-cheeked, and her eyes were a velvet brown. Her hair, which she kept severely brushed back from her high forehead, though the odd curly tendril was inclined to escape, was as dark as her mistress's. She wore her modest maid's dress beneath her long, dark-blue cape and on her head a neat, if somewhat old-fashioned, bonnet with a small brim. She was almost four years younger than her mistress but in her somewhat severe garb looked older.

"Now then, Mrs Maddox," Mrs Cheers said pleasantly, "what can we do for you?" A handmaiden hovered behind her, dressed in black as she was, ready to haul rolls of material from the back regions of the shop and throw them upon the "fabric" table for Mrs Maddox's inspection; to pin her into something; to run and fetch a bonnet or a muff or a net of gold chains to complement Mrs Maddox's choice of material.

Mrs Maddox smiled artfully and Mrs Cheers's heart sank, for she knew that smile, not just from Mrs Maddox but from a dozen of her customers who wanted something from her; in other words, a complete wardrobe by the morning, but nothing showed on her smiling face.

"I come to throw myself at your feet, Mrs Cheers, with the hope, and belief, that you can work a miracle for me." Kitty's smile was quite brilliant. "I have, unexpectedly, been invited to a house party this weekend and . . . well, you will no doubt have heard of my . . . accident . . ."

Of course, who hadn't heard of the wilful Mrs Maddox's accident which, half of Liverpool said at the time, was her own fault, for should she have been riding when she was with child?

"And since then . . . well, you can see for yourself, Mrs Cheers, I have lost some weight. I have the gown you made for my brother's wedding which fits me but, as for the rest, my maid has been forced to alter them for the time being, taking a tuck in here and there but really I cannot take myself off to Brook Hall . . . Aah, you know the Olivers?"

"Oh, yes, Mrs Maddox. Both Mrs and Miss Oliver are customers of mine."

"I thought I saw the work of an artist in their dresses. We were at Aintree together."

"You are very kind, Mrs Maddox, and if you will tell me what you require I shall start at once. My fitter will call at your home in the morning."

"But I need them for Friday, Mrs Cheers."

Mrs Cheers smiled as though at the impatient demands of a small child. "And you shall have them, Mrs Maddox. One fitting will be enough and on Friday morning I will personally deliver the garments to your house, making any small alteration that is needed. Now then, evening gowns: how many? Three perhaps. Afternoon gowns, three again, for one can't be seen in the same one twice. A couple of walking costumes, for I believe the grounds at Brook Hall are quite extensive. And will there be tennis? Yes. And then there are hats . . ."

"Yes, and I dare say a new pair of breeches and a

jacket for riding. And some silk shirts, cravats, that sort of thing."

"Mrs Maddox, may I give you a word of advice?"

Mrs Maddox lifted her nose in the air. "Yes, of course." But her manner said there would not be much chance of her taking it.

"There will be . . . society people there, Mrs Maddox. The *cream* of society and it is simply not done to wear anything but a conventional riding habit. Some of the ladies, including, I believe, the Empress Elizabeth of Austria, who has been known to ride with the local hunt, are fanatical about the correct riding clothes. They ride gallantly and have wonderful seats despite riding side-saddle. I fear if you were to—"

"I don't believe the Empress of Austria is to be a guest this weekend, Mrs Cheers." Kitty was at her most arrogant. "And if she were it would make no difference to what I wear. I cannot abide the tight riding habit and side-saddle that ladies are expected to use so if you will set your mind to the garments we have discussed I would be obliged."

Mrs Cheers bowed to the inevitable, telling herself it was no wonder this hoity-toity madam had come off her horse and lost her child if that was her attitude. *And* no wonder that there were rumours whispered about Liverpool that her husband was never at home and had been seen in the company of the rich and beautiful widow of a ship owner!

The outfits were delivered in time for Emma to pack

them carefully in the large trunk and half a dozen other leather boxes that were to go with them, and be stowed in the carriage. The servants were whipped up to a state of such high excitement Mrs Ullett was heard to say that you'd think they were to go with Mrs Maddox. Every few minutes one or the other would pop a head out of the kitchen door that led into the front of the house, all of them hoping for a glimpse of Mrs Maddox in one of her new outfits.

"You've never seen owt like them," Emma had told them, inclined when she was excited or distressed to slip back into the north-countrywoman's way of speaking. And she was excited! She had never been away from Meadow View in all her working life. Her family lived within walking distance at Fazakerley, perhaps two miles, and those two miles were the sum and substance of Emma's travels. She'd been overwhelmed when she'd come as scullery-maid to Meadow View, staggered by the size of the kitchen, the gardens, the stable yard which was all she saw of her place of employment for three whole years. When she had been set to cleaning the front of the house, the drawing-room, the dining-room, the library, she had been frozen at first to the edge of the rich velvet carpet across which she had been expected to walk.

Now, seven years after she had begun as a lowly scullery-maid, she was accustomed to the comfort and luxury that was so taken for granted at the Maddox home. And here she was on another journey, one that made her heart leap with fright and her chin tremble a bit, for she wished with all her heart that her mam could see her now as she climbed into the carriage beside Mrs Maddox.

But the shocks were not yet over. Sauntering down the front steps, his hands in his pockets, a cigar clamped between his lips, was the master. The other servants, those who had made some excuse to gather at the front door to see the mistress off, stepped hastily to one side.

At once Emma found her hand gripped by that of her mistress, a grip so fierce she almost cried out. Mrs Maddox's face was still all the colours of the rainbow, having turned from purple-blue to plum, and was now fading somewhat from plum to green to yellow. She looked a real sight, she said, but Mrs Cheers had found her a hat with a high brim tilted rakishly to one side which almost hid it. Not that she particularly wished to hide it, she had told Emma defiantly, acting as though it were a war wound to be worn proudly. Her husband had struck her and she wanted nothing more than to tell the world what a brute he was, but her own pride, which hated to admit that she had let a man get the better of her, kept her silent.

"So, may one ask where you are off to?" he asked, smiling engagingly, just as though she were some acquaintance whose destination he must politely ask about but was not really interested in. The servants began to drift away, for if there was to be another battle they did not want to be caught in the crossfire.

"I am . . . to stay with some friends for the weekend,"

she answered loftily, but Emma definitely felt her flinch as she said the words, just as though she expected him to fly at her, or at least flay her with harsh words. He did neither.

"Really," he said, "how very nice. I hope the weather is kind to you." Then, flicking the ash from his cigar, he went inside.

It seemed he didn't care. He didn't even ask after the condition of her face which, Kitty supposed, would have been too much to expect. Not that it mattered, for she had decided on the night he had struck her that their marriage was over. A poor thing it had been, half-hearted on both sides. In fact she had wondered why he had married her in the first place since there must be dozens of pretty and docile young women who would suit him much better. Well, she must make a new life for herself, something that would fill her days, her endless days, and it seemed she had found it in the company of her new friends.

The journey was uneventful. Since it was no more than seven miles from Walton to Brook Hall, which was on the west side of St Helens, it had been decided that she would travel by carriage. The weather was fine and they drove with the hood down, Kitty shaded by an exquisite lace parasol that she had purchased at Mrs Cheers's salon. As they drove through the village it seemed as though half the inhabitants were out to stare as she went past, nodding and smiling, for it appeared Mrs Maddox had fully recovered from her accident. Where was she off to, they wondered, looking as pretty as a picture with her maid beside her? But what was that on her face? they whispered to one another. Surely she'd not had *another* fall! Mr Armitage hurried from his shop doorway, a smile all over his rubicund face and she bowed to him graciously. He was still hoping to sell her one of his guns, she supposed. Well, he might have the chance now if she was going to take up the life of a sporting country gentleman! She'd need a good horse, a hunter, she supposed, and a good gun. How exciting life was to be, she told herself as they bowled along narrow country lanes drenched in the scent of honeysuckle and wild guelder roses. Buttercups were in flower, starring the ripening fields in gold, and butterflies, their wings tipped with orange, hovered in the warm sunshine as though the wealth of flowers was so great they could not decide on which to alight.

They passed through small villages, the cottages built of stone and the roofs warm with the colour of stone slates. They stood alone, or in a row, usually fronted by a strip of green, their gardens bright with country flowers, orchards to the side. Smoke drifted with barely a movement from the chimneys, the air was so still and children stopped their games to watch the grand carriage go past.

She did not speak and neither did Emma. Though she would have admitted it to no one, even to herself, she felt . . . How could she describe it? Empty, was that it, the euphoria slipping away? And the strange thing was she didn't know why. Surely it couldn't be to do with the carelessly indifferent way Ben had wished her away. What Ben did or said or thought was of no importance to her and really, she must pick up her spirits before she got to the Olivers' place or they would think her a dull weekend companion. She was looking forward to it, she told herself sternly. She was excited, enchanted to be going somewhere that had nothing to do with her past life, nothing to do with Freddy or her parents or her husband. This was hers. She, with Michael's help, had brought this about and, by God, she was going to have the best weekend of her life.

The gates to Brook Hall stood open as though she were expected, which of course she was. A long avenue of hoary old trees, huge and magnificent, led away round a bend and when the carriage turned that bend there was another bend. They passed through a woodland, oak and birch and yew and still there was no sign of the house. They crossed a stone bridge over a busy stream and then they were out of the woodland, surrounded by rolling parkland on which deer browsed and rabbits nibbled the grass beside them, neither alarmed by the other.

The drive continued through massed walls of rhododendrons, still awash with colour from rosy lilac to a glowing blood red and then, quite incredibly, the house was there. An old house that looked as though it had grown from the very soil the trees had been nourished in, old and venerable and yet stately, imposing and yet welcoming. It looked somewhat like a castle with a crenellated roof from whose many chimneys smoke rose passively in the still morning air. It was built of small, honey-coloured bricks and yet there was a touch of pink and carnation, even cream, tinted there. The windows were many, long and gleaming, and though Kitty had no idea when it was built she knew it was very old.

Even before the carriage drew up to the steps leading to the arched front door, they were all there to meet her: Vannie and Grace, Tam and Jimmy and Michael and a milling group of servants who at once pounced on her luggage under the direction of a suave and disdainful butler. The butler opened the carriage door and held out his hand, but before she could wipe the astonishment from her face Tam was there, shouldering aside the black-suited servant, a warm smile on his handsome face, a wicked gleam – oh, yes, she knew it was wicked – in his smoky, blue-grey eyes. There were other people, guests, she supposed, who all seemed as pleased to see her as the Olivers and she was almost carried up the steps and across the threshold into a square hallway which was so big it had two fireplaces to keep it warm in the winter, one on either side. A wide staircase bisected it, leading upwards to an equally wide gallery along which she could see many doors; but before she could be gathered up and taken to wherever they fancied she stood stock still and straightened her back and shoulders. She was not going to be treated like some new toy the Olivers had acquired and, since it was new, was to be played with, which was how she felt at this moment. She was herself, Kitty Hayes – not Kitty Maddox – who had always decided her own course of action. She had been carried away with the novelty of the past few days, she admitted that, but from now on they must be made to see that she was not to be treated as a child.

"Come, Kitty," Vannie was saying, "come and meet some people, our friends and, we hope, yours too. They've been dying to meet you."

"Why?" Kitty said shortly and was amused by the sudden look of bewilderment on the faces about her. "Why should they want to meet me so particularly?"

"But you're such good fun, Kitty. You proved that the other day at the races," Tam purred, like some big cat with its quarry in its sights. "We're expecting you to amuse us this weekend, for we are so *bored* with one another, aren't we?" looking round the circle of faces, all of them young, for confirmation.

"Tam, you are a scream, really you are, but I'm no different from any other woman."

"Oh, but you are, my Kitty-Cat."

"I'm not your Kitty-Cat, Tam, nor anybody's." Her voice was tart. "But if you are prepared to accept me as I am and not some diverting skylark you have discovered then I'm sure we'll all get on famously."

Grace and Vannie shrieked with laughter, turning to the others with cries of, "There, didn't we tell you? Isn't she a darling?"

But Kitty frowned. "Really, Vannie, it was not that funny. Now, won't you introduce me to your friends, then I would be glad to be shown to my room. Is my maid here?"

She looked about her for Emma and found her patiently waiting just inside the front door. Her luggage was being carried up the stairs by a horde of servants and she wished to follow it and take Emma with her. She smiled in a friendly fashion at Clive and Roger, at Caroline and Harry, at George and Charles and Florence and Elizabeth, to name but a few, many of whom seemed to have a title and then, as they began to drift away to whatever they had been up to before she arrived, she was taken upstairs to the room that was to be hers. It was at the front of the house overlooking the magnificent formal gardens. The room was charming with gas wall brackets festooned with crystal, and decorated in peach silk and white lace. There was a Chinese carpet of peach blossom and pastel-tinted clouds; the furniture was pale and polished and everywhere gleamed the evidence of great wealth.

"Where is my maid to sleep?" she asked the trim upper chambermaid who was directing the transporting of her luggage.

"She has been allocated a room with the servants of the other guests, madam," the maid answered frostily, for surely any house guest with anything about her would know that.

"No, I don't think so," Mrs Maddox, as the maid had been told to call her, answered.

"I beg your pardon, madam. It is the custom—"

"I don't give a fig for customs. Where does that door

lead to?" indicating a closed door on the far side of the spacious room.

"It is a small dressing-room, madam, shared by the . . . the occupant of the bedroom beyond."

"Really. Then if you would be good enough to give orders for a bed to be put in there I would be obliged."

"Well . . ."

"At once, please. And is there a lock on the door to the bedroom of the other occupant?"

"Yes, madam, but—"

"Thank you, that will be all. My maid will see to my things."

"Yes, madam." The maid bobbed a peeved curtsey then muttered something beneath her breath, longing to get back to the kitchen region to describe to her colleagues the imperious woman with a black eye on her like a prize-fighter who had put one over on Mister Tam!

"You have something to say?" Kitty was at her most haughty and Emma turned away to hide her smile. Really, the more she got to know Mrs Maddox, the more she liked her. She wasn't letting any insolent maidservant, who thought she was better than most, dictate to her. "Yes?" she enquired icily.

"Nothing, madam, only that luncheon will be served at half past one."

She was treated like royalty. No matter what she did or said they thought she was a "hoot", or a "scream", or a "good sport" and she began to enjoy herself, since what can be more pleasing than to be told what a wonderful creature you are, how stunning you look, how amusing you are and what a magnificent seat you had in the saddle. They thought her riding outfit was splendid, outrageous, like her, but splendid. The weather was superb and during the "Friday to Monday" as she learned it was called they had tennis parties and tea parties on the lawn where a great number of cucumber sandwiches, scones and rich cream, chocolate cake and rich fruit cake were consumed. The ladies wore huge hats and afternoon frocks in pastel tints, delicate cream, near whites and the faintest shade of lavender, but none was as elegant and lovely as those worn by the young and outspoken Mrs Maddox. She played tennis with the gentlemen in an outfit that could only be described as *risqué*, showing her ankles and bare arms, with a small hat that looked like a jockey's cap jammed on her turbulent curls; and, of course, her riding breeches and silk shirts caused a sensation the first time she sauntered down the stairs to the stables where she was put up on a fierce-looking bay which she soon had on a tight rein knowing its place. She rode in what was described as a steeplechase from the hall to the church, the spire of which could be seen in the distance, then back again, leaping great hedges and gates and was the first lady to come in behind Tam Oliver.

The next day most of the ladies spent their morning in the deep armchairs scattered about the square hall in their expensive, town-made country clothes, chatting, writing letters and flirting with Michael and other young

gentlemen who were kept for the purpose of amusing the ladies, since most of the gentlemen, and Mrs
Maddox with Vannie and Grace, had gone off to shoot.

There were cries of amazement and congratulation
when it was made known that Mrs Maddox, their
brilliant Kitty, had actually brought down a dozen
birds!

There was luncheon at noon, a light meal, with
another sent out in hampers to the sportsmen. Tea was
at five seated round the fires in the hall, the ladies having
changed into elaborate tea gowns and after tea whist
was played until nine when dinner was served. There
were gowns by Worth and other famous designers,
diamonds flashing, pearl chokers of great value, rubies
and emeralds on every female neck and hand. The meal,
never fewer than ten courses, would be superb and
the conversation quick and witty, sometimes crude,
for these people were all well known to one another.
But none was more witty than Mrs Maddox who was
the toast of the weekend.

The only person who did not seem totally pleased
with the way things had gone was Tam Oliver.

"No luck?" his wife asked him, her arm companionably through his as they walked up the front steps after
having seen the delectable Mrs Maddox on her way.

"No, she kept that bloody maid of hers by her at all
times, but not to worry. There'll be other occasions.
What about you?"

She smiled like a cat at a saucer of cream. "I can't
complain."

17

Michael was the only gentleman among the dozens she met who did not make a fuss of her. He was always polite, charming, amusing but he did not beg for her favours as the others did. She supposed it was because he was far too busy entertaining the lady guests who gathered, if not at Brook Hall, then at Clive and Elizabeth's place, at Roger and Caroline's place, at Henry's place or George's place, or indeed any one of the well-to-do homes to which she was invited. He was very young, of course, though he did not act like a man still not yet twenty. He was sophisticated, suave, absolutely at his ease with the ladies when they required a fourth at whist, and with the gentlemen round the billiard table; on the grouse moor or seated superbly on one of the splendid mounts from the Oliver stables. He always seemed to surround himself with women older than he was, married women for the most part, handsome and smiling with great good nature, at everyone's beck and call but unperturbed by it and she supposed that he had no choice.

His father had died before he was born, he told her, leaving his mother without support though some kind people – about this he was somewhat vague – had taken her in and looked after her. When he was born they had continued to do so, for she had been in frail health, and, having no children, though it had not been done in a legal way, had adopted him as their own. When he was ten years old his mother, whom he had adored, his face soft as Kitty had never seen it, had died and he had continued to be a son to his benefactors. He had been sent to a famous public school where he had met many of the chaps with whom he now socialised, but – here he smiled and shook his head impishly – he had not been a "good" boy. He had been wild, gambling away his allowance until his stepfather, as he always thought of him, had refused to pay any more of his debts. He had been "sent down", or expelled, whatever, and his stepfather had washed his hands of him. So here he was, earning a living in the only way he knew how, which wasn't a bad existence until something better turned up.

"Something better? What are you expecting?"

They had been alone in the conservatory attached to the sunny side of Brook Hall. She had come down early, knowing that most of the guests would be changing for dinner, though from the shouts from the billiard-room it seemed some of the young men were playing the fool in one of those inexplicable games young men get up to. She had felt the need to slip into the drawing-room, which would be empty at this time of the evening, and play the piano. She had touched the keys very gently, since she didn't want anyone to hear her, a soft piece from a Brahms piano concerto, but Michael had surprised her. He had stood leaning on the piano for about five minutes but she did not feel like an audience so she had closed the lid and suggested they move into the conservatory which led off the drawing-room.

The conservatory was a room where peace and tranquillity, which did not rule in the rest of the house, were to be found. Lady Oliver rarely went there, for it was the sort of room that was added to the house merely because it was fashionable. It was filled from glass wall to glass wall and up into the high domed ceiling with rare and exotic plants, an explosion of colours with a pleasing fragrance which was not overpowering. There were tiny, brightly hued birds in white wicker cages, a small fountain, whose sound formed a pleasant background to conversation – when any took place – and comfortable white wicker chairs heaped with brightly coloured cushions set round tables covered with lace cloths.

"I am always the optimist, Kitty."

Michael was smoking a cigar, the smoke wreathing about his head and she was surprised when a pang of something she was not willing to call painful, but which disturbed her none the less, brought back a picture of a large, smiling man with dark hair whose expression had always been an enigma to her.

"But what if it doesn't?"

Michael drew deeply on his cigar and grinned audaciously and as she had done when she met him and on several occasions since, she had a feeling of *déjà vu* as though this moment, or this man, had been part of her life in the past.

"Believe me, it will."

And then Tam had come stalking in, like a panther, graceful and indolent, but with an expression that said he was not sure he liked the picture of Kitty Maddox and Michael Northwood, who was only a guest here after all, and on sufferance at that, with their heads together in what looked like an intimate conversation.

"Now then, what's my beautiful girl doing in the company of this young reprobate?" There was laughter in his voice, for he was joking, wasn't he? *Wasn't he?*

"Don't be a fool, Tam," she said lightly, getting to her feet, for the private moment was over.

"Well, darling, I'll forgive you for that remark and for holding private conversations with this ne'er-do-well" – casting a quizzical glance at Michael – "if you'll promise to take a walk with me in the gardens after dinner. It is a balmy night. There's a splendid moon and it's just right for romance. I promise not to pester you for kisses though . . ."

"Do stop it, Tam. If your wife could hear you . . ."

"Now then, my pet, you know Vannie wouldn't mind. She has her own . . . entertainment and will not even notice."

"Behave yourself, Tam. You do say the most outrageous things and you don't mean them at all. Look, here's your mother and—"

"Very well, my sweet. We'll finish this conversation later. You know how I adore you." And he smiled his most disarming smile to let her see that he was not in the least offended.

Later she managed to avoid him and his advances which were, she was beginning to admit, becoming more and more urgent, by the simple expedient of staying close to where the "fun" was, where the crowd was, the dancing and larking about which always ended the evening before the discreet pairing off of the sexes began. As he whispered in the more receptive ear of a guest, the wife of a minor aristocrat, she managed to slip away to the safety of her room, and Emma who stood stoutly and bravely between her mistress and the young master's amorous advances. She and Emma, as far as mistress and maid could be, had become friends, sharing small talk, gossip that Emma had picked up among the other servants, small jokes at the expense of some of the guests, though Emma was never less than politic in what she said about her mistress's friends.

It was several weeks later that they all decided that it was time she had a good horse, asking in a delicately tactful way if she could afford it. Not that they begrudged lending her one from their own stables, she must know that, but it was imperative to have a decent mount, a decent hunter, since the hunting season would be upon them before they knew it. When she remarked off-handedly that if she couldn't afford it her husband certainly could, they all laughed in that almost hysterical way they had, for wasn't she the wittiest thing.

"You'll get a decent hunter at Doncaster, my pet," Tam remarked, laying a possessive hand on her arm. There were the usual dozens of guests about the dinner table which seemed to be an accepted thing nearly every weekend at Brook Hall, and, as usual, she was seated next to him. So far, apart from the kiss in the carriage on their return from Aintree he had done no more than flirt and single her out for his partner in any party game. His conversation was often two-sided, as though what he said had a double meaning, which was understood by them all, even Kitty, and it seemed to be generally accepted that she was Tam's property. She often laughed about it with Emma after the bedroom door had been shut firmly, and laughingly in his face, for it really was amazing the way the gentry seemed to treat these . . . flirtations, if that was not too mild a word. When Tam danced attendance on Kitty, Vannie Oliver merely smiled and turned to some other gentleman who appeared to be only too happy to entertain Tam's wife while Tam dallied with the wives of other gentlemen.

And his father and mother, Sir Arnold and Lady Oliver, who presumably had the same light-minded outlook on the world as their three children, sat and watched quite amiably, aware of what went on under their roof but not seeming to care overmuch. The Olivers had been an ancient family who had grown poorer every year, very hard pressed to support themselves in the way "landed" gentlemen were used to until coal had been found on the Olivers' vast acres. A pit manager had been appointed and as the pit wheels and slag heaps of the mine were situated well away from the hall and were seen by no one, or at least anyone who mattered, not even the hunt that rode across his land, it meant no more to Sir Arnold than a welcome source of revenue. A *considerable* source of revenue!

They played games. Children's games which were often, in Kitty's opinion, dangerous, but when had danger ever stopped her from doing something she thought might be fun? Snapdragon was one. A large shallow dish was set in the centre of the carpet with enough inflammable spirit to fill it, matches to set it alight and a handful of currants to throw into the flames. The object was to snatch out a currant, bare-handed and then swallow it and whoever swallowed the most had won. Kitty, in the flamboyant scarlet brocade gown that Mrs Cheers had made for her, and with no jewellery to enhance her smooth white flesh of which she showed a good deal, and which needed no adornment anyway, and her mop of midnight curls which Emma kept cut short for her, as daring and unafraid as she had been all her life, won more times than any lady, and often the gentlemen as well. They thought she was superb in her recklessness, some of them so drunk they fell about laughing helplessly, flopping like landed fish on the carpet and some part of Kitty's mind, which remained cool no matter what madness she was taking part in, wondered why they acted as they did. She supposed that common sense was something she had inherited from her mother, who would have been appalled, not only by the wildness, but by the sheer lunacy that took place under the roof of Brook Hall; and as for the goings-on after the lights were out, well, it was quite amazing, or so Emma had told her, as shocked as a well-brought-up girl has a right to be, even if she was from the lower orders, when gentlemen crept along corridors and knocked on doors behind which other gentlemen's wives were accommodated.

Sardines was another favourite game, particularly with Tam, for if Kitty was "it", hiding in some dark cupboard while the others counted to a hundred before they ran about to find her, and if he could get to her first, who knew what liberties he might be able to take. He had not done so yet and he was not to know that it was doubtful he ever would, for on the night her husband had struck her she had sworn that a man would never take liberties with Kitty Maddox again!

They travelled by train to Doncaster, first class, naturally, and stayed with some friends of the Olivers who seemed to have "chums", as they called them, with whom they could put up in almost every part of the country. The St Leger meeting at Doncaster, where, again, they saw the Prince of Wales who bowed to her and twinkled merry eyes but did not speak, was a proven ground for showing and selling good horses. With Tam's help and the encouragement of all the noisy party, she purchased, for the astonishing and outrageously extravagant amount of three hundred pounds a beautiful black mare, tall and brave in the hunt but hard to handle, or so the trainer confided to Tam. He wasn't sure that Mrs Maddox could manage her, he said, and was surprised when Mr Oliver threw back his head and roared with laughter.

"Did you hear that, my pet?" he chuckled to Kitty, and the rest of the party, putting a possessive arm about her. "He's not sure you can handle her. What d'you say, shall you give him a demonstration?"

"I would if I had my breeches," Kitty began, but Tam, who had drunk a lot of champagne, was not to be put off.

"Nonsense! What do you want with breeches, my love? Mr Hollingate does not believe the mare is a fit mount for a lady. Too wild, he says, but we know better, don't we? Why don't you show him?"

That ride was the talk of the sporting set, the racing set, the well-bred and moneyed set who had come to look at what was for sale. They had all heard of the outrageous Mrs Kitty Maddox; who hadn't in their social world? Those who knew him wondered what her husband was thinking of, allowing her to flaunt herself about with the mad Oliver set, but then he was no saint, brazenly associating with the lovely widow who was often seen on his arm.

Kitty smiled. "Hold her steady and help me up then."

"Please, Mrs Maddox, I don't advise . . ." But Kitty Maddox had been flung a challenge and had she ever turned away from a challenge in her life? They stepped back to give her room and to avoid the flying hooves of the offended hunter, even Kitty's hard-playing, wild-riding, hell-raking, newly found friends, as Tam cupped his hands to receive her foot and threw her up into the saddle, the skirt of her expensive walking dress of coffee-coloured foulard des Indes bunched up wildly around her. The lovely line of her profile, her throat and breasts which in the last few weeks had become fuller and rounder, were etched against the white painted stable walls as she threw back her head and laughed.

"Open the gate, Tam," she cried, holding on like grim death to the reins, applying pressure to the snaffle and the corners of the mare's mouth. Some of the men and women not of their party, who had come from other parts of the country and who did not know her, or her reputation for wilfulness, stared in disbelief, for she was barelegged apart from her fine stockings and the smart pair of high-heeled walking shoes she had on and when, astonishingly, she raised her arm in a military salute they began to cheer and clap, for there was nothing this sporting set liked better than pluck.

"Dear God, she's an original, that one," Vannie murmured, her hand on her husband's arm.

"That's why I want her," he told his wife, who smiled.

"She'll kill herself," someone else said to his neighbour, but on the whole those who watched were inclined to shout their approval and wish her well on her wild dash beyond the stables and along the run where the horses were exercised.

She was gone for no more than ten minutes but when five had gone by Mr Hollingate wanted to send out a search party. He was not overly concerned with the mad bitch who had taken off on one of the finest hunters in the owner's stable but with the bloody animal which did not belong to him since he was only her trainer.

"She'll be back shortly," Mr Oliver kept telling him as he hung about the gate through which Mrs Maddox had bolted. They were drinking champagne, fetched from the back of the waggonette in which the party had driven from wherever it was they were staying and though Mr Hollingate knew their host and many of his guests he did not like the way they were drinking about his expensive bloodstock.

She came thundering back down the path on which she had set off at a wild pace, but though the mare was galloping at her top speed the woman on her back was in full control. Mr Hollingate had never seen anything quite so beautiful as the woman and the horse who seemed to move as one entity and he was forced to admit that they deserved one another.

The mare clattered to a halt, her bridle caught at once by a groom and Mrs Maddox slithered down from her back and straight into the arms of the man who, it seemed, was not her husband.

"I want her," she said directly into his face and for a moment they all thought he was going to kiss her, there in front of his wife, and though it was accepted that Tam Oliver and Kitty Maddox, if they were not lovers now, soon would be, it was not done to flaunt it.

"You shall have her," he said, his blue-grey eyes flaring in the bright sunlight directly into hers, and I shall have you, those eyes told her.

"I shall call her Havoc."

They all began to laugh then, for was that not just like Kitty Maddox? Havoc! The name suited her, the mare, and the way of life the pair of them would have together on the hunting field.

"Well done, Kitty."

"That was marvellous, my dear."

"I've never seen a finer bit of horsemanship."

"By God, I couldn't have done better myself, Kitty."

And so it went on, music to her ears, their admiration and approval filling the inner pockets of her being which were so terribly empty, smoothing the jagged corners of her soul which had been cauterised by her husband's bland indifference when she met him in the hallway on her way to her carriage yesterday morning.

"Off again then?" he had drawled and something inside her, she didn't know what, seemed to shrivel. She was suddenly conscious of being drained of emotion, of a feeling of inertia, then the expression on his face, an expression that told her that he didn't give a damn what she did, stiffened her spine, and she pasted a brilliant smile on her face so that for a second or two Ben Maddox was transfixed.

"Indeed, as you see. We are off to Doncaster to buy a hunter."

"Really. Well, good luck. Will we see you before the weekend is over?"

"I doubt it. There is a party of us going to stay with some friends of Tam's. Tam Oliver, that is."

"Of course. Well, I must be off, I have plans of my own for the weekend."

And so the good wishes, the shining approval, the whole-hearted and enthusiastic praise which was poured over her dispersed the coldness that had lain like a lump of lead in her chest ever since. These people thought she was worth while. They valued her. They thought she was beautiful, accomplished, courageous, amusing, good company, all the things no one else had seen in her, right from the young man Freddy had become when he had chosen Ciara above her, to Ben Maddox who despised her as whole-heartedly as she despised him!

The autumn came and with it the start of the hunting season. Almost every day she was out with the Burton Hunt on her big black mare, dressed in her outlandish outfit which the ladies and gentlemen of the hunt, those who were not close friends of the Olivers, did not care for. Ladies were expected to wear a black riding habit, which consisted of a chamois undergarment into which she would be sewn, a full, divided skirt, a double-breasted well-fitting jacket, a top hat with long streamers, and to carry a small riding whip. But the Olivers were an old family, influential and wealthy and there was not a lot the traditionalists of the hunt could do about it, especially as Sir Arnold, an enthusiastic fox hunter himself, provided most of the foxhounds, plus the huntsman and would lend a mount to anyone who was without one from his extensive stable.

She took to it like a duck to water, which naturally, Tam said, they all knew she would. She was "blooded" on her first day out, being the first lady to reach the kill and had even laughed as they daubed her face with the dismembered tail.

She became a good shot, shooting driven partridges, grouse and pheasants in their hundreds that first season. Sir Arnold said she was an asset to the party, since landowners vied with one another to produce the biggest bags of game on their estates.

But it was at the parties in the evenings that she was the biggest success, for as the weeks and months went by, Christmas spent at Brook Hall and with no idea where her husband might be, she regained all her old statuesque beauty so that she began to find it increasingly difficult to hold back the ardent demands of Tam Oliver.

But it could not last. There was a small room behind the back parlour at Brook Hall where the Olivers' old nanny sat and dozed by the fire, ready, should it be needed, to hand out the sal volatile for a lady who might feel faint after so much rowdiness, to put a stitch in a torn hem, to provide a degree of privacy in which to recover from a wounded heart, for there were many in the raucous company Nanny's charges invited to their parties. Not all of them were house guests and the cosy, fire-glowed room was a haven in which to pull together whatever it was that ailed them. Kitty did not want Tam to see her disappearing up the wide stairway to the landing where her own bedroom lay, for there was no doubt he would follow her.

She slipped without being seen into Nanny's parlour, and was having a stitch put into the torn hem of her gown which Jimmy had stepped on, when the door opened, snapped shut again and Tam stood there, smiling, his eyes narrowed with an expression that told her that this time, and without Emma's support, she would need all her inventiveness to talk him out of what was very obviously on his mind. She wondered, almost with despair, how she had managed it up to now.

"Good evening, Master Tam," Nanny said, turning to put away her sewing box then moving her table, on which stood her tray of tea and biscuits, a little nearer to her. "Is it a good party, dear?" She peered lovingly at him through her short-sighted old eyes.

"Yes, Nanny, a wonderful party and getting better all the time. Now then, why don't you go to bed? I'm sure you must be tired and no one will need you any more tonight."

He did not take his greedy eyes off Kitty all the while he spoke to Nanny.

"Well, I don't know, Master Tam. I usually wait until your mother comes."

"Never mind that, Nanny, go to bed."

"But, Master Tam, I . . ."

"*Go to bed,* Nanny. This lady and I want to be alone, don't we, my pet."

"Tam, behave yourself. You're drunk and so am I, but

not enough, so the sooner we get back to the others the quicker I shall have a glass of champagne in my hand. Come along . . ."

"I don't want to come along, my love." Tam's voice was soft, dreamy, thoughtful as though he were considering what would be the best way to go about this . . . this final stage of his seduction of Kitty Maddox. He had never had to wait as long as he had waited for this woman, which was perhaps why she had become almost an obsession to him. He had allowed her to escape him many times, enjoying the chase which was a novelty to him but he had waited long enough and now his patience had been rewarded. He had her trapped in this small, out-of-the-way room where he would make it his business to see that they were not interrupted. He knew she had avoided it but in his arrogance he believed that he only had to kiss her, to get his hands on her, to get her in his arms and she would be as eager as he was.

Nanny slipped discreetly from the room, closing the door quietly behind her.

Kitty let him kiss her with the hope that a couple of kisses might satisfy him. What else could she do since he had the key, which he had just turned, in his pocket? She would escape him, make no mistake about that. When he began to think he had her, that she was his; when he relaxed and let down his guard she would knee him in the belly and when he was down take the key from his pocket and race back to Emma and safety.

His mouth was hot and wet and she hated it. She

could not get out of her mind, and her revolted senses, the feel of another mouth, just as hot, but with a sweetness, a thrilling, caressing touch that had filled her with pleasure.

"Sweet . . . sweet," he was murmuring, taking her stillness for compliance, bending her back over his arm as his mouth slid down her throat to the top of her breasts. "God . . . oh, God, I've waited for this . . . waited and at last . . ."

"Stop it, Tam. Take your hands off me," she hissed, beginning to cuff him about the head as his right hand invaded the neckline of her low-cut gown, cupping her naked breast. Disgusted, she began to struggle but he was strong, an athlete, used to being in the saddle for hours, to controlling a wild horse, to playing tennis or cricket, to walking across the grouse moor and his strength was gaining on her.

She managed to free herself for a moment, or, more to the point he allowed it, his eyes gloating as they fastened on her high, peaked breasts, which his fumblings had revealed. She stood away from him, the first tinge of fear trickling through her veins, for she was becoming aware that there was a chance she was about to be raped here.

"I won't be forced, Tam, so give me that key and—"

"I'll not force you, my darling. You know you want it. You've been leading me on for months now and, by God, I'll not be put off a moment longer."

It was at that moment that the door knob was rattled and an insistent voice demanded why the bloody door was locked. A man's voice, blurred with drink, as they all were, but not to be put off.

"Go away, you daft bugger," Tam shouted. "Can't a man have a bit of peace in his own bloody house. Get the hell out of it."

"Tam, you'll have to open the door, old chap."

"No, I bloody well won't. I'm busy." He smirked at Kitty and reached out a tentative finger to her nipple.

"Is . . . Kitty in there with you?" the voice asked apologetically and Kitty recognised it as Clive Barrie.

"Of course she is, aren't you, my darling, and she's staying here. Now, sod off, there's a good chap."

"Tam, you don't understand. You must let her out."

"Must!"

"Yes, Tam. There's a man here with a message from her husband and he says he must speak to her urgently."

18

The carriage her husband had sent for her was waiting at the door, Sir Arnold told her, his voice and manner somewhat vague as though he were not awfully sure why she needed to leave so late in the evening. Her maid was packing her trunk, Lady Oliver added, and as soon as Kitty had changed, which really she should since she couldn't travel in her evening gown, her coachman would drive her wherever she wanted to go. Now, she wasn't to worry her pretty head, Sir Arnold chipped in, really she wasn't. The note had said her father had been taken ill and that she was to go to Riverside House as soon as possible, but not that he was in any danger. Her husband, that vague and unknown quantity who none of them had ever met, had gone on ahead, the note said and would meet her at the station in Manchester if she would send a telegraph to let him know which train she was to catch.

The message really had put a dampener on the party

which had been tremendous fun and none was more conscious of it than Tam Oliver. His frustrated male ardour was racing through him like a river in flood and he didn't know how to contain it, since he had had little practice in self-restraint. But for this bloody message that ardour would now be assuaged, or so he told himself. He had had her half naked in his arms and a little bit of persuasion would have done the trick. Kitty Maddox belonged to him. Kitty Maddox would have been his. Everyone knew he had first claim on her. He had been lusting after her for months now and tonight he had been on the point of having her and now God alone knew when he would get another chance.

"Yes," Kitty said vaguely. The tail end of the evening, not just this last shock, had been punishing. She could still feel the hot breath and hands of Tam Oliver, the smell of the brandy he had drunk, see his gleaming, predatory eyes as they had devoured her in the cosy room, a room which was the personification of the naïve and spinsterish innocence left by the old lady and which he had tainted with his greed. Had it not been for the message from Ben and the timely arrival of Clive Barrie to inform her of it, he would have torn her clothes from her and violated her. She had played with him for months, believing she had control of him, slapping him away playfully, jokingly telling him to "behave" when all the while the playful kitten she thought she was dealing with was in reality a full-grown leopard.

She was filled with a mixture of emotions and second to worry about her father was a growing fury. A furious disbelief that she had allowed a man to treat her as Tam had done and a rage that he had had the bloody cheek to do so. She had the strange need to shout her rage and revulsion across the room to him, even to leap at him demanding what the hell sort of woman he thought she was? How dare he? *How dare he?* Well, she could do nothing about Tam Oliver at the moment. Her father was ill and she must go to him, but, by God, she'd have something to say to him when the time came.

Her frenzied thought must have shown in her face.

"Are you all right, my dear?" Lady Oliver asked her. "Would you like me to call your maid to help you?"

She made a great effort to put what had happened in Nanny's room to the back of her mind. "No, really, it is just . . . Well, my father has suffered for years with his chest; that is why he and my mother had been spending the winter in Lytham. The air is much better for him, you know. I can't understand why they were back in Manchester." She shook her head, trying to clear it, knowing she should be getting changed and taking the carriage back to Meadow View and then the early morning train to Manchester but somehow she couldn't seem to get her brain working as it should. She was aware of the murmuring figures about her, of the somewhat impatient guests who, she was sure, were longing for her to go so that they might get back to their evening's entertainment, but she was unsure, dithering as to the best action to take which was not like her at all. Her father was ill and she should be flying to his side, but a strange lifelessness had her in its grip and she couldn't seem to escape it.

"Come along, Kitty," a voice said at her elbow and, thankfully, or she might have sat there for ever, a strong hand took hers and lifted her to her feet. "You've had a shock but you'll be all right in a few minutes."

She turned and looked into the unruffled face of Michael Northwood which was on an exact level with her own. He smiled at her reassuringly and she felt a small measure of relief that someone was taking control. He began to lead her away towards the door but a bellow from the window, where a moody Tam Oliver lounged with his buttocks on the edge of the sill, brought them all – for the guests had started to mill about – to an uncoordinated halt. They had begun to move towards the billiard-room where a raucous game of the usual foolish kind had been interrupted; towards the dining-room where a lavish supper was laid out, towards the motionless figures of servants who held trays of drinks, for they found they needed a stiff one after the fuss and bother of the last half-hour, but Tam's astonishing roar stopped them in their tracks and they turned questioningly towards him.

"What d'you think you're doing, lad?" he thundered at Michael, and Vannie was seen to grimace and shake her head anxiously as though to say she had seen this coming. She had known Tam was besotted with Kitty Maddox but it was not done to let others, at least in public, see what an effect the woman had on him.

Both Michael and Kitty turned.

"She can't go alone, not in the state she's in. She's had a shock," Michael said mildly.

"No, of course she can't. You're right, but I shall go with her. Come, Kitty-Cat, let's go and see if that woman of yours is finished and then we'll be off."

There was a concerted gasp from the onlookers, for it seemed that, hedonistic and self-indulgent as they were, they still had a certain code. Tam Oliver might take Kitty Maddox to be his mistress. He might sleep with her beneath the same roof as his wife and their four children, but their code, perhaps unspoken, said these things, which they all understood and indulged in, were to be done discreetly. They were not to be flaunted, brought out into the open, espcially before one's wife and parents.

There was a long silence and as it trailed on and on, Tam Oliver came to his senses. He was still inflamed with his lust for Kitty Maddox but he had been trained, as all boys of his class were trained at school, to show self-control and leadership, to take a beating with a smile, to be a man, to be true to the conventions of his social equals and for a terrible moment his male lust had betrayed him. That moment was over. He must not court disaster, by which he meant Kitty Maddox shunning his friendship or he would never get another chance to have her. He must cover up his slip the best way he could and he must do it by letting the lad, who was *his* lad after all, for did he not rely on the good offices of Tam Oliver, and other gentlemen like him, for the very food he put into his mouth. He must let Michael escort

Kitty to her father's bedside. Michael would not dare to put his hands on Tam's property, not if he wished to live the good life Tam and his family allowed him to share with them. They were his livelihood, the Olivers and the Barries and the rest of their set. He knew which side his bread was buttered and would behave accordingly.

"Of course, what am I thinking of? Do forgive me. I'm letting my duty as a gentleman override my duties as host. I do apologise," bowing and smiling to his friends who at once all relaxed. "I was concerned only with the safety of a guest. Michael is just the man to see Kitty safely home."

"I don't need escorting," Kitty was heard to say tartly, but she was ignored.

Twenty minutes later she and her maid, with Michael beside them, drove away from Brook Hall to the collective good wishes of the guests who came to see her off on the wide front doorstep before hurrying back inside to continue with the fun.

"How is he?" were the first words she spoke as she hurried through the open door, held by Tilly, into the hall at Riverside House.

Tilly stared at her in dismay, for it was over a year since Miss Kitty had left them and they had forgotten her forceful ways.

"The doctor's with him, Miss Kitty, and Mrs Hayes. They say he's had a better night but . . ."

She was halfway up the stairs before she became aware of the group of people who had come to the door of the drawing-room as she entered the house. Her husband was among them. Freddy was there, and Ciara, and even in the midst of the chaos, the confusion, the anxiety, some part of her mind not occupied with terror for her father noticed that her half-sister was pregnant. Why had no one told her that Ciara was pregnant? She was surprised by the bolt of pain that shafted through her, wondering what had caused it. So many things perhaps. Freddy's choice of Ciara as a wife. Their impending parenthood. The loss of her own child which Ben had valued and which might have made a difference to the life they now both separately led. The loss of her childhood which, though she had not been her mother's favourite, had been warmed by the love of her father who lay upstairs, perhaps on his deathbed.

Ben must have seen the expression on her face and read what it meant.

"Come down, Kitty." His voice was surprisingly gentle. "The worst is over."

"What was he doing back here?" Her anguish made her voice hard and angry. "You know his chest complaint is aggravated by the damp, sooty air of Manchester. What was he thinking of?"

Her eyes were drawn to Freddy who had begun to shift uneasily. He had his arm round his wife's bloated figure and Kitty, though she felt she should be, was not ashamed of the momentary elation that swept through her, for Ciara did not look her usual dainty self.

Freddy, as though he were doing his best to hide, stood fidgeting behind his wife. He looked guilty, embarrassed, shamefaced. He shuffled his feet and would not look at her, and it was then that she began to understand what had brought her father back to Manchester.

As she always had since she was a toddler she went at once on the attack.

"By God, it was you, wasn't it? You couldn't manage the mill and the warehouse and so Father had to come back and sort it all out for you. After all these years under his supervision you still couldn't handle—"

"*Kitty!*" Ben's voice, though it was not loud, for they were in a house of sickness, was sharp enough to bring her to her senses and she turned to him, her face as white and stricken as though she had been greeted by her father's death. "This is not the time, Kitty," he continued. "Come into the drawing-room and the maid will bring you some fresh coffee. In fact we shall all have some."

For the first time she noticed that, but for her half-brother Sebastian, all her family were clustered in the drawing-room doorway, including her Aunt Jennet who was no relation but was her mother's oldest friend. Her half-sisters Anna and Marguerite appeared to be clinging together for support, pale and frightened and they turned as one when Ben moved to escort them back to their chairs, glad of his strength and his reassurance that everything would be fine and they must drink their coffee and wait for the doctor to come and give them his report. He smiled at them and at once Kitty could see they felt better, smiling a little themselves, glad of his support and encouragement. Again her wayward mind thought its own thoughts and one of them was that she wouldn't mind a bit of comfort and support herself.

She came slowly down the stairs, pausing on the last tread, trailing the hem of her pale beige woollen gown over which Emma had put her into a three-quarter-length chocolate-coloured velvet coat trimmed at the neck, the wrist and about the hem with pale brown fur. She scarcely remembered what had happened since she had been rescued from Nanny's cosy room by Clive Barrie. The wild ride to Meadow View and the equally wild carriage ride to the railway station in Liverpool to catch the train to Manchester. She knew a carriage had met them there and she remembered shrieking to Brewer, her father's coachman, to drive like the wind. Emma had been beside her, as she always had been during the past year, ready to be whatever Kitty wanted her to be: lady's-maid, friend, confidante, a comfort and life-raft to which Kitty was only too happy to cling. Michael, calm, cool, quietly efficient as he dealt with sending the telegraph, removing the luggage from the railway carriage, tipping porters, finding the Hayes' coachman in the chaos about Victoria Station, his voice telling her that everything would be all right, to which she had asked, rudely she was aware, how the hell he knew that!

She stepped down from the bottom tread and there he was, a well-groomed and courteous young gentleman, standing patiently beside Emma, waiting to be told, as Emma was, how he could be of assistance. Should he go now that he had delivered her safely to her home? his raised eyebrows asked her but she shook her head, managing a smile. Putting her arm through his she led him into the drawing-room where Tilly was serving fresh coffee.

"This is Michael. Michael Northwood. Michael was kind enough to bring me home. He was a guest at your wedding, Freddy. He came with Jimmy Oliver, if you remember."

"Aah, Jimmy, of course," Freddy said vaguely but it was plain that nobody, including himself, could remember the handsome, politely smiling young man whose arm she held, which was surprising, for Michael was not the sort of man you could overlook.

"These are my sisters, Anna and Marguerite, my brother Freddy and his wife Ciara. This is my mother's friend, Miss Williams. And, of course, my husband," waving her hand in Ben's general direction as though throwing this last in as an afterthought.

There were polite murmurs. An effort was made to engage one another in subdued conversation, though Kitty found she could not join in. She hung about by the doorway into the hall, prowling restlessly back and forth, biting her nails and chewing her lip and when she heard footsteps on the stairs hurried out to greet the doctor and her mother.

"Mother, how is he?"

Her mother, in that way that was very familiar to Kitty, just as though Kitty's energy and loud voice were things she could not cope with just now, held herself slightly aloof, though she did offer a cool cheek for her to kiss.

"Doctor Croxley will tell you, dear. Shall we go into the drawing-room."

"But, Mother . . ."

"Patience, dear. Let us all sit down and then Doctor Croxley will . . ."

Nancy Hayes had taken several steps into the drawing-room, her face tired but tranquil, for it seemed her beloved husband was to recover, when she caught sight of the young man who hovered at the back of the room looking as though he had no wish to intrude in a family crisis but was not sure where to go. She looked at him with what seemed to be dawning horror and those about her watched in bewilderment as every vestige of colour drained from her face.

With a faint moan she crumpled to the floor.

"Get him out of here," she hissed, glaring past the solicitous figure of Jennet Williams to the young man who stood by the window.

"Who, dearest?" Jennet asked, clearly bewildered, as they all were. And worried too, for though Nancy Hayes had been up all night with her husband and her reserve of strength had been stretched to the limits, it was not like her to faint. Her old friend Jennet knew that only too well. They had known one another for getting on for thirty years. They had suffered great hardships together, hardships not even Nancy Hayes's husband knew about. Through it all Nancy had borne up and not only borne up but had borne them *all* up, carrying them through adversity to the calmer waters of her marriage to Josh Hayes. Now, or so it seemed, she had fallen by the wayside. Not exactly gone under but her mind seemed to have lost itself in some maze.

They were all anxious and mystified. Her two youngest daughters knelt by the sofa to which Ben had carried her after he had scooped her up from the floor where she had fallen, getting in the way of the doctor who still waved under her nose the vial of sal volatile he always carried in his medical bag, and who begged them sharply to stand away and give Mrs Hayes some breathing space. Nancy Hayes frantically turned her head away from the sal volatile's pungent fumes, showing that she had at least recovered from whatever it was that had struck her down. Kitty hovered behind them all, unsure what one was supposed to do for a woman who had fainted. She glanced at her husband and then at Michael as though for inspiration but they were both gazing at her mother, Ben with what seemed to be great sympathy, though the expression on Michael's face was less easy to read.

"Who?" her mother shrieked and with such force they all instinctively looked towards the ceiling as though the sick man upstairs might hear her. "Him, that man. Dear God, Jennet, are you blind?"

Eight pairs of eyes all turned to look at Michael, for it was at him her trembling finger pointed. He shrugged apologetically, his young face creased, for he was a gentlemen and it was not his way to cause distress to a lady.

"I'm so sorry," he murmured, "but I seem to have upset your mother. Shall I go?"

Tilly, who had been hanging about in the doorway wringing her hands, as anguished as the rest of them over poor Mrs Hayes who surely had enough to deal with with the master, turned at once towards the front door, ready to throw it wide open. Perhaps if the gentleman, poor soul, was to leave, Mrs Hayes would get over her fit of hysteria and they could all concentrate on the master, but it seemed Mrs Hayes was still struggling with some demented thoughts of her own.

She sat up slowly, her face still ashen.

"Lie still, dear lady," the doctor advised but she took no notice. Her daughters, all four of them, stared at her dumbstruck, for none of them had ever seen their mother anything other than calm, controlled, in charge of their lives and hers.

"Sweet Jesus," she whispered, holding on to Jennet Williams's hand as though it were the only sure thing in a world gone mad. "Sweet Jesus, I thought it was all over years ago but he's come back, Jennet. Can you not see it, you of all people who suffered with me at his hands?" With her free hand she fingered the almost invisible scar that she carried on her cheek.

Jennet turned again to gape at the young man in the corner who surely, her expression said, was far too young to have harmed Nancy Hayes in her distant past, but even as she looked her expression changed and she put her hand to her mouth.

"It's . . . no, it cannot . . ."

"Dear God!" Kitty suddenly exploded. "Will one of you tell me what the dickens is going on? And will either you, Mother, or you, Doctor, give us news of Father. Is he to—"

"Mr Hayes suffered a congestion of his lungs but he has recovered somewhat, though he must rest, of course," Doctor Croxley said importantly, glad to interrupt this peculiar madness that seemed to have inflicted itself on Mrs Hayes. "My advice is to get him back to Lytham as soon as possible. He should not have been in Manchester at this time of the year."

"No, he shouldn't," Kitty pronounced bitterly, "and what I would like to know is why he was here in the first place. Freddy was supposed to—"

"I won't have you blaming Freddy." Ciara swung clumsily closer to her husband and on her face was the expression that she always turned on Kitty. There was indignation, resentment, spite, for in her opinion Kitty had always been allowed to get away with things that a well-brought-up young lady like Ciara, who had tried and tried to be good, had never managed.

"And anyway, do you care what happens to anyone in this family, let alone Father? Gadding about the county without a thought for his health. When did you last go and visit him? You care more about those fast friends of yours than—"

"How dare you criticise me, or my friends. At least I have some, you stupid little—"

"*Kitty.*" Again Ben's voice cut through the vituperations that each sister was intent on heaping on the other's head. "This is not the time for these recriminations. Have you forgotten your father is ill and will not benefit from scenes such as this? So, if the doctor says it is all right, Kitty, I imagine he would be glad to see you."

Suddenly subdued, Kitty bowed her head and at a nod from the doctor began to make her way towards the doorway, but it seemed her mother had merely been waiting for a lull in the tirade to carry on where she had left off.

"Where have you come from?" Nancy Hayes's voice cut harshly through the doctor's instructions to Kitty on how she was to behave in the presence of her sick father. It was as though he were babbling some nonsense that had nothing to do with what was going on here. The doctor's face registered his annoyance and surprise, for Mrs Hayes was usually the most gracious of ladies. Kitty came to a halt in the doorway.

"Do you mean me, Mrs Hayes?" Michael Northwood asked smoothly.

"I do." She lifted her head in the same imperious manner that her eldest daughter had inherited. Jennet clasped her hand, giving the impression that, though she was a head shorter than her old friend, she would defend her to the death. Anna and Marguerite were in a state of considerable shock, for not only was their father very poorly, snatched at the last moment from death's door, but their mother had gone mad. Their usually placid life had been severely rent apart in the last two days and they didn't know how it was to be mended.

But there was worse to come.

Michael Northwood sighed. Ben Maddox had a sudden urge to move across the room and stand protectively beside his wife who was still hanging about in the doorway. She looked quite haunted and he felt his love, which he had successfully interred in a deep hole, then covered with a heavy rock – which often weighed him down – stir as though trying to lift that rock. The young man looked . . . satisfied. He was almost, not quite, smiling, and from her position beside her diminutive friend he distinctly heard Mrs Hayes moan deep in her throat.

"I lived in Rainshough until I went to school, Mrs Hayes. The River Irwell runs . . . quite close to the village as you may know."

"I can't bear it, Jennet, really I can't."

"Dearest, hold on."

"After all these years . . ." For just a moment Nancy Hayes seemed to sag but the strength, culled from God knows where, of Jennet Williams held her up. The other occupants of the room, even the good doctor who would have said, if asked, that there was not much in this world that he had not seen or that would surprise him, found they were holding their breath. Marguerite was crying silently, probably unaware that she was doing so, the tears running in a silvery stream across her fresh young cheeks.

"I was born there and raised by an elderly couple, not my parents, of course, since my father was dead, drowned, I was told, before I was born, and my mother was an invalid. I was lucky, I suppose, considering my . . . er, background, to have had such a privileged upbringing. But now that I am returned to my . . . Well, how would you describe it, Mrs Hayes?"

"I will not try, Mr . . . er . . . I will just repeat that I wish you to leave my home."

"Aah, I cannot do that, Mrs Hayes." He thrust his hands in his trouser pockets and sauntered forward, then bowed from the waist towards her.

"Haven't you and . . . and your parents done enough to us? Get out . . . *get out*." Nancy Hayes's voice rose in a shriek and Doctor Croxley reached out a hand to her, horrified not only to be a witness to whatever family drama was being played out here, but by the state of Mrs Hayes, and, if he had heard that last shriek, the state of his patient.

"Not until I have wished my . . . uncle a speedy recovery."

"Oh, dear Lord have mercy," Nancy whispered.

"In case you have not guessed it," the handsome young visitor went on, turning to smile at the appalled and totally silent group about him, "my name is Michael Hayes."

19

"We can't keep it from him, Mother. It will be a ferocious shock to him, as it has been to you, but he must be told. Michael is his nephew. His own flesh and blood. His sister's child."

"And the son of that bastard. Thank God we found *his* body or I would be haunted by the fear that he would come back, too."

Ben spoke reassuringly, leaning forward to emphasise what he was saying. "They are both dead, Mrs Hayes. The father and the mother of this . . . this man who says he is your nephew and can do you no harm."

"No, they have done that in abundance in the past." Nancy Hayes's voice was bitter and her hand clenched convulsively in Jennet's. "She . . . Milly did her best to come between Josh and me. She was jealous. She didn't think I was good enough for her brother. She resented the children, because of who they were and when she met O'Rourke . . . well, I can only think she lost her wits. He was no longer the handsome, charming young Irishman who had pestered me, but a man who had . . . he was coarse, gross. She was an ageing spinster and somehow he must have . . . Dear God, it sounds obscene but he must have swept her off her feet."

They were seated in the drawing-room. Nancy, Kitty and Ben, Jennet, Anna and Marguerite, Freddy and Ciara and had it not been for Ben, Kitty was forced to admit, her sisters and her mother would have gone to pieces. She supposed he was used to taking control, since he was at home in the world of business and had learned that a man who is indecisive and weak, a man who shilly-shallied like her brother Freddy, she thought dispassionately, gets nowhere in this world. It was Freddy's weakness, his inability to get a grasp of the business that his forebears had built up over the past hundred years that had brought them to this crisis. He could not be blamed for the appearance of Michael Northwood – or Hayes, as she supposed she would have to get used to calling him – but it was his fecklessness that had brought her father back to the polluted air of Manchester and caused his collapse.

Doctor Croxley had advised that they must keep this staggering news from his patient until he was stronger. Another good night's sleep would do him a power of good, so perhaps tomorrow, or the next day – he would let them know – they could break the news of his nephew's return.

Ben had seen to everything. He had quietly gone about the task of putting Michael into a decent hotel, since it was evident that his mother-in-law could not, at this precise moment, stand the idea of her husband's new-found nephew spending any more time under her roof. She had accepted, reluctantly, that he would have to be integrated into the family; her husband would insist on it, as he had never forgiven himself for what had happened to his sister, and that she would have no choice but to allow it, but she needed time, she said. The doctor could say what he wanted but she needed to get Josh back to Lytham, to get him stronger before she broke the news to him that this young man was his sister's child. It had been a terrible shock, one she would need time herself to get over but in the meantime she would appreciate it if he was got out of her sight as soon as possible, she told her son-in-law.

The carriage had been ordered and Michael Hayes, smoking one of the expensive cigars Ben had offered him and leaning back among the velvet-padded luxury of Nancy Hayes's splendid victoria, had waved a languid hand as it drove off down the drive. It was a low-built vehicle with an elegantly curved body and a small leather hood to protect a lady from a shower and as Ben watched him go he had the distinct impression that the young man had landed exactly where he had planned and exactly where he was meant to be.

"Shall I expect the carriage tomorrow, Mr Maddox?" he had asked Ben smilingly as he climbed into it. "Perhaps about eleven. That will give you all time to talk about me, and more to the point, decide what is to be done with me." His smile was charming.

They had dined splendidly as usual, though Cook said she didn't know which way to turn and how she could be expected to prepare anything like a decent meal with all that was going on in the house she didn't know. Tilly had told them of the identity of the young man who had brought Miss Kitty home, her face as white as Cook's apron. She had described in graphic detail what had happened in the drawing-room though they had heard Mrs Hayes's cries even through the closed doors. Tilly had been employed at Riverside House for over twenty years and, along with Cissie, who had then been scullery-maid, and Ivy, could remember that appalling day when the accident happened and now, it seemed, it had come back to haunt the poor master and mistress. What was to happen now, they asked one another and how, which was worse, would it affect the master who lay so poorly in his bed? An improvement, Miss Williams had been kind enough to tell them, but a long way from being recovered, and now this.

"Will you have another cup of coffee, Mrs Hayes?" Ben asked the silently staring figure of Nancy Hayes, his face concerned. Kitty couldn't get over how kind he was to everyone, even Freddy, who drifted about as though he couldn't get his bearings in this whole sorry mess. Even his wife was neglected as he wandered from here to there, staring out of the window at the darkness beyond, moving to the whatnot to finger a nymph or a shepherdess until Kitty irritably told him to stop fiddling about and sit down. It was bad enough without him sulking all over the place; after all, this was his fault.

No, not the revelation about Michael – at whose name she saw her mother wince – but his father's collapse and it was no good him looking indignant because he *was* to blame. It did occur to her that he was wondering how this sudden materialisation of a cousin whose existence they had been unaware of might affect *his* and his brother's inheritance. The business, which had been passed from father to son for several generations, would go to Freddy and Sebastian, with a settlement for herself and her sisters, she supposed, but now, with her father's nephew to consider, things would probably change and not in Freddy's favour.

As Freddy poured himself a brandy, taking it moodily to the window where he took up his position again, Ben assisted Ciara to a special chair that had been brought for her, since her back was aching, she complained, lowering her into it as though it were his child she carried. Anna and Marguerite were smiled at and fussed over, asked if they were warm enough and could he ring for the maid to bring Anna a warmer shawl since he had seen her shiver. Her Aunt Jennet, who clung to her mother like a limpet in her determination to give her comfort, was helped to coffee and sugar and cream and even, if she felt like it to warm her and steady her nerves, a drop of brandy. He was polite to Kitty, offering her a chair by the fire but apart from that he didn't speak to her. She could fend for herself, she supposed, which was understandable after the last year and the fragmentary lives they had lived at Meadow View. She wondered idly why, if that was how she looked at it, she should feel this need to . . . to what? Have him fuss round her as he did the other ladies? What nonsense, she told herself firmly, settling back in her chair and waiting for someone to say something.

At last her mother did, her voice soft and hesitant.

"I feel I ought to . . . to tell you something about the young man's father . . . and his mother. I don't know how much you already know."

"Dearest, don't upset yourself," Jennet begged her. "If you don't feel like it . . ."

Ben leaned forward again and took her hand, since he knew exactly what she was going to tell them. "Really, Mrs Hayes, Miss Williams is right. There is time enough for explanations later. Your husband seems to be improving."

Which was true. He and Kitty had been up to see him, propped as he was on a pile of pillows to aid him in his breathing. He had smiled and held out a thin hand to Kitty and she had taken it with strange gentleness, leaning to kiss his pale, unshaven cheek.

"Father . . ." Then she couldn't speak and, amazingly and just for a moment or two, her husband had taken her other hand and held it.

"It's all right, my lass. I'm not going for a while yet so there's no need for that long face."

"Oh, Father." She was unprepared for the flood of love that surged through the very bones of her for this man who she knew had not fathered her.

"Now then, Ben, take her downstairs and send my

wife up, will you? We've been married for twenty-two years nearly and I still can't bear her out of my sight."

"You're a fortunate man, sir."

"I know that, lad."

But now Nancy Hayes began to talk, a sort of vague, faraway kind of talking as though she existed on some level of consciousness that concentrated her thoughts and her voice into one narrow, backward-looking channel.

"We were poor – well, more than poor: destitute – when my mother left us, my sisters and me. I was nine. Mary and Rosie were younger. We starved for a while until I managed to get us a job at Monarch Mill."

She did not mention the heroic struggle she had, at the age when a child expects to be cherished by loving parents, just to keep herself and her sisters clean, never mind clothed and fed, when there was nothing but one water tap to be shared with dozens of other cottages in the alley where they lived.

"Yes," she went on vaguely, "your father's mill, but we worked hard bringing in enough wages to keep body and soul together. We did the work of grown women, as did many of the children but I didn't mind. We were independent. But I wanted more than that for me and my sisters so on a Sunday I took them off to Sunday school and we learned to read and write and add up. We spent our days, not in the street games the other children in Church Court played, but in the library getting ourselves an education. When the time came we moved on from the mill to a shirt factory, for

I had this idea that if I could go into business for myself we could better ourselves even more. But we needed to be taught how to sew, to make shirts and waistcoats and we did, thanks to my friend here." She turned and smiled at Jennet Williams. "Apart from when I met your father the day I first saw Jennet Williams was the best day of my life."

"Nancy . . ."

"Hush, you know it's true."

She looked away and stared into the fire which glowed softly on her pale face, giving her an appearance of ruddy health, putting a shadow on her scarred cheek.

"I also became . . . acquainted" – her voice suddenly hard and malevolent – "with a young man called . . . Michael O'Rourke. He was the one who gave me this," fingering the scar on her cheek. "He lived in Church Court and something in me caught his eye and he would not leave me alone. He was a big, handsome Irishman and believed that any girl would be overjoyed to have his attention and when he finally realised that I did not want him, he took me . . . by force."

Anna and Marguerite, who sat one on either side of Ben Maddox, recoiled as though a bullet had been fired into both their chests. They gasped in horror and at once Ben put his arms about them, holding them close, shushing them softly. Jennet held her friend's hand and gazed compassionately up into her face and Kitty wished with all her heart that it was she and not Anna or Marguerite who sat huddled against Ben Maddox's strong chest.

"You were born nine months later, Kitty, but as if that were not enough the beast turned his attentions to my sister Rose and you, Ciara, were the result."

She took a deep breath then let it out on a slow and gentle sigh. "But I had done well with my business. I had hired sewing-machines and . . . well, that is another story; and of course your father and I had met and married by then. We were very happy, the past not troubling us until . . . until Michael O'Rourke came back into our lives. He . . . well, there is no way to soften this tale. He made himself pleasant to your father's sister, Millicent. She thought he wanted to marry her, which he did until Josh told him there would be no money. He had . . . Dear God, this is hard, Jennet."

"I know, dearest, but it is almost done."

"Is it? Is it really? I don't think so. This man, this evil man who is father to Kitty and Ciara is also father to Michael Hayes."

There was a long terrible silence broken only by the heartbreaking sobs that came softly from Marguerite. They all waited for Nancy Hayes to finish her tragic tale. There was more to it, they knew that.

"When Josh told him he would get nothing if he married Millicent he, Mick O'Rourke, ran away down the garden. There had been a great deal of rain that week and when he was cornered by the men who had been told to see him off the premises . . . he slipped in the mud and into the floodwaters of the river. Millicent, who was clinging round his neck begging him to take him with her, went with him into the river and, worse than anything, Josh's younger brother Arthur valiantly jumped in to save her . . . and drowned too. They found his body, and Michael O'Rourke's, but not Millicent. It seems she survived, for that was her son we saw today. He does not need to prove it with documents, for he carries his father's face with him, as you do, Kitty. I am amazed that no one saw it. Even you, Ben, who are more discerning than many. The eyes, the hair, the smile . . ."

No wonder my mother does not like me, Kitty thought as she watched the calm, almost impassive expression that folded itself about her mother's face and figure. She has told her tale, it said, and so she had done her duty. She did not really care what the outcome would be, how it might affect her own children, one born out of wedlock and three in her marriage to Josh Hayes. Josh Hayes was all she cared about. They could all go and jump in the river, along with Arthur, if only her husband survived, even the three who were her husband's legitimate children. She would whisk him off to Lytham at the first opportunity and if she had her way would not even tell him about Michael Hayes. She would have to, of course, but if she could have kept it to herself and sworn her family to do the same, she would have done so.

Nancy stood up, smiling at Jennet with great affection as she let go of her hand. "Stay the night, dear, why don't you, or would you like Brewer to take you home?"

"I think I'll go home, dearest. Bridget will be wondering where I've got to."

"Of course. Anna, ring the bell, will you, darling. Now then, Jennet" – putting her arm through that of her friend and strolling with her towards the door – "will you come over in the morning? I would be glad of your support if I am to tell Josh. I fear it can't be put off; that's if the doctor agrees. I shan't have that man in my house, of course."

"Of course not, Nancy, but won't Josh want to . . ." The question was left delicately hanging in the air.

"See him?"

"I would have thought so."

"Well, perhaps when we get back to Lytham, but I will not have him here. This is my family's home, the home I came to when I was married and I will not have . . ." She could be heard talking softly to her friend as Tilly brought Jennet's cape, then opened the door to where the carriage waited for her on the drive.

Kitty sat on, waiting for whatever was to happen next. Her sisters had recovered somewhat from the shock of what their mother had told them, though they still clung like frightened children to Ben. Ciara sighed dramatically, for was she not the one who was to have a child and, in her opinion, deserved more in the way of attention from *somebody*. Freddy helped himself to another brandy and Kitty wondered why she had not noticed before how much weight he had put on since his marriage and how . . . flushed his face was. He didn't look happy, which she had put down to the guilt he felt over his father's illness, and then the shock about Michael, but somehow she thought it was something else entirely.

Her mother came back into the room and at once Ben stood up, moving towards her.

"Is there anything I – we – can do to help you, Mrs Hayes? Kitty and I will . . . will stay the night, if that is all right, just in case there might be . . ." His voice tapered off and it was very evident that he had no faith in Freddy's abilities in an emergency.

"Thank you, Ben. You are very kind, and of course you must stay. I'll tell Tilly to prepare a room for you but there is just one thing."

"Of course, you have only to ask."

"I'm going upstairs now." She turned enquiringly to Kitty who watched her with some surprise, for what on earth did her mother, who thought she was a wild and feckless child with no sense of responsibility, want from *her*?

"Would you play something, dear? Something tranquil, soothing, for your father to hear. You know how he loves your playing. We will leave the doors open for a while and it may help to get him off to sleep."

"Of course, Mother." She sprang to her feet and crossed to the piano. She opened the lid and sat down at the keyboard.

"I wonder . . ." she mused, flexing her hands and wrists, then, with an instinct that came from her love for her father she began to play a soft Brahms lullaby, the lovely music floating up to the ceiling and through it to where he lay.

* * *

"I won't trouble you for long," Ben said to her distantly as they shut the bedroom door behind them. It was a guest bedroom, large, comfortable and airy, dominated by the large double bed which had been turned down. A fire had been lit and the room was already warm but there was no warmth in Ben Maddox's heart, it seemed. "I'll give everyone time to settle down then I'll go."

"Where to?" she asked carelessly. "Not that I'm concerned, you understand, but my mother would be."

"Kitty, since when have your mother's feelings meant anything to you, or indeed anyone's." The words were spoken quietly and with little interest.

Where had that considerate man gone, the one who had been so kind to her mother and her sisters, to Jennet and even Ciara? This man was a stranger, aloof, polite, but uncaring as one might be with a passing acquaintance. He wandered to the window, twitching aside the heavy velvet curtains and peering into the darkness, giving an impression of a gentleman waiting as long as courtesy demanded before he left, which was exactly what he was. A courteous gentleman trapped for a moment with someone he barely knew.

"My mother would not notice if you slept on the rug outside her door she is so wrapped up in my father and his health, but the servants . . . ."

"Oh, come now, Kitty, the servants mean nothing to you and I must admit that personally it does not matter to me what they say, or what curiosity might be aroused by you and me sleeping apart, but I do not want to give your mother any more worry, about the state of *our* marriage, that is, than is necessary."

"I doubt she'd care. I have never been high on her list of concerns." Kitty flung herself into the chair by the fire, kicking off the house shoes she had put on when she arrived. They had none of them changed for dinner but she had been wearing tightly laced high boots for the journey which she had discarded. She pulled a small round pouffe covered with embroidered velvet towards her and put her feet on it, wiggling her toes in the warmth from the fire, unaware that her husband, who surely hated the sight of her, was watching her covertly from beneath his lashes. He had lit his inevitable cigar without asking her permission, which he had long giving up doing. It was clamped between his white teeth. His hands were thrust deep in his trouser pockets, his jacket was open and pushed back to reveal the immaculate whiteness of his shirt and he lounged gracefully against the window frame, one leg crossed over the other. His hair, which had an inclination to curl when he pushed his hand through its brushed smoothness, fell across his forehead in an untidy fringe.

The clock ticked and the fire crackled and the rosy glow from it whirled in swathes across the white ceiling. Ben tapped his foot irritably on the thick carpet, but he continued to watch her as she stared moodily into the flames of the fire. She looked unhappy, which was not unusual in the circumstances, he supposed, but there was a droop to the corners of her mouth, like that of a despondent child, which he found heart-rending. He supposed she was missing the excitement of the life she led. The attention of the gentlemen who admired her, and he wondered, with something like an arrow to the heart, how many of them she had slept with. How many had shared that slumbrous passion, that wanton loveliness, that enchanting sexuality that she had brought to their bed. How many had seen her as she was now, her face in repose, vulnerable, thoughtful, her mind dreaming of something she had never revealed to him. The firelight had turned her dark hair to coppery black, glossy and tumbled and touched her lips to a full poppy red. Her hands twined restlessly about one another and he had an overwhelming urge to go to her, kneel at her feet, take those hands in his and still their spasmodic plucking.

He made a harsh sound in his throat and she turned, startled.

"I'm off then," he told her curtly, straightening up and striding across the room. He didn't care who saw him leaving his wife's room at midnight, or where he ended up, for that matter, wishing he was in Liverpool and in the soft and comforting embrace of the ship owner's widow.

Ben spent the night in the drawing-room, stretched out on the sofa, not sleeping, for his wife's face kept painting itself on his closed eyelids. He kept the fire in, since the maid had left a scuttle full of coal. He smoked one cigar after another and drank nearly a bottle of brandy which had not the slightest effect on him. He was as sober when he got up as when he had lain down, but as the dawn began to skim a subtle pink glow on the rim of the earth he fell asleep. Even in sleep he couldn't escape her, dreaming that she was lying in the arms of another man who grinned at him over her bare shoulder.

This is how she is with me, the man said. She is not yours any longer and never will be, and he moaned in his dream, for he knew the man spoke the truth.

The maid who came to see to the fireplace and dust and clean the room was considerably startled, as he was, when he rose from the sofa.

"Oh, sir," she stammered, "I din't see yer there. I'm sorry, sir, I'll go an' . . . ."

He tried to escape from the depths of the dream which was still clear in his head, and still cut his heart to its core, smiling to allay the girl's fears, for though she knew him and who he was, her timid expression said she had never before spoken to the man who was Miss Kitty's husband.

"No, please, I beg of you, get on with your work, I'll go and . . ."

Where should he go? Where in this world was there to go to get away from the love he felt for his wife who did not return it and never would. Where should he spend the time until breakfast? Where should he wash and shave? It was perhaps these mundane, ordinary, everyday matters that brought him at last to his rueful senses.

He smiled at the little skivvy and she smiled back at him hesitantly.

"There wouldn't be a cup of tea brewed, would there? What is your name?"

She beamed, for he was saying something she understood.

"Mary, sir, an' I just this minnit put kettle on. D'yer want me ter fetch yer a cup?"

"I would be eternally grateful, Mary." And though she didn't understand the words Mary was made up with him.

She scuttled away, leaving her dustpan and bucket, telling him she'd not be but a minute and when she brought him the steaming cup of hot, strong tea liberally laced with sugar, which was how *she* liked it, she stood and watched him drink it with the greatest satisfaction.

"There is just one more thing, Mary." He smiled at her and she thought she had never seen such a lovely white smile.

"What, sir, another cuppa tea?"

"No, Mary, but I would be very grateful . . . pleased, if you'd mention this to no one."

"What, sir?"

"Finding me asleep here on the sofa. Can we keep it our secret?"

"Oh, sir . . ." she breathed and for the remainder of the day, though the rest of the household seemed to be draped in worry and sadness, she went about with a smile plastered to her face. Even when Cook asked her what the devil she was grinning at she didn't tell.

20

The next day was one of those winter days that are a blessing to the heart. The sky was an arch of azure blue, a blue that happens only when the air is so clear that if a swirl of starlings were to fly on the wing at a thousand feet every detail of their feathers would be discernible to the naked eye. A day so clear that a rabbit would be detected on the other side of a field, or a fox making its way back to its den after a night's feeding.

But there was nothing to be seen on the move. There was nothing in the sky, not a cloud nor a bird, just the ball of the sun which was a disc of golden rose above the bare, black outline of the trees. The intense cold during the night had laid a thick layer of hoar frost across the grass and every blade, every stalk, every quiet bush and tree stood like a white sentinel, diamond-draped where the sun lit it. The ground was rock hard and Mr Tinker, the gardener, and Archie, his lad, at Riverside House had given up trying to work outside on the brussels sprouts which were at their best, and gone off to the relative warmth of the greenhouse to have a look at Mr Tinker's infant bedding plants.

The grooms, Charlie and Richie, with Charlie's dog, Tizzy, who never left his master's heel and treated the horses with supreme indifference, stood in the stable door and scratched their heads, for should they bring their "beauties" out on such a cold day? It was a bit of a tricky one but they decided a good gallop round the paddock would do them no harm. Brewer, the coachman, whistled softly through his teeth as he curried one of the carriage horses, unaware that he was awaited impatiently by the young man he had driven to the hotel in Piccadilly the day before.

Michael Hayes arrived at Riverside House in a hired hansom cab, since no one had thought to send the carriage for him as he had requested. But then no one except Ben had known of the request and as Ben Maddox was a shrewd judge of character as well as being a shrewd businessman he had decided that until the young man had proved himself worthy of it by his actions, and entitled to it by birth, he was not to have the Hayes' privileges and the Hayes' wealth handed to him on a plate.

Michael was immaculately dressed in a knee-length double-fronted frock coat of black with black and grey striped trousers well fitted to his muscular legs. Over his shoulders he had slung a woollen chesterfield. He carried a top hat and a short cane. He looked exactly what he was, or what he imagined he was, a young gentleman about town, of the gentry class born and bred.

He was shown, as one would show a guest, into the drawing-room and told by the polite maid that she would see if the mistress was at home.

The mistress was at that precise moment up in the bedroom she shared with her husband, her husband's hand in hers, the doctor and Ben Maddox standing beside the bedside in readiness for whatever state he was flung into by the announcement that his sister's son had risen from the dead, so to speak. Doctor Croxley, pleased with Josh Hayes's improved condition after a peaceful night's sleep, had decided that his heart was sound enough to stand the shock, but had thought it prudent to have the obviously reliable gentleman who was Kitty Hayes's husband standing by to deal with Mrs Hayes should the news cause a relapse. He kept to himself the thought that it was a strange thing when the son-in-law and not the son of the family was considered the one to perform this duty but Mrs Hayes had asked for it and the doctor had agreed with her. Freddy Hayes was a nice chap, good-natured and eager to please but he was just not to be trusted in an emergency. He was likely to become as upset as Mrs Hayes and one needed a cool head in a crisis.

The room was warm, for warm air helped the patient, whose damaged lungs were fragile, to breathe more easily, a comfortable room, spacious and well furnished but there was an air of tension about it which manifested itself in the rigid stance of Ben Maddox, though he did his best not to show it, and the slow metronome ticking of the clock which seemed to herald the coming of something that the patient might not care for. Mrs Hayes wore a look of harrowed distress, though, like Ben, she did her best not to let her husband see it, only the doctor maintaining that air of detached kindness that is the hallmark of the profession. It would not do for a medical man to reveal his private worry, would it?

When Mr Hayes was told the news Doctor Croxley had thought for a terrible moment that his patient was about to have a heart attack, and then a stroke. His mouth fell open and he turned the most ghastly shade of mushroom. His eyes became a dead flat grey, losing all their bright intelligence, their humour, the warmth that he had always associated with the man who had been his patient for many years. His hands clutched his wife's in a grip of iron, afraid to let them go, since he might not get them back again and then where would he be his appalled expression seemed to ask? He appeared as if he were about to choke and Mrs Hayes surged forward, moaning his name, then, just as quickly, under his skin flowed a tide of red blood and dreadful sounds emerged from between his lips. He tried to speak but his words came out in what sounded like groans of anguish and the doctor moved closer to the bed.

"Josh, darling, I'm here . . . I'm here," Mrs Hayes began to babble and Doctor Croxley leaned over his patient, ready to take charge while at the same time Ben Maddox put a gentle restraining hand on Mrs Hayes's arm, for it did no good to have a fainting woman getting in the way.

"It's all right, old man," the doctor said calmly, "just take deep breaths. There's no need to speak just yet. It's a shock, but I made the decision that you were strong enough to stand it so don't let me down. That's it, deep breaths . . . calm breaths . . . good man. I'm going to give you a sip of something that will help but there's no need to speak. Your wife is here and so is Mr Maddox so you are in good hands." Gradually the swollen colour receded from the sick man's face and his breathing became easier. His eyes lost their blankness and filled with an expression of unbelieving wonder and his hand relaxed its grip on his wife's. He turned to look at her, then back to the doctor and Ben Maddox and he began to smile incredulously.

At last he spoke coherently. "I can't take it in. After all these years . . . we thought Milly was drowned."

"I know, darling, but it seems she wasn't."

"Why didn't she come home?" He shook his head in bewilderment, the movement kinking his grey hair up about his head on the pillow.

"We don't know, Josh, but I'm sure the . . . young man will tell us her story, and his. But not until you feel up to it, my love."

Nancy Hayes's voice was warm with the devotion she had for her husband but at the same time there was uncertainty in it. Josh Hayes caught it, for did he not love her with the same devotion she had for him? He knew her story. He knew her hatred for the man who had almost ruined not only her life, but her sister's and, in the end, had killed his own sister and, through his sister, his own younger brother. This could not be accepted with unconditional joy. Much as he longed to see his sister's boy, to welcome him back into the family that had been denied him for so long, and where he rightfully belonged, for the sake of that family he must go slowly. He was a good man and his first reaction had been an overwhelming gladness that something had been retrieved from the tragic events that had killed his sister and his brother; that in some way he could make it up to them by giving this unexpected new member of the family part of the inheritance that would have been theirs.

But his wife and his own children must be considered. That he owed something to this young man was undeniably true but he must not go blindly, emotionally rushing into what might have many pitfalls.

And the first was the question of Michael Hayes's true parentage. It was all very well Nancy saying that he was the double of Kitty, though not of Ciara who was fairer and whose eyes were a different shade of blue; enquiries must be made, not only of the young man, but of his past and the right man for that, the *only* man for that was his son-in-law, who had proved such a stalwart in this matter and whom Nancy seemed to trust implicitly.

"Shall I see him?" he asked somewhat tremulously, looking from one concerned face to the other, and it was plain that he was afraid.

Ben looked enquiringly at the doctor, raising his eyebrows.

Doctor Croxley considered his patient, pulling his lip indecisively. The draught he had given him had relaxed him. In fact he looked as though a good sleep might be in order before any new stress was foisted on him. Perhaps tomorrow when Mr Hayes should show even more improvement would be soon enough, though he knew Mr Hayes was very eager to see this unknown nephew of his.

He made his decision. "I think we might wait until tomorrow, old chap. You are improving nicely and by the end of the week should be able to make the journey to Lytham where, if I have anything to say about it, you will remain for the rest of the winter. If I see you in Manchester again I shall wash my hands of you. Now then, have a nap while your wife and Mr Maddox discuss what is the best thing to be done about your nephew. We will talk to him and explain the situation and then perhaps tomorrow, depending on how you are, we might let you see him."

It was as though, much as he wanted to see Milly's boy, if he *was* Milly's boy, Josh Hayes was relieved. He was tired and all he wanted at the moment was to have his wife's hand in his while he drifted off to sleep.

But there was one more thing that must be attended to. With an apology to his wife and the doctor, he beckoned Ben to remain in the room.

"Come closer, old chap," he murmured, as though afraid that they might be overheard. What Josh Hayes said to him was never revealed, except perhaps later to his wife, but when Ben came down the stairs to greet Michael Hayes there was an expression of satisfaction on his face.

Ben was as immaculately and correctly dressed as Michael Hayes. With the help of his little friend in the kitchen who was the only servant up at that time, he had been shown to a bathroom on the first floor where he had bathed and shaved and, finding his suitcase still in the room where he had spent the first night after the message came from Nancy Hayes, he had changed. No doubt last night when he had been given a bedroom which he was expected to share with Kitty his luggage had been overlooked. That was another difficulty to be got over. Somehow he had to make it known that he and his wife needed separate rooms, though it was going to be awkward, to say the least!

It was clear that Michael Hayes was somewhat put out at being kept waiting as though he were a casual caller. The maid had even left him with his hat and coat, as was the custom for someone who was not a close friend. He did not like it. He was a member of the family now, at least in his eyes, and should have been shown immediately into their midst but there was no one about except this poker-faced, keen-eyed man who had turned out to be Kitty's husband.

Nevertheless he rose to his feet politely, letting it be known that he was a gentleman and had the manners of one.

"Mr Hayes," Kitty's husband said pleasantly enough,

holding out his hand in a friendly but formal manner. "I'm sorry to have kept you waiting but the doctor has just been and I—"

"I'd like to see my uncle," Michael interrupted impatiently. "I think I have that right. I have been waiting."

Ben felt the antipathy grow in him as the young man bristled waspishly. It was not just that he did not trust this smooth chap who evidently thought himself already one of the family, but he was also a member of the "set" with whom Kitty spent so much time: the Olivers and their hard-drinking, hard-riding set whose wild reputation was trumpeted about Lancashire and which would undoubtedly rub off on Kitty, if it had not already done so. He didn't know, really, why it mattered to him, for he and Kitty, though they lived in the same house and shared the same name, were strangers to one another and did one concern oneself with a stranger? This jackanapes was part of that breed of drawling idlers living on their land rents and who had never, and *would* never do a hand's turn in their lives. They lived solely for pleasure, their own, and Ben Maddox despised them. He let it be seen in his contemptuous expression.

"Mr Hayes, you must appreciate that Mr Joshua Hayes has been ill and is not yet recovered enough to—"

"I will not disturb him for long."

"I'm afraid that won't be possible at the moment. The doctor has forbidden any excitement and has in fact given him a sleeping draught so—"

"Has *my uncle*," emphasising the last two words,

"been told of my existence? Or even that I am here? I don't think his wife was—"

Ben Maddox could be as hard and exacting as any man and Michael Hayes's constant and offensive interruptions were making him increasingly angry.

"Mr Hayes, I don't think you realise how ill Mr Josh Hayes has been." His feeling of animosity towards this young man made him stubbornly determined not to call Josh Hayes by the name of "uncle". His nephew he might be and his appearance seemed to bear it out, for his likeness to Kitty was very evident, but until he, Ben, had fulfilled his father-in-law's request to find out what he could about the lad he had no intention of treating him like some privileged member of the family, as Michael Hayes obviously thought was his due. For instance, why had it taken all these years for him to come forward? Why, as soon as he learned who he was, had he not come at once to claim kinship with the Hayes family? There was some mystery here that he, as well as Josh Hayes, who was no fool, wanted to solve and until then he was to be kept in line. His arrogance was an affront, though really, should he expect anything else from Kitty's half-brother?

"The shock of being told that his sister lived," he went on smoothly, "and not only lived but gave birth to a child, would be enough to distress the healthiest of men and Mr Hayes is not in the best of health. Perhaps if you were to call again tomorrow the doctor might give his permission for you—"

Again the young whippersnapper interrupted him.

"Then I'll have a word with Kitty, that is if you have no objection. She and I, as well as being related, are good friends. We have shared—"

"I don't know where my wife is at the moment, Mr Hayes," Ben said, his voice and temper only just under control. "She and her family" – of which you are not yet a part, his manner implied – "as you can imagine, are distressed and are seeing no one." He was sure that this was true of Anna and Marguerite who were the proper stuff of young, well-brought-up girls who knew the correct way to act in any given circumstance but he could not say the same about his wife. She might be out riding, for Josh Hayes kept a decent stable. She might be walking somewhere, perhaps down by the river, but he was pretty sure she wouldn't be moping about the house. Not Kitty. He had been told she had been in to see her father earlier in the day but her restless nature would have taken her somewhere she could exercise, work off whatever it was that drove her.

As though his thoughts had called her to him, Kitty strode into the room and at once her face lit up, not at the sight of him but of Michael Hayes. Ignoring him she slowed her pace, sauntering towards the handsome young man, shaking her head and beginning to smile. She was dressed for outdoors in a walking outfit of midnight-blue wool edged with pale-brown fur round the neck and the hem of the coat. She had sturdy boots on but no hat and her hair swirled in a bounce of glossy black curls about her head. With her came three dogs, a black labrador, a golden retriever and a black and white

English setter. They moved restlessly about the room, sniffing enquiringly at the legs of the two men. Ben bent to scratch their heads but Michael moved in a finicky fashion as though afraid they might deposit something offensive on his trousers.

Kitty appeared not to notice. "I've been for a walk with the dogs. It really is a splendid day, one just made for riding, don't you think? We went through the woods and then down to the river. It was glorious." And so was she with poppies in her cheeks and her eyes as blue and brilliant as gemstones and the truth of it was in the eyes of both the men who looked at her.

"But enough of that. I just can't believe it," she went on wonderingly. "That you and I are related, I mean. We talked of nothing else last night after you had gone and I didn't sleep a wink my mind was in such a whirl, though I must admit in certain quarters the fact of your existence was not well received. The girls, my sisters, who are typical of their class and upbringing—"

"*Kitty!*" Ben said warningly but she seemed to be unaware of his presence or, if she was, cared not a jot for it, or him.

"They will come round. You are such a charmer you won't be able to help themselves. You are related to them, of course, to Freddy and Sebastian, to me and Ciara. Isn't it a hoot? Honestly, if I'd known I had such a handsome brother I—"

"Kitty, this has gone far enough. We only have this young man's word that he is your father's nephew and until we—"

Kitty turned on him scornfully. "Stuff and nonsense. You only have to look at us together to know we are blood. God knows why nobody recognised it. Now, have you seen Father?" she said to Michael, taking his arm in a way that further infuriated Ben.

"No, this gentleman won't allow it."

Kitty turned and stared in amazement at her husband. "Won't allow it? And what, pray, is it to do with him?"

"It is not I who won't allow it," Ben said through clenched teeth, "but the doctor. If you have a word with your mother . . ."

"I shall, believe me. Now, Michael." Turning her back on Ben Maddox as though he were no more than a servant who had spoken out of turn, she drew Michael towards the door. "Let me ring for Tilly to get rid of your hat and coat and then you must come and meet my sisters and Freddy and his wife. Properly, I mean, and then I must have a word with Mother about putting you up. There is no need for you to stay in a hotel when we are—"

"Kitty, I must ask you to leave this alone. There are certain things that must be investigated."

"Investigated! What things?"

"He means me, Kitty-Cat. They don't believe I am who I say I am. Well, this chap doesn't, even though your mother recognised me at once last night."

Kitty turned again and looked at her husband with barely concealed dislike. Her lips curled so that the edge of her eye-teeth showed in what was almost a snarl.

"Goddammit to hell and back, Ben Maddox, what's

it to do with you?" She was incensed and her eyes narrowed hazardously as they swept up and down the length of his tall body as though assessing his fitness to be among decent people. "Who the hell d'you think you are, telling my family what they are, or are not to do? My father will be furious when he hears of your high-handed attitude with a man who is undoubtedly his nephew." The hot flare of her temper took her by surprise, though it did not seem to disturb the man who was her husband.

"Well, that remains to be seen. I think if you check with your mother, and your father's doctor, you will find that—"

"Will you stop drivelling on about—"

"Kitty."

A quiet voice from the doorway cut off the tirade that was just about to explode in earnest from Kitty Maddox. They all turned, Kitty and Michael and Ben, and at once Michael was the smooth, well-bred young gentleman in the presence of a lady, bowing his head and smiling.

Nancy's head moved a fraction in his direction, though her face was set in stony lines. She was dressed with her usual elegance in a soft, dove-grey gown of wool. Her hair, a riotous tumble of brown curls when it was let loose, was brushed smoothly into a meshed net of velvet. She held herself like a queen so that even Michael Hayes was momentarily hushed.

Not Kitty! "Mother, will you sort this out? I cannot believe that Ben is doing his best to keep Michael from seeing Father."

"That's right, Kitty. He is having no visitors at the moment—"

Michael broke in and even Kitty frowned a little at his rudeness.

"I am not a visitor, Aunt Nancy, I am—"

Nancy drew herself up, her face set and white as a marble bust, her eyes flashing and her mouth drawn into a hiss of anger.

"Don't you dare call me that, you insolent little sod." She had evidently dredged up the obscenity from what had once been a normal part of her childhood. "If you must address me my name is Mrs Hayes to you. You may, or may not be my husband's nephew but you are no relation to me."

"I am to your daughter, *Mrs Hayes*. She and I share a father and—"

Nancy Hayes, who had always been the epitome of a perfect lady to her daughter, again reverted to her early days when she had had to fight for not only her own existence, but for that of her two younger sisters.

"You may convince my husband that it is only fair to bring you into this family, since . . . I will admit you have a likeness for . . . for Kitty's father. I can even see Millicent Hayes . . . some expression she had, but let me tell you, you slimy little toad, she was as evil as Mick O'Rourke and though, if it is proven that you are who you say you are, I shall have to accept it for my husband's sake, I will make your life so bloody miserable—"

"*Mother*, please."

Nancy Hayes whirled to face her daughter, her face a livid scarlet and Ben Maddox could see why it was that Nancy Hayes had dragged herself from the gutter, as it seemed she had, to become the ladylike wife of one of Manchester's most prominent businessmen.

"Don't you 'mother' me, Kitty Maddox. You have no idea what this man's father did to me . . ."

"My father as well, Mother."

"True, and that is why I—"

"Why you've never liked me much, is that it, Mother?" Kitty's face was quite desolate and yet there was a look in her eyes that told Ben that she was not beaten, not even by what seemed to be her mother's dislike. She'd fought all her life for affection and though she'd had it from Josh Hayes, who was not even her father, his love had been much diluted by what he gave to his wife. She had clung to Freddy, believing that at last she had someone of her own but he had turned from her and chosen another woman. Her marriage to himself had been a disaster, due in no small part to her own wilfulness and so what was left to her but people like the Olivers, like this man who purported to be her half-brother. No wonder she was eager to cling to him; to have him recognised; to flaunt him about the county as her long-lost brother.

Nancy Hayes let her shoulders sag as though in great weariness and she looked her age all of a sudden. Ben wasn't sure what that was but she had always been a beautiful woman. Now she seemed haggard, lifeless, lost, even broken and he watched as Kitty moved a little as though she would go to her mother in comfort. But too much had been said. Too much withheld over the years and she stayed where she was.

"The doctor has said that perhaps tomorrow you may see my husband, Mr Hayes, so if you would call in the morning—"

"But, Mother, surely we can find a bed here for Michael? There is no need for him to go traipsing back into Manchester."

"Kitty, when will you learn to keep out of what does not concern you? This is my house, my home, and I shall say who is to be a guest in it. Michael Hayes is not one of them and if I have my way never will be. Your father may decide that this man is his sister's son but I will never, never accept him as a guest under my roof. Is that clear?"

"*Mother!*" Kitty's wail of dismay cut Ben to the heart but he held himself aloof. He liked Michael Hayes as little as did his mother-in-law.

"That is my final word. Now, if you will ring for Tilly to show Mr Hayes out I would be obliged. Lunch will be served in half an hour."

Nancy Hayes had made an enemy of her husband's nephew and, like his own dead mother, he was unforgiving of those who crossed him. She had not only crossed him, she had insulted him and he would not forget.

21

Joshua Hayes was many things to many people. He was a devoted husband whose love was returned a hundredfold by his wife. He was a kind father who was fond of his children, even his stepchildren, among whom he counted Kitty and Ciara though Ciara was child to neither him nor his wife. He was looked on as sharp-witted and experienced in his trade, which was cotton, a man who knew every job in his own mill, and could perform them all when he was younger. He was a decent employer, fair with his mill workers, indeed with all those who worked for him, including his servants at Riverside House. He was respected by every man with whom he did business, for he was honest and had integrity. He was well liked, though he had a reputation for being soft-hearted when faced with a cry for help.

But one thing he was not and that was a simpleton. He was not naïve enough to accept on blind faith that the young man who had presented himself as his sister's

son *was* his sister's son. Which was why he had sent Ben
Maddox to Rainshough to find out all he could about
Michael Hayes, as he called himself.

The village from which Michael Hayes said he came
was no more than a straggle of cottages, an ancient
church, a public house calling itself the George and
Dragon, all set about a small green on which a few geese
strutted. Though it was barely midday there was nobody
about, projecting a general air of desertion which was
not unexpected, for it was beginning to snow. Smoke
plumed from every chimney and lamps were already
lit, throwing out an orange glow which at least gave a
feeling of cheer in the dreary day.

It was a bit late in the year for snow, Brewer, the
Hayes coachman remarked as he huddled himself
deeper into his many-caped greatcoat, and after the
heavy frost they'd had the day before, too cold an' all.
Nevertheless, as Ben alighted at the George and Dragon,
for what better place to start with his enquiries than the
village public house, the few drifting snowflakes were
beginning to stick to the already frozen ground.

The locals, most of them farm labourers, hedgers
and cow men, making the most of the lousy weather,
were having a dinner-time pint and, since it looked as
though it was coming on to snow, had agreed with one
another that one more would not be out of order. Well,
you couldn't work in a bloody snowstorm, could you?

As one man they stopped talking and even drinking, turning to gaze in astonishment at the toff who
stepped smartly into the taproom. They stared at the

long box-coat he wore, the like of which they had seen only on the gentry in church, at the well-polished boots and the top hat he carried. What the devil was he doing here? their expressions asked. This was the haunt of the working man, a taproom with sawdust on the floor, a good fire halfway up the chimney, sturdy, well-polished farm tables and chairs to sit on, though most men crowded about the bar, so what could this gentleman be doing on their territory? They were tucking into pies, made by the landlord's wife, rich and juicy with meat and gravy, pickled eggs and onions, cheese and fresh baked bread, pease pudding and faggots, all good country fare which filled a man's belly at a cost he could afford. A barmaid, arms folded, leaned her capacious bosom on the bar, exchanging banter with a customer, but her mouth fell open as she gawped at the newcomer, and the landlord, if it was he, looked disapproving. This was not the sort of place where gentlemen drank and his regular customers might not like it, for it would inhibit their own enjoyment.

"Good morning," Ben said politely enough, nodding at the circle of faces that was turned to him. "A cold day," rubbing his hands together and sidling up to the fire where he stood with his back to the flames. They watched his every move.

"Mornin' sir," the landlord answered, for one did not speak rudely to a customer. "What'll it be?"

"I'll have a whisky, if I may, and perhaps one of your meat pies. They look and smell delicious."

"Right you are, sir. Will yer sit?"

"After I've warmed myself, thank you. Oh, and my coachman will be in in a minute. He's seeing to the horses. Serve him with what he wants, will you?"

"Right you are, sir." He raised his eyebrows at the barmaid who pulled a face.

Brewer, knowing his place, sat at the other end of the room to Ben and, recognising one of their own, the men there were soon engaged by him in conversation. Brewer was of farming stock and could talk of ploughing and planting, of calving and harvesting, of the price of seeds and the growing of potatoes, the weather and what a bugger it was at times and, having been primed by his master, was quickly becoming knowledgeable about the families, working class and gentry, who resided in and around Rainshough. He scoffed half a dozen of the pies, pleasing the landlord's wife, who liked a man with a decent appetite and especially one who appreciated her baking. He washed them down with half a dozen pints of good brown ale, which was potent stuff, with no apparent ill effects, earning the landlord's grudging respect.

The gentleman, a more dainty eater, the landlord noted, ate a meat pie and drank a couple of whiskies and seemed content to sit by the fire, gazing into the leaping flames and taking little notice of the rest of the taproom occupants. He even took out a newspaper and, shaking it out, began to read.

Gradually, though they were still curious, they became used to him, deciding he had come in for a warm in this mucky weather, and who could blame him? The general hubbub rose again.

The taproom emptied at last, leaving only Ben and Brewer and when Brewer stood up and sauntered across the room and sat down beside his master, the landlord and the barmaid, who was vigorously wiping the bar top, took little notice. They did not hear what the stranger's coachman said to the stranger and when Ben spoke up they were somewhat startled.

"I'm looking for Northwood House," he stated, his voice pleasant, his manner polite. "Is it anywhere near here?"

The landlord finished polishing the glass tankard he held, then replaced it carefully on its hook above the bar before answering with the countryman's deliberate and cautious manner, especially to a stranger.

"Aye, that's right." His voice was non-committal.

Ben smiled. "Does that mean it is or it isn't?"

"Well, that's not really—"

"Sir Algernon is a friend of mine but I seem to have lost the directions he gave me on how to reach his place."

"Well, sir, yer shoulda said." The landlord leaned on the bar, his manner confidential. "'Tis only on the edge o't village, so to speak, no more'n half a mile as crow flies, though yer not going by crow, are yer?" He laughed at his own joke and Ben smiled good-naturedly.

"Not in this weather. I doubt if even the crows have left their nests today."

They all looked towards the small, mullioned window, watching with varying degrees of interest as the snow whirled in a mad white dance past the glass, sticking here and there before sliding down to the sill where it had begun to collect.

"Aye, 'tis gonner be bad. Well, as I said, if yer take the first right up Peartree Lane, then go on fer about . . . oh, I dunno, 'ow long would yer say, Dolly? 'Alf a mile, yer'll come ter Northwood House. Yer can't miss it. Lane goes nowhere else."

"Thank you, landlord, but before I go could I trouble you for another whisky for myself and my coachman. To keep the cold out, and have one yourself."

"Well, that's right kindly of yer, sir, an' I will."

They were all sipping their whiskies, quiet and companionable, when the stranger spoke up again, his voice slow and musing.

"I was wondering whether Sir Algernon's son will be at home?"

At once the landlord slammed his whisky glass down on the bar top with a force that suggested it had offered him some unforgivable insult. His face turned purple and the barmaid, who was about to polish the already gleaming brass pumps, turned to look at Ben with consternation.

"Nay, don't mention that young bugger's name round 'ere, sir, if yer don't mind. That's if yer want ter gerrout alive. There's men round 'ere'd like ter see that little sod strung up, so they would. If yer a friend of 'is—"

"Believe me, landlord, I am not." Ben's voice was rock hard and something in it stopped the landlord's ranting, or what at least might have turned into something nasty.

"Well then, yer'd best gerrup ter Northwood House an' we'll say no more. That lad's name's like red rag to a bull in these parts, the randy little sod, an' after all what Sir Algernon an' Lady Northwood did fer 'im, an' 'is mam."

"His . . . mam?"

The landlord who had been just about to down the rest of his whisky turned to look suspiciously at Ben. "Aye, an' if yer a friend o' Sir Algy's yer'd know about that little runt's mam. So what's yer game, mister?"

"No game, sir. I am just attempting to find out something about a young man who has come into my life . . . my family's life before he does any damage. I must apologise for misleading you. It was an underhanded trick but this Michael Northwood, or Michael Hayes as he is now calling himself, is claiming . . . Well, it's a long story but I have been commissioned by my father-in-law to find out something about his background."

The landlord pulled his lip and stared broodingly at Ben as though weighing up the truth of his story, then, as it seemed to fit in with what *he* knew about the little sod he relaxed and leaned his forearms on the bar.

"What d'yer wanner know, sir?"

Ben's voice was crisp. "I don't want to trouble Sir Algernon and Lady Northwood, perhaps distress them further . . ."

"Yer'll not do that, sir. Leastways, not wi' Lady

Northwood. The poor soul died last back end, God rest 'er. Broke 'er 'eart, that little swine did."

"I'm sorry. I didn't mean to stir up . . . perhaps it's as well if I don't get to see Sir Algernon. As you may have guessed I don't really know him, only through—"

"That little bugger."

"Yes, I suppose so. So won't you tell me about that little bugger?"

It was well into the evening before Ben and Brewer got back to Riverside House. Though Rainshough was no more than five miles, if that, from Broughton, the snow had risen to blizzard-like proportions and the journey took twice as long coming back as it had done going. When the carriage drew up before the front door of the house the horses could barely walk they were so weighted down with snow and Brewer was no more than a large, shapeless, unrecognisable statue of white perched above them on his seat. Put a carrot in his face and he could have passed for a snowman, Tilly told them as she waited for him at the back door where Mr Maddox had directed him. Charlie and Richie took immediate charge of the horses, clucking and soothing them as they were led into their stable while Brewer staggered to the back door of the kitchen. He was almost blinded, his eyebrows bearing a shelf-like layer of snow which had frozen, even his moustache hidden beneath a covering of frozen white. He was barely able to speak, merely repeating in a hoarse whisper, "Christ . . . Mrs Hodges . . . Christ," as the women took him into their sympathetic charge. His clothes were frozen and stiff and they had to bang at him with the carpet beater to loosen it, poor devil, and when, finally, they had him down to his combinations – and hang the immodesty of it – he could do no more than hunch over the kitchen fire with Mrs Hodges's warm shawl about his shoulders and shiver uncontrollably, barely able to hold the mug of hot tea laced with whisky she thrust into his hands.

Ben Maddox had fared better, since he was protected inside the carriage but he was so cold Nancy ordered Dulcie to run him a hot bath. An enormous fire blazed in his room – not the one in which her daughter slept – since his mother-in-law was aware by now that Ben and her daughter had not shared a bed the night before. He lay in the bath which he kept topping up with hot water, drinking a whisky toddy, drowsily wondering how he and Brewer would get through the rest of the evening without blundering into a drunken sleep! He had lost count of how many whiskies he had downed! And how was he to tell Josh Hayes what a bastard, in every sense of the word, his nephew was?

It was an hour later. He had eaten the food sent up to him and when he presented himself at Josh Hayes's bedside he was dressed casually in an open-necked shirt and warm woollen jumper, a tweed jacket and cord breeches tucked into his riding boots. He could hear voices in the drawing-room and the sound of his wife's laughter and the thought went bitterly through his head that she would laugh when the trumpet of death sounded! Then just as he was striding along the top hallway Kitty began to play what he thought might be a little lullaby by Brahms. She softly played a few bars of the melody, her laughter gone, the sound of the music strangely haunting and sad. Her mood seemed to have changed from one moment to the next, from merriment to melancholy and her fingers fell with compassion on the keys. He felt himself hesitate, wanting to stop and listen to her. It was the only time his wife was gentle, tamed, the wildness, the recklessness gone, although he had heard her play some fierce things, strident even, but not like this and he knew she was playing for her father. It was as though only when her fingers were on the keys and her mind lost in the beauty of the music, did she lose her mad need to defy all that she had been brought up to believe – though she had taken no notice – was the correct way to be.

He knocked at his father-in-law's door and when it was opened Nancy Hayes stood there, smiling a little. Her face was still pale, strained, but calm, for it seemed her husband had spent a peaceful day and the doctor had given his permission for him to be told the truth, whatever it might be, about his sister's boy.

Josh was propped up against his pillows, a slight flush reddening his cheeks but his intelligent eyes were keen and it was evident he was eager to hear what his son-in-law had to tell him.

Ben took a deep breath, then let it out slowly and as he did so he saw the hopeful anticipation leave his father-in-law's face. Josh's shoulders slumped and he sighed sadly. He turned to his wife and took her hand, his face losing the little improvement that had glowed there.

"It's not good news, is it, lad?" he said quietly. "I can tell by your expression."

"No, sir, I'm sorry, it's not."

"Out with it then."

"There's no doubt he is who he says he is."

"Dear God, I knew it. He is so like his father," Nancy moaned, rotating on her heel to stare into the bed hangings and at once her husband turned to her in concern, patting her hand before returning his gaze to Ben.

"Yes. Though it is many years since, they remembered the day. I was told that they . . . some farm labourers working in a field beside the river found your sister, sir. She was in a bad way, half drowned and . . . well, they took her to the nearest house which was Northwood House, the home of Sir Algernon Northwood. He and his wife brought in a doctor and a nurse and looked after her devotedly. Apparently they are known for their charity. Eventually, though she was half demented, so the story goes, she gave birth to a boy."

"Michael?"

"So it would seem. But she . . . she never recovered. She was an invalid, her mind affected by what she had suffered."

"Oh, dear God . . ."

"Josh, darling, you are not to blame yourself. You did not—"

"I know, but if she had just come home we might . . ."

"No, no. Please don't upset yourself."

Josh Hayes threw his head back on the pillows, his throat muscles working, his face anguished. He clung to his wife and Ben had time to wonder how a man, or a woman for that matter, came to rely so totally on another human being.

Josh pulled himself together with a superhuman effort then turned back to his son-in-law.

"There's more, isn't there, Ben?"

"Yes, sir."

"Go on, let's get it over."

"The boy was wild and . . . well, not to put too fine a point on it: bad. The Northwoods brought him up; they had no children of their own and they doted on him, and, from what I hear, ruined him. He was to be their heir. Not to the title, of course, but to the estate. His mother had died when he was young and her death seemed to drive him over the edge. He had always been intractable but his mother's death made him worse. They sent him to school in the hope that a bit of discipline would do him good but he was expelled. Even at fourteen he was bad, with women, gambling . . ."

"Sweet Jesus, was there not a drop of Hayes blood in him?" Josh moaned, putting his hand to his eyes. "My mother was the sweetest, kindest—"

"As was Arthur and you as well, Josh," Nancy said, doing her best to comfort her distraught husband.

Ben knew he had to go on. He could not let Josh

Hayes sink into a pit of despair and self-flagellation but he must be told the truth, for if this young man had no check put on him he could do untold damage to this family. In his opinion he should be disowned, turned away from their door and left to drive himself on the destructive road he seemed to have chosen. But somehow he had the most awful dragging feeling that it would not happen. Josh Hayes was a decent man who held himself responsible for his family and was not this young bastard his own sister's child? But he must go on, for there was more.

"His stepparents did their best but they were elderly and had no control over him. He got a girl, a farmer's daughter, into trouble and they took care of it, but when he seduced the young daughter – fifteen she was – of a prominent family, friends of the Northwoods, then refused to marry her saying she . . . she was . . . I'm sorry, I cannot repeat what he said of her, they gave up. They turned him out and he went, taking a great deal of money with him, stolen from his stepfather. They say the scandal killed Lady Northwood."

There was a long and dreadful silence. From downstairs came the strain of some light air. Ben did not recognise it since he knew little of music but in the room there was nothing but heaviness.

At last Joshua Hayes spoke and the words surprised neither Nancy Hayes nor Ben Maddox.

"Despite all you have told me, Ben, and I thank you for your trouble and your truthfulness, I must see him."

"No . . . no, Josh, please, I beg you," his wife pleaded. "He'll bring nothing but trouble, you know he will."

"We don't know that, dearest. The lad has had no proper home influence; with his own family, I mean, and perhaps if he had a job . . . He might be a great help to Freddy."

"Josh, he is Michael O'Rourke's son. You know what his father did to me and—"

"Kitty is also O'Rourke's child, darling, as is Ciara."

"And they both have some . . . weakness in them, you know that."

"But not badness, Nancy, and perhaps with a loving family about him . . ."

"This is because of Milly and Arthur, isn't it?" Nancy asked bitterly. "To make up for what happened to them."

"Well, in a way, I suppose it is, but we must give the lad a chance, don't you see?"

Ben shifted uneasily and they both turned strained faces towards him.

"Sir, if you take my advice you'll have nothing to do with this young man. There seems to be no doubt he is your nephew and I suspect he will produce some document to prove it. Perhaps a birth certificate. We know now why he did not come to you before. He was expecting a great inheritance from his stepfather and he did not need you. But since then why has he been knocking about with the Olivers and their set? He actually came to Freddy and Ciara's wedding but did not make himself known to you. He is clever, devious, and

I suspect that he kept out of the way of anyone – you, Mrs Hayes – who might recognise him, while he had a look round to see what the situation was here. Was there wealth? for instance. Was it worth his while insinuating himself?"

"Hey, steady on, lad, he is my nephew," Josh said stoutly, squaring his shoulders. And with those words both Nancy Hayes and Ben Maddox knew that whatever they said Josh Hayes was determined to give his nephew the chance he thought he deserved.

The blizzard which raged for twenty-four hours gave Josh Hayes and Ben Maddox, who was determined to try and change his father-in-law's mind, a breathing space, for there was no way for Michael Hayes to get from his hotel in Manchester to Riverside House. Bury New Road and indeed all the streets leading from the city were blocked with four feet of snow which had drifted against walls and buildings to a height of six or eight feet. Broughton and all the outlying suburbs were cut off, trams were snowed up in their depots, milk was not delivered, for it was impossible to get the floats out of their sheds, let alone deliver milk, which they hadn't got anyway since the farmers, after milking their beasts, had no choice but to pour it down the drain. Fortunately Mrs Hodges had a store-room bursting with food, cured hams and bacon and fowl, vegetables and fruit tarts which Mrs Bright made from the fruit Mr Tinker struggled to deliver to the kitchen door.

Ben thought he would go mad, cooped up in the

house with the Hayes family, for though he was fond of Anna and Marguerite, they were just children to him even though Anna was eighteen. Freddy, whom he had known at school, was younger than him too, and not just in years. His marriage seemed to have unmanned him, if such a thing could happen to a man whose wife was to give birth any day now, by the size of her. He hung about his wife's skirts and seemed incapable of holding a conversation with anyone but her. And Ciara appeared to have no interest nor concern for anything but her own state and her impending ordeal which she talked of at great length. That is until Kitty turned on her and told her if she didn't stop drivelling on about it she'd hit her.

Ben was worried about his own business. What he had come to do here was done. There was nothing else to be said, it seemed, for Josh Hayes was bent on at least *seeing* his nephew and nothing Ben or Nancy could say would change his mind. There was nothing to keep him at Riverside House now. As soon as the snow had gone Joshua and Nancy were to take the train to Lytham where, Josh said gravely, he hoped Michael might visit them and they could discuss what needed to be discussed.

Ben was in the library, a two-day-old *Times* in his hand, reading it for the second time and wondering what the hell to do with himself when, glancing through the window, he saw that the outside men were getting ready to clear a path down to the gates. The sun shone on the breathtaking beauty of the white, umber-shadowed garden. Every tree stood sharp against the clear azure sky, their branches heavy with a patina of glittering ivory scattered with sequins. The rolling lawns rippled with crisp, untouched snow and the plants stood frozen in pearl and silver. Squirrels who should have been hibernating, looking for nuts, scampered along the branches of the trees, scattering little puffs of snow like smoke.

It was unbelievably beautiful but as he watched the men tramped across its purity, spades over their shoulders, their breath wreathing like smoke about their capped heads, their cheerful voices splintering the enchantment of it all. They had the dogs with them, the three of them floundering comically through the snow which was as deep as their large bodies.

He smiled. Then, as he was about to return to his newspaper the figure of his wife came round the corner, just as comically floundering in the deep snow. He could hear her voice, though not what she said, and her high laughter. The dogs turned as one and began to lollop across the lawn to her and before she could set herself they had her down in the snow. She was dressed in a serviceable skirt of wool and a three-quarter-length coat. A bright red scarf was fastened about her neck and on her head she had a tam-o'-shanter of the same colour. She wore stout boots and a pair of leather gloves. She looked quite glorious, the colour the cold had put in her cheeks as bright as poppies.

He sighed in exasperation, for wasn't it just like Kitty to get involved, and yet at the same time he could not help but smile. How she loved *fun*. It didn't matter what sort of fun; if it smacked of a good time, Kitty was all for it. She struggled to her feet, shouting something to the men who waved to her, then she was down again as the black labrador reared up against her.

He didn't know why he did it. He didn't even think as he raced towards the small panelled hallway that led to the side entrance. There was a stand there, as he remembered, which contained oilskins, weather coats, riding crops, walking sticks and several sizes of wellington boots. Shrugging himself into a coat and finding a pair of boots that fitted him, he opened the door and stepped out into the magical fairyland of the garden. It must have been magic that made him do it, he decided afterwards. Moving round to the front of the house he was in time to see Kitty staggering under the impact of the retriever this time.

"Can anyone join in?" he shouted, bending down to mould a handful of snow into a snowball.

She turned, her mouth open in amazement and when the snowball hit her in the chest she began to laugh.

"You devil, I'll get you for that one. See, Jess, go for him, girl, and you, Holly." Then, scooping up the snow into a snowball, flung it at him just as the dogs struck him. He was on his back when she reached him, the dogs beginning to bark with excitement, all three snapping at the snow she was throwing at him.

The noise, not just of the dogs, but of Kitty and Ben Maddox, who rarely spoke to one another, shrieking with laughter, brought Freddy and Ciara to the window of their upstairs sitting-room and Anna and Marguerite, with their mother beside them, to the window of their parents' bedroom. Ben was begging Kitty for mercy as she stuffed snow down his collar, his arms up to defend himself and when he put them round her, pulling her down on top of him, then kissed her soundly, they were all open-mouthed with astonishment.

They were even more bewildered when Kitty sprang to her feet and, hurrying as best she could, disappeared round the corner of the house.

22

To say she was startled by the kiss was a massive understatement. It took her breath away, and her wits, and for several seconds she lay on his chest looking down into his eyes, so deep and velvety a brown, so filled with an enigmatic expression that she was unable to read, she felt paralysed by it. The whole incident with the dogs and the snowballs had probably lasted for no more than five minutes. The kiss and that exchange of incredulous glances, incredulous at least on her part, for no more than five seconds but those five seconds had seemed so absolutely right, so amazingly natural, she could feel even now as she ran away from it and away from him, a smoothness of something sweet run through her veins like warm honey. How ridiculous! How absolutely damned ridiculous! she said to herself, her breath fast in her throat, her heart thudding in her breast, her booted feet making slow progress in the softness of the deep snow. As she floundered towards the side entrance her thoughts were considering every moment from the one when she had turned to catch the full force of the snowball he had thrown in her chest; to the grin of boyish glee on his face; to his laughing words winging across the undulating quilt of snow; his shout of laughter at her astonishment.

"Can anyone join in?" he had asked and then proceeded to do so, not waiting for her permission as though sensing it were not needed, and without a moment's hesitation, totally forgetting the gulf that had yawned between them for months, she had responded with a spontaneity which, now she thought about it, astounded her.

What the devil had she been thinking about? she asked herself furiously as she flung open the side door, crashing it against the wall and then closing it to behind her with the force of a tornado before racing up the hallway towards the stairs. Snow from her boots left slushy imprints on the linoleum and she almost slipped as she flung herself at the bottom step of the staircase. Dammit, they had barely exchanged a word since last May when she had taunted him about her new friends and he had hit her, and then . . . of course . . . how could she forget what followed? She had hated him for the humiliation she had suffered at his hands but for the sake of the servants, the family, and the appearance of marital harmony which was required in their class and which Ben seemed willing to keep up, despite their separate lives, they had stumbled on together.

She had the Olivers and the others, Clive and

Elizabeth Barrie, Roger and Caroline Norris, Harry and George and Charles and Grace and the rest and Michael, of course, all the people with whom she had shared the thrill of the hunting field, the bay of the hounds, the huntsman's horn and the thunder of hooves. She had joined the shoot with them on the "Friday to Mondays" to which she was invited, revelling in the crack of the guns on the grouse moor, the pheasant drives, and all the other autumn and winter sports they seemed to thrive on, as she did. Before her father's collapse and her sudden summons to Riverside House they had begged her to join them in Scotland, an invitation to which she must give careful consideration, since the Olivers would be there, among others.

There was the unfortunate incident in nanny's room at Brook Hall which must be considered. Was she to treat it as an insult to her as a lady and therefore never to be forgiven, or was she to pretend it had all been a big joke, one of Tam's whimsical nonsenses and therefore to be laughed at and forgotten? She knew it would have to be faced up to, and resolved. It had been a serious mistake on her part, since she should have read the signals correctly instead of believing it to be no more than a bit of fun. An acceptable flirtation, one of those that went on all the time in their circle. Well, she knew better now, and Tam must be made to see he should look elsewhere if he wanted what he had wanted on the night of the party. And he must be made aware of it before she went to Scotland where they were to hunt the stag. The journey would mean a couple of weeks away from Meadow View. She was looking forward to it, especially after what had happened this morning. Ben would not miss her. He had his own amusements and . . . well, whatever it was he did without her: she suspected another woman, for Ben was a virile man. They had fallen into a pattern that suited them both, hadn't they? Neither questioned the other about their pastimes or whereabouts. Neither cared what the other did, or so she told herself, and now in the time it takes to blink an eye he had impulsively put his arms about her and his lips on hers and she didn't know how it had happened.

Emma nearly jumped out of her skin as her mistress flung herself into the bedroom, showering wet snow all over the carpet, and once again crashed the door to behind her. Emma had one of Mrs Maddox's petticoats in a froth of lace and white lawn on her knee and was placidly putting a stitch or two in the hem where the frill had come loose. She was sitting before the fire in the low chair, a button-back sewing chair with no arms especially designed for the purpose. Apart from the anxiety of Mr Hayes's illness Emma was quite enjoying her stay at Riverside House where the Hayes family resided. The servants accepted her. They liked to gossip. Who was walking out with who in the big houses of Broughton. Innocuous chatter about the two young ladies of the house who were of marriageable age and who were both attractive, well dowered, well educated – as far as young ladies of their class were – and brought up to be the proper wives of the many young gentlemen who had begun to come courting. The excitement of the forthcoming birth of an infant to Mr Freddy and Miss Ciara, as she was still called despite her wedded state, for it would be a joy to have a child in the house again. They sat round the kitchen table and drank tea when their day's work was done and told her about Master Sebastian's achievements at school, about all the doings of the family and she had relished it. It was like having a holiday, she told them, if it wasn't for Mr Hayes's illness, she added hastily, guiltily.

"Oh, madam!" she said now, putting her hand to her breast as her mistress erupted into the room. "You didn't half startle me." She stood up respectfully, folding the petticoat and laying it on the small table beside her. What the dickens was up now? was her first thought, for Mrs Maddox never did things by half and everything that happened to her had the proportions of a minor hurricane, which was how she had stormed into the room.

"Dear God . . . Dear good God," Kitty hissed through clenched teeth, striding from the door to the fireplace where she kicked the coal scuttle in temper.

"Pardon, madam!" Emma almost stumbled over a footstool in her haste to get out of the way of the virago who was her mistress. Mrs Maddox looked as though she might not only kick the coal scuttle but land a fourpenny one on Emma.

"The bloody nerve of the man," Kitty went on, spluttering and scarlet with fury. "After all this time and after what happened before, he has the effrontery to attack me again and with a dozen gawping men watching with great interest. Probably thinking it a huge joke and running off to spread it round the servants hall at this very moment. I'll never forgive him, Emma, never. To show me up like that is beyond belief. Has he no restraint, no shame? Dear heaven, I could strangle him, really I could."

"Who?" Emma managed to warble but Kitty was past answering a reasonable question. She feverishly began to unbutton her coat which she threw in the general direction of Emma who managed to catch it before it hit the carpet. Her tam-o'-shanter was next then she began to tug and swear at her bright red scarf as it became entangled round her neck.

"Let me, Mrs Maddox," Emma said, the coat over one arm, moving to help with the unravelling of the scarf but Kitty Maddox was struggling with something inside her that made her want to hit out and poor Emma had her hands slapped down for her pains. Again she backed diplomatically away from her mistress's temper.

"And that's another thing," Kitty spat out, her eyes accusing as though Emma were guilty of some grave offence. "I just cannot abide being called 'madam' or 'Mrs Maddox'. D'you hear me, Emma, and if you call me either again I shall dispense with your services. My name is Kitty and I would be obliged if you would address me as such."

Emma's jaw dropped. She couldn't keep up with this hopping from one thing to another which took place in her mistress's head. She knew something had happened in the short time Mrs Maddox had been outside, something that sounded as if it were to do with Mr Maddox, but really, what next. Call her *Kitty*! Emma was deeply shocked and it showed on her face. Confusion chased shock, and disbelief chased confusion to be followed by a stern expression which displayed itself in a lift of the head, something like Kitty's own imperious gesture, a slight narrowing of the eyes and a pressing together of the lips into a firm, thin line.

Kitty recognised it at once. Kitty had often thought that the reason she and Emma got on so well was that Emma, though obedient and respectful, could only be pushed so far. When it happened her sound common sense and strength of will broke through those layers of obedience to which she had been trained since the age of twelve, and even before by her mother. When she decided that enough was enough, that Mrs Maddox was being a fool, that she was being totally irresponsible and needed a jerk on the reins like an unbroken colt, she was quite capable of giving Kitty a piece of her mind. Tactfully, of course, since they were mistress and servant but nevertheless she made her opinions known. She was honest and loyal and Kitty, who had known no friend unless you counted Freddy, admitted that she respected her, that she was fond of her and that Emma returned the feeling. But for Emma she might not have survived the traumas of the past year. But for Emma she would have had no receptacle for the outpourings, much of it angry, of her heart. But for Emma she would have had no one to laugh with, to share the often acerbic, sometimes ribald but always humorous comments and observations she made on the subject of her new friends. For despite her gladness that they accepted, even admired her, she had no illusions about their airs and graces and their positive belief that there was no one quite so grand as they were.

"Well, Emma, you evidently have something you wish to say," Kitty remarked tartly, putting on an imperious air to match Emma's, which she knew did not impress Emma one bit, "so out with it."

"Indeed I have, madam, and if you wish to do so you must fire me but I can't call you by your first name as though you an' me were equals."

"Piffle."

"No, not piffle, Mrs Maddox. You are mistress of Meadow View, wife of a well-known businessman and I am your servant. My pa is a farm labourer an' yours owns a mill with goodness knows how many folk workin' for him. My mam does a bit of sewin' and yours is a lady and mistress."

"She wasn't always."

"I know nothing of that, Mrs Maddox," Emma retorted primly, "but she is now. We come of working-class stock and you're gentry."

"What rubbish!"

"No, it's not rubbish and anyroad, what would the others think if they heard me calling you by your first name?"

"The others?"

"You know who I mean, madam."

"I can't say I do, Emma."

"Give over. At least be honest."

"The other servants I suppose you mean?" Kitty waved her hand airily, then wandered to the window to peer into the garden where, it seemed, judging by the cascade of drips that was falling from the roof gutter, the snow was beginning to thaw. The men were still making a pathway to the gate, though from the look of it it wouldn't be needed if the thaw set in, and the dogs were bounding about, chasing every spadeful of snow the men threw to one side. Of her husband there was no sign.

"Aye, the other servants. A right fool they'd think me, an' gettin' above meself, an' all, if I was to—"

Kitty sighed dramatically, cutting through Emma's remonstrances.

"I suppose you're right."

"I am, an' you know I'm right. Anyroad, what brought this on?"

Kitty was aware that while she was arguing with Emma, and over such a silly thing, she was shoving to the back of her mind the strange event that had taken place in the garden, but it wouldn't do. She must face it and who better to face it with her than Emma?

"It's him," she said abruptly.

"Oh, aye." Emma knew exactly who the "him" was by the scathing tone in her mistress's voice. "An' what's he done now?"

"He . . . threw a snowball at me."

"Dear heaven, is that all?" Emma sighed just as dramatically as her mistress, casting her eyes heavenwards as though at the antics of a naughty child. What a storm in a teacup, her attitude seemed to say, but she was caught unawares by the soft, almost wistful note in her mistress's voice.

"And . . . he kissed me."

Great God, as her old pa used to say, what now? These two who were her master and mistress seemed to be always at odds with one another, and though, naturally, she never heard *his* side she had seen the way he looked at her mistress when he thought no one was watching him. They hated each other, or so they would have her believe, since she was the one who had listened to it, to the shrieks of rage and roars of anger, though come to think of it, they must have heard it in the kitchens and drawn their own conclusions. She it was who mopped up the mess after some catastrophe laid waste to their relationship. She was the one who had nursed her mistress when she came off that horse, when she had sported that black eye, had kept the questions from the other servants at bay, who had accompanied her on her wild adventures with those hunting friends of hers. She wasn't daft, or blind, and had seen how it was with that Mr Oliver who lusted, there was no other word for it, after Mrs Maddox. Aye, she saw it all, and more besides but she kept that to herself.

"Well, that doesn't seem so bad," she said delicately.

"But I don't know why, Emma. For weeks, months,

he has kept his distance. He even refused to share my bed, as you well know, when we came here."

"Aye, lass, I know that, but happen there was a reason."

"What reason, Emma?" Kitty turned imploringly to Emma, her face strained with some emotion Emma wondered at. "I would not have refused him. For the sake of the family, of course," she added hastily, "but just for a couple of nights we might have, could have, managed."

"He didn't know that, madam."

"For the love of God, will you call me Kitty?" Kitty's voice was high and sharp and for a moment Emma feared there would be hysterics, the mistress was so wound up. "We are friends. I . . . I reveal to you all the . . . all my innermost feelings and you will insist—"

"I'll call you Miss Kitty, then, as the servants do here. Will that do?"

"I suppose so. It's better than madam."

"Very well, Miss Kitty. Oh, for dear's sake, won't you sit down. You make me dizzy with your jittering about."

Kitty turned in amazement, staring at Emma who had herself sat down again in the sewing chair and taken up the petticoat. Her face was a picture and Emma, after threading her needle, began to smile, then to laugh.

"If you could see your face, madam . . . I'm sorry, Miss Kitty. But if you an' me are to be real friends then I must say what I mean. I promise to treat you with the respect you deserve if you'll do the same for me."

"Well, Emma Taylor, I've never been spoken to—"

"You can't have it both ways, Miss Kitty. I'm your maid and I shall continue to be your maid but if you want to confide in me as a friend, as you have done in the past, you know you have, then you must be prepared for a bit of give and take. At least in private. And that's another thing, I'll not address you as Miss Kitty in front of the others so if you expect me to you can forget it. Give me the sack if you must, but that's the way it's to be."

Kitty closed her mouth, then opened it wide and began to laugh, a long peal of merriment that her husband heard with astonishment as he passed her bedroom door on his way to his own.

Joshua Hayes was still in bed, he and his wife having breakfasted together from a small table set by his bedside, transferred from a tray that Tilly had brought up from the kitchen an hour since.

With the privilege of an old and trusted servant she began to speak before the table was even laid. "Now Mrs Bright ses she don't want to see a scrap left, sir, if yer don't mind. Mr Tinker fetched those peaches over and says ter tell yer they're straight from the hothouse this morning. And Cook's made the porridge with cream and yer not to argue but to eat it all up. If it were up to her and her cooking she'd have you out of that bed before the week's end, sir, an' no mistake. Now will I pour your coffee, Mr Hayes? Oh, I forgot, Mrs Bright ses yer to drink that milk . . ."

"Tilly, Tilly . . ." Josh Hayes held up his hands in

laughing supplication. He had had another peaceful night with the help of the draught the doctor had given him and his chest was less wheezy. He had managed to shave himself this morning with a bit of tender help from his wife and was beginning to look more his old self, Tilly thought. She'd had strict instructions to report back to the kitchen, for they were all very fond of Mr Hayes and they'd be right glad he was picking up. As long as that handsome lad didn't upset him again, the one who had turned up with Miss Kitty and who, amazingly, was supposed to be the son of Miss Milly who'd drowned years back and who'd been a right bitch if ever there was one. If it hadn't been so sad and so crushing a blow to Mr Hayes they might all have said "good riddance" at the time, though not to Mr Arthur who'd been another one such as Mr Hayes, kind and . . . well, soft-hearted, she supposed they'd call him. A lovely chap was Mr Hayes, like his mother who'd been the kindest mistress anyone could hope to work for, and they all hoped that Miss Kitty's husband, who seemed to have a bit of something about him, would deal with this lad, whoever he was, and save Mr Hayes the worry of it.

It was Tilly who answered the door bell an hour later. The snow had thawed during the night, leaving great sweeps of mucky grey slush at the side of the drive and in untidy heaps on the lawn. The bushes and shrubs poked their heads through the deeper snow which still lurked at the edge of the woodland and a few trees retained a sliver of melting white along their broad branches. Mr Tinker and Archie, with the help of a couple of the stable lads who had already cleared the stable yard, were setting the garden to rights and in a patch of pale sunlight were to be seen exclaiming over the golden heads of new blooming crocus.

The four of them turned to stare unobtrusively at the cab as it disgorged its occupant, nudging one another, for wasn't it that young chap who claimed he was kin to the family? Good-looking fellow and when you had a close look at him you could see the likeness to Miss Kitty.

Tilly's face, as though she knew there was going to be trouble, hardened and her eyes took on a flinty look when she saw who was at the front door. They'd not have Mr Hayes upset again, choose how, so she'd just fetch Mr Maddox, for there was no way she could stop this supercilious chap from coming over the doorstep. Mr Maddox'd see to him. She had no choice but to ask him in, telling him she would see if the mistress was at home, her tone frosty. She showed him into the drawing-room where Miss Anna and Miss Marguerite were sitting by the fire, a bit of embroidery in their hands. They looked up and at once were seen to blanch, to edge backwards into their chairs, one on either side of the fireplace.

Michael Hayes smiled, a slow, charming smile which told them he wouldn't hurt a fly and they had nothing to fear from him. He didn't know what had been said to them; what reports of his past and his hopes for the future had been divulged, but they were quite safe with him for was he not a gentleman and knew full well the dainty susceptibilities of a lady. There was no one else in the room except the three dogs who rose to their feet and stiffened their legs defensively. They had had a sniff at him the other night and with that instinct that dogs possess had sensed he was not to be trusted. The English setter, of a somewhat more timid nature than the other two, sidled over to lean against Anna's skirts and growled low in his throat while the retriever and the labrador remained watchfully standing.

"Heavens." Michael's smile widened. "What a fierce beast. I do hope he is not going to attack me."

"Oh, no," quavered Anna. "He is very placid."

"I'm happy to hear it, but please, don't let me disturb you. The maid showed me in here but I was not aware that it was occupied. Would you like me to wait in the hall?"

Again he smiled and was rewarded by one in return. A small, hesitant smile, to be sure, but a smile nevertheless. She shook her head and he noticed how her glossy curls bounced against the soft childish flesh of her neck. The younger one did not speak.

"I was wondering whether Kitty was about," he asked, keeping his distance and certainly not being so presumptuous as to sit.

"No. I think she's in her room," the one he thought was called Anna quavered, but she had relaxed somewhat as though this gentleman, for surely that was what he was, who it was reported was . . . well, her cousin, she supposed, was of no threat to them.

"And Kitty's husband? Has he returned to Liverpool?"

"No, he has not," a harsh voice from the doorway answered. The two young girls put their hands to their mouths and their soft grey eyes, the same lovely shade as their father's, became as big as saucers. They had heard that Ben, whom they both admired tremendously, had begged their father not to see the young man who said he was his nephew, though naturally they had not been told why. Their mother became cold and distant when he was mentioned, by Kitty, of course, her face as pale as it had been on the day he had come with Kitty and she had fainted at the sight of him. There was a mystery about him, they knew that, and now that Ben was here to deal with him, in whatever way he was to be dealt with, they felt a little thrill of excitement run through them. They were young, innocent, protected, impressionable. He was so handsome, so pleasant, so well mannered, they could hardly believe that whatever he was supposed to have done could be too wicked. That merry twinkle in his eye, that soft smiling curl to his mouth, the way he spoke, surely could not be the mark of anyone but a gentleman?

"I thought you were told you could not see Mr Hayes until he was a great deal better," Ben said, his voice implacable, his manner implying that it would give him a great deal of pleasure to throw him out.

But Michael Hayes appeared not to mind. He smiled. "Since when has it been your place to tell my uncle's guests . . . no, his *relatives*, when they may or may not visit him? I am here on perfectly legitimate business and I would be glad if someone could tell him I am here."

"I believe that message has already been taken to him but that does not mean you can see him. The doctor—"

"Dear Lord, you will keep trotting out that excuse." He turned to grin infectiously at the two girls who were watching the exchange with bated breath and though Ben made some sound of denial in the back of his throat they both smiled shyly at him.

"I think it might be wise if you were to go to your rooms, girls," their brother-in-law told them, and so well brought up were they they both rose obediently.

"He certainly likes to give orders, doesn't he?" Michael chuckled, treating them to an audacious wink at which they both began to giggle. "And he isn't even in his own home. Now then, as it seems he has not been informed, would one of you like to run up to my uncle's room and tell him—"

"Marguerite, Anna, I would be glad if you would go to your rooms until this man has left the house."

"I think perhaps it might be a good idea if you were to obey him . . . er, Marguerite, is it, and Anna?"

Shyly they owned up to their names.

"Only I do believe your brother-in-law is about to do me a mischief and it might not be fit for a lady's eyes."

For a second or two they looked alarmed but when he winked again and smiled that lovely smile of his they realised he was joking and with another giggle, since he was so amusing, they glided from the room.

At once Michael turned to Ben and his face was like stone, as were his eyes, those blue and brilliant eyes which shone from the face of Ben's wife, this man's sister, there was no doubt of it. He still smiled, that smile asking Ben what he thought he could do about it, for was not he, Michael Hayes, kin to this family? By blood which was stronger than the ties of marriage which were all that united the man who had married Josh Hayes's daughter.

Ben felt the cold anger rise in him, an anger that was directed not just at Michael Hayes, who thought he had a perfect right to walk into the life of this family and be accepted, but at himself who really had no power to stop him. He knew, knew it in his bones, that Josh Hayes, who was not a well man, would be unable to turn away from his dead sister's son, no matter what tale of horror Ben had brought from Rainshough about his nephew's past. He would make some excuse, blame himself as he seemed to blame himself for his sister and brother's deaths. He should have let the woman marry the bastard who had eventually killed her but then would that not have led to further disaster? There was nothing Ben Maddox could do about it. Nothing. Only watch this young bastard like a hawk. Protect the sick man upstairs, protect his wife and his family in any way he could and, by God, if it took him until the end of his days, he would see that no harm came to any member of the Hayes family through this arrogantly smiling limb of Satan!

23

Joshua Hayes's nephew, who had come back from the dead, or so it was rumoured among the business community of Manchester, was given a position at Monarch Mill side by side with Joshua's own son, plus an allowance to match. He was to learn the business, it was said, though surely not from Freddy Hayes, who was a bit of a numbskull where the cotton trade was concerned, where anything to do with the world of commerce, manufacturing and profit-making was concerned, but it seemed Joshua Hayes, who was an astute man and, naturally, had been aware of the falling off of trade since his son took over, had it all in hand. A new manager was taken on, one who knew the cotton trade from the floor up, the spinning- and weaving-rooms where he had learned his trade, the buying of the raw yarn to the selling of the completed garment, the cost of it all and the profit that might be expected and would have the whole lot under his capable thumb. A good man who had not come cheap but whose value was inestimable. And not only that, it was reported that Josh Hayes's own son-in-law, who had found the man and who was no fool himself in the world of industry, was frequently to be found at Monarch, keeping his finger on the pulse. Joshua Hayes, who had had a bit of a scare in February with that bad chest of his, had more or less retired to Lytham, but now he could relax, or so it was assumed, though from the start the gentlemen who had cause to associate with his nephew thought him an arrogant young bastard and wondered, with his attitude towards "trade", as it was called in scathing tones by those who thought themselves above it, how long he would last in the competitive world into which he had been introduced.

Ben Maddox was among them.

He would not forget that day when Michael Hayes had come as soon as the snow had thawed sufficiently for a cab to get to Riverside House, determined on see-ing his uncle, and on this occasion it seemed he would succeed. The meeting had been dramatic, emotional, what Ben had seen of it, whipped up by the newcomer's superb acting, Josh Hayes's sincere feelings of remorse, and his wife's tight-lipped anxiety.

The bedroom door was open as Ben led the way along the landing to Josh's room, just as though the man in the bed, who wanted nothing more than to begin the process of making up to his nephew for the dreadful tragedy of what had happened to his mother, Josh's sister, couldn't wait to get on with it.

Michael hesitated in the doorway and for an appalled moment Ben could have sworn the young bugger had managed to bring tears to his eyes which did not go unnoticed by his aunt and uncle. Josh was visibly moved but Nancy tightened her already tight lips and her grip on her husband's hand.

Dashing a hand across his face, Michael stepped into the room, standing for a second or two to allow his uncle time to absorb the family likeness. Not particularly Josh Hayes's family, though there was, as Nancy had said, something of Millicent Hayes in the way he held his head, but his likeness to Kitty which, now that everyone had been told of it, was very obvious. They had all asked one another, Ben included, why they hadn't noticed it, but there it was. The colouring particularly, of the eyes and the darkness and thickness of the curling hair.

"Sir?" he enquired delicately and Ben had to hand it to him, it was exactly the right thing to do. Diffidence, to start with at least. A certain modest charm which Ben knew did not exist, the modesty at least, a deference to an older man, a sympathy for the older man's frail health. It was exactly the right note to strike and this time there were tears that were genuine in Josh Hayes's eyes and his throat was clogged with something emotional as he held out his free hand to the man he recognised as his sister's child.

"Michael . . . oh, lad, I can scarce believe it. Come here, closer; closer where I can get a good look at you. Dear God, Michael, this is a happy day and one I never thought to see. Look at him, dearest." Turning for a bare second to his wife who looked as though she wished she had a knife in her hand, for there was no doubt if she had she would dearly like to stick it in this young upstart. This was how his father, Mick O'Rourke, had looked all those years ago when he had lusted after Nancy Brody. Smiling, smiling and filled with his own belief in his ability to get what he was going after. With his father it had been her. With his son it was her husband, or at least what her husband was going to provide him with. He bowed courteously in her direction, a sop to his uncle, she was well aware, for Michael Hayes knew to a nicety how Josh Hayes depended on and was influenced by his wife and though he cared nothing for her, or how she judged him, it would not do to cross her in front of her husband.

They clasped hands, Michael O'Rourke's son and Nancy Brody's husband but it was not enough for Josh, who was overwhelmed by this joyous moment and reaching up he put his arms about his nephew's shoulders and strained him to him. Michael suffered it, as overwhelmed as Josh, or so he pretended.

Ben stood by the open doorway and his heart sank, for it seemed the appalling tale of seduction and desertion, of gambling and thieving, of a life of debauchery which Michael, despite his youth, had lived, was of no account to his uncle and he wondered how much of it was due to family affection, or how much was caused by the tragedy all those years ago for which Josh felt himself in some way to blame.

"Come and sit by me, lad," Josh was saying. "See, Ben,

will you fetch Michael a chair and put it here," indicating a spot close to the bed. "Ring the bell, darling," to his anxiously hovering wife, "and ask for coffee – or would you prefer tea, Michael? – and we shall have a good talk. I want to know about your mother, my sister. Dear God, if you knew how distressed I was to hear . . . well . . . Ben had the story from . . . the village where . . . where . . . and he told us. I'm sorry, but I wanted to . . ."

It was very evident that Josh Hayes was embarrassed, not knowing how to tell his nephew that he had had his past investigated and for a moment a frown creased his brow, for that past had been far from innocent. Then it was gone and Josh patted his nephew's hand, a gesture that did not go unnoticed by his wife who appeared to wince every time Michael's name was spoken.

Michael turned his gaze on Ben for a moment and his eyes changed from the warm concern he would have his uncle believe he felt to the implacable frost of one who knows he is looking at an enemy. Then he smiled that triumphant smile of his which said that despite all Ben's efforts and what he had found out about his past it appeared to make no difference to his uncle who still clasped his hand and gazed at him as though he were returned from the dead. As though Michael were his uncle's brother and sister all rolled into one and here, at last, was his uncle's chance to redeem himself for the past.

"I'll leave you to it, then," Ben said, knowing that for the moment there was nothing more he could do. He had nothing further to say on the subject and if he had, if he tried to warn Josh that he was playing with fire, it would make no difference. His only hope was that Nancy might influence her husband, persuade him to move slowly before he brought this young devil into the family. There was an old adage that a leopard never changes its spots and Ben had an appalling feeling that in this case it would turn out to be true.

"Right, lad, and thanks. I might see you at dinner if I can persuade that fusspot of a doctor to let me out."

"Oh, no you won't, my lad," his wife said firmly. "It's far too soon."

"Rubbish, my love. Seeing Michael like this has given me a new lease of life and besides, we will want to introduce him properly to the rest of the family and I want to be there when we do. And ask Tilly to have a room made up for him, will you, dearest? There is no point in his staying at a hotel when we have enough rooms and to spare. He is family, after all."

As Ben turned to leave the room Nancy Hayes cast a despairing look at him, a look in which was written her dread of what was to come, her fear for her husband since she knew, none better, that this young man would break her husband's heart all over again. That he would take and take and take and give nothing in return and what would that do to her beloved Josh? The entreaty in her eyes cut Ben to the bone, for in a strange way, though Kitty was supposed to be the image of her dead father, he could see Kitty's face in her mother. Kitty had never implored him to do anything for her, ever. She was a strong, wilful, independent woman who would regard it as weak to depend on a man for anything, but he had it in him to think, wrongly he knew, that he was doing this for Kitty. He was protecting her from some evil, an evil she knew nothing about, but *he* knew and it gave his heart which would always be hers, a modicum of comfort. Nancy Hayes was imploring him to do something, she didn't know what, to save her husband and her family from the badness that was surely to come and for her sake and for his wife who despised him, he would defend them from the malignancy this young man would undoubtedly inflict on them. Josh Hayes could see no further than his dead sister and brother. He would be blind to the corruption Michael Hayes would bring if not watched but Ben Maddox's eyes were wide open. His and Nancy Hayes's.

He nodded, a slight inclination of the head which told her she was understood. That she could trust him to protect them all, as he had vowed to protect them downstairs and he was rewarded by a slight relaxing of her stiff shoulders and a sigh which, though soft and almost unnoticeable, was one of relief.

They were a merry party who sat down to dinner that night, due to Kitty and Michael more than anyone.

The table looked splendid, Ben heard Mrs Hayes murmur to Tilly and Dulcie who were to serve them. They both looked gratified and indeed it was a work of art, for it was set with the Hayes Crown Derby ware and silver cutlery, reflecting the light from the flickering candles which Nancy preferred. Nine places, each bordered with an array of gleaming knives, forks and spoons, four delicate crystal wineglasses and immaculate napery, each napkin folded and arranged in wings with a rosebud in its heart. There were rosebuds decorating the length of the table and hanging at its corners in a swirl of ivy. In the centre of the table was a tazza piled with an intricate pyramid of nectarines and peaches, figs and grapes, green and black, and many other fruits grown in Mr Tinker's hothouses. It seemed Joshua Hayes had wanted to show his nephew that he was special, that he was someone for whom only the best was due and Nancy, despairing and afraid that if she baulked at it, which she had longed to do, it might upset her husband's frail health, had fallen in with Josh Hayes's wishes. He was on the mend and she wanted to keep it that way even if it meant entertaining the hated son of a hated man from her past.

They entered the dining-room, a dazzling and handsome family group, Kitty on Michael's arm since even Michael, who should have taken his hostess into dinner, could not quite bring himself to approach the frozen figure of Nancy Hayes. It was obvious that she wanted to be as near as possible to her husband should he need to cling to her and would have sat beside him at the dinner table if it had not looked a trifle odd. Freddy accompanied his wife and it was left to Ben to bring in the pretty sisters, one on each arm, both flushed and excited, for it seemed their new cousin was to be a cherished member of their family. They were too young and unworldly to sense the undercurrents at the table and could see only the attractively smiling young man who was, Ben had recognised, already making himself especially pleasant to Marguerite! No one else had noticed, for Josh was too intent on his charming, well-mannered nephew and Nancy Hayes was too intent on her husband whom she watched like a hawk.

Freddy was slightly on his guard, he didn't know really what about. He was not a greedy man, nor acquisitive. His father was a very wealthy man, despite the small falling off of profits over the past six months, and there was more than enough to go round. Sebastian, who had proved to have an academic turn of mind, was showing early signs that he might not wish to join his father's firm when he left school. He had stated a desire to go on to university and Freddy thought it might be an advantage to have another member of the family by his side in the business. Especially if this Michael turned out to have a head for commerce which, sadly, Freddy admitted he did not.

Ciara, who sat beside him doing her best to disguise her enormously protruding stomach with her napkin, for their guest was an exceedingly attractive, attentive young man, ate her way steadily through the many delicious courses Mrs Bright had concocted for this special meal. Ciara was eating for two, though she didn't say this out loud, for it would have been in poor taste to draw attention to her pregnancy to a young, unmarried gentleman. She seemed to wear a permanently frowning expression these days and was seen to whisper time and time again into her husband's ear, complaining of something or other, Ben supposed, since why should she alone suffer the aggravation of bearing a child, her sour features said. He noticed Michael, after the first polite greeting, totally ignored her since she could do him no good.

The two girls, Marguerite and Anna, sat one on either side of Michael, shy and blushing when he addressed them, giggling as young girls were inclined to do at every witticism, hanging on his every word. He was obviously well versed in the art of drawing young ladies out of their shells and made a great deal of effort to extract from them, especially Marguerite, Ben was quick to note again, their opinions on everything to do with art, books, music, riding, the theatre of which they were very fond, they told him, in fact every subject that did not tax their innocence or knowledge of the world beyond the walls of Riverside House.

Nancy Hayes sat at the foot of the table, scarcely taking her eyes off her husband who, despite Doctor Croxley's dire warnings that he would not be responsible for his patient if he came downstairs to dinner, had done so just the same. He seemed tired, pale, and ate little but it was very evident that he was enjoying every moment of this, what he called family reunion and if only Seb could have been here it would have been perfect. Ben, along with Nancy, watched him not only with anxiety but with amazement that he seemed able to put to the back of his mind . . . No, *out* of his mind the dreadful reports Ben himself had brought back from Rainshough about Michael Hayes. It was as though none of it had ever happened. As though Michael were an upstanding young man of good character who could do no wrong, and again Ben could only put it down to his obsessive need to make amends to his dead sister and brother.

Kitty sat next to Ben and opposite Michael and the witty repartee they kept up, since they knew one another well, it seemed to say, and were used to such badinage in the circles in which they moved, had the rest of the diners – except himself and Nancy – in gales of laughter. They had drunk champagne, of all things, in the drawing-room though again Nancy had declined, he noticed, to be drawn into this general celebration, saying very little except to ask Josh not to overdo it, to tell her if he felt tired, not to drink too much champagne and other such worried and wifely things to which Josh, for once, took absolutely no notice. He seemed to be elated, not just by the champagne but by his nephew's charming ways, his beautiful manners, his deference to the ladies, his kindness to Nancy though she seemed to be unaware of it. He was polite to the servants, respectful of himself and Ben and ready to be friends with Freddy which, with what Josh had in mind, though he had said nothing as yet, was all to the good.

Kitty looked quite magnificent, Ben noticed with a catch in his heart. She wore a rich satin gown in pale ivory, the bodice cut daringly low and fitted like a skin over her breasts. It had tiny puff sleeves and a skirt that was swathed over her flat stomach to a bustle at her back which was constructed of a series of satin flounces, each one edged with lace, like a frothy waterfall from her waist to the hem. She wore no jewellery but her glossy, tumbled curls were scattered in some clever way with dozens of tiny seed pearls. As she leaned over the table to talk to Michael Ben could see down her bodice almost to her nipples and he knew Michael could do the same. In fact, his eyes were constantly drawn there, smiling appreciatively. The other ladies, all expect poor Ciara, looked pretty as young girls do in their white dresses and pale sashes and Mrs Hayes, as always, was dressed elegantly but simply in a dress of grape-purple silk.

It was all very impressive, the understated luxury, the comfort, to which the Hayes family were well accustomed, and more than once Ben saw Michael glance round him with great satisfaction. It was all here, the great wealth of the Hayes family, a wealth to which he would one day help himself and when his glance caught Ben's he made no attempt to hide it. What could Ben Maddox do to stop him insinuating himself into his own family? the gleaming, slightly narrowed eyes asked him, the small smile asked him, the slight raising of the eyebrows asked him.

"Tell them about that time you brought down a hundred birds with a hundred shots in one morning, Michael. D'you remember at Clive's place when that Lord somebody-or-other was most put out because you had beaten his record. He lost a few guineas on it, didn't he?"

"I believe he did, Kitty, but I'm sure your parents, and

your lovely sisters, don't want to hear about my poor exploits."

"Oh, pooh, don't go all modest on me, Michael. I thought it was a hoot when he called you a . . . what was it?"

"Kitty, behave yourself." Michael's voice was amused but it was clear that he was not pleased with the way the conversation was turning. "You tell them about Havoc and that day you bought him."

"Havoc?" Josh ventured curiously.

"Yes, my hunter, Father. I call him Havoc."

"Well, my dear, that seems an appropriate name since you have never been one to walk calmly through life, has she, my darling?" turning to smile at his tight-lipped wife.

"Father, really, anyone would think I had led a wild and reckless life." Kitty laughed, throwing back her head to reveal the lovely line of her throat.

"And have you not, my dear? Your courage from being a toddler has always frightened us to death."

"Well, it is my belief that if you are not prepared to take a risk you will never know how exciting life can be. Is that not so, Michael?"

"I have heard you say so before, Kitty-Cat, but some-times—"

"Fiddlesticks, Michael. You are as mad as the rest when it comes to a dare, especially one that has money on it."

"Kitty!" Michael Hayes's hands clenched about his knife and fork and his face took on a brief expression of fury but it was gone in a flash. "Have you told your family about the day you met the Prince of Wales?" A remark that instantly drew their attention away from his own exploits.

Anna gasped. "The Prince of Wales! Kitty, you have met the Prince of Wales? Where? What did he say? What is he like?"

"He's . . . well, Michael, how would we describe him? Portly, stout, a bit like a pouter pigeon with a beard?"

"That's it exactly, or a cock strutting about a farm-yard."

"Oh, I like mine the best. He is not handsome, far from it. He is short and plump, as I said, bulbous-eyed and weak-chinned."

"Kitty, that is most cruel," her mother said sternly. "Remember he is the future king."

"That makes no difference to his appearance, Mother. But he is genial and he held my hand for too long. But then he is a ladies' man as we all know, though it is said he is tiring of Mrs Langtry and that she has taken up with—"

"Kitty." Her mother's outraged voice broke again into Kitty's laughing remarks, for she was conscious that her young and innocent daughters might be impressed by what Kitty thought of as her own sophistication and knowledge of the world.

"But where did you meet him, Kitty?" Marguerite cut in. Both she and her sister led the protected lives of young girls of their class, but who had not heard of the wicked Prince of Wales? He was a gambler and lover of other men's wives and even they had heard of the lovely Lillie Langtry through gossip picked up from the servants and the thought that their sister, who was a daredevil herself, had actually met him, thrilled them inordinately.

"At Aintree. My . . . some friends of mine invited me to the races and it—"

Nancy Hayes cut in smoothly, for the conversation was taking an inappropriate twist she did not care for, turning to Tilly who was listening as avidly as Anna and Marguerite. It was many months, in fact the day that Master Freddy married Miss Ciara, since Miss Kitty, with her flare of excitement, her explosive talent for stirring up the household to fever pitch, her ability to turn to chaos the simplest occasion, had been over to Riverside House and though they had groaned with exasperation when she had lived beneath its roof, for who knew what mischief she would be up to next, they had missed it, and her. Wait until Tilly told them in the kitchen that their Miss Kitty had actually met the Prince of Wales, and of course they would want to know all about the young man who was the master's nephew. She and Dulcie would be besieged when the meal was over by the other maidservants, begged to reveal every detail of what was said, and the pair of them were busy storing it all up in their heads so that what one missed the other would remember.

"I think you can serve the coffee in the drawing-room now, Tilly. And will you tell Mrs Bright the meal was excellent."

"Thank you, madam, I will."

They moved slowly into the drawing-room and as Ben followed the laughing figure of his wife, who still hung on to Michael as though he were a lifeline of entertainment in a barren and boring family evening, he realised that he himself had not spoken one word throughout the whole of dinner.

Ben took breakfast early the next day, and alone, for he was to catch the first available train back to Liverpool. He had, after all, his own concerns to see to. He had decent and experienced managers in all of them but he was anxious to check that everything was ticking over as it should and as he expected it to. Joshua and Nancy Hayes were to return to Lytham in a few days' time, if the doctor agreed, but before they did Joshua had indicated that he wanted to have a private word with his son-in-law. It had taken place last night in Joshua's study, while in the billiard-room a hilarious game of billiards was taking place between Freddy, Kitty, Michael, Anna and Marguerite. Ciara had taken herself off to bed since, though she knew the others thought her fanciful, she really did feel poorly and was not receiving the attention she thought was her due.

It seemed Kitty and Michael knew many variations of the game of billiards which seemed to involve a great deal of laughter, a certain suppleness in handling the cue and though it was quite proper since it was played out in full view of the two maidservants who were standing ready to serve more coffee to those who required it, or brandy to Master Freddy and the young gentleman, they could not quite overcome the feeling that there might be something not quite ... tasteful about it. The young gentleman and Master Freddy drank a great deal of brandy and though Master Freddy quickly became befuddled and silly, Mr Hayes's nephew remained suave, elegant, immaculate and totally in control of himself.

Nancy Hayes moved restlessly round the study, fingering this and that, turning in what seemed to be great nervousness as her husband outlined to Ben what he wished him to do about his nephew. Though he was quite determined on the plans he had devised, it was apparent that she was not and for more than an hour Ben and Josh Hayes argued about it until it became clear that not only was Joshua Hayes's mind set in concrete, he was worn out and wished to go to his bed. Several times she had interrupted, beseeching Josh to think again, to reconsider, to sleep on it, to remember what terrible reports Ben had brought back from Rainshough, but each time Joshua's face became more rigid. He seemed to have decided that those reports, though Ben had not been lying about what he had been told, were not necessarily the truth. Had not the villagers exaggerated? Were not all young lads a bit wild and was it not their way to pursue a willing maid? Had he not done so himself and Freddy was the result? He knew the weaknesses of the flesh, at least among young men, and had, in his youth, gambled on this and that, unknown to his father.

Ben watched them go carefully up the stairs, Joshua's

arm through Nancy's, their heads close together and marvelled that a man could be so short-sighted, and that the woman who loved him was willing to welcome into their lives a young man she knew to be as wild and degenerate as had been his own father. To preserve Josh Hayes's health and state of mind she was prepared to forget those words that she had spoken on that first day she had met Michael Hayes.

The love of a woman was a wondrous thing, so strong and unyielding in its protection of the beloved, Ben thought as they disappeared from his view.

He waited until he was sure Josh and Nancy Hayes were in their room before beginning to follow them up the stairs, but as he stepped on to the first tread he heard the music, come from his wife's fingers, drift from the drawing-room. It was a tune he knew which began with the words: "Believe me if all those endearing young charms . . ." the notes rippling softly, and though he could not have said why, he had the feeling she was alone as she played. Her sisters had retired before their parents, coming into the study to kiss them goodnight, so presumably the two young men were drinking themselves into a stupor over the billiard table.

He was tempted to go back, to stand in the doorway, casually, of course, and listen to her play, but instead he moved further up the stairs and sat down on a tread in the dimness which the downstairs lamps did not reach. For half an hour he listened to her play but when she stopped and came upstairs herself there was no one and nothing there except a whiff of cigar smoke.

24

"There is absolutely no need for you to put yourself out, dear."

"It's not a question of putting myself out, Mother. I just thought I might take some of the strain out of the journey."

"It's not necessary, dear. With Anna and Marguerite to help us we shall manage perfectly. I have reserved a first-class compartment which we will have to ourselves so your father can rest if he needs to. Besides, the journey is only a short one. I shall take Tilly with me since she is so dependable, and one of the grooms, Eddie, I believe, will accompany us to see to the luggage. He will come back the next day so—"

"So what you are saying, Mother, is that you don't want me, or my help, in getting Father back to Lytham?"

Kitty's face was set in a rigid expression of pretended indifference which was meant to convey to her mother that she was not in the least hurt by her refusal of Kitty's help, though she was, deeply. It was meant to convey to her mother that this action on her part was only to be expected, since when had Nancy Hayes ever turned to her daughter for anything? That it meant nothing to her for she and her mother had never got on, had never seen eye to eye, had not, in fact, been particularly fond of one another.

Looking from the window she could see her father, a daughter on either arm, strolling in the pale spring sunshine across the lawn. They stopped to speak to Mr Tinker and Archie who were hoeing the warming earth in the flowerbeds which were crammed with narcissus and primula, with hyacinth and a purple, yellow and white rainbow of crocus. Her father said something that made them all laugh. The three dogs bounded about the lawn, playing "silly beggars" as her father called it, chasing their own tails like puppies, and again the group on the lawn laughed. It was a cheerful scene, but for some reason Kitty felt her heart grow sad as though their delight excluded her, a feeling reinforced by her mother's refusal of her offer of help.

They were in the bedroom her mother and father shared and there were piles of neatly folded garments on every chair and across the bed. Emma, who had been called in to help with the packing, exchanged a look with Tilly. Tilly knelt at an opened trunk, carefully packing a gown of Mrs Hayes's with layers of tissue paper and both the maids did their best to look as though not only were they invisible, but deaf as well. Tilly, who had known Miss Kitty longer than Emma, sometimes thought, and the other servants agreed with her, that though Miss Kitty had been a little hellion in her childhood and young girlhood, Mrs Hayes was hard on her at times. Miss Kitty had always had a good heart despite her reckless ways and, well, Tilly believed she had softened in the past year and the others agreed with her. Now whether it was to do with that lovely husband of hers without whom this family might have foundered in the past weeks, the baby she had lost, or just that at last she was growing up, Tilly didn't know, but she was certainly a great deal easier to get on with. Mind you, perhaps it was nothing at all to do with her marriage. It seemed that even that might be a bit rocky, for they had all been shocked to discover that Miss Kitty and Mr Maddox had not shared a bed while they were at Riverside House so what were they to make of that, they had whispered to one another.

"You are so involved with your new social life," Mrs Hayes went on, "and I don't want to interfere with your plans, dear, that is what I'm saying. You must be eager to get back to Meadow View and your life there. To your friends and your husband whom I'm sure you've missed. It was good of you to stay so long."

"Mother, I was worried about Father, surely you knew that. I didn't want to leave him until he was well out of the woods. Now that the doctor has given the go-ahead for him to be moved I thought . . . perhaps I might be of some help."

Nancy Hayes turned an ironic look on her daughter

and her eyebrows rose slightly. The look said quite
plainly that she didn't believe her. When had Kitty
ever considered anyone but herself? All her life from
being an infant she had raged and screamed if she
did not get what she wanted, and at once, caring not
an iota for who might be upset by her demands. She
had struggled through life, and *with* life in a constant
battle against those who had her in their charge and it
was very evident Nancy had no reason to believe she
was any different now. True, she had been surprised
that her daughter had remained at Riverside House for
so long, wondering why, but now that she and Josh and
the girls were to go to Lytham, and stay there for good
if Nancy had her way, there seemed to be no reason for
her daughter not to return to her own home, to her
own husband, who had been back in Liverpool for
over three weeks now.

"Dear, that is most kind of you, but really, we shall
manage beautifully. Now that everything is settled, I
mean with . . . with that man . . ."

"I know who you mean, Mother, and why you should
take against him just because of who his father was
seems most unfair."

But then what else had she expected from her
mother, her mother who had never shown more than
a lukewarm cordiality towards herself? She supposed
it was for the same reason: because of the man who
had fathered them both, both she and Michael and
whom her mother still hated with a deadly loathing.
It had been tricky, if that was the word, during the

week Michael was at Riverside House. Her mother had managed to avoid speaking to him and in fact had more than once risen from the table when he sat down. She had taken to eating in her room, though Joshua had dined with the family and it was not until Michael had moved into the rooms that had been found for him on Bury New Road that she had returned to take her meals with her family.

Ciara was finally to be mistress of Riverside House. The nursery had been painted and refurbished in readiness for the new arrival, due any day, and, or so Nancy announced firmly, it was high time that the next generation of the Hayes family, the younger generation, was left to follow on in the way it should be. Josh Hayes had done his duty, as his father had before him and it was up to Freddy now to carry on. That he was to have his cousin to help him meant nothing to Nancy Hayes as long as she did not have to be a part of their lives. Joshua had interviewed the chap Ben had sent over from Liverpool and who was to be manager, a decent man who had married late and had a young family to support. Josh had been somewhat surprised to see him, for he was of the opinion that if he suited Ben Maddox, who was a shrewd judge of character and no one's fool, then the man could only be the right one for the job. But that was like Ben. He was not a man to take things for granted and the fact that Josh Hayes had trusted him to find the chap did not mean he would take it upon himself to employ him without consulting his father-in-law.

Michael had been given an office of his own at Monarch Mill, with a magnificent mahogany desk, numerous filing cabinets, the room lined with shelves on which books covering every aspect of cotton were stacked, and on the walls two portraits, one of Joshua Hayes's father and the other of his grandfather. When Kitty had visited him towards the end of his first week there she had found him sitting on the windowsill, one leg bent, his foot on the sill, his arm across his knee and his chin on his arm as he stared moodily out into the busy yard. There were papers on the desk, neatly placed by some careful hand in the centre of the blotter, but it seemed to her they had not been touched.

He leaped to his feet when she was shown in, his face breaking into a merry smile. He crossed the room to take her hands, holding her arms out wide to get a good look at her, his eyes sweeping her from head to toe.

"Dear God, Kitty-Cat, have you any idea how pleased I am to see you and looking as beautiful as ever. If you only knew how I have suffered. The boredom is crucifying me and that's no exaggeration. I'm heckled from morning till night by that man."

"What man?" She disengaged her hands and stepped back from him. She was somewhat startled by Michael's attitude, for though she knew he might find it hard to settle down to the life of a young businessman after the hedonistic ways the Olivers had introduced him to, this was a wonderful opportunity for him. He was to be part of a thriving family enterprise and its success would rebound on him. He might even become a partner, her father had hinted, if he shaped, with all the advantages, financial and otherwise, that would bring him. Still, it was early days yet, she told herself. He certainly looked the part in his narrow grey striped trousers and black frock coat, though his merry, impish grin would have looked more the part at one of the Olivers' riotous evenings.

"I think his name's Hardcastle which is enough to turn anyone against him, wouldn't you say? He drags me from here to there and back again, all of them the most god-awful places you ever saw with machinery that deafens you and these creatures. . . What creatures? Well, spinners and weavers and such, or so I believe. They look like nothing I've ever met before; but will you listen to me boring you with stuff that isn't worth thinking about. Come here and give your brother a kiss, if you please, and let me breathe in that wonderful perfume you're wearing."

"Now watch what you're saying, Michael. I had more than enough of that from Tam Oliver with his flattery."

"Jesus, Kitty, it's not flattery, believe me. You look absolutely divine."

She knew she was looking her best. She had on a silk gown the colour of cherries over which was carelessly draped a pale grey velvet cape edged with pale grey fur. Hats were small this year and she had had hers made for her by Mrs Cheers's clever milliner. It was no more than a puffball of soft grey fur to match her cape, tipped saucily over her eyes with long satin ribbons of grey hanging to her shoulder blades and from which her dark curls escaped. Michael eyed her appreciatively. "If you weren't my sister I'd . . . Well, as you say, enough of that. It's just so good to see someone from the past."

"From the past! But Michael, you've only been here . . . what? Less than a week." Her voice had a touch of dismay in it.

"I know!" He groaned dramatically, clapping his hand to his forehead and rolling up his eyes so that she could do no more than laugh at him. "Anyway, what time is it?"

Kitty glanced down at the tiny pearl-encrusted fob watch that was pinned to her bodice. "It's almost twelve."

"Right, that's it then. Time for luncheon and I know just the place to take you. I've done a bit of investigating in the past week. Well, there's no point in having a decent allowance if one can't find somewhere to spend it." He reached for his overcoat and top hat, linking his arm in hers and drawing her towards the door.

"But what about Mr What's-his-name?"

"Oh, to hell with him. If he wants me he can whistle. I haven't had so much as a chuckle since you and I last saw each other. Mind you" – he grinned outrageously – "I have had other . . . entertainments. Those rooms of mine are very comfortable and very convenient. I'm having them refurnished, at Uncle Josh's expense, of course – no, he told me to so don't look like that – and at the weekend I'm going over to Chester to have a look at a hunter a pal of mine wants to sell. Why don't you come with me? It would be great fun, or would that husband of yours object?"

"Whether he does or he doesn't is no concern of mine, or yours. But you know I can't. I feel as though I should behave myself at least until Mother and Father have gone to Lytham, though I must say the prospect of being alone with Freddy and Ciara is one that doesn't exactly fill me with glee."

"When are you going back home?"

"Probably tomorrow since it seems I'm not needed at Riverside House any more." Her voice was bitter and Michael looked at her understandingly, for he was not the only one to reason that Nancy Hayes cared for none of the children Mick O'Rourke had fathered and that included Ciara Hayes.

"Cheer up, Kitty-Cat. Let's go and get tiddly at the expense of Monarch Mill. Oh yes, didn't I mention that I am to have an expense allowance, since Uncle Josh seems to think, owing no doubt to my wit and charm and boyish good looks, not to mention my breeding, that I might make myself useful, eventually, by entertaining prospective buyers? Let's pretend you are one, shall we?"

They dined at the Albion Hotel which Michael said was not up to the standard of the Adelphi in Liverpool but Manchester was so terribly provincial with its obsession for commerce, what else could you expect. They laughed a good deal, causing heads to turn to look at the handsome young couple who were making something of a spectacle of themselves to the obvious annoyance of those around them. Despite Michael's gloomy forecast they had a splendid luncheon, drank a bottle of champagne and tumbled out of the hotel at almost half past three. They were a vivid pair, with their identically brilliant azure eyes, their dark, gleaming curls and everyone who watched them evidently thought so. They were related, of course, and of the upper class which often thought it could do as it pleased, but their high spirits were somewhat out of place on a weekday afternoon on a cold day in Manchester at the beginning of March. They were seen to exchange a kiss on the cheek as the young man helped the young lady into a cab, waving extravagantly to one another until the cab turned into Market Street.

She had been home for no more than a couple of hours when the sound of galloping hooves brought her to the window of her bedroom where she and Emma, or to be honest, just Emma, were unpacking and sorting out her clothes. Emma kept up a monologue, which seemed to require no response on her part, on what should be done with this or that, the state of certain undergarments which needed a stitch or two, these boots to the boot boy for cleaning, that pile for the laundry-maid, her furs to be put away for the summer or did Miss Kitty think it might be a cold spring in which case Emma would leave them out for a week or two.

"Dear God, Emma, how should I know and if I did would I care? Do what you like with the damned things. One presumes it would not be impossible to get them out again if winter returns. Just make sure my riding things are out and ready for tomorrow. I mean to take Havoc out first thing. In fact I might just go down to the stables and have a look at him now."

It was then that she heard the sound of horse's hooves and when she saw who it was her face lit up.

"Bless him, it's Jimmy. Jimmy Oliver. Thank God! I was beginning to believe I should have gone to Chester with Michael." A cryptic remark that went right over Emma's head.

There had been, naturally, no sign of Miss Kitty's husband when they drove up the drive in the carriage, though several housemaids stood at the front door to welcome their mistress home, glad to see her, or so it seemed.

"Good morning, Mrs Maddox, welcome home, madam," Tansy murmured, sketching a curtsey, while Elspeth and Clarrie, having done the same, picked up the smaller bags which the coachman had shouldered to the steps. A telegraph had been sent to Meadow View telling Harrison which train to expect them on but even if Mr Maddox had seen it it was not likely he would remain at home to greet his wife. His business came first, of course, and God knew he would have more than enough to do, Emma told herself, – wondering why Miss Kitty looked so disappointed – what with looking after Mr Hayes's affairs, the state of which had been of great interest in the servants hall at Riverside. They all knew that Mr Maddox was more or less in charge of the mill in Manchester now. It was all very well saying that Mr Hayes's newly found nephew was to give Mr Freddy a hand but it didn't matter how many hands were involved if none of them knew what the hell they were doing, as seemed the case.

Emma sat back on her heels and watched as her mistress hurried lightly across the room and out on to the landing. She heard her run down the stairs and the sound of her excited voice as Elspeth opened the front door. Emma sighed deeply, a troubled look on her face. They were home now and with nothing to think about but her own boredom and how to alleviate it what mischief was her mistress to get up to now? It was Jimmy Oliver who had come to call and though he wasn't as bad as his brother for devilment he wasn't far behind and where was it going to lead this time? The young squire, they called Tam Oliver, who rode to hounds, shot grouse and pheasants in season, drank brandy and claret, played cards in low company, it was said, and was unfaithful to his wife. Emma had seen it with her own eyes. She had seen what those society people with their London society ways got up to and she feared for her mistress, she really did, since she knew how Miss Kitty was inclined to get into trouble if she was left to go her own way, which she would if she was bored.

Kitty put her arm through Jimmy's and drew him into the drawing-room, her grin of delight telling him he was more than welcome on this dreary day of her return to her marital home. It wasn't dreary at all, actually, for the March sun, pale and uncertain, shone on the great swathe of nodding daffodils, only just beginning to open, which stretched beneath the trees and out from the woodland across the lawn in haphazard clumps. There were primroses budding in their crowns of green leaves. Birds were busy with their nest-building activities and on the elm trees bordering the gardens, blossom was opening wide showing little antlers and filaments.

"This is a wonderful surprise, Jimmy," she said, her pleasure at having someone, anyone, really, she supposed, call on her so soon after her return making her sound more enthusiastic than she meant. She had not forgotten, how could she, the narrow escape she had had with this man's brother, but just the same it was good to have *someone* who was pleased to see her home. "How about tea, or would you like something stronger?"

"Don't ask daft questions, Kitty. I'll have a glass of that whisky I see on the sideboard."

"Help yourself, and then you can tell me how the dickens you knew I was home. I haven't been in more than a couple of hours."

"Oh, one has one's ear to the ground, you know." He grinned wickedly and raised one eyebrow and she thought how like Tam he was. Alike in many ways, vigorous and full-blooded except that Jimmy seemed to be a copy of the original mould and was therefore somehow a little less. A little less charming, a little less handsome, a little less attractive to the ladies and she supposed it must have been difficult for him to live in the shadow of his exciting brother. But she'd always liked him. Perhaps because he was not so overpoweringly male as Tam was. He didn't mind having a gossip, as one woman might do with another. Not that he was feminine in his ways, far from it. She'd seen him making a play for many a pretty woman but he was more discreet about it than Tam. He was a brave horseman, willing to take a risk at a bad fence or a tall hedge, a wide and dangerous ditch, but somehow the flair that Tam had was missing in Jimmy.

"And what does that mean? Don't tell me you have one of my servants in your pay? My husband wouldn't care for that."

"When did what your husband think matter to you?" He sipped his whisky, leaning indolently with one elbow on the mantelpiece, his legs crossed at the ankle, his grin wide and audacious, for they all knew what Kitty Maddox thought of her stick-in-the-mud husband. She sat down on the sofa, arranging the skirts of her dress about her, smiling up at him.

"Oh, believe me, it doesn't but I am intrigued. I wonder what you are here for, Jimmy Oliver? Surely you haven't ridden over just to welcome me back?"

"And why shouldn't I, Kitty-Cat? We've all missed you, especially Tam."

At once the laughter left her, the pleasure she had felt at his visit dispersed by the image of Tam Oliver sending his brother to sound out her feelings about what had happened in Nanny's room at Brook Hall, for that was what it seemed this visit was all about. She stretched her neck, straightened her back and lifted a haughty head, making it very plain she had no wish to hear Tam Oliver's name in her home, then she frowned, for why had Jimmy mentioned his brother in that way? There were only two people who knew what had happened, or perhaps three if you counted Clive Barrie who had knocked on Nanny's door that night and who must have known who was in there and what was going on. He had brought her the message from Ben and in some way had known where to find her. Did that mean . . . surely they were not *all* . . . ?

Jimmy must have recognised the horror on her face, for at once he knelt down before her and, placing his glass on the hearth, took her hands in his.

"No, Kitty-Cat, you're wrong. No one else knows of . . . what Tam tried to do, only me and Tam. He told me himself. He was absolutely devastated by what he had put you through. He was drunk, Kitty, or he wouldn't have tried it on. He's a terrible flirt, you know that, and will tease a lady into giving her a kiss but, Jesus, he has no need to *force* a woman. They love him, Kitty, and though it sounds crude there's more than one who would lie down and . . . well, you know what I mean. He lost control. You're a very lovely woman, you know that. And really, Kitty-Cat, you should not have been there in the first place."

Throwing off his hands she leaped to her feet, almost knocking him to the floor and for a moment a look of irritation crossed his face, for though he might not be as blessed with arrogance as Tam, he was an Oliver after all and did not like to be treated as though he were of no importance by some woman who came from a family in "trade". A member of the manufacturing classes whose family, though now as wealthy as his own, had no name, no pedigree, no background beyond weavers and spinners and the manufacture of cotton.

"So that's it, is it? What your precious Tam did to me was my own fault."

Jimmy hurriedly got to his feet. He had been given this commission by his brother and he must fulfil it and it was no good getting out of sorts with the woman just because she was not immediately ready to forgive and forget, which is what Tam wanted. "Tell her anything you bloody well like, old chap, but get her back into the fold. She bloody well haunts me, Jimmy, and until she gives in to me I'll know no peace. Get on your damn knees if necessary, but persuade her it was all a big mistake," which was what he was trying to do. He could understand his brother's obsession with this lovely, high-spirited woman, but he had not reckoned on her bloody-minded determination to tell Tam, and him, to go to the devil. Manufacturing class she might be but she had a high opinion of herself which he must feed on.

"Kitty, please, I put that crudely. Forgive me."

"I was in the room merely to get the hem of my gown fixed."

"Tam got his signals crossed, Kitty-Cat, for which you must forgive him. He obviously thought it was an invitation to—"

"Well, it wasn't, and you can tell him to go to hell."

"Kitty, please, can't you forgive him this once? It'll

never happen again, really it won't. We had such fun, didn't we, you and Tam and Vannie and all the others. Come on, you can't deny it, can you? We've got plans for all sorts of things and we would be desolate if you wouldn't join us. Please, Kitty, say you'll at least think of it. We're getting up a party for the Grand National and the whole of society will be there for the week. We've been invited to banquets and parties and we are longing to include you. Brook Hall will be overflowing with amusing people. Please, sweetheart, don't turn us down. Think of the fun we'll have and I can absolutely guarantee you'll have no trouble with Tam. In fact, I'll let you into a little secret."

He smiled and put his finger to his lips and she could not help but smile back a little. They were fun, these people. They were amusing and what else was she to do with herself if she turned them away? She had spent wonderful weekends with them. She had laughed and danced and flirted and forgotten about the quiet man who was her husband but who did not want her to be his wife. Her life would be empty without them and surely . . . *surely* Tam Oliver would behave himself now. She had shown him her true feelings. She had resisted him and his advances and even if he resented it, there were still the others who wanted her to be a part of their lives.

"What is it? This secret?" she asked him, sighing as though at the tantrums of a spoiled child.

"Promise you'll keep it to yourself. And certainly not a word to Vannie."

"Well?" Her voice was impatient.

"He's . . . well, you won't be offended . . ."

"Oh, for goodness' sake get on with it, Jimmy."

"He's fallen rather heavily for the wife of a major in one of the Liverpool regiments. The major, as it happens, and conveniently for Tam, is on duty in Ireland, leaving the field clear for Tam. He's a rogue, good old Tam, but really, you can't help but smile, can you?"

"He didn't make me smile, Jimmy."

"Of course he did. Time and time again. Now, Kitty-Cat, say you'll come to Aintree with us. Can I tell Vannie and Grace you'll be in touch? Your room is ready for you, and one for your maid next door to your own. You see how we think of your every wish?"

He winked at her and despite herself she could not help but smile and though she told him she would think about it and he was not to take it for granted she would come, they both knew she would.

25

She awoke to a feeling of wellbeing, a feeling that
something good had happened, or was about to happen, then, remembering yesterday, realised that it was
both. Henry, who had howled when it seemed Artie
was about to take him back to the stables and so had
been allowed to stay, lifted his head and, seeing she
was awake leaped to his feet and began a determined
attack on her face with his tongue. She laughed and
tried to push him away but he wasn't having any of
that nonsense, lying across her as he waited for the
inevitable game to begin.

"Get off, you daft thing. Behave yourself." And,
contenting himself with another rapturous kiss, the
dog subsided against her.

She lay for several minutes staring raptly up into the
draped silk curtains of the four-poster bed, those that
curved up into what she called the imperial crown then

she stretched languidly, yawned and reached for the bell to ring for Emma.

Yesterday the servants had seemed pleased to see her, she thought, but the only truly enthusiastic welcome she had received had been from Henry, who had been in the charge of Artie, the stable lad, while she had been away. The young beagle had gone wild with joy, leaping to fantastic heights in an attempt to lick her face. She had bent down to him and he had knocked her on to her behind, to the vast amusement of the watching servants, who, she could see it in their faces, were telling themselves that their time of peace was over, for the mistress was back. She had raced about the garden with the rapturous dog, not even bothering to change from her smart travelling outfit, putting holes in Wilf's lawn with her high heels, much to his sour-faced reproach.

For half an hour she had been delighted to be home, then, the excitement wearing off, she had begun to mope about the place with Henry at her heels, wondering how she was to fill her days.

She had believed her friendship with the Olivers and the rest of their circle was at an end, since she had been certain that she and Tam Oliver could never get on, could never resume the light-hearted relationship they had once known. Tam had struck her as a man who would never forgive an affront to himself as a member of a family of breeding, nor to his masculinity which she had thrown in his face. She had shown him vigorously in Nanny's room that his advances were not only unwanted but distasteful to her, slapping his face, struggling to get away from him, fighting and scratching and spitting her disgust and but for the intervention of Clive would have definitely come off worst. She had not seen him since and had barely given any thought, in her worry over her father, to what was to happen when the emergency was over.

Now, with Jimmy's visit, it looked as though Tam was truly repentant for what he had tried to do to her. He had been drunk, Jimmy had said, which she knew to be true, though she had never ever seen him lose control of himself as he had done that night, no matter how much he drank.

Still, there was always a first time, she supposed, and if he vowed, as it seemed he had done to Jimmy, that he would not repeat the offence then she was perfectly willing to forget it. He had a new prey, it seemed, this attractive young wife of an officer serving in Ireland and if that was so he would leave Kitty alone, or at least treat her in the same courteous and friendly way he did the other ladies in his party. What could be simpler? She really did want to be included in their busy social life, in their rich, luxury-loving, fun-loving coterie, and it seemed they were eager to have her join them again.

The hunting season was coming to an end but taking its place would be race meetings, the Derby, Ascot, the St Leger at Doncaster. In early summer the gentlemen would don cricket flannels, the ladies play tennis or croquet. There would be boating to fill the long summer afternoons, tea on the lawn, all the entertainments a good hostess provides, and then later, at the end of the summer when it came time for the culling of the red deer which bred so prolifically, they were all to migrate, or so she had been told, north of the border to shoot grouse and stags. The whole year would be filled with endless parties and dances, weekends spent at one stately home or another, the Henley Regatta of which they had promised her she was to be part, as a spectator, of course, and the thought made her sigh with pleasure. She would wait a day or two to send a message to Jimmy Oliver, let Tam dwell on his misdeed for a bit longer, then she would go wherever she was invited.

But today she meant to take Havoc out, perhaps for a gallop along the sands from Bootle to Formby Point. Though the curtains were still drawn there was a fine golden light edging them and she sensed that the day was as pleasant as it had been yesterday, just the day to lean over Havoc's neck and encourage him into a full-stretched gallop. Not that he would need encouraging, for though the grooms would have exercised him, along with the rest of the horses, they would not have given him his head as she did.

There was a tap at the door and Emma entered carrying her morning tea.

"Good-morning, Miss Kitty," she said, placing the tray on the bedside table, then moving to the window and drawing back the curtains. Kitty was right. It was a fine and sunny day and rays of golden light spread across the delicate blue of the plain carpet. They fell on the polished satinwood of the dressing table and tallboy and reflected in the silver-topped scent bottles and hairbrushes and all the lovely, shining things Ben Maddox had once put there for his bride.

"Good-morning, Emma, and what a lovely morning it is, too. What time is it?"

She sat up in bed, not bothering to reach for her wrap since there were only herself and Emma in the room. The sunlight, the sun still fairly low in the sky, touched her bare shoulders, their smooth flesh the colour of rich buttermilk, and tangled in her hair, putting highlights of copper in its rumpled darkness.

"It's barely seven thirty, Miss Kitty." Emma poured her mistress a cup of fragrant tea, passing it to her, giving the dog a glance of disapproval before she began to move this and that, unnecessarily, for she had tidied the room last night while Miss Kitty was taking her bath.

"And that animal shouldn't be on the bed. You don't know where he's been. There's rats in them stables and everyone knows rats have fleas."

"Rubbish. But if you feel so strongly about it ask Artie to give him a bath. He's staying in here with me from now on, is that clear?" She began to feed the eager animal with bits of broken biscuit.

"Oh, aye, crystal clear." Everyone in the house, with perhaps the exception of the master, knew that if Miss Kitty said a thing was so, then it was. "An' them biscuits're for you, not that animal."

"Don't be such a grump, Emma. It's a lovely morning and I'm off out. I can't believe it's so early, and d'you know, for some reason I'm absolutely starving. It must be the Liverpool air. They do say, coming straight off the river, it is considered to be very bracing."

"Do they indeed? Well, it's certainly put the roses in your cheeks. I haven't seen you look so well for weeks. You must have slept well."

"D'you know, I did."

"Are you glad to be home then, lass?" Emma asked softly, wishing with all her heart that Miss Kitty's good looks and apparently boundless health were due to the anticipation of seeing her husband. She knew they weren't, of course. That beggar who'd come galloping up the drive on his wild horse was the cause of it, she knew that only too well. Not him in particular but the expectation of the invitations, now that they knew she was back, that would come flooding in from those wild-riding, hell-raking friends of hers. The contemplation of the parties, the excitement, the fun-filled madness they considered necessary to get through their days and nights had rejuvenated her. They'd be off again soon, there was no doubt about it, gallivanting about the country from one house to another, from one party to another and though Emma wouldn't for the world desert her mistress she did wish she was more like the usual young married women Kitty Maddox's sort of people produced. But that was not likely, was it, with the master off God knows where on the path of his own pursuits and Miss Kitty tearing about in search of something he could not, or would not, give her.

She was in the breakfast-room, striding with her long trousered legs towards the sideboard before she realised that she was not alone. The maids, having been told by the master that he would serve himself, had returned to the kitchen and Ben Maddox was just about to tuck into a hearty breakfast of bacon, eggs, mushrooms and tomatoes.

He was as startled as she was, his fork, which had just speared a piece of perfectly cooked bacon, hovering halfway to his mouth.

"Oh," she said, hesitating for a moment as though she'd half a mind to turn and come back later, then her lips firmed and her chin lifted, for she had as much right to be here as he had.

"Good-morning," Ben managed to say politely, though he had a distinct feeling the food he had just swallowed was stuck somewhere between his mouth and his stomach. He knew she was back, naturally, for the house had been filled with that strange tension she seemed to generate, but he had never known her come down so early. In fact, she was very rarely here to come down early. Most weekends he spent on his own, drifting rather pleasantly about the place, reading the Sunday newspapers, inspecting what had been done in his gardens and surrounding grounds during the week, walking in the woods with the beagle of whom he had become quite fond in her absence. It was Sunday today. She had had a visit yesterday from one of those madcap friends of hers, so he had heard from the stable lad who had cared for the visitor's animal, and now, here she was, looking as magnificent as only she could in her outrageous breeches, her well-cut tweed hacking jacket, her immaculate cravat, her highly polished chestnut-coloured boots. Only her hair struck the wrong note though even that was very attractive, tumbling in a thick cap of dark and glossy curls about her head, over her brow almost to her eyes and touching the collar of her jacket.

"Good-morning," she answered, her voice toneless.

She helped herself to a bowl of porridge which she brought back to the table, sitting at the far end as far away from him as she could get. A place had not been set for her there so she whisked a lace-edged linen table mat from halfway down the table, some cutlery and a napkin. Sitting down, shaking out the napkin, she began to spoon the rich and creamy mixture into her mouth. Ben continued with his breakfast, glancing at her from time to time but not speaking, and the awkwardness between them was a tangible thing.

Tansy popped her head round the door to ask if Mr Maddox wanted a fresh pot of coffee and, as she told them in the kitchen, nearly had a fit when she saw Mrs Maddox sitting there as large as life. Not speaking, either of them, but seated at the same table which none of them had seen them do for many a long month.

"Yes, bring fresh coffee, Tansy. I'm sure Mrs Maddox would be glad of some."

"Thank you, I would," Mrs Maddox answered, speaking as though her lips were sewn together, Tansy reported.

"Can I serve you with anything, Mrs Maddox?" Tansy asked her anxiously.

"No, thank you, Tansy. Just bring the coffee and leave it. I'll help myself."

"Will I bring fresh bacon? Cook could fry you—"

"No, thank you. What is on the sideboard will do."

"Very well, madam." And bobbing a hurried curtsey Tansy fled the room.

Ben wiped his mouth on his napkin and cleared his throat and Kitty looked up expectantly. He reached for the butter and marmalade, spreading both thickly on his toast before speaking.

"I take it you're to ride," he said, his voice cool but pleasant.

"Yes, and you?"

"Yes."

Another silence broken only by the chink of cutlery on plates and from the garden a warble of a blackbird which was heralding the spring with its joyful song.

"A nice day for it."

"Yes, I thought so. I'm to take Havoc down to the sands."

"He's a fine horse. I had a good look at him while you were away. Having received the bill from the dealer I thought I'd better inspect what I'd spent my money on."

She looked up quickly but he merely smiled wryly and lifted one of his eyebrows.

"You approved then?"

"Oh, indeed. You made a good choice."

"It wasn't really my choice. I had some advice . . ." Her voice trailed off uncertainly.

He seemed unruffled by this. "Well, it was good advice. Tim and John were very impressed."

She grinned. "I didn't buy him with them in mind."

"I'm sure you didn't."

The strained atmosphere had relaxed somewhat. It seemed to Kitty that perhaps, if they both made the effort to be civilised to one another, their loveless marriage, the arid desert of their relationship could be got through without too much acrimony, even with a degree of common courtesy. They both had a life, which need not impinge on the other and if they could act, if not as friends, then well-mannered acquaintances, their lives would be so much more congenial. Ben evidently was of the same opinion and though their conversation was stilted, at least they were able to sit at the same table and converse!

They drank a cup of coffee, their elbows on the table, barely exchanging a glance but chatting in a desultory manner of trivial, inconsequential things. The state of Joshua Hayes's health which had improved immensely and his return to Lytham with his family. The possibility of Anna becoming engaged to Edward Lambert, the grandson of old friends of the Hayeses and who had been a frequent visitor to Riverside House while Ben and Kitty were there. He had been doing his best to court Anna for months now and did Kitty think she would take him? They admired the spring glory of the garden which was down to the hard work and genius of Wilf, the head gardener; the training of Henry who should by now have learned to walk to heel, the coming of the

Eisteddfod Grand National Welsh Festival to Liverpool. Today's newspaper reports of the arrival of General Gordon at Khartoum which was in imminent danger of being besieged by the fanatical religious leader known as the Mahdi.

Kitty found to her own astonishment that Ben was extremely well informed on this matter, one, she had to admit, she had not been aware of and for half an hour she listened and questioned him on the subject. Except for him no one had ever talked to her like this before, plainly expecting her to understand what he was saying, about *serious* stuff, about things that women were not supposed to be interested in, that women were not supposed even to understand, and she found she liked it. She was quite put out when Tansy came in to ask if there would be anything else they required.

"Are you on your way to the stables?" Ben asked casually as he held the door open for her.

"Yes, I'm very eager to see Havoc."

"I thought you might be. But where on earth did you get such a name for him?"

"What's wrong with it?" It seemed she had taken no offence, for she was smiling as she walked before him down the narrow passage that led to the side door and the stable yard.

"Nothing, I suppose. I've heard worse. As long as he doesn't create it on the hunting field."

The stable yard was a beehive of activity with horses being groomed, the carriage washed and polished, the grooms hissing and whistling at their work, cats stalking imaginary rats and Henry prancing on his back legs in an effort to greet them both, despite having spent the night on Kitty's bed. There was the smell of a clean, well-tended stable lingering on the air, not offensive as might be supposed but one to which those who rode and loved horses were very well accustomed. The coachman, the grooms and stable lad had been at work since six o'clock, for they knew Mr Maddox insisted on a well-groomed horse and an immaculate carriage without a speck of dirt, inside or out. Each horse, even the mowing pony, was thoroughly cleaned from the tips of its ears to the soles of its hooves to free its coat from all accumulated scurf, dirt and sweat. Even their ears were gently massaged until they were warm and then wiped out with a damp sponge. Most particular, was Mr Maddox, who knew his horseflesh, and it showed in the magnificent health, strength and beauty of all his animals.

The two thoroughbreds pricked their ears and turned to see the new arrivals. Havoc's coat shone like wet coal and Kitty was astonished at how alike he and Marcus, Ben's stallion, were in appearance.

"It struck me, too," Ben said, his hand on Havoc's arched neck. "I was tempted to trace the line of Havoc to see if there was any relationship."

Kitty's hand lingered near his, both of them suddenly aware of it as they smoothed the hunter's shining coat. The grooms, their faces a mixture of amazement and plain idiocy, listened to this exchange between their master and mistress who, it was said, rarely spoke a word to one another if they could help it. Ever since the mistress had taken out the master's horse and killed his child when she came off it he had not forgiven her, or so they had been led to believe, and yet here they were chatting pleasantly to one another with every appearance of amity.

"Well, I'll be off then," the mistress said, turning to one of the grooms to give her a lift into the saddle, but the master was there before them.

"Allow me," he said politely, cupping his hands to receive her bent knee.

"Thanks," the mistress said airily, turning the eager horse towards the gate that led to the drive and the lane beyond.

"D'you mind if I ride along part of the way?" they heard the master say as he leaped up into the saddle of his own horse and followed on her heels.

"Not at all," she answered, then, putting her heels to Havoc's flank she urged him into a trot.

"Well, bugger me," said Tim, taking off his cap to scratch his head. "Wait till we tell 'em in the kitchen. They'll never believe it. I never thought I'd see't day when them two'd go ridin' tergether. An' as nice as pie wi' one another. 'Appen they're . . . well, I dunno . . ." His voice trailed off wonderingly as all of them, even the dog, stared after Ben and Kitty Maddox.

They were not exactly riding together, for Kitty put Havoc to the gallop the moment they got beyond the gateway. Being Sunday, the lanes were almost deserted, for the working man likes to take his ease beside his own fireside on his day of rest, perhaps prepared to take a stroll down to the pub for a midday pint while the missis cooked the Sunday dinner.

Though he could have overtaken her, or thought he could, Ben kept a couple of lengths behind her, going like the wind between hawthorn hedges which were already beginning to show the misty green of young leaves. They flew past fields in which cattle the rich colour of bronze, heads down, were cropping the grass among a profusion of early buttercups. The air was flecked with passing rooks and jackdaws who gave violent tongue to make sure everyone below knew of their passing, but the two riders were too preoccupied with their race even to notice them.

The village of Walton-on-the-Hill went by in a blur and then they were on Bootle Lane and it was here that Ben decided to give Kitty a run for her money. The hooves of the two horses dashed like great hammers against an anvil and sparks flew from the cobbles over which they galloped. With a whoop of exultation he gave Marcus a light flick with his crop, urging the stallion into even greater effort, slowly drawing up to Havoc and then, just as slowly, for Kitty had guessed what he was up to and was urging the hunter on, going past her. His bent arms moved up and down like wings, his hair flew from his head in a wind-whipped banner, his jacket flapped, and as he went he turned and grinned at her and she grinned back, her teeth a white slash in her rosy face.

"I'll catch you," she shouted, "see if I don't."

"How much?" he yelled back.

"Five guineas."

"Done!"

He reached the sands at Bootle no more than a tail's length in front of her, drawing to a thundering stop that scattered the sand in a high arc. Ben jumped from Marcus's back, bending down for a moment, his hands on his knees, trying to catch his breath, laughing at the same time, then moved as though to give Kitty a hand but something, some instinct, stopped him. She slid from Havoc's back and, like him, bent for a moment, dragging deep breaths of air into her lungs. The two horses had great drools of spittle trailing from their mouths, their hearts pumped and their flanks heaved but their loyalty and strength had been proved.

"Well done, but I'm sorry to say you owe me five guineas," Ben said when he had got his breath back.

"We could double it on the way home."

"Well, you may be up to it but I doubt these animals are. I think before we move another foot we should give them a breather, don't you?"

"You're right, I'm sorry."

Leaving the animals untethered, since it was apparent that they were not likely to wander for a while, they sat down on the sand and fell silent. The arch of the sky was a pale and lovely blue with a feathering of gauzy clouds across the river above New Brighton.

There was shipping of every kind on the river, the dancing, silvered river, hurrying to catch the tide, the movement of the ships keeping the waters constantly on the swell and sending wavelets of white foam to the water's edge. There were seagulls crying as they let the breeze carry them over the water and oyster-catchers were searching at the water's edge for cockles and shrimps, strutting importantly in their distinctive black and white like so many noisy gentlemen in evening suits.

For a while they were both engrossed with the scene before them, then slowly Kitty began to feel the tension evolve between them. He had lit a cigar and she found she was watching his hands which were clasped about his bent knees, the cigar between his fingers. They were brown, strong, long-fingered, the nails cut short. There was a faint scattering of pale brown hairs on the back of them which disappeared up the cuff of his sleeve. He leaned forward to tap ash off his cigar and the back of his neck above the collar of his jacket was exposed, brown like his hands, smooth, his dark hair curling crisply into the nape. His back was broad, straining the seams of his jacket and where it fell open she could see his thighs, strong, muscled, taut beneath the smooth fabric of his breeches.

She stood up so abruptly he looked up at her in surprise.

"I think I'm going to ride up to Formby Point," she told him, her voice turning cold, for her thoughts had alarmed her.

"D'you think you should, so soon, I mean? I think both the horses could do with a few more minutes' rest, not to mention me."

"Well, that's up to you but—"

"Kitty, I would advise—"

"Really, Ben, I have no need of your advice where my animal is concerned." She turned to give him a haughty stare and watched as his face, which had been open and . . . and what? She didn't know, but now it was closing up into that tight mask with which she was familiar.

"Besides, he needs some exercise if I'm to join the hunt at the weekend. The season is at an end and I . . . well, Jimmy Oliver was over yesterday . . ."

"I heard," he answered stiffly.

"Oh, of course, I forgot you have the servants trained to spy on me and my friends."

"Friends! Dear God, is that what you call them."

"They are *my* friends and they have invited me."

"Ah well, it is your choice."

"So it is, as your choice of . . . friends is your affair."

"And what is that supposed to mean?" Though of course he knew very well.

"Let us just agree to keep out of each other's lives, shall we, as we have done for the past year almost. Ever since you struck me."

"Bloody hell, Kitty, are you never going to . . . ."

She didn't know what he was going to say and she didn't wait to find out, since she knew whatever it was would hurt her.

"I'd be obliged if you would give me a leg up," she said icily.

"Of course." He was just as icy, his face frozen into a mask of what looked like hatred and when he had her in the saddle she galloped off towards Formby Point as though the devil himself were at her back.

26

She saw the woman first. She was so lovely, so delicately exquisite that heads were turning to watch her go by, both those of the gentlemen and the ladies, staring after her with an almost comical air of awe and disbelief on their faces, as Kitty did. She wore a small stylish bonnet decorated under the brim with white silk lily-of-the-valley. It was tipped forward over her brow and she had masses of pale silk hair arranged in a froth of glinting curls at the back of her head. Her eyes, which smiled up into those of the man beside her, were an incredible blue-green, cloudy and mysterious and surrounded by long, silken lashes. Her skin was ivory-tinted and her mouth a soft, rosy red. She wore a dress of pale-blue silk and about her shoulders was an exotically patterned crimson shawl. She was not tall but her figure was perfectly proportioned.

Kitty could hear the appreciative murmurs of the gentlemen in her own group and was smiling, agreeing with them and when she turned to the "lucky dog", as she heard Jimmy Oliver call him, and to whose arm the lovely woman clung she felt as though every drop of blood in her brain had left it, seeping away to other parts of her body and leaving her faint and sick. Her heart lurched into her throat, choking her, and her knees began to buckle and had she not had her arm through Michael's she would have stumbled.

The man was Ben Maddox. Like the woman on his arm he was smiling, a warm smile, a gentle smile, looking down into her flower-like face, saying something to her, something that made her tip her head back in laughter. She tapped his hand with her fingers as though in reproof, holding his upper arm tightly against her breast. They sauntered on slowly towards the grandstand, oblivious to all those about them, many of whom were business acquaintances of Ben Maddox and who stared in amazement.

"Is something wrong, Kitty-Cat?" Michael asked her, bending his head and smiling mockingly down at her and it was at that precise moment that Kitty began to see her half-brother as his true self. "You look as though you've seen a ghost. It's only your husband, after all, with his mistress. You knew about her, didn't you? Besides, you led us to believe you don't give a damn anyway. You don't, do you?"

"Of course not," she managed to gasp, cursing herself for allowing her distress to show so obviously, and cursing him for his maliciousness. Her heart was fetching up painfully against her ribcage, as though it were trying desperately to get out, to escape the bewildering pain it felt, and she found it hard to draw in a deep, life-saving breath. Short, shallow gasps then, just enough to keep her conscious, to keep her upright, smiling, though her face felt as though it were set in concrete. Her whole body was suffering such a pang of sheer physical anguish she found herself rushing forward to escape it, dragging an amused Michael along with her until they had caught up with the others of their animated group. Tam was there, on his arm the simpering, girlishly pretty Mrs Eva Hepworth, wife of the luckless Captain Jack Hepworth whose regiment was serving in Ireland. Vannie was whispering and laughing provocatively into the smirking face of a certain Major Gerald Cranshaw, nicknamed, for some reason, "Gus" and who was Vannie's latest conquest. Grace Oliver, since she was single and must therefore be more circumspect than her sister-in-law, had two languid young gentlemen one on either side of her and there were several other fashionable young ladies and gentlemen in the party, strolling in the mild sunshine towards the grandstand. Jimmy Oliver, who never seemed to favour one particular lady over another, was one of them.

So this is jealousy, then, Kitty thought wonderingly. How strange I have never felt it before. Perhaps small sips of it, childish sips taken when Freddy turned his boyish smiles on someone other than herself. Perhaps larger draughts forced down her throat when Freddy chose Ciara for a wife instead of her. But nothing like this, nothing like the great choking mouthful that poured down her throat and threatened to engulf her like the crash of rollers on a stormy sea.

It was a pleasant day for March, fine and mild, and the course was crowded. They had come on this special day, this day of the Grand National, not only the ordinary inhabitants of Liverpool and the gentry of the vicinity, but most of the élite of the sporting men of the nation who had arrived from all parts of the country, for this was one of the most famous racing events of the calendar. From abroad they came too, for Aintree was acknowledged to have the best turf and was renowned for its size and the comfort in which spectators might watch the races.

Ben and the pretty woman were sauntering some way ahead of them, stopping now and again to look at the lists of the runners the bookies had pinned up on their stalls and Kitty saw the woman point with her gloved hand at some name she seemed to fancy. Ben shrugged and laughed, then taking some money from his wallet handed it to the bookie. He gave her a ticket which she put in her reticule, saying something to her which made her put a hand to his face. He turned his mouth into it and kissed the palm before tucking it once more into the crook of his arm. Kitty felt as though a saw-edged knife had been plunged into her heart, damaging it irretrievably. She made a small sound in her throat but there was so much noise about her no one heard it. She must bear her pain in silence. No matter what might happen this day she must bear her pain in silence.

"We're going straight to the grandstand, everybody," Tam called over his shoulder.

"We're right behind you, laddie," Jimmy answered, putting his arm through Kitty's on her other side, for which she was grateful.

"Are you all right, Kitty-Cat?" he whispered in her ear, genuinely concerned, for Kitty's strange behaviour at the sight of her husband had not gone unnoticed.

She flashed him a brilliant smile from beneath her pretty parasol, twirling it light-heartedly, lifting her head to a queenly angle. "Of course." She laughed. "Whyever should I not be?"

"That's the ticket, old girl. Don't let them get you down."

"Who?" she asked curiously, and though her heart still throbbed and she felt inclined to shiver despite the tender warmth of the spring-like sunshine, she knew she must get through this day without making a fool of herself. Without anyone knowing how she suffered. Kitty Maddox upset over the sight of her own husband with a pretty woman on his arm! Never! Kitty Maddox gave not a tinker's toss what her husband did, nor who with. As little as he cared about her and despite the fact that she felt the same about him, and though it was highly indiscreet of him, a married man, openly to escort another woman under his wife's nose, what did it matter? Society, who liked its members to be somewhat more circumspect, might not approve of Ben Maddox "carrying on" with another woman – and *her* reputation would be in tatters – but Kitty Maddox, his wife, whose own reputation was none too intact, didn't give a damn. Though it cost her every shred of strength and willpower, and her own bloody-minded pride, she would not let them see she cared.

A slow realisation of what was happening, born in the moment she had seen her husband bend his head with evident affection to another woman, was moving through her, making its way from her wounded heart up to her slowly thawing mind which had frozen with disbelief. She had become heartbreakingly aware that something tremendous, awe-inspiring, terrifying, had happened to her in that split second it had taken for her eyes to recognise it and for her heart to acknowledge it and she didn't know what she was to do about it. She only knew that as soon as possible she must be allowed quiet, seclusion, a space somewhere with no one in it – perhaps Emma – in which to recover her composure, though how in the name of God she was to do that she couldn't imagine. The noise, the colour, the movement and cheerful laughter swirled all about her and she had the feeling she was in the centre of a swiftly moving kaleidoscope. The gowns of the ladies were in every shade of the rainbow and all in the very height of fashion. There were rose-coloured silk and crimson brocade, primrose bombazine, cornflower-blue gauze, saffron-coloured muslin and emerald-green lace. There were coffee-coloured velvet and sapphire faille and lemon satin, leno of amethyst purple and ottoman silk in hyacinth. Their skirts were a waterfall of frothy, lace-edged elegance draped from tiny, corseted waists, threaded with ribbon and beads, the bodices high-necked and hugging the figure. The hats were a mass of many-coloured flowerbeds and their parasols pretty bits of lacy nonsense threatening to poke the eye out of any careless onlooker, and it all swirled about Kitty Maddox like a child's vast spinning top.

The gentlemen were easier, for they were in the traditional black and white and grey. A tall silk hat and frock coat, high white cravats, white waistcoats, grey striped trousers, white kid gloves and each carried a pair of binoculars about their necks. They led the ladies towards the grandstand where a spacious dining-room was set out with tables laden with the kind of food the well-to-do expect to find wherever they go, and with fluted glasses of the finest champagne. They all shrieked with foolish laughter, at least those in Kitty's party did, Kitty among them, for they were having *such* a good time.

They wandered into the handsome salon, glass in hand, an enormously long room with full-length windows down one side from where the guests might view the whole one and a half miles of the racecourse and look across the sloping velvet lawns to the sweeping panoramic views of Walton-on-the-Hill.

Hundreds of spectators crowded the gallery to see the graceful dash of sleek horses line up to begin the race and in the excitement not one person, except the lovely woman who stood beside Ben Maddox, whose binoculars were trained on the start, noticed the fine drawn lines of pain about the mouth of Ben

Maddox's wife. Her own soft mouth was sad and pity-
ing.

Kitty saw none of it. Her face was pressed close to
the window and her eyes followed the long, glossy
stream of lovely horses as they pursued a line to the
first and longer brook, then angled back when it met the
Leeds-Liverpool Canal. The well-known Canal Turn.
They flowed back over the second brook, across the
flat then returned to the grandstand to go round the
course for the second time. The horses came – those
who had not fallen – to a paling surmounted by a
high, jagged hedge behind which was a ditch: Becher's
Brook, named after the horseman who first fell there.
The winner streaked past the winning post.

Kitty saw only a vivid reflection in the window as
her husband turned to the woman beside him, his face
creased in a huge grin of delight, his arms open wide to
draw her into his embrace.

"You did it, you little devil. You picked the winner
and just because you liked his name. Well, that's ladies
for you, bless 'em. Never mind form or any such nonsense. Any pretty name will do."

Over the head of the dainty little woman in his
arms Ben Maddox saw his wife watching and his eyes
widened with shock, for though he was well aware
that she was there, he had not expected her to be so
close. Then they became hard and expressionless as
they swept contemptuously over the raucous, rowdy,
half-drunken group who surrounded her.

For a moment or two he stood cradling the lovely

woman in his arms, then very deliberately he bent his head and put his lips against hers.

"Come, darling," he said, "let's go and collect your winnings."

She stumbled into her bedroom at Brook Hall, standing for a blind moment with her back to the door like a vixen who has missed the snapping teeth of the hounds by a hair's-breadth. Her head was up, her hands, one on either side of her, flat against the door, her eyes a dull, haunted blue and Emma, who had risen from her chair by the fire, put her hand carefully on its back to steady herself, for it looked as though steadiness were about to be needed. Something appalling had gone wrong. For a dreadful moment it occurred to her that Mr Oliver had been up to his old tricks again, but then they had only just returned from Aintree – she had seen the carriages on the drive from the window – and what could he have done to her mistress in full view not only of all their friends and relatives, but half the local gentry of south Liverpool looking on? There was to be a dinner party for sixty people this evening to which some of the most illustrious names of the county were invited. Lord and Lady this, the Earl and Countess of that and after the hectic goings-on of the day the ladies would want to rest and bathe before they changed for dinner. In about an hour's time, after she and Miss Kitty had discussed which gown she would wear, which jewellery if any, for Miss Kitty was not one for jewels, how her hair was to be arranged, Emma would remove from behind a screen in the corner of the room the huge, flat, but deep tin tub, painted to match the colouring of the curtains, and place it before the fire. It had a lovely, woolly bath-mat of the same tone with an enormous bath towel to match. The housemaids would bring numerous and immense cans of hot water, fetched up the stairs to the bedroom door by an army of men-servants. Brook Hall, unlike Meadow View, had not been modernised and though there were several water closets hidden discreetly in cupboards here and there, most of the guests preferred the convenience of chamber pots in their own rooms. Bathrooms with running water were unheard of. What did they need with such things when there was a staff of almost a hundred servants to fetch and carry, empty slops and clean up after the family and their guests?

Emma took a hesitant step towards her mistress, her own face blanching to the same pallor. She put out a hand, though they were still several feet apart, but Miss Kitty appeared not to see it. She had removed her pretty bonnet, holding it by the ribbons but, with her reticule and parasol, it fell to the floor as Kitty folded over, her arms across her stomach and was violently sick on the Olivers' splendid carpet.

"God almighty!" Emma whispered, leaping forward to catch her as she staggered upright. "What's happened to you? In the name of God you look . . ."

"Emma . . . Emmma . . ." Kitty moaned.

"What is it, darling?" In her appalled concern Emma quite forgot their respective positions. "See, come and sit by the fire. Oh, never mind the mess. One of those housemaids who are for ever hanging about can clear it up. Sit down and tell me . . . Did you eat something? Them oysters can give you a bad stomach as soon as look at you. My mam wouldn't let one in the house, not that we could afford . . . and then there'd be champagne flowing, I suppose. Oh, lass, you're shivering. Put this shawl round your shoulders. I'll ring the bell for the maid to see to that" – indicating with a careless gesture the stinking mess by the door – "and then you can tell Emma what's up."

It was more than something she'd eaten, Emma could tell that. Usually when an upset stomach has emptied itself of whatever has upset it, the sufferer, though inclined to shake and sweat, begins to recover, but Miss Kitty just sat, transfixed by something only she could see, her pinched face as grey as the ash that spilled from the fire into the grate. Her eyes were enormous, almost black with some unimaginable horror and Emma was frightened, for it took a lot to reduce Miss Kitty to the state she was in now. In fact, Emma had never seen her in such a condition. She was courageous, defiant, bold, challenging, so that no one, except perhaps Emma, knew that sometimes she was hurt and afraid. She laughed in the face of adversity, so what adverse thing had come on her today to reduce her to this sick and shaking creature who crouched, head bent, over the fire.

The chambermaid came and went with her mop and bucket, glancing curiously at the little tableau by the fireside, her mind filled with thoughts of pregnancy and, if it was so, who the father might be. Of abortions, perhaps, for these society ladies were not found very often in their own husbands' beds and could not afford to be caught out with an unwanted result of their philandering.

Emma knelt before her mistress. "Tell me," she said simply, stilling and chafing Kitty's hands which had the touch of fluttering snowflakes about them.

"I can't bear it, Emma." Her voice was soft and despairing.

"What, lass, what can't you bear?"

"I didn't know I cared, you see. Well, I didn't, not then. I thought we were like Tam and Vannie: they seem to manage, even to like each other even though they are both unfaithful. It works for them. Why can't it work for us?"

"Us?"

"Not that I've ever been unfaithful, you know that."

Oh, yes, Emma knew that. Miss Kitty might be wild and uncaring of what others thought of her but she herself knew she had done nothing, and never would, to shame herself, or her husband, which was strange really considering the mad bunch she went about with. She was always the centre of a group of admiring gentlemen, making them laugh and shake their heads with her flippancy, her impetuosity but when she closed her bedroom door at night she was always alone.

"I knew, of course I knew, that he had . . . someone, but I never saw her. She had no face, no form, no shape, no colour. She was just a woman, someone who saw to his needs since it appeared I couldn't. But she's not now, Emma. She's real, flesh and blood. I've seen her and . . . Oh, sweet Jesus, how am I to stand it, for he loves her. He loves her, Emma, and what am I to do?"

Her voice rose to a devastated wail and Emma flopped back on her heels, her face slack with growing bewilderment and at the same time the beginnings of understanding. What was she saying? What was her warm-hearted, reckless, hot-tempered mistress owning up to? Surely . . . surely not that the sight of her husband with his mistress had driven her into this pit of despair? She didn't love him, that was the trouble. She never had. God in heaven, she'd told Emma so a hundred times and if that was so, which Emma had no reason to doubt, then why was she in such a state?

"She's . . . lovely, Emma. Dainty, fair, sweet-faced. The exact opposite of me. She looked kind . . . and Ben couldn't take his eyes off her. He loves her."

She clutched at Emma's hand with such force Emma winced in pain. "When I pictured her, if I ever did, she was always some . . . some painted, overdressed person, you know what I mean. The sort of woman who . . . is paid for that sort of thing. A woman with no reputation to lose; but she's not. She's a widow, I was told, but surely she's ruined by what Ben has done to her, although she didn't seem to care. She loves him, she must do. And he must love her to put themselves in such a position."

"No, lass, no. He doesn't love her."

"Why not?"

"Because he loves you, lass. I've seen it."

"Rubbish, Emma."

"No, not rubbish, Miss Kitty. I've seen the way he looks at you."

Kitty obviously thought this statement not even worth considering since it was, to her, so patently unbelievable.

"Emma, how am I to manage? They all saw it this afternoon."

"Saw what? Who did?"

"The Olivers, Michael. They saw how it distressed me. I almost fainted; they are all laughing."

"Why should they laugh?"

"Because there is no more foolish a sight than a woman who finds her husband with another and cannot control her . . . her jealousy. I was jealous, Emma. I wanted to drag her away from him, to hit her. Oh, dear, dear God, to hit him for hurting me so, to scream with pain and . . . and betrayal. Heaven help me, Emma, what does it mean?"

There followed a long, quite appalling silence while the two woman stared into one another's shocked eyes. The unimaginable had happened. The shock of seeing her husband, whom she did not love and who did not love her, with a pretty woman on his arm, one she had convinced herself meant a great deal to Ben Maddox, had triggered off some sleeping thing within her, bringing it to life, bringing it into the sharp light of day and revealing to her the true state of her heart. And it was too late. It was true that Emma had believed that once upon a time Ben Maddox had loved his wife. When he imagined no one was looking at him, Kitty particularly, his glance had been yearning, sad, filled with his love and his longing but that had been months ago. Since then he appeared to have lost interest, to be totally indifferent to what she did and, if what Kitty Maddox said was true and he had found love elsewhere, who could blame him? A man needs a woman, just as a woman needs a man and somehow these two had, somewhere along the way, missed each other on the path of love. Their ways had crossed, certainly, but not at the exact time it was needed. When he had loved her she had despised him and now, when the time was right for her, what she had found at last to be worth while in the false sham of the life she led, he had moved on to another place.

"I must go home, Emma," she said softly. "I can't stay here . . . with them. Perhaps later, when I am . . . better I will. But just now I need to be . . . at home."

It was a measure of her desolation that for the first time since her marriage she was calling Meadow View "home".

"Right, lass, home is best."

"Will you tell them?"

"Of course. I'll go and see Mrs Oliver. Tell her you've been taken poorly and will leave in the morning."

"They'll know why."

"Why should they and anyway, do you care, Miss Kitty?"

"They are all I have, Emma. I must have something . . ."

Kitty sighed and lifted her head to stare sightlessly into what surely was to be her bleak future.

"Oh, Emma, did you ever think . . . ?"

"No, Miss Kitty, I never did but . . ."

"Yes?"

"Perhaps if the master was to see you at home, at Meadow View, he might . . ."

"Don't, Emma, don't try to give me hope. He loves her. Even I can recognise true love when I see it."

No, not really, you can't, my lass, Emma said to herself as she turned to the screen in the corner and lifted out the tin tub. That man who's your husband truly loved you, even as short a time ago as Christmas. I've watched his face . . . that time in the snow, for instance, but you were blind to it and now look at you, bent over with the anguish of loving a man who no longer loves you.

27

She lay in her bed where Emma had put her. Emma had bathed her as though she were an ailing child, and brushed her hair, then, kissing her gently on the brow, like the mother of an ailing child would do, had left her to go downstairs to advise Mrs Oliver that Mrs Maddox was not well and would not be down to dinner. The chambermaids had emptied the tub and tidied up the room, bobbing curtseys, efficient and unobtrusive but watching all the same as Emma readied her for bed. What was up with her? they would ask one another, since it was only just twilight and here she was being put to bed.

She wished she could weep but her eyes were hot, dry and, strangely, she felt feverish. She didn't know how she had got through this day but somehow she had. She'd managed to laugh and exchange the banter which these people who were her friends used to communicate with one another. These people who were her friends! Dear Lord, could she call them that? Friends! They had all seen Ben with his mistress and how the sight of them together had affected her, but not one had so much as given her a word of sympathy, a look of compassion, a comforting hand. In fact they had laughed, not at her but at the spectacle Ben Maddox was making of himself, which they thought, highly entertaining though it might be, was not the thing to do in public. They all had their little dalliances, flirtations, but really there was a way to go about these things which they all respected and one certainly did not flaunt them in the face of society. Tam had his Eva, Vannie had her Gus and there were a dozen little affairs of the heart, light things that went on at Brook Hall and other weekend parties which meant absolutely nothing to those involved. A bit of fun with no hearts broken, but what Ben Maddox was up to was really quite immoral in their opinion. Still, he was in trade. He might mix with the high-born gentlemen with whom he was on nodding acquaintance but he was not one of them. They were of the patrician class whose ancestors had been privileged and powerful, whose education had been expensive, exclusive to their class. They believed themselves to be vastly superior to the rest of humanity. They had been born to greatness and Ben Maddox had worked for what he had and though he might be convinced of his own rightness they were not. He was of the working class, despite his wealth, as Kitty Maddox's father was of the working class. What *they* had inherited, he had laboured for, so what else could you expect of such a man? And privately they agreed they were quite amazed by Kitty who had, for several awkward moments, shown an embarrassing, a middle-class inclination, to let everybody see that she cared about her husband's association with his woman.

And the fact that she was not to dine that evening would give them further fuel for gossip, she thought. What a curious world she moved in when a woman who suffered pain at her husband's faithlessness should be thought peculiar, raising eyebrows and curling lips contemptuously. When their own escapades with this woman or that man were, to them, quite normal. Everybody in their circle had a lover, for they had to alleviate their boredom in some way, usually somebody else's husband or wife and it was considered completely acceptable. Even she, a few hours ago, had scarcely given it a thought. She was aware that they had seriously believed that she and Tam were more than good friends and had it not been for her father's illness it might have developed into . . . well, she didn't know, for the idea was abhorrent to her. She supposed if she had been introduced to some attractive gentleman who had shown interest in her, a man who in his turn attracted her she might have . . . No . . . no, she thought wearily, she would *not*. She would not and the reason for it, for her quite circumspect behaviour, circumspect in their eyes, was that buried deep inside her where even she had not thought to look, was the feeling she had for her own husband. Something tiny and hidden, hidden too deep even to have a name really, had awoken, stirred and, at the sight of Ben and his mistress together and in such intimate circumstances, had blazed into life, burning her, scorching her and she didn't know what to do with it, or about it.

She remembered the nights they had spent together in the deep privacy of their marriage bed when she had pressed herself wordlessly against him. She had wrapped her long legs about him, welcoming his warm mouth, deliciously sweet on her tongue, his hard body capturing hers as she flowed over him and under him, his kisses on her mouth, her cheeks, behind her ears and below her chin, racing her and himself towards an explosive orgasm of pleasure which left them both breathless, and sometimes laughing at the incredible joy of it. They would fall asleep in one another's arms, limbs embraced and were often considerably startled when they woke to find themselves still clinging fast together.

And now that rapture she had known but not valued was shared with another woman. Kitty had thrown it carelessly away, considering it to be useless and her heart was breaking at the loss of it and the loss of the quiet, humorous man who had, without her even realising it, offered it to her.

Even last week when they had ridden out together to Bootle sands there had been a . . . a question mark shimmering in the air between them. But she would not recognise it for what it might have been. She had, in her usual fashion, taken offence at something he had said, she couldn't even remember what it was now. They had exchanged bitter words . . . yes, she remembered she had reminded him of when he had struck her and when he tried to speak she had flung herself on her horse and galloped off in high dudgeon.

Why? Why? Why had she not . . . ? Dear God, she didn't even know what question she was asking herself. Tomorrow she would perhaps, when she was home, when she would have the quiet – Kitty Maddox longing for quiet! – and the seclusion of her peaceful sitting-room, the burgeoning spring of the gardens to walk in, Henry at her heels, long rides on Havoc, she would scrape herself together and . . . Well, she didn't know what but she would find it. She would find something. She supposed when she had recovered from the shock and was able to hide her feelings from them she would take up the life she led with the Olivers and the Barries and the rest of her social circle, but until then she needed to be on her own.

She must have slept, for when she woke she was in total, pitch darkness. Even the fire seemed to have gone out, the only contrast in the room the outline of the windows where starlight glimmered. Why were the lamps not lit? Why had one of the numerous chambermaids not been in to see to the fire? What time was it and where was Emma? Emma was her lifeline to reality, her lifebuoy holding her up in stormy seas and while she had slept it had gone dark and Emma was not here. She had been in such a state of shock and sorrow she hadn't noticed what time Emma had slipped away, promising to be no more than a minute, to let Vannie know there would be one fewer for dinner. Should she ring the bell to summon a maid? The fire needed seeing to and . . . and . . . Dear Lord, why did she feel so apprehensive?

She sat up in bed. She was not sure she knew how to light the lamps and until she did she had no idea what time of the evening it might be. Really, she was being very foolish, dithering about like this, trembling in her bed as though . . . as though . . . Oh, God, where was Emma? She needed Emma.

Feeling her way out of bed she made her way hesitantly across the vast expanse of velvet carpet to the fireplace where she seemed to remember seeing a candle. There was a glimmer in the grate where the last of the coals flickered, and reaching to the mantelpiece she found a tall box of spills and the candle. Taking a spill she managed to light the end which she put to the candle and as it flared into life so did her room. Empty, quiet, threatening somehow, though she knew that was silly. Well, there was only one way to find out what was going on. Why no one had come near her and where Emma had got to. She just couldn't imagine her lounging in the servants hall, a cup of tea in her hand, not Emma, whose first thought was always for her mistress. By the light of the flickering candle, which she held to the pretty enamelled and jewelled boudoir clock, she saw it was almost nine o'clock.

Pulling the cord to summon a chambermaid she reached for the soft white blanket that Emma had tucked up round her neck, and dragging it off the bed she wrapped herself in it, for the room was going cold.

Within seconds there was a discreet knock on the door and when she called out a little maid entered, bobbing her curtsey as she had been trained to do. She looked enquiringly at Kitty, smiling politely, then, as though suddenly aware that something was wrong, she frowned, looking about the bedroom which was not only dimly lit but cold.

"Madam, oh, madam, what has happened? Has no one been to light your lamps and what's happened to the fire? Dear me, this won't do. Whatever can have happened? Did your maid" – wherever she might be, the unspoken words said— "not see to your needs before she left?"

Within minutes there was a bevy of maidservants scurrying round the bedroom, remaking the fire until it blazed merrily, lighting all the lamps, straightening the bed, begging her to tell them what they might bring her, for they had heard she was not quite herself. A tray of tea perhaps, a boiled egg, or could Cook whip her up an egg custard to tempt her appetite? The head chambermaid was fulsome with her apologies, for was it not the custom of Brook Hall to make sure that every guest was treated like royalty. It was not their fault, they all knew that, for her own personal maid should have seen to it that Mrs Maddox had every available comfort that was to be had and there was a lot of it at Brook Hall, but to be left with no lamps lit and the fire out was most appallingly slipshod and they were sure, though they didn't say as much to Mrs Maddox, that the housekeeper on whose shoulders all responsibilities rested would have something to say to Mrs Maddox's maid, though she was not, strictly speaking, one of hers.

"Will you find my maid for me, please, er . . ."

"Jackson, ma'am," the head chambermaid murmured.

"Jackson. I can't begin to imagine where she could have got to. It's . . . well, several hours since she left to tell Mrs Oliver I would not be down."

"The message came through to the kitchen that there would be one fewer for dinner, madam."

"There, then she must have seen Mrs Oliver."

"I would say so, madam. Dinner is just about to be served."

"Well, she must be found. She might have . . . well . . ."

"Yes, madam?" the maid said politely, but it was apparent from her expression that she had a fair idea where Mrs Maddox's maid might be. She was a very attractive woman; many of the footmen and valets, those who travelled about with their masters and those who worked at Brook Hall, had remarked on it. With her mistress safely asleep in her room she most likely thought she might take up the offers one or two of them had made to her. At least, that was what she thought, but first they must get Mrs Maddox comfortable and warm and tucked up back in her bed. She certainly did not look well. She was pale and drawn, her lovely hair which normally rioted about her head like a dandelion clock quite quenched by some illness she seemed to be suffering and as soon as . . .

The door was open slightly, for there had been a great deal of toing and froing with maids bringing in bedwarmers, coals, a tea tray and when it was pushed wide with a great deal of violence several of them stepped back quickly to make way for the woman who entered. Well, entered was not really the word. She fell in, staggering across the carpet with such force she knocked over a small chair. She stood in the centre of the room, her head turning this way and that as though she were not sure where to go, or indeed what to do next.

For an appalled moment there was silence, for who on earth was it who had invaded Mrs Maddox's now cosily glowing bedroom. The woman looked as though she had been cornered by a crazed beast, her clothes torn and hanging from her in so many tatters her white flesh could clearly be seen through several rents. Her hair flared about her head in a snarl of curls so that she looked as though she had been dragged by it through the proverbial hedge, and backwards too. She wore no shoes and where were her stockings, for her feet were bare. She was moaning, her face like paper, ghastly, all sunken grey hollows and protruding bones and yet she had been so bonny, a real country lass with apple cheeks and a magnificent breast, much of which was on view at this moment. Her eyes, when she turned to them, were as flat and colourless as hoar frost but without the sparkle. She was like a beast at bay, some strange sound coming from her throat and her head slowly lowered itself until it hung down as though in the deepest shame. Just as slowly and quite gracefully she sank to her knees, her arms about herself and began to rock backwards and forwards in the age-old manner of a sorrowing woman.

With a crash that made them all jump a foot in the air one of the maids dropped the bowl of water she had been just about to carry downstairs. It hit the doorpost and the bowl broke, spattering its contents all over the maid's boots. She began to cry, not because she hurt but because she was frightened. They all stared at the apparition in the centre of the carpet, even Mrs Maddox rooted to the spot in the bed where they had tenderly laid her. Her face was like suet, her eyes staring and quite wild as she studied the intruder, then, as they all backed away towards the wide-open door wishing to God they were anywhere but here, she began to moan.

It was as though the sound in her own throat which she had not known she had made, brought Kitty back to life and in a moment she was out of the bed and kneeling before the figure of the woman who was crumpled on the carpet.

"Emma," she whispered and in the doorway, which they were all trying to get through at the same time, the maids hovered and stared, the young one beginning to be hysterical.

"Emma . . . darling," Mrs Maddox said surprisingly, for this was her maid, that they had deduced, and what mistress calls her maid, "darling"? "What . . . ?

Who . . . ? Dear God, what's happened to you?" She didn't know how or why but, could you blame her, she had a picture of Emma crashing about in the woods at the far side of the gardens, savaged by some beast that lurked there, for what else could have caused the bruises, the bites, the scratches which, now that she was close to her, Kitty could see on Emma's white flesh?

The upper chambermaid sprang to life and with a sharp word and a wave of her hand sent the maids scurrying with instructions to send up Mrs Jagger, the housekeeper, for this was something that . . . Well, who or what had done this to Mrs Maddox's maid must be found. It must be a madman, some escapee from a lunatic asylum who had got into the grounds, even the house and he must be found. The men-servants must be sent out in a search and the rest of the household warned, for who knew what lurked in the grounds, or even, God forbid, in the house?

Kitty stood up and gently lifted Emma to her feet, then, with an instinctive movement, she put her arms about her maid and held her to her. "Come, darling," she was crooning. "Come and sit by the fire. See, you" – turning to Jackson – "fetch that tea and . . . and . . ." What? What did Emma, who must have been mauled by a wild beast, need at this moment? Again her instinct told her it was not all these maids gawking at her and especially the frozen-faced, grandly efficient housekeeper who ran Brook Hall and all the servants in it with an iron hand.

"Leave us alone, please," she said to the chamber-maid. "We don't need Mrs whatever she's called. Bring hot water yourself and then I'll let you know whether a doctor is needed. Tell no one, if you please. I don't want all and sundry trooping up here to question her. Leave us alone and when I'm ready I'll ring."

"Very well, madam, but I feel—"

"I don't give a damn what you feel. Just go."

The chambermaid sketched a curtsey, smirking to one side, for already she had begun to picture what had happened to this woman's personal maid, who always gave the impression she was a cut or two above the others. She was struggling in the arms of some man, a man she had egged on and then, finding she had got more than she'd bargained for, fighting for her honour in which it looked as though she had not succeeded. Not tell Mrs Jagger indeed! Of course she must tell Mrs Jagger and Mrs Jagger must inform the mistress, though it might be a bit tricky in the middle of dinner.

Just as Emma had bathed her earlier in the evening, Kitty bathed Emma, gently applying a sweet-smelling salve, one she always kept in what she called her medicine chest, since she liked to be prepared for a cut or a bruise when she was out riding. She brushed her hair and held her close, for Emma had begun to shake and whimper, then, putting her in one of her own plain nightgowns, she laid her in her own bed and held her hand until she saw her eyes begin to droop.

"That's right, darling, sleep. I'll stay here and then when you've had a rest you can tell me . . ."

"It was him." Emma's eyes flew open and tears began to flow from beneath her long lashes. One of her eyes was already swelling where a heavy fist had landed. The bed shook with the storm of her anguish and she clung to Kitty as Kitty had earlier clung to her. "He raped me . . ."

Kitty felt the ice move into her veins just as though someone had opened one up and injected it with ice water. Something inside her lurched in terror, of what she didn't know, for surely the worst had happened. Her heart began to pound so that she could hardly breathe. Nausea rose in her throat, choking her. Oh, sweet Jesus, her mind whispered, oh, dear sweet Jesus, what has he done to her? For of course she knew exactly who Emma was mumbling about through her torn and bruised lips.

"He was . . . on the top hall when I . . . I came back from seeing Mrs Oliver. They hadn't lit the lamps yet and . . . you know how dim it is . . . There's a linen cupboard . . . He didn't speak and neither did I, but I thought he wanted me to get something for him, so . . . I went in. Then . . . he hit me. He was like a madman. Oh, Kitty, I thought he was going to . . . to kill me. He was so angry . . . wild. He kept saying things that didn't make sense . . . about you . . ."

"Darling, don't talk, I'm going to send for the doctor."

Emma clutched at her hands frantically. "No, please. No doctor, Kitty . . . not here."

"But, darling, you may be hurt . . . inside."

"I am. But no doctor. There's nothing to be done. Please, just take me home. I want to go home."

"And you shall, as soon as the carriage can be ordered. We can have Doctor Drysdale to look at you."

"Yes, but not here."

"No, darling, but first I want you to drink this. Remember, you gave it to me when I was . . . poorly last year and couldn't sleep. You have a rest while I make arrangements and then I'll take you home."

"Yes . . . home . . ."

She held Emma in tender arms until her eyelids began to droop, watching her poor bruised face, smoothing back the tangle of her hair, tucking the soft white blanket up about her neck. Whether it was the shock, her injuries or the draught Kitty had given her, she fell into the deep sleep nature provides to heal those who are hurt.

Kitty stood for several moments, trying to get her breath, for she felt as though she herself had been punched in the ribs and winded. The icy rage that had infiltrated her body as Emma mumbled her tragic story was beginning to leave her and in its place was a fury so hot and hating she didn't think she could contain it. She was in pain with it, for this was all her fault. Her own stupid pride had convinced her that she could control Tam Oliver. She had believed Jimmy when he told her that Tam was involved with the officer's wife and indeed he seemed to be. That he was genuinely sorry for the loss of his usual gentlemanly behaviour, and that his obsession with her was over, but he had just been biding his time, hiding behind the smokescreen of his supposed infatuation for whatever her name was and when he thought he had her, when he thought he had Kitty Maddox cornered, he had continued what he had started on the night the message had come to say her father was ill.

But he had made a mistake. Emma was the same height as Kitty. She was dark and had a good figure. She had not been wearing an apron or cap but an elegant plum-coloured dress which had once been Kitty's and he had mistaken her for Kitty. There would be no light in the linen cupboard and in the few moments when the door was open as he had pushed her inside he had not recognised that he had the wrong woman.

She might have known he would not give up. He was a man used to his own way. All his life he had been indulged and had come to believe that it was his God-given right to do as he pleased, especially with women. A man who insisted on it. He had persisted in his belief that she, Kitty, was just acting out a bit of female foolishness, a pretended reluctance, skittishness that most women had in abundance, giggling and coy, but meaning him to carry on with his seduction, naturally.

But she had fought him and Emma had obviously fought him and it had only added to the titillation. He might even have realised at the end that he had got the wrong woman but as that woman was merely a servant, what did it matter? Men of his class were convinced that women of Emma's were fair game but, by God, he was going to be made to realise that it made no difference to Kitty Maddox. Herself or Emma, it made no difference: Tam Oliver was going to regret this day for the rest of his life, for Kitty Maddox would make sure of it.

So strong was her killing madness, her violent rage, she was trembling. She had no thought for anything, now that Emma was safely asleep, but her need for revenge. No, not for revenge but for justice. Justice not only for Emma but for all the other young serving girls who had been taken down by their masters or their masters' sons but here was one who wasn't going to get away with it. Him first, shown up for what he was before his fine friends, then home and the doctor, and then the police.

She could feel the heat of her body turning her flesh to a rosy pink and even her hair seemed to stand on end with wrath. Flinging open the door she raced towards the head of the stairs, no slippers to her feet, no wrap, just a vengeful figure in a voluminous nightdress which, though it wasn't exactly transparent, revealed the shape and shades of her beneath it. It was a pretty thing, made of the finest lawn, embroidered in white thread with wild flowers, all the seams joined by drawn threadwork and it clung to her figure as she ran lightly down the stairs.

The hallway was softly lit, warm and luxurious, furnished with deep armchairs and sofas, costly rugs and exquisitely turned tables, with lamps and flowers and pale, watered-silk walls. A log fire flickered in the enormous stone fireplace and leaning over it, replenishing it a young footman glanced up in surprise as the flying figure in white went by him.

"What . . . ?" he blurted out, for he was convinced it was a woman dressed in a nightgown, but how could that be? As he stared after her, watching her go through the wide doors that led to the dining hall, the butler, followed by several footmen, came through the green baize door from the kitchen passage. They were carrying silver platters piled high with whatever the guests were to have for their second course and as he moved ponderously, majestically towards the dining-hall doorway the butler was just in time to see . . . Good God, were his eyes deceiving him, but was that pretty little Mrs Maddox who, they had all been told, was sick in her bed, entering the dining hall in her bloody nightgown? He stopped in confusion and the footmen behind him crashed into him and for an appalling moment chaos reigned as silver salvers went everywhere, splattering their contents over immaculate uniforms and polished boots, not to mention the carpet, which had cost hundreds of guineas, but Kitty Maddox didn't see it. She didn't see the seated row of open-mouthed, slack-jawed, elegantly dressed ladies and gentlemen at the highly polished table, for her whole being was concentrated on the lounging figure of Tam Oliver who, she wasn't surprised to see, carried a deep scratch on his left cheek.

"What the devil . . ." she heard someone say. She thought it might be Major Gus Cranshaw whose thigh was being stroked by Tam Oliver's wife but though several footmen moved hesitantly forward to intercept her, for surely she had lost her mind, none was quick enough to reach her.

She stopped at his chair and he got slowly to his feet. He was laughing at something one of the ladies had said to him and the smile was still on his face but his eyes were as cold and as flat as a cobra's. He turned away from her for a moment, shrugging his broad shoulders, his eyebrows raised to the others as though to ask what the hell was wrong with Kitty Maddox, but when he turned back to her she hit him so hard across what she now recognised as his cruel face that he fell back into the lap of the lady next to him.

"Dear God, Kitty." Vannie Oliver leaped to her feet, appalled and concerned, for she had not yet been told of the fracas upstairs, since Mrs Jagger thought it prudent to leave it until after the dinner party. After all it was only a servant who had been . . . well, whatever had been done to her.

"Kitty, my dear, whatever is wrong and" – Vannie's eyes moved in fascination over Kitty's white nightdress and her bare feet – "and why are you . . . See, let me ring for your maid."

"Thank you, Vannie, but my maid is indisposed. You see, she has just been raped by your husband and is not quite up to it."

There was a horrified gasp about the table and one or two of the ladies of a more delicate nature put their hands to their mouths and moaned. They remained rigid in their chairs though, as they did their best, since they were ladies and gentlemen, to pretend this unfortunate thing was not happening to their host and hostess. They most of them knew Kitty Maddox and were aware that she was sometimes wild and reckless, but really she must have lost her mind, had some sort of a brainstorm. You could see that their host was absolutely livid and it was with the utmost difficulty he was keeping his hands off Kitty Maddox.

Vannie put her hand to her throat and staggered back against her chair. "Kitty, darling, you don't know what you're saying," she began.

"Yes, I do, Vannie, and you can't pretend you don't know what a . . . a bastard your husband is. He pursued me relentlessly but I said no and now this has happened and I'll never forgive myself." She whipped round to Tam Oliver, whose face was twisted in a snarl of rage. "You thought it was me, didn't you, Tam? You thought you had trapped me in that linen cupboard."

"Linen cupboard . . ." Vannie said faintly.

"Oh, yes, and if you doubt that this has happened I beg you to question your chambermaids for they saw Emma stagger . . . Oh, dear God . . ." She put her hand to her mouth and her eyes widened with horror. "He nearly killed her . . . he must have beaten her. He's a beast, a bestial thing who needs locking up."

"Get out of my house," Tam roared, and several of the footmen moved forward, for surely he was going to strike the woman in the nightgown but she had turned away contemptuously.

"Oh, don't worry, I'm going, and at once, and tomorrow you may expect a visit from the police, for I mean to report you for the sick and evil bastard you are. I believe rape is an offence that carries a prison sentence. Now then, I shall expect the carriage to be at the front door immediately and one of the men to carry my maid down to it. Don't bother to see me off and don't expect to see me again, except perhaps in court."

28

"Kitty, can't you see how impossible this is? I know the constable—"

"The constable is a dolt and I would be obliged, with your influence, if you would arrange for . . . for an inspector to call on me. We need someone higher up in the police force to deal with this. Someone who isn't terrified at the mention of the name of Oliver. The doctor who examined Emma says she was . . . taken against her will."

Kitty swallowed convulsively and bent her head, putting her hand to her eyes for a moment to shut out the sight of the man who stood before her. He was so stern, so . . . so stiff-necked, so oppressive and yet so . . . breathtaking. Sweet Jesus, why had she not seen it before? He took her breath away. He was not handsome but his face was strong, compelling and completely masculine. His eyes were warm with concern, not for her she knew that, but for Emma, turning to a deep chestnut, fringed with thick brown lashes and his mouth, which at the moment was not smiling since this was a serious matter, was well cut, curling and sensual. He was doing his best to be what she wanted him to be but she could see he was only being polite. She wondered why she was holding this conversation with him, for though he was a basically decent man he did not really want to be involved with anything that had to do with her. She was no longer a part of his life. He loved another woman and though she knew he would do what he could to help Emma, if such an action was possibly within his power, it was not because of any consideration for her, Kitty Maddox, but because he was the sort of man who had a weakness for defenceless creatures, a tendency to rescue a kitten or a child in distress, to be kind to animals and small children, creatures who had been hurt and Emma was such a one. In other words he was a good man placed in an awkward position and she could see he was uneasy, not only with her but with the situation.

Dear God, what had happened to her in such a short time? Why had chance, fate, destiny, whatever name you cared to put to it, turned, in the time it took to blink an eye, her supreme indifference to the man who was her husband to a painful love that was blurring her mind when she should be thinking not about herself or even him but about Emma. He lounged against her fireplace, his hands in his pockets, his face carefully blank, his eyes looking somewhere over her head as though he didn't really care to consider her face and even as she burned with a fiery determination to see Tam Oliver brought to justice, her heart beat agonisingly and longingly, despairingly, wanting Ben's arms about her, wanting his hard, protecting body against hers, his lips smoothing her forehead in the way of a man who loves a woman. He did love a woman but it wasn't her and she must find the strength to accept that but, by God, it was hard to see him standing there, awkward, uncomfortable, wishing to God he didn't have to be involved.

The man who leaned against her sitting-room fire-place moved uncomfortably. He wanted to go to her, take her in his arms, kiss her and soothe her and tell her he would make everything all right and yet how could he after what had happened yesterday. But she was evidently much distressed, and who could blame her after what had been done to her maid.

He had been tossing restlessly in his bed when the clatter of the carriage on the drive had drawn him to the window. He had spent several hours with Helen after they had returned from Aintree, eating the fine dinner her cook had prepared, then taking her to bed and making love to her until she moaned with pleasure, but something inside him, though he too had shuddered into an orgasm, had not been satisfied and he had made some excuse and returned to his own bed at Meadow View.

It was just on midnight and the sound of furious voices, servants calling out, Kitty giving orders, feet running up and down stairs and then the sound of a horse being ridden furiously down the drive had brought him out of his room and down the stairs just in time to see Kitty and a couple of half-dressed maidservants almost carrying her maid, bundled up in Kitty's own fur-lined cloak, up the stairs.

"Hell's teeth, Kitty, what the devil has happened?" he had blurted out, staring in horror at Emma's bruised face, as the clustered servants were staring, their own expressions appalled, for surely poor Emma had been attacked by some wild beast.

But Kitty had brushed him and them aside like a swarm of troublesome flies. "There's been . . . an accident," she said shortly. "Tim has gone for the doctor."

"An accident? What sort of an accident?"

"I'll tell you later when the doctor has been. Now, if you'll excuse me, I must see to Emma."

Though it was still dark, a streak of paler grey lined the horizon above the trees. Fires had been lit, coffee brought, the constable who had been summoned, somewhat perplexed as to what Mrs Maddox wanted of him, had gone and so had the doctor who had given Emma something to make her sleep and informed Kitty that he would call in later. Speculation was rife in the kitchen where the maids congregated, for what had happened to poor Emma? they asked one another. But the two people who could have answered were keeping it to themselves.

Ben sighed and reached for his coffee which stood on the mantelpiece, wondering how in hell's name he was to convince Kitty that really she was wasting her time. It was a sin, an appalling state of affairs, but that was what life for a girl such as Emma was like. The trouble was it was her word, a woman of the working classes, against that of the son of a baronet and Ben Maddox, who knew these men and their appetites, and their total belief in their own right to slake them wherever and whenever they felt like it, knew what Kitty asked of him was quite out of the question. Tam Oliver was known for his excesses, a bastard of the first order, one of the very worst examples of his class and upbringing. He was like them all, reared in the belief that as a member of the ruling class he was entitled to anything his privileged birth told him was his due, but he also commanded a great deal of influence and power and Kitty had no idea of the risk she was taking in besmirching his good name.

"She is much torn about and needed to be . . . stitched and one of her . . . her breasts was so badly bitten—"

"God in heaven!" Ben turned away in disgust and pity, reaching for his cigars, then, when he had lit one, dragging the smoke deep down into his lungs. "The man is an animal. No, that insults animals."

Kitty looked up at him eagerly. "Then you agree that I must go on. That we must have justice for Emma."

Ben sighed and sat down next to her on the sofa. Surprisingly, he took both her hands between his own and for a breathless moment her heart jumped in her breast; then, as though remembering the deep division that stood between them he let them go and stood up again, moving to stare out of the window into the lightening garden.

"Kitty, it will be all over Liverpool what happened at Brook Hall, what you *allege* happened at Brook Hall."

Kitty leaped to her feet and began to stride up and down in front of the fireplace, kicking her skirt back at each turn, her face bright and furious, her eyes snapping like blue lightning. She had not changed out of the gown she had thrown on in the bedroom at Brook Hall and her hair had not been brushed since she jumped out of the bed where Emma had put her. She looked wild, demented, ready to hit him if he stood in her way.

"Alleged! Alleged! Dear God, he raped her. He threw her skirts over her head and simply took her like a dog will take a bitch. She . . . she had known no man and when she fought him he hit her. Oh, I know taking a woman of the lower classes against her will is nothing to make a fuss about, at least in the circle you seem to move in but—"

"Stop it, Kitty. You know that's not true. I have never taken a woman by force in my life. I am just trying to tell you that there will be little sympathy in Liverpool for what you are bent on doing. At least among those who matter."

"Oh, yes, there would be. The *gentlemen* who no doubt think Tam Oliver is a hell of a fellow and can't help wondering what all the fuss is about. She is only a servant after all but I think there is something you should know. That *they* should know."

"Yes?" he asked guardedly.

"Emma wasn't meant to be raped. I was! It was me he was after."

She lifted her head and stared directly at him. He probably didn't care overmuch, only in the way any decent man would care about a woman who has been brutalised by some predatory male, and when he turned away and stared out of the window as though that were not the issue here it seemed to prove it. She did not see the way his rigid shoulders bunched, nor the way his hands, clenched into fists in his pockets, moved savagely as though in great need of smashing themselves into someone's face. His lips were clamped in a thin white line about his cigar and his brown eyes were dark and sombre, with an expression that was hard to define. Rain beat against the window, making patterns on the glass which were reflected on his pale face and it seemed he could not speak.

At last he did. "How do you know that?" His voice was harsh, rasping curiously in his throat.

"Because it was not the first time. Once – that day my father was taken ill and a message came – he had cornered me in . . . well, it doesn't matter where but had one of the guests not knocked on the door he would have . . . stripped me. He was ready then to put his fists in my face."

"And yet you went back there?" He turned and leaned his buttocks on the windowsill, his arms crossed, his face calm and expressionless as though her answer were really of no concern. "You returned to his house and exposed yourself to his insult again. Do you know,

Kitty, you never cease to amaze me. You are so head-strong, so self-willed, so filled with your own invincibility you were willing to put not only yourself in danger but Emma."

"No . . . no, Ben." Her voice was passionate in her own defence. "Jimmy came. He told me Tam was sorry . . . he lost control, he said, he was drunk."

"And you believed him. I have been known to get drunk, Kitty, as have thousands of other men but we do not go about attacking defenceless women." He spoke quietly, his back to the window so that his eyes were shadowed, the expression in them hidden from her.

Kitty stopped pacing, turning away from him and staring into the fire. She put both hands on the mantelpiece and leaned forward and her own voice was low and soft.

"So, are you saying I should let it go?"

"No, I'm not saying you should let it go. I only want you to be aware of what you are taking on. They will close ranks against you, the gentry. They will lie and they will be believed."

"I don't give a damn about that, Ben. I only care about him and what he did to Emma. Are you saying you won't support me?"

"No, I'll help you any way I can but I don't think it will be enough. I wasn't there."

"But the servants, the maids who saw her . . ."

"Will prove nothing, Kitty. Anyone could have attacked Emma and are they likely to speak up against their master? Not if they want to keep their jobs, they're not. They won't have to lie. All they have to say is they didn't see it happen. And you know what they will say?"

"Who?"

"All of them. Can a woman, a servant, a member of the working classes who are known to be obliging—"

"*Ben!*"

"Can a woman like that be raped? They will be furious with you for even bringing it to the attention of the police. They will say these things occur with tedious regularity. That she should have picked herself up and said nothing. After all, can one rape a woman who puts herself in a dangerous position wandering about the estate in the dark of night asking for trouble."

"It took place in a linen cupboard off the hall in the house where Emma had every right to be. She was not wandering about the—"

"They will say that you, as a gentlewoman should not trouble the constabulary with a sorry episode such as this."

"And if he had raped me, Ben, what then? If I, as a gentlewoman was attacked?"

"As my wife you . . ."

"Would be believed?"

"Yes, I suppose so."

"And you would defend me."

"Yes."

"But you know Emma. You know she is a good woman. That Tam Oliver is a bastard so why . . . ?"

He passed a hand across his face and turned away

again to stare out into the slanting rain. It was almost light now. There was no one about except for young Joey, the gardener's lad, a piece of sacking draped over his head, running for shelter across the lawn on his way to report to Wilf. The trees which were coming into leaf dripped dismally and from the leaden skies, which gave the appearance of hanging drapes of dirty grey cloth, the rain fell steadily. He should be on his way to his office. There were many matters that needed his attention and he had promised Josh Hayes that he would get over to Monarch Mill to speak to young Michael Hayes who, it seemed, showed up whenever he felt like it, which was not often, and find out what was going on. Not that he needed to be told what was going on, for the young bounder was making it perfectly obvious that though he was not averse to taking the generous allowance his uncle made him he thought it was beneath him to work for it.

And Freddy was not much better. Ciara had given birth to a daughter a few weeks back and it appeared that she really could not manage without her husband constantly by her side. She had a nanny and a nursery nurse to care for the infant besides the hordes of other servants in the house but unless Freddy was with her, she said, she really could not cope with a baby. She needed time to recover and surely, now that Michael was there and Ben was overlooking the running of the mill, Freddy could be spared to be with his wife who had been through such a dreadful experience.

And now this. He knew if he turned he would find

Kitty glaring at his back in that determined way she had, wanting her own way, as she had always done, believing that he should dash down to the police station and stir them all up. Even go with them to arrest Tam Oliver, but it was out of the question. Already he knew it would be whispered that Emma Taylor should be dismissed, for how could decent girls be expected to work in close contact with a girl who had been raped. It was a disgrace. She was disgraced and should go at once to do whatever women like her did in such circumstances, but Ben was forced to smile, a small, rueful smile which was reflected in the window pane, for he knew that his Kitty would never allow it. That she would fight tooth and nail in defence of her maid and if they didn't like it, the other servants, then they could all go to hell, she would say.

His Kitty! What had made him say that? he wondered, for she was not his, and never had been. He loved her, of course he did, and always would, but the very things he loved in her kept them apart. The sad thing was that he could never let her see it, what she meant to him, or it would destroy him when he saw the disbelief, the amusement, the amazement in her eyes. He had loved her from the first moment he laid eyes on her but her spirit was too strong for him. She seemed incapable of accepting love, of letting herself be loved and so he had shut her out, slowly and painfully, and it was only at times like this when she showed her own warmth and compassion and vulnerability that he almost let it overcome him.

But there were other women in the world, warm-hearted women. He could not live with Kitty and he could not stop her from going hell-bent for leather down the mad path the Olivers took her. Tam Oliver had wanted her and had almost had her, so she was telling him, and if he, Ben Maddox, had been a stronger man, perhaps a harder man, a less warm-hearted man, he would have forced her to his own will. He should have locked her up and thrown away the bloody key, but would that have made her love him? If he had gone to Brook Hall and smashed Oliver's bloody teeth down his bloody throat, would it have made any difference? He loved her steadfast good humour, her quick temper, her hot-headed, self-willed resolution, her loyalty, and he wanted nothing to change in her, ever, but he could not live with her.

He was going to leave her and set up home with Helen and the thought was, at one and the same time, torturing him and yet comforting him with its promise of peace. It was a measure of the love he knew she bore him that Helen would immediately give up whatever freedom and reputation she had to be with him. He might even be able to get one of these easier to come by divorces if Kitty agreed and he saw no reason why she shouldn't, for she certainly didn't want him. He had said nothing to her yet, or to Helen. He didn't know why he hesitated, but he knew Helen loved him and he was extremely fond of her and she would welcome him in her life as Kitty never had. He supposed he sounded self-pitying but he was tired of it, of the appalling half life he led and he must, if he was to know anything like happiness, do something about it.

But first he must get this mess of Kitty's cleared up. He must settle her, convince her to give up this mad idea of hers of bringing Tam Oliver before the magistrates. He didn't suppose for a minute that she would grieve over his going. He would give her a generous allowance, let her have Meadow View and she could continue her wild and reckless way of living in any way she wanted. He didn't suppose the Olivers would welcome her into their home again but there were others who would and, anyway, was it any of his concern any more?

He turned from the window and looked at her, expecting defiance, that head-held-high hauteur she flaunted whenever she thought she was in the right and what was he to do about it, but she was drooping on the sofa, her head back against a cushion, her eyes brooding sadly into the flames of the fire. He watched her, his eyebrows drawn down in a frown of surprise. A muscle in the curve of his jaw jumped. His hair, which needed cutting, fell over his forehead and he put up a hand to brush it back and as he did so she looked up at him, an expression of such sadness in her eyes his heart was moved to something he knew was not pity.

"What is it, Kitty?" he said gently, wondering as he spoke what was the matter with him, and her.

She sighed, then, with a great effort, or so it seemed, she smiled. She was about to speak and he felt himself waiting for her words with more interest than he cared to admit, just as though they might mean something important to him, when there was a small tap on the door.

They both turned towards it and when Tansy entered and dropped a curtsey both of them felt what could only be called disappointment.

"Yes, Tansy? Is it Emma? Is she . . ."

"Oh, no, Mrs Maddox, Emma's still asleep. Clarrie's with her. You have a visitor but I wasn't sure you were . . . at home."

"Who is it, Tansy?" For it was barely seven o'clock in the morning and who on earth would call at this time? Before Tansy could speak, or even turn round to glance back into the hall, a tall figure brushed past her, smiling imperturbably, though the smile dropped somewhat when he saw Ben.

"It's only me, Kitty-Cat," Michael Hayes murmured, "come to enquire after the patient. I know it's early but there was such a bloody fuss at Tam's place I thought . . ."

Ben straightened his tall frame and his face became dark with anger. There was scorn in his eyes and a contemptuous curl to his strong mouth, but when he spoke his voice was as soft and sweet as honey.

"That is kind of you. Did your masters send you or is this a family call? I'm surprised that they are at all concerned about the violation of a young woman, only a maidservant, of course, by the master of the house. Is his conscience pricking him, then, or is he afraid that my wife is about to drag his name through the mud?"

"Don't be ridiculous. Do you imagine Tam Oliver

would do such a thing, a gentleman? Good God, of course he is concerned, but only with the need to find the man who did this to your . . . your maid."

"How dare you come here talking such absolute bloody nonsense. He is known for a rake and a black-guard and I myself only just escaped his attention by the merest chance. I don't care to have you in my house drivelling on . . ."

"Kitty, please." Ben moved towards her and took her arm and she was so surprised she let her voice trail away. "This man can do nothing, and would do nothing if he could. The Olivers are his friends and as long as he is of their company . . . Well, even your family, of which he is a part, would not want to know him. But perhaps now that he is here he might care to accompany me to Manchester where many things await our attention at the mill. Or are you engaged with something today, Mr Hayes? Perhaps another day at the races or is it the hunt, the season for which is coming to an end."

"Now see here, Maddox—"

"No, *you* see here, my lad. You are a working man now, earning a working man's wage and have no time to be jaunting all over the bloody county with those who have nothing better to do."

"Is that so? Before we go any further I am not your *lad*. My uncle employs me—"

"Then bloody well get about what he employs you to do." Ben's lips strained against his teeth in a grin of bitterness, for this man was one of those who had wooed Kitty to the sort of life they led, to the sort of life she had led and which had brought about this tragedy and he could not forgive it. "I am to visit your uncle in the next day or so and I believe he would not be pleased to hear that you have not been seen at the mill for weeks. Neither has your cousin, of course, so between you you are doing your best to ruin a fine business and I will not have it."

Michael's face sneered obscenely. "*You'll* not have it! And who are you to say what my uncle—"

"Your uncle has made me a director of the firm – did you not know that? – and has given me legal powers to hire or fire whom I please. I'm sure when he hears you are not pulling your weight he would not be surprised to find you among the latter. Just as I would get rid of any man or woman who did not earn their wage, I swear I'll get rid of you. Your allowance which enables you to live like a young lord would stop and what would the Olivers think of you then?"

Kitty felt her husband's hand, hard and determined, on her arm as though daring her to say a word in defence of her half-brother. But what had happened last night to Emma and what was happening here, Michael's effrontery in calmly riding over, not to pass on any message from the Olivers who would not apologise if Emma had been murdered by one of them, but to pretend family concern was making her blood boil in her veins. He had done nothing last night, as he should have as her half-brother, to smooth her passage back to Meadow View. He had remained at table with the rest of the guests just as though Kitty were really nothing to do with him, and if she was, his first loyalty was to his good friends.

Michael seemed lost for words but she could see he was livid, and very tempted to tell Ben to go to hell in a handcart, for how dare he criticise a member of the Hayes family who, after all, owned Monarch Mill. She could feel herself beginning to lean on Ben's strong arm and had time to wonder with that part of her brain that was not exhausted, shocked, filled with shuddering horror at what had been done to Emma, and guilt, for it should have been her, why he was being so . . . so kind to her. So supportive, but she supposed it was because he loathed Michael Hayes and all his kind.

"Well, I'll get off then, if my good wishes are to be ignored," Michael said in the manner of a petulant schoolboy and she wondered in her tired mind why she had thought him so fascinating, so amusing, such a wonderful companion.

"So you are not to come to the mill with me then?" Ben asked him mockingly. "I am to tell your uncle you are too busy at the moment at the tail end of the hunting season to attend to your duties at the mill."

"For God's sake, man I'll be there as soon as . . . well, tomorrow first thing. I must get home and change, and so I'll wish you good-day." He threw a look of positive loathing at Ben then turned his false anxious gaze back to Kitty. "May I say something to the Olivers, Kitty? They were very concerned about your wellbeing . . ."

"*My* wellbeing! I was not the one Tam Oliver raped."

"Kitty . . ." Ben put a warning hand on her arm but she shook it off.

"But you may say this to them. Tell them they've not heard the last of this, for I mean to take it further. In the meanwhile I hope they rot in hell for all eternity."

"Well, that told him," Ben grinned wryly as Michael flung himself from the room. "You really are—"

"What? What am I?" And she grinned too, for this little episode seemed to have drawn them together in some strange way, made them allies.

"I was going to say you were like a warrior queen dismissing some insolent minion who had displeased you."

"He had, but if he and they imagine I am just going to let this go they are sadly mistaken. I'll hound that bastard through every court in the land to get him what he deserves. I believe what you said, of course. It makes sense, for what can I do against people like the Olivers, but that doesn't mean I can't try. They can't be allowed to do this to us and get away with it. I mean to see the top man in the constabulary and . . . a solicitor would be useful, wouldn't you say so?"

"Oh, undoubtedly, but don't be disappointed if he won't act for you. Don't be disappointed if you can't find anyone to act for you, Kitty. The Olivers—"

"Damn the Olivers, Ben, and damn you if you won't help."

She lifted her head and stared at him through narrowed eyes in that defiant manner he was so used to seeing. But there was something there, a ripple of something . . . what? He couldn't describe it but it swam through the incredible blue-green of her eyes then it was gone and he knew it was nothing he would care to recognise. He had stopped looking for that months ago.

"I didn't say I wouldn't help."

"You're all the same, aren't you? You *gentlemen*. You stick together through thick and thin. After all, Emma is only a working-class woman and so is not—"

"Stop it, Kitty."

"No, I won't stop it and I won't stop hounding Tam Oliver. Not until—"

He cut through her angry voice like a hot knife through butter, saying the only thing that would reach through her furious rage.

"Have you considered asking Emma how she feels about this . . . vendetta?" His voice was icy. "Have you for one moment put aside *your* feelings and considered hers? Perhaps it might be wise, since if she won't agree to it there is nothing you can do."

Turning on his heel, ignoring her shocked face, he left the room.

29

Ben Maddox proved to be right, for no matter what Kitty said to her she could not persuade Emma to see the police inspector she had summoned to Meadow View and who was at this moment striding restlessly about her downstairs drawing-room.

"Please, Miss Kitty, can't you just let it go? I don't think I can bear the thought of standing up in front of a lot of people . . . gentlemen . . . and describing to them what was done to me. I don't even want to be interviewed by the policeman downstairs, let alone say it all in a courtroom."

"I'll be there, Emma, and Mr Maddox, and we'll help you. The doctor will testify—"

"Yes, that I was raped but not who raped me. He doesn't know."

"But I do, Emma, and I can say so."

"But it didn't happen to you, Miss Kitty. Kitty, oh, Kitty, it didn't happen to you so how can you help me?"

"I can tell them what a good person you are. What a decent woman and Mr Maddox has a lot of influence."

Though she spoke these last words confidently she could not help but remember Ben's rigid face when he left the drawing-room earlier. She didn't honestly believe what she had said about gentlemen sticking together, for she knew Ben was as genuinely horrified as she was at what had happened to Emma but he was a man of the world, a realist and he knew how difficult it would be – nay, virtually impossible – to get this charge of rape against the son of a baronet even into court, let alone get a conviction, but she couldn't bear it if nothing was done. She wanted it blazoned across the newspapers, every one in the land. Talked about and . . . She wanted Tam Oliver to suffer because of it. She would not forget his contemptuous face, his sneering smile, his pretence to his guests that he didn't know what this mad woman who had accosted him in her nightdress was talking about. He had treated her as though she had lost her wits and for two pins would get her locked up in the local lunatic asylum, but it was he who would be locked up for his wickedness, she'd see to that.

"And besides," she went on, "Tam Oliver's reputation will go before him. I'm sure you're not the first woman he has . . . done this to. Dear God, he tried to rape me, Emma and I'll say he did. I'll stand up and say so. Oh, darling, don't you see, I can't bear the thought of him getting away with it. Laughing to his friends who'll think he's a hell of a fine fellow and after what you have suffered."

"I know. I know that but don't you see, I want to put it behind me, not drag it out for weeks, months, have everyone know what . . . Oh, please, Kitty, can't you see? You're doing this for yourself, not me."

"*Emma!* That's not true."

"It is, Kitty. I'm nothing but a maidservant but you're a lady and you can't stand the idea of a man like him taking a woman, *forcing* a woman and you are eager to expose him. If it had happened to you they might do something, for you're the wife of a powerful man but what is it going to do to me? Even if they send him to gaol, which is unlikely and you know it, how am I to live with it afterwards?"

There was a long, heavy silence. Kitty leaned back in the chair that she had pulled up to Emma's bedside, *her own* bedside, for Emma had been put in Kitty's bed while Kitty had spent the night, to the servants' amazement, in the small dressing-room on the narrow bed where her husband had once slept. They knew something dreadful had happened to Emma. How could they not with her bruised face and the doctor coming and a police constable and now, pacing about in the drawing-room, a police inspector, the top man, it was said. They were all agog with curiosity but Mrs Maddox was saying nothing and Mr Maddox had stormed out of the house hot on the heels of that young chap who was Mrs Maddox's brother, so what was to happen next?

The police inspector, who had come only because Mr Ben Maddox was one of the wealthiest and most influential gentlemen in Liverpool, was not at all pleased when Mrs Maddox came quietly downstairs and told him politely that his services were not after all needed and she was sorry to have bothered him. His constable had told him the gist of what Mrs Maddox had said earlier about her maid and as he bowed over her hand he told her he thought she was doing the right thing in letting the matter drop. Far the best to patch the maid up and give her a few guineas and send her home to her mother.

He was shocked and offended when Mrs Maddox exploded, there was no other word for it, and told him he was a disgrace to his uniform and if it was in her power she would have him drummed out of the force. Would he leave her house at once, she had thundered. She would ring for the maid to let him out, then she marched out of the room as though he were nothing but a lowly constable and not worth her consideration.

It was some weeks later when it was realised that Emma Taylor was pregnant.

"I'm sorry, my dear, but it is quite out of the question for you to stay here with us. There is really not enough room since your father needs total peace and quiet—"

"Hey, steady on, my love. You make me sound as though I'm on my last legs. There is a spare bedroom and I'm sure Kitty's maid could share with one of the other girls."

"No, darling, you really must let me, and Doctor Croxley, be the best judge. You know how unwell you were last winter and you still need a rest after lunch. The front study is needed for this purpose. A comfortable sofa has been put in there for your father's use," she explained to Kitty, "so we truly are a bit pushed for space. Anna and Marguerite are forced to share a bedroom as it is and it really would be too much for Josie and Dolly to look after guests."

"Really, sweetheart, you can hardly call our daughter a guest, can you, and I'm sure she and her maid would not mind mucking in for a week or two."

"It might be more than a week or two, Father," Kitty began, but her mother took up the challenge, holding out her hand to her husband who took it, rather, Ben thought, who was a polite listener to this conversation, like a small child who is not quite sure how to manage without its mother. Josh Hayes looked a lot better than he had earlier in the year, his prolonged stay in Lytham with its bracing "ozone", its wide sweeping beaches and its reputation for its health-giving properties having improved his enormously. But he still leaned on his wife, if not literally, then metaphorically speaking, turning to her at her every word.

Ben, Kitty and Emma had taken the train to Lytham where, outside the railway station, he had hired a hansom cab to take them to West Beach where the Hayes' house stood. Elm Cottage had been rented and then bought by Josh Hayes's mother and father even before Josh and Nancy were married and had been a favourite holiday place ever since. Lytham was well known for its lovely golden beaches, its sparkling waters which were clear and safe and, with the help of the bathing-machines drawn up on the edge of what was known as the Green, were popular with swimmers. Further north towards the newest watering place, the town of St Anne's, were stretches of wild dunes heaped with billowing sand, for it was a windy shore, the sand covered with long, wiry grass and golden gorse, with wild briars and forget-me-nots. The air was bright and pure and filled with the sounds of chirping linnets and it was declared in the *Manchester Courier* and the *Liverpool Mercury* that a run down to the seashore was a wonderful safety valve for those businessmen, and their families, of course, who worked under the high pressure of commercial and industrial life.

It was a fine day and though Emma was silent and pale and Ben, who wanted to chat to her father about one or two business matters, had nothing to say to her, Kitty felt her spirits rise somewhat. It was early April, and everywhere she looked trees and shrubs were bursting into bud. Blossom erupted like lacy clouds in orchards and gardens, white and pink and beautiful. Lilac was bursting into flower and in every garden great sweeps of trumpet-headed daffodils carpeted the neat lawns and under the spreading branches of the trees. Primroses clustered thickly among them and even a butterfly or two could be seen dancing in delirious joy against the cobbled walls of the gardens. Ash trees and sycamore trees were in flower and high in the sky, so high it could be seen only as a small, quivering dot, a skylark sang its heart out.

"There, you see, my darling," Nancy Hayes went on,

addressing her husband with such loving tenderness Ben felt the need to look away. He had never in all his years seen a couple as devoted as Nancy and Josh Hayes, to the exclusion of everybody else in their lives, even their children and their new grandchild who, Nancy admitted, they had not yet seen. The pandemonium of an infant in the house might, just now, she had explained, set her husband back, but perhaps when the summer months came and they, meaning the child and her nursemaid, could get out more, Freddy and Ciara and Cecily, which was what the child was to be christened, might come over for a few days. The girls, Anna and Marguerite, had been invited to stay with friends in the Lake District so Freddy and his family might come then. It was, of course, out of the question for Josh to travel to Manchester.

"Where are the girls, Mother?" She knew her mother would not like her daughters to know what had happened to Emma.

"The day being fine they have gone for a walk in Lowther Park Gardens with Mr and Mrs Arnold Rimmer and their son and daughter. The gardens really are beautifully laid out and in the summer they are to play tennis and croquet there. There are some very nice families here now, like the Rimmers who are from Oldham, just the sort of person I want the girls to mix with and many of them take the air in the park. You really must try to get a look at it. Perhaps before you go home this afternoon."

Kitty knew her mother was talking merely to avoid

the real reason for Kitty's visit which she knew she was not going to like.

She would never forget the look of total horror on her mother's face as Josie ushered her, Ben and Emma into the spacious drawing-room at the front of the house which looked out over Lytham Green and had a splendid view of the windmill. She had risen to her feet and for some unaccountable reason moved to stand beside her husband, taking his hand in hers.

"Kitty, Ben, what a delightful surprise, but I do wish you had sent me a telegraph. We are considering installing one of those new telephones which will be very convenient providing one's friends have one as well. Perhaps you might consider it, Ben, then you can give us plenty of warning if you are to visit. Are you to stay long? Shall I tell Dolly to inform Mrs Blane that there will be two more for lunch? Really, you look well, my dear, and so do you, Ben." The whole time she spoke her eyes never once touched on Emma who stood quietly by the door. Emma might not have been in the room for all the notice she took of her and Kitty supposed that it was not surprising, since Emma, strictly speaking, should not have been ushered in with the family. Into the kitchen with the other servants, that's where she belonged, but there was absolutely no way that Kitty would abandon Emma who, though she was decently dressed and her condition did not show as yet, was obviously not herself. She trembled against Kitty, hanging her head as though in great shame and it was all Kitty could do to prevent herself from putting her arm about her and leading her to a comfortable chair by the fireside.

Ben came to her rescue. He strode across the room to where Josh was struggling to get out of his chair and took his hand. "No, sir, don't stand up. I shan't keep you long but there were several matters that I felt needed bringing to your attention so I have come over with . . . with my wife to have a chat. I must catch the three thirty train back to Manchester so I won't keep you long."

He turned politely to his mother-in-law. "I believe there is something Kitty wishes to discuss with you, Mrs Hayes, but before she does I wonder if you have a place, perhaps with a fire, where her maid might rest. Emma has not been well of late which is the reason why Kitty and she are here. But a cup of tea and some degree of privacy would be very welcome."

"Of course." Nancy studied her daughter's maid more closely, then turned back to her husband and her son-in-law, her face anxious and Ben wondered at the obsessive way she treated Josh Hayes.

"Perhaps if she were put into the study. I believe Josie lit the fire there and then, if you feel the need, you and I could go to my sitting-room, Kitty. I have a small one upstairs – this house is not big, you know – and you can tell me your news."

Emma, who had begun to shiver, not with cold, Kitty was aware, but with shock and fright, for it was only this week that, having missed two of her monthly courses, she and Kitty had realised what appalling thing had happened. Mrs Hayes had not made her feel welcome.

In fact she made it quite clear that not only was Emma a damned nuisance so was her own daughter. But she settled obediently where Miss Kitty put her, inclined in her distress to go where *anybody* put her, drank the cup of tea the curious Josie brought her, Josie clearly amazed that a lady's-maid should be given such special treatment, then dozed fitfully as she had been told to by Miss Kitty.

"Mother," Kitty began briskly after she and her mother were seated in her mother's comfortable armchairs. She had hardly had time to take off her travelling coat before she began and she could see the disapproval on her mother's face. But then she was used to her mother's disapproval, had been all her life so she waded right in, for this seemed no time to be beating about the bush.

"A dreadful thing happened several weeks ago."

"Now then, Kitty, if it is going to upset your father I don't wish to be a part of it. You know how his heart is and—"

"Mother, for God's sake, he seems perfectly fit to me and why you continue to treat him as though he were a semi-invalid I can't imagine. It can't be good for him to be coddled—"

"Don't you speak to me like that, girl. As though I don't know what is best for my own husband. I have nursed him through—"

"I know you have, Mother, and I apologise. I promise Emma and I will be no trouble. We will share a room."

Her mother stared. "Share a room with your maid! I never heard such . . . Dear Lord, what is wrong with her that you feel the need to treat her as though she were a member of the family? And if you must have a holiday with her there is a small house for rent at the other end of the beach. It would suit you admirably, but why there is a necessity to make such a pet of her is beyond me."

"She is . . . my friend, Mother and I'm extremely fond of her. I couldn't say all of this in front of her which is why I wanted her to take a rest and she *needs* a rest after what was done to her."

"Done to her?"

"Yes."

"What?"

"She was raped, Mother, and she is to have a child. I'm sorry, I know you suffered the same."

Her mother recoiled. "How dare you mention that to me, now, after all these years. After I have rebuilt my life and wish for nothing more than to forget it."

"How can you forget it when I sit here beside you? The result of that rape. I believed you would be more . . . sympathetic, having gone through what Emma is going through."

Her mother stood up and began to move blindly across the room, reaching for the handle of the door and flinging it open. She stood back and indicated that Kitty was to leave.

"Mother, please, listen to me. We only want to get away from Liverpool for a few weeks."

"Then take the house I have mentioned. I'm sorry, but you cannot stay here. Do you seriously expect me to expose my innocent daughters to . . . to this? A woman who is to have an illegitimate child."

"You had an illegitimate child, Mother. Me! Surely there is some compassion in you."

"Hold your tongue. I must think first of your father. Who knows how it might affect him and, besides, we have no room."

Nancy Hayes was halfway down the stairs when Kitty caught up with her, standing before her so that she could go no further. She tried to speak in a low voice since, despite what her mother said, she was concerned with her father's health which could still be fragile but her mother was becoming more and more agitated, trying to push her aside.

"You know that's not true, Mother. It is merely an excuse to keep Emma from under your roof."

"You may stay for lunch," her mother was saying, in a high voice not at all like her, "but then you must catch the train back to Liverpool with your husband or have him make arrangements for you to rent . . ."

By this time both Ben and Josh were crowding in the doorway to the drawing-room, Ben looking mystified and Josh beginning to be agitated.

"Dearest," he said to his wife, "what are you saying? Go back to Liverpool with Ben when she has just got here?"

"Darling, I have just been explaining to Kitty that we have no room, that it would be impossible—"

"That is not the reason, Mother and I'm surprised at you, really I am. I had expected sympathy for Emma since you suffered the same dreadful violation when you were a girl."

"Stop it, stop it at once. I will not have you discussing such a thing in front of your father, nor your husband. Have you no regard for my feelings?"

"And have you none for Emma's? Surely you will know how she feels and I wanted to get her away from the pointing fingers."

"Then you must take her elsewhere. The maids would refuse to work with a girl who has been . . . interfered with. And as I said you cannot expect your sisters to consort with a woman who has been—"

"As you were, Mother, but your friends and family did not turn away from you."

"God in heaven, what is going on here?" Josh Hayes roared. "I don't know what it is, Kitty, but the moment you enter a house it is as though a whirlwind has swept through the door. Haven't I enough to contend with after what Ben has just told me? My son sitting at home with his wife, holding her hand when he should be at the mill . . ."

"Josh, darling, please don't upset yourself. It will all be sorted out," his wife pleaded, doing her best to get by Kitty and put her arms about him.

"And my nephew who I took in off the bloody streets is not apparently doing what I am paying him to do but is larking about the county with that fast set."

"The Olivers. It was Tam Oliver who raped Emma and it is his child she is to bear. But it was not Emma he was after, Father, it was me. That is why I feel totally responsible. In the dark he mistook Emma for me and dragged her into . . ."

Even as she spoke Kitty knew she had made a terrible mistake. Her father put his hand to his throat as though he were about to choke and his face turned a bright puce as the blood rushed to his head. Ben swore softly as he put out his hands to catch him, but he was not quick enough and Josh Hayes slid slowly down the door frame until he was slumped on the floor, the blood still exploding in his brain, his eyes fixed in terror on his wife.

Nancy Hayes began to scream.

Josh Hayes lay upstairs in his bed, his eyes glittering fiercely, glaring out of his twisted face, one eye higher than the other, his mouth drawn up into what seemed to be a perpetual sneer, the weeping Josie told the others in the kitchen. Mrs Hayes hung over him doing her best to understand what he was trying to say, but he was making such awful noises, noises that terrified Josie when she took up the "pobs" which was all the doctor would allow poor Mr Hayes to eat. Bread and hot milk, and perhaps a drop of weak tea. Mrs Hayes was in such a state they all thought she wouldn't be long behind her husband. Not that he was dead, or anything, but she doted on him to such an extent that if he should die she'd follow him within the week, they were convinced.

And what a scene had taken place in the hallway after the doctor had come and been taken up to Mr

Hayes's bedroom where Mr Maddox had carried him. Mrs Hayes screaming that she never wanted to see Mrs Maddox again and she'd best take herself and her wickedness with her and if her daughter said one more word in defence of her maid, who stood trembling like an aspen tree by the study doorway, she'd hit her. If her father died she'd never forgive her, she screamed, and when the two young daughters of the house had crept, trembling, over the doorstep, come from their pleasant walk with the Rimmers, it had been pandemonium, with everyone crying at once, Mrs Hayes prostrate at the bottom of the stairs where she awaited the doctor's report, the only calm one among them Mr Maddox, and thank God for it.

He took the young ladies outside into the garden where he introduced himself to the Rimmers who assured him they would be more than happy to take them to their house further along West Beach until the doctor thought it was suitable, or their father well enough for them to be allowed home. He disappeared for an hour, no one knew where, while Mrs Maddox and her maid sat in the study, for by now Mrs Hayes had been admitted to her husband's bedroom. When he came back there was a cab waiting outside the door.

"Come, Kitty, Emma," he said, just as though they were off for a stroll along the green. "I have rented a house on East Beach and arranged for you and Emma to go there at once. It would not be fitting for you to go back to Meadow View at the moment. This will give you time to think what you are to do; but your mother is right, you can't stay here. I had not thought about the girls. I should have, I know, for they are only young and with Emma as she is . . ."

With Emma as she is! What did that mean? Josie and Dolly and Mrs Blane wondered. But without a word Mrs Maddox and her maid, with their personal belongings, were put in the cab and driven off.

But that was not the last they were to see of Mr Maddox. He was back within the hour, enquiring after Mr Hayes and wanting to know of the doctor if Mr Hayes was well enough to see him.

"Of course he's not, man," the doctor answered irritably. "He's just had a severe stroke. He can't even speak. His wife is with him and I am about to give him something to make him sleep."

"Nevertheless I think he will sleep a great deal easier if he hears what I have to say. He does not need to speak. Merely nod his head, or shake it. I take it he can do that?"

"No, Mr Maddox, I won't have it. I cannot be responsible."

"You may be there beside him all the time, Doctor, and may put a stop to it if you think it is necessary but I happen to know there are certain things Mr Hayes wants me to do and I must do them before it is too late."

Only the doctor and Nancy Hayes heard what Ben Maddox asked of Josh Hayes, his big hand smoothing his father-in-law's hair, his voice gentle as he bent over him. They saw the striving leave Josh Hayes and his face and eyes become peaceful as he nodded his wishes to his son-in-law.

The next day, though he was not as he should be, far from it, he had had a good night's sleep and was able to put his mark to the legal document which the local solicitor had drawn up and which was witnessed by the doctor.

Nancy Hayes came down the stairs to see Ben off the premises and though she was strained and pale, inclined to tremble through lack of sleep, she smiled at him and he was to wonder what it was that she held against her eldest daughter, for it was a sweet smile, and kind.

"Thank you, Ben," she said simply. "You have put his, and my mind at rest and he will improve because of it. You are welcome at any time to call on him but there is one thing I must insist on."

"Yes, Mrs Hayes?" He held her hand compassionately.

"That you come without your wife. She is to blame for this and I never want to see her again."

30

The banging came from somewhere far off, she didn't know where, but it was persistent, frantic, it seemed to her and she knew it was Tam Oliver trying to get out of the gaol at Walton in Liverpool where she and Emma had sent him. Dear God, she'd never get over it if they let him out, not after all the heartache he had caused. She turned over in bed, frantic and gasping, and as she did so the light sleep she was slowly coming out of became complete wakefulness and she knew the banging wasn't a dream. Someone was knocking on the front door and the night beyond her half-drawn-back curtains was still pitch black.

Stumbling from her bed, catching her toe in the hem of her nightgown and nearly falling over Henry who Ben had brought over last weekend, she reached for the candle and matches she kept beside her bed. She had never quite got the hang of lighting the lamps by which the rooms were lit, leaving it either to Tansy or Elspeth who had been brought over, with Henry, and who were to look after their mistress for as long as she decided to stay in Lytham. They were as excited as children, the pair of them, for this was like a holiday, since neither had ever been further than a ferry ride to New Brighton on their afternoon off.

By now, of course, Emma's "trouble" was known to them all.

She lit the candle with trembling fingers then glanced at her watch which she had put on the table beside her bed. It was ten past three!

Henry began to bark now that she was up as though his courage had suddenly come to him with her beside him. She shushed him and wavered uncertainly towards the bedroom door which she opened, stepping out on to the upstairs landing to find she was not alone. The two maids and Emma were all emerging from their bedrooms, Emma's at the front next to hers, Tansy and Elspeth, who shared one, at the back of the small house.

"Someone's at the front door, madam," Tansy quavered, pulling her sensible woollen dressing-gown more firmly about her.

"Yes, I realise that, Tansy. You'd better see who it is."

"Oh, madam, what if it's burglars?"

"Burglars would hardly bang on the front door to be let in, would they, Tansy? Now go down and let whoever it is in. We are all right behind you."

She and Emma had been at Foxglove Cottage for

two weeks and in that time the weather had been spring at its best. A pale golden sun had shone day after day from a sky which was that washed blue that comes only as winter leaves and spring arrives. Everywhere trees sprang, almost overnight, into full leaf, gardens erupted with early summer flowers long before their time, delphiniums of every shade of blue from the palest to a deep purple, old-fashioned pinks and border carnations and even wild sweetbriar in the hedges and thousands upon thousands of daisies starred the lawns.

They went for long walks along the green, she and Emma, taking the prancing Henry on his lead. Already because of the spell of warm weather bathers were being drawn down to the dancing, silvery waters in the bathing-machines pulled by sturdy horses. There were sailing ships and steam ships, moving up to the docks at Preston or dropping off cargoes at Lytham. Families strolled in groups along Lytham Pier, going out to sea without sailing in a boat, as they called it. Ladies sat in deckchairs, swathed in their elaborate gowns and wraps, taking the air, if not the exercise, parasols over their heads to protect their complexions from the damaging rays of the sun, though Emma and Kitty gave not a thought to such things and did not care that their faces became a warm, golden brown. Little girls rolled hoops and little boys flew kites and at the water's edge they built sandcastles and paddled their white feet in the water which was believed to be good for them.

They walked for miles, going as far as Ansdell and

even St Anne's. They leaned against the railing listening to the tide's "singing" as it passed over the sand and shingle and watched the bonneted, aproned women cockling on Horsebank, which had once been a green pasture for cattle. With the fresh breeze in their faces they clambered up and down the sandhills at Starr Hills, laughing like children as they avoided the rabbit warrens, and the devastation of the last few weeks was forgotten for a brief half-hour. They took a tour round Lytham Lighthouse which was situated on Starr Hills to the south of St Anne's before walking on to St Anne's itself which, it was said, had only a few years ago been nothing but shippons, slaughterhouses, stables and whitewashed cottages, and where there had once been green fields were now wide, clean streets, fine shops and the mansions Manchester businessmen had built. They sat in St George's Gardens, resting before the walk back, or, if Emma did not feel up to it, took a cab outside the railway station on St Andrews Road back to Foxglove Cottage.

Emma had to a certain extent lost that look of desolate despair which had sent her reeling into a shocked state that had been difficult to drag herself out of. But she had done it, for she was a sensible woman who knew that time could not be put back and besides, she had such perfect trust in Miss Kitty. She knew she would never be abandoned. She knew she would be cared for during her pregnancy and the birth of the child. She didn't want this child. What woman would want a child that had been conceived in rape? But she knew Miss

Kitty would find a solution. Perhaps a childless couple to adopt it, and then, though she knew she would never be as she was, in her own eyes and in those of her fellow servants, again there was nothing to be done about it and she must just get on with her life. She was enjoying, if one could enjoy anything in the circumstances into which she had been flung, these days with Miss Kitty which were giving them both a breathing space, a time to make plans, to decide what they should do next. And she was not the only one who needed an arm to lean on, for she knew Miss Kitty waited every day for a word from her mother about the state of her father's health. She would have walked along East Beach and on to West Beach and knocked at the door of Elm Cottage if she had not been so afraid of upsetting her father and so Emma quietly let her see that, as Miss Kitty was always there to steady Emma when she was in despair, she would do her best to do the same for Miss Kitty.

When they opened the door Charlie Whitehead, who was groom and coachman for Mr and Mrs Hayes at Elm Cottage, nearly fell into the hallway. His face was as red as a ripe tomato and his breath was so harsh in his throat he couldn't speak.

"Oh, Lord," Elspeth whispered, her hand to her mouth, for it must be bad news and her mistress thought so too, because she went as white as a newly ironed sheet.

"What . . ." she managed to say, no more, as Charlie did his best to regain his breath, leaning forward, his hands on his knees.

"Yer ter come at once . . . Mrs Maddox. The master's asking for yer."

"Oh, God, has he . . ."

"Nay, I don't know. I were sent ter fetch doctor an' then you. Mrs Hayes ses ter be . . . ter be as quick as yer can."

He was propped up on his pillows, his breath labouring to get in and out of his chest, his face a dusky, mottled red, his eyes mere slits in his swollen face.

The doctor, who was leaning over the bed, his fingers on his patient's pulse, spun round as she flew into the room as though to ask who was this whirlwind who had come to disturb his dying patient, while beside the bed Nancy Hayes turned a face of cold dislike on her daughter whom she blamed for this.

"Mother . . . thank you for . . ." Kitty stammered, her eyes on her father who, she thought, was trying to smile.

"I did not want this," her mother said harshly and her husband weakly raised his one good hand to quieten her. "He wanted to see you."

The doctor tutted, for though he knew nothing on this earth could save his patient and that his daughter's presence could do him no harm now, he would like Mr Hayes to go in peace.

She knelt by the bed and gently took his hand, stroking the back of it as though he were a child she was soothing to sleep. There was nothing she could say. She could think of nothing he might want her to say and so she said the first words that came into her head.

"I love you, Father." She pressed her lips to the back of his hand and bent her head over it and heard him mutter something in the strangulated voice his stroke had caused.

She looked up at him, her eyes brimming, the tears splashing on the back of his hand and was overjoyed – had the occasion not been so harrowing – by the look in his eyes. He could not speak but his eyes did, telling her she was loved, and, if forgiveness was needed, forgiven. He did not blame her for this, as her mother did, for he had always known his health, after years and years in the filthy air of Manchester, was poor, but he was leaving her with his love for her intact.

"Father . . ." He was not her father but he always had been and she would always love him for it.

She told him so again before the doctor lifted her to her feet and led her from the room. One of the maids, weeping quietly, sat her in a chair by the fire and put a cup of tea in her hand which she drank obediently and just before the doctor came down the stairs to tell her Josh Hayes was dead, Ben was there, holding out his arms to her and she flew thankfully into them as she received the news. Her face was buried in the curve beneath his chin and so when the doctor spoke the words it was as though Ben took the brunt of them, not her.

"Come, sweetheart," he said, amazing her, "I'll take you home. I've a cab outside."

He put her in it and climbed in beside her, gathering her once more into his arms and holding her close. She did not weep but she could not control her trembling. It shook her body in great shudders and rattled her teeth so that her head ached with it.

Emma was at the door to meet her, ready to take her upstairs to her bed which, she said, had been warmed for her, but Ben Maddox smiled his thanks and shook his head. He walked past them all, the thunderstruck servants, his arms supporting her and when he reached the bedroom, with infinite care he undressed her and put her in her bed. But she shook so hard, with shock and grief, he understood that, he knew he could not leave her. Taking off his outer garments he lay down beside her and gathered her into his arms, stroking her back and murmuring small sounds which had no meaning but were meant to comfort.

"Ben . . . Ben . . ." Her breath was sweet and warm against his throat. He felt himself begin to respond with that damned part of him that didn't give a bugger about his bloody mind which was telling him to do the right thing with this sorrowing woman. Groaning inwardly at the madness of it but unable to stop himself, he placed his lips gently on hers. Jesus God, this should not be happening but she was so warm, so womanly, long and slender but curving against his body as he remembered from so long ago. She shifted her body, doing her best to get even closer to him in her need for comfort . . . *comfort!* Was that what she wanted, was that what he wanted to give her? He didn't think so. His male body rejoiced in it, for it told him that he was holding a willing woman in his arms and, by God, what could be better than that. The hot, sweet smell of her whipped his blood through his veins and without further thought, for who, man or woman, has time to think, for God's sake, at a time like this, he discarded his own clothing, whipped her nightdress from her and made love to her with the frenzy of a man who has been incarcerated and without female company for months. They both cried out as he entered her and she continued to moan deep in her throat so that he knew that since the last time he had touched her, no other man had. He rejoiced in it. It was just as it had always been, the pair of them trembling and unsteady with the rapture of it, the passion he had known with no other woman, the fever of possessing one another. He did not speak and neither did she and when it was over he held her in his arms until she slept. His own face was wet, with her tears and with his own, for he knew he had taken advantage of her frailty, her vulnerability and the weakness of her sorrow for her father and he was ashamed.

He had meant to do no more than hold her, to assuage her natural misery but he had lost control as he always did when he was near this beloved woman. When would she know the content, the peace, the serenity she so badly needed, this brave, defiant, hot-headed, wilful, sweet-natured wife of his? When would he? When would she ever find the happiness she deserved? She did not love him. He knew he had taken advantage of her tonight but it had been done with goodwill on his part. Only her needs, and not his own, had been uppermost in his mind but his body had said, well, to hell with that, and now look what had happened. She slept peacefully, gaining strength for what was to come, but he knew he could not give it to her, only in the way he just had. That was all she had ever wanted from him.

He was gone when she woke and she did not see him again until the day of the funeral. He stood among the mourners at the graveside of the church where Nancy and Josh had married, where he and Kitty had married, and it was a measure of his trust in her, his belief in her strength that it was her mother he supported and not her. Freddy cried and so did his sisters, and Ciara gave a sensational performance as a bereaved daughter, but Kitty was dry-eyed. She did not even wear a veil, which many of those who gathered to see Josh Hayes on his way, and there were hundreds, thought was disrespectful, but she was all in black, elegant and very slender, her head high and her eyes staring at something only she could see. At her back was that half-brother of hers, the one who was supposed to be learning the business at Josh Hayes's mill, his head bowed respectfully, his black suit immaculately tailored.

The will was read right after the funeral, since Mrs Hayes wanted to get back to Lytham where she intended to live out her days. It was a simple will, one drawn up, apparently, on the day Josh Hayes had suffered his stroke. He left his widow the house at Lytham and a generous allowance, and Riverside House was deeded to Freddy, he was now a family man. His two daughters, Anna and Marguerite, were to have splendid dowries and an allowance for life which would make them very desirable in the marriage market. His mill, his shares in the railway, coal mines in St Helens, shipping, his warehouse, in fact everything he and his family had worked for over the generations and which added up to a considerable fortune, was to be divided equally between his two sons, Sebastian and Freddy and his daughter Kitty.

His nephew, the son of his sister who had come back into the family only a few months ago and had been given his chance by his indulgent uncle and who was sure to be a beneficiary in his will, was never mentioned.

Kitty sat before her open bedroom window at Meadow View and smiled at the irony of life. What was it that made it twist people about, shaping them to its own whimsical fancies, or was it the people themselves who did that? Had she shaped her own destiny years ago when she had fallen in love with Freddy Hayes, convinced they would marry and live happily ever after? It had devastated her when he had chosen Ciara, causing her to rush into marriage with Ben. She had not known Ben and she had certainly not loved him and he had not loved her, so why then had they married? She knew why she had married him and it was simply to escape the knowledge that Freddy did not want her and that everyone knew he did not want her. But why had Ben married *her*?

And why had Ben made love to her the night her father had died, after the months of barely speaking to one another? Of both of them knowing that their marriage was a sham? That was the mystery that puzzled her the most and though it had been a great comfort to her in her grief on that night, and more than that, she was honest enough to admit, she could not help but wonder why he had acted as he had. He had been . . . was the word *kind*? Had he thought to comfort her with an hour of good, honest lust, take her mind from her father's death and her mother's dismissal in the pleasures of their bodies? He was sensitive, a man of many different layers, a complex man, a man of humour and sometimes arrogance. A strong man who allowed no one to see the real Ben Maddox, which was why she could honestly say she did not know him at all, so why had he made love to her with such . . . such passion? It had not been faked, but then perhaps it was true what they said about men that, put beside a willing female body, of a personable appearance, they could make love as easily as animals, regardless of their feelings. He was a true man, strong, masculine, with his feet planted firmly on the ground of reality and her life, she knew now, would be hollow without him. They had barely lived as man and wife and by that she didn't mean in their bed, but in their day-to-day life and yet the pain of his loss, if she did not get a good grip on herself, could send her crying to Emma who was the only one to know of her feelings. It sounded so foolish but on the night her father had died Ben had been ardent, as eager as she had been to take warmth and pleasure from her, to give it to her, and as she had fallen asleep in his arms she had thought, hoped, believed that perhaps . . . perhaps something might come of it. It hadn't, of course, at least not in the way she meant. His eyes had shone a deep, unreadable brown, glowing as the horse chestnuts that scattered about the garden in autumn. His hands had been demanding, hard. He had been rough with her and yet gentle as though his one aim had been her need at this moment of her great sorrow.

She had not been surprised when he had gone from the house when she awoke, for it might have caused great embarrassment to them both after the great tearing rift in their marriage, which had never been mended, since neither of them had attempted to mend it. She had accepted that she loved him, that he had given her great joy, that he was a good man who had found happiness with another woman, and though it broke her heart all over again to think of him going from her bed to that of the lovely woman she had seen him with at Aintree, what else could she expect.

It was four months since her father had died and in that time she and Emma had returned to Meadow View and on most evenings her husband had been absent from the dinner table. She dined alone, or sometimes she and Emma had a light meal before her sitting-room fire, for Emma was lonely without the companionship of the other servants which had vanished when it was discovered what had been done to her. Kitty didn't think it was deliberate cruelty. They just didn't know what to make of her, for Kitty herself treated her as a friend, spending all her time with her, walking, taking rides in the small gig which Tim and John, the stable lads, had unearthed for her from the back of the old stables. A light gig which either one of them could manage and did, driving into the village and sauntering up the main street under the curious scrutiny of the villagers who had, of course, become aware that Mrs Maddox's personal maid was to have an illegitimate child.

It was August now and the weather, which had been so superb while they were in Lytham, continued to be fine and hot and it was time she stopped hanging about and got down to the garden where Henry was waiting for her.

She rose from her chair, her hand for a moment on her belly, then, with a smile, she hurried from the room and made her way to Emma's.

Ben Maddox was in his study when they appeared round the corner of the house, their arms linked, their heads together in deep conversation. The dog ran about them with a ball in his mouth and now and again Kitty bent down to take it from him, throwing it with a young man's aim and strength, far across the garden. Emma, who was five months into her pregnancy, was looking plump and pretty, the way women were supposed to be when they were carrying a child. She was calm now, for he had been told that she meant to let her baby go for adoption when it was born. She would make a new life for herself, Kitty had told him, since she wanted no reminders of Tam Oliver in her life, and neither did Kitty, he suspected. He had been amazed at the way she had given her time, her whole attention to Emma, never leaving her, taking her with her wherever she went, even into Liverpool in the carriage to visit her dressmaker. She had been seen nodding and smiling at acquaintances, making sure that they saw her maid beside her, her maid who had been raped and was to have a child and who she, Kitty Maddox, would never abandon. She had not seen her mother, or her two sisters, for her mother would not allow it, since the day of her father's funeral. Freddy and Ciara had made it plain that while she dragged "that woman" about with her she was not welcome at Riverside House but she didn't seem to care. In fact, he had never seen her look so . . . happy, he supposed. She moved about the garden and the house. He had even met her with an armful of flowers which she was about to arrange for Emma, she had told him. He had heard her play the piano and had, as he had done before, crept down to listen as her clever fingers made the keys sing with Brahms, Debussy, Mendelssohn and lighter tunes, the words of which she and Emma roared forth as though they hadn't a care in the world. He didn't know why he had worried about the night he had spent in her bed on the night of her father's death, for it did not seem to have disturbed her in the least. She had accepted it, responded to it, then forgotten about it, as a man will do with a light woman who means nothing to him.

He sighed, for he intended to tell her tonight. He had bought a house down on the shore about three miles out of Liverpool, rural and placid with views over the river to the Welsh hills and in the east across open fields and beyond to where the Pennines rose, and as soon as he had told Kitty, and Helen had sold her own elegant Regency house in Upper Duke Street, they meant to move into it together and hang the scandal. It would not particularly upset his life, since men were tolerant of other men who set a mistress up in a house, but Helen would never again be received in any home in the upper-class social circles in which she now moved.

He leaned his buttocks on the back of an armchair, his hands in his pockets, a cigar clenched between his teeth, the smoke from it making him narrow his eyes. The two women continued to saunter across the lawn in their light summer dresses, pretty and graceful against the glossy green of the lawn and the outburst of colour that edged it. Emma was laughing and Kitty let go of her arm and danced a few steps ahead of her, turning to face her, darting this way and that like a child teasing another. She was evidently trying to persuade Emma into something she was reluctant to do and Ben could not help but smile, for was there anybody who could stand against Kitty – except perhaps her own mother – when she was in this merry, impish mood. He wondered what it was she was trying to make Emma do? Probably something completely outrageous like climb a tree or go for a swim in the small lake that could just be seen shining at the end of the woodland.

Emma stopped and threw back her head in gales of laughter, then flopped down on the lawn where the dog instantly jumped on her and began licking her face with the enthusiasm of his kind.

Ben moved forward and opened the window so that he could hear what all the fun was about, his own face breaking into what he knew would be laughter, for really Kitty was so . . . so . . . entertaining. She had a knack of turning the most ordinary pastime into a joy. She kneeled down beside her maid and tried to drag the dog off, crying to him to behave and would Emma please stop laughing, since she really thought she was going to . . . well, she said, she wouldn't tell her what it was that was about to happen but she had become aware that her . . . bladder was not quite as reliable as once it had been. Did Emma find that?

He didn't hear Emma's answer, for both women had calmed down somewhat, their voices quieter, sitting, their legs folded under them as they put their heads together in what seemed an earnest discussion on something they alone shared. The dog lay down and yawned, then rolled over on his back, inviting one of them to scratch his belly.

He knew he had heard something very important in the last few minutes but for the life of him he couldn't decide what it was. There was something the two women on the lawn shared and if he put his mind to it, fetched it out of the fog in which it struggled, he would have the answer. The smile had gone from his face. The laughter died and he straightened up slowly. For almost five minutes he continued to watch them. He was perfectly still as though the slightest movement might disturb his thoughts and send him off in completely the wrong direction and it was not until Kitty sprang to her feet and held out her hands to Emma that the fog cleared.

"I can get up by myself, Miss Kitty. Providing I turn on to my knees and have something to hold on to. Heavens, I'm only five months but you mustn't pull at me. Not now. Not as you are."

"Rubbish, Emma, I'm as strong as a horse."

She turned as Emma straightened up. Putting her hand to her eyes she stared off into the wood at something that had caught her eye, saying something to Emma and as the tall, graceful length of her was outlined against the woodland, he saw the slight roundness of her belly as her light gown clung to her.

31

The young girl flew along the path, the skirt of her pretty muslin dress swinging, the flowers on her bonnet bobbing, skimming past surprised groups strolling in the sunshine who turned to watch her hurry by. You could tell that she was doing her best to be circumspect, to act as a young lady should, but her face was white with excitement and the man who was watching from behind a dense thicket of bushes groaned and gritted his teeth in what seemed to be extreme irritation.

She came to a halt as though in some confusion, again making passing people stare in surprise and the man cursed softly under his breath. Goddammit, she couldn't have made more of a spectacle of herself if she had held up a banner advertising her intentions, but he swallowed his exasperation and did his best to put a warm smile on his face.

"I'm here," he murmured from his hiding place in the shrubbery and at once she turned towards him, a blissful smile on her face. Dear God, what next? he thought. His name perhaps and a darting movement into the bushes, pushing aside all before her in total unawareness of who was looking, and who, if they were, might know who she was. But she was here now, out of sight of those taking an afternoon's promenade in Lowther Park Gardens.

"I thought I'd never find you," she whispered, trembling a little as he pulled her into his arms and covered her soft, rosy lips with his own, shutting her up and calming her down. She was lovely, sweet, young and inclined to babble, which annoyed him immeasurably but this had to be done properly, or at least what he considered to be "properly", and getting her away from here without anyone seeing them go would take a lot of ingenuity and a great deal of luck. He had a hansom cab with the hood down waiting just outside the gates on Church Road opposite the church. From there they would go swiftly to the railway station and catch the next train to Preston where they would change to the North Western Railway to Lancaster and on to Windermere. That's the place they, those who would certainly search for her, were most likely to look, that's if they followed the trail he was deliberately laying: the romantic district of the Lakes, and that's where he meant to be found.

"Did anyone see you go?" he asked her, keeping her in his arms so that he might more easily control her.

"No, I slipped out at the back while Cook was in the pantry."

"Clever girl." He kissed her again. "Come, sweetheart, we'd best make a move," he continued, taking her hand and peering out through the screen of the shrubbery to the path that led to the gates. "Right, all clear. Now, walk sedately. See, take my arm; there is no need to draw attention to ourselves by hurrying. Don't be frightened, my darling, you are safe with me and always will be. Look, there's the cab. That's it, good girl, in you get. The railway station please, cabbie and as quick as you can."

The first Kitty heard of it was when the cab came hurtling up the drive. Throwing some money at the cab driver, Ben leaped up the steps to the front door, almost knocking over Tansy who had hurried to open it.

"Oh, sir, is there anything wrong?"

"Where's Mrs Maddox?"

"She's . . . I think she's in the garden with Emma. They are . . ."

"Fetch her, will you, and at once."

"Yes, sir. Oh, sir, is anything wrong?" she said again, for most of the servants at Meadow View had been with him and his family for a long time and felt they belonged and could therefore ask questions and were entitled to be worried.

"Quickly, Tansy, there's a good lass, and when you've fetched Mrs Maddox will you pack me an overnight bag. You know what I'll need: a change of shirt and . . . But hurry, Tansy, there's not a moment to lose."

"Oh, sir." Tansy put her hand to her mouth and

hurried along the side passage and out into the garden. Dear God, what now? her flustered thoughts wanted to know. It must be something dreadful for Mr Maddox to be in such a state and him usually so calm and in control. A cool head, had the master, which had been needed a time or two with the troubles this family, meaning the mistress's family, had known.

Ben stood for a second in the hallway doing his best to calm himself. It was not like him to get in a panic, but the thought of innocent little Marguerite in the hands of that evil bastard was almost more than he could bear. He wanted to snarl and hit something, preferably Michael, but he must pull himself together and get over to Lytham as soon as possible, for that was where the trail started. It was only two hours since it was discovered that Marguerite was missing and half an hour since he had received the frantic telegraph from his mother-in-law. He had to think . . . *think*, which was bloody difficult, as to where she might have been taken, where the most likely place would be. Try to put himself in the mind of the man who had taken her, for whatever his purpose was it would not be straightforward. He was devious, clever; look at the way he had picked on the most innocent, trusting, unworldly of the sisters, a child of just fifteen. Oh, God, think, think. He must put his brain to working out . . . The trouble was his mind had been snarled up for the past week, barely able to function at any level even in his place of business, let alone deal with this.

Ever since he had discovered that Kitty was pregnant

he had floundered in a honey-sweet morass in which was mixed unbelievable joy, deep despair, a pain that was almost physical on what this would do to Helen who loved and trusted him, and a hope, a small, persistent ray of hope that . . . that would not let him rest. Hope for what he couldn't bring himself to consider, for it was so unbelievable. He was waiting, he had realised that a day or two ago, for Kitty to tell him herself, for she must be . . . well, it was the end of April when her father had died and it was on that night that he had made love to her. It was August now, almost the end, so four months and yet she had still not said a word. He was aware that he and she, even after that enchanting night in her bed, were still divided, going their separate ways but she was always perfectly pleasant when they did happen to dine together. She had changed so much. The wildness seemed to have gone and she moved about the house with a serenity he had thought caused by *Emma's* pregnancy, content to stay at home, not even riding out on that hunter of hers. He had often watched her and Emma and the dog strolling about the garden, sitting sometimes in the shade of the trees with a book or what, astoundingly, looked like a bit of sewing. The last time she had been carrying a child she had pulled savagely against all restraints, cursing the need to be careful, to lead the life a mother-to-be must lead and in the end she had rebelled and look what the result had been.

So what was different about this one and why hadn't she told him? He had been waiting all week, scarcely going out even to Helen's place, so that he might be available when she finally revealed her condition, which she must soon. If he had seen it then the servants must have seen it so what the devil was in her mind?

She came running into his study and he wanted to steady her, tell her to sit down and be careful but instead he sat down himself, hoping she would do the same. She didn't.

"What is it? Is it Mother . . . or . . . Tansy was very upset and seemed to imply that something awful had happened." She was slightly out of breath as though she had run from the garden but she looked quite radiant, blooming, he supposed, his heart a cold stone in his breast.

He stood up since she wouldn't sit down.

"It's Marguerite . . ."

"Oh, God, not an accident. What?"

"No, not an accident." There was no way to tell her except with the simple truth and he prayed that the shock would not have an adverse effect on her condition. Women were frail creatures, he said to himself, then almost smiled, despite the circumstances, for could such a word ever describe Kitty Maddox.

"She's run away—"

"*Run away!* Marguerite!" Her voice was incredulous.

"With Michael Hayes."

She sat down then, slowly sinking into the leather chair, her lovely colour gone, her eyes haunted, for it seemed history, family history, was repeating itself.

"I wondered where he was," she whispered. "Why he had been so quiet after the reading of Father's will. I thought he had gone back to toadying after the Olivers but all the time . . . Oh, sweet Jesus, Ben, what are we to do?"

"We must try and decide where he would have taken her and get there before it's too late. Before he . . ."

"Don't. She's only fifteen."

"Kitty, you have a good brain, intuitive, sharp. What d'you think is in his mind?"

"Money, of course, and a lot of it, but more than anything else, revenge."

"Yes. Scotland, d'you think? Gretna Green . . ."

"It's a possibility but . . ." She paused and bit her lip. "He's too clever. That would be too simple. He'd know we'd come after him and there's a waiting period surely, before a wedding can take place."

Ben Maddox was a shrewd man. All his commercial life he had stared men in the face, keen-eyed and sharp-minded as they tried to convince him that black was white and vice versa, and though Michael Hayes was devious, black-hearted and clever it would take a better man than him to hoodwink Ben. Kitty was narrow-eyed, her teeth worrying her bottom lip as her mind ran on the same lines as her husband's. She had seen Michael Hayes at play, watched him deceive many a pretty woman with a word and a suggestion which, on the face of it, had seemed quite plausible and which had got the better of them and gained him the upper hand.

"There's only one way to find out, Ben, we must go to Lytham and—"

"No, Kitty, not you. You must stay here. In your . . ."

He had almost said in your condition you can't go gallivanting about the country, probably rattling about in trains and cabs and God knows what else. This was his child and, by God, he was going to see it born alive this time, but something, some instinct warned him not to let Kitty know he knew her secret. Besides, he wanted *her* to tell him of her own accord. Again he didn't know why, for what good would it do their ailing marriage? The child made a difference, he realised that now, and how the hell he was going to break the news to Helen he didn't know, but he must, and he and Kitty must try to shape some solidity into their lives, if only for the sake of the child. *The child*. Even just saying those two words in his head warmed his cold heart until it glowed with something sweet and loving and . . . But this wasn't the time to be rhapsodising over what was to come . . . what *might* come. Marguerite must be considered first.

"Don't tell me what to do, Ben Maddox," Kitty was saying as she rose from her chair. "Marguerite is my sister . . . half-sister and I'm coming with you. They say two heads are better than one."

"No, Kitty, I absolutely forbid it," he began, his voice harsh, but she merely smiled and shook her head.

"How are you to prevent it, Ben? You surely know by now that I do as I please."

He groaned and passed his hand across his hair which immediately fell over his forehead again. Kitty saw the movement and took a step forward, wanting to smooth the lock of wavy hair back again, perhaps touch his cheek and tell him how grateful she was for his presence, for his concern, for him. He had been there at exactly the right moment in all the adversities of their lives, the Hayes family. Steadfast, reliable, steadying them all with his calm strength, smiling sometimes to let them know that it would be all right. Freddy was her father's son and Marguerite's own brother and yet it occurred to no one to turn to him for help. He was back at the mill and under Ben's strict supervision and the guiding hand of the managers of each of the departments of the manufacture of cloth was shaping up at last but in no way could he be relied on. He was under his wife's thumb and always would be and to set him the task of finding Marguerite, or even of *helping* to find Marguerite was not even considered.

Ben did not try to stop his wife from accompanying him and neither did her mother try to stop her daughter from entering the house on West Beach, despite their differences.

Nancy Hayes was barely recognisable as the mature but still beautiful woman she had been before the death of her husband. With her two daughters and the kind support she had received from the friends she and Josh had made in Lytham, she had pulled together a life for herself and her daughters, totally unaware that one of them had fallen into the clutches of the man she hated, as she had hated his father, more than any other in the world. She had despised him, spurned him when her husband had brought him into the family and he had not forgotten, nor forgiven her. He probably blamed her for his uncle's actions in cutting him out of his will. This was his revenge, and his saving, for Marguerite would be a very wealthy young woman on her marriage.

It was when, as the twilight was falling, she had found Anna pacing her bedroom with constant stops to peer from the window that the story came out. It seemed Anna knew about Michael but had thought her sister would come to no harm, for, whenever they met, Anna had always been no more than yards away but somehow they had made their plans under her very nose and Marguerite had . . . had that afternoon simply not been there, where she should have been.

It proved unbelievably easy, so easy that they began to realise that a trail was being laid out for them to follow. They had questioned every cab driver who plied his trade from the railway station and even the horse-drawn family omnibus employed by the London and North Western Railway to transport families and their luggage to their lodgings or hotels on the promenade.

Yes, one cabbie said, after several hours of chasing two or three others on their fares about the town, he remembered the young lady and gentleman. Picked them up outside Lowther Park Gardens by prior arrangement with the gentleman. Toffs they were . . . oh, aye, no doubt about that. Yes, they took the train. Where to? Well, he'd heard the gentleman say they'd go first class to Preston. Oh, aye, in quite a loud voice, the cabbie thought, and Windermere would be lovely in this weather. Oh, aye, those were his very words.

He thanked Ben, his eyes goggling, for his generous tip and went home to report to his missis that he'd had the best day in years, what with one toff hiring him to hang about and wait to take him and his lady friend to the station and the other questioning him on the matter.

He had had her two days when they found them, for there was more than one hotel in Windermere and in the surrounding towns that were part of the Lake District. It was a time for holidays and everywhere was crowded, Lake Windermere a glorious wash of pleasure boats and sailing boats but it was not there that they were found.

They were in the bedroom Michael Hayes had taken, in the bed where he had kept her for two nights, Marguerite's eyes terrified, not only of the man who had used her like a whore but of her own sister and brother-in-law who would not want to know her now that she had been shamed. She had trusted him implicitly. Michael had told her time and time again that they would be married and though she had begged him to arrange it, as he had promised, before they . . . they . . . he had swept her off her feet and into the bed and, as he called it, made her his own! It was to have been a magical experience, for she loved him so much but he had hurt her and she had wept for her mother and he had been angry. He had asked her to prove her love for him and she had done so and still he had not been satisfied, cursing fluently when she had begged him not to make her do such dreadful things and please to take her home to her mother.

He sat up in the bed as Ben, who had bribed the porter

for the key, with Kitty beside him, entered the bedroom. Marguerite began to cry with the broken-hearted appeal of a child, doing her best to cover her nakedness which Michael seemed bent on displaying.

"Mr Maddox . . . and Mrs Maddox . . . how delightful." He grinned, reaching for a cigar from the box that stood on the table by the bedside.

"Mr Hayes," Ben answered him without expression. "And would this, by any chance, be Mrs Hayes?"

"You probably think she should be, Ben. If you and my sister would care to wait downstairs while we get dressed," running a possessive hand across Marguerite's trembling shoulder, "perhaps you and I could discuss it over a drink."

"I don't think there is any need for that, lad. It's straightforward enough. You have violated my sister-in-law."

"Oh, hardly that, sir." Michael smirked. "She came willingly."

"Believing you were to marry her?"

"Which I intend to, at the earliest possible moment. She is, after all, damaged goods and no use to any-one."

"Is that so?"

"It is definitely so, Ben."

"If you call me Ben once more I shall smash your teeth down your throat, but as it is I think I prefer to leave it to these two gentlemen I have brought with me for the purpose. Gentlemen . . ."

He stood aside and so did Kitty, and Michael Hayes

began to cry thinly, not exactly a scream for it was too weak and terrified for that, and while they began systematically to reduce him to bloody pulp, concentrating on his face which, after all, was his fortune, Kitty bundled the shocked and terrified Marguerite into the nearest clothes she could find and hurried her from the room.

Ben stayed to watch then told the men to stop. "We want to be able to get him to Liverpool without too much trouble. Give him a drop of this when he comes to and if anyone should enquire say that he is to be . . . married and has been celebrating."

"Wha' abou' 'is face, Mr Maddox?"

"Put your cap on him and keep the peak well down. When you get to Liverpool keep him somewhere handy until I get there. Understand?"

"Oh, aye, we do right enough, sor." They both winked, blowing on their bloody knuckles, the figure of Michael Hayes hanging, head down, between them.

"I'll see you right then, lads."

They took her home to her mother who, having experienced something similar in her own girlhood, was standing waiting in the doorway to receive her. Ben carried her and she hid her face in his shoulder, clinging to him with desperate, drowning hands as he took her up the stairs to the bed which her mother had prepared for her.

"Has she . . . ?" Nancy Hayes whispered to her son-in-law and he knew what she meant.

"I'm afraid so, but she's your daughter, Nancy," calling her by her Christian name for the first time. "She's strong and she'll mend."

"Shall . . . will she need to see a doctor?"

"Not at the moment. She's been through enough without another man . . . well, you will know what I mean?"

"What if she . . ."

"Let's wait and see. Give her a great deal of love, Nancy, and let her see she's not to blame. And remember, no one knows of this but you and Anna, Kitty and me."

"And him?"

"You'll not be troubled with him again. By this time next week he'll be on a boat to Australia."

"Thank God, and thank God for you, Ben Maddox. He was looking after us when he sent you into our lives."

"Now, Nancy, none of that. We'll be up to see you at the weekend and perhaps if you were to keep in touch with Kitty," letting her know she owed him a favour and he was mending a few fences that had been broken over the years. "We'll be anxious to hear if . . ."

She did not embrace her daughter, her eldest daughter who waited patiently in the drawing-room, but she took her hand as Kitty and Ben left. She was speechless, but telling her that this support in which Kitty had played a part would not be forgotten.

She sat quietly in the corner of the carriage on their

return journey to Liverpool, staring out of the window with unfocused gaze. He could see she was tired. There were huge dark stains beneath her eyes and she was pale. They had spent last night in a bedroom in a small hotel in Bowness, she in the bed, he on the sofa, barely speaking, but with a strange accord between them which said words weren't needed at this moment. He had listened to her light breathing – they had both discarded only their outer garments – which had deepened as she fell into whatever dreams she dreamed and he marvelled at the strange and silent harmony into which this adversity had plunged them. They had spoken of nothing but Marguerite and rescuing her from Michael Hayes's evil clutches but she seemed to have – what was the word, mellowed? – become softer in her distress for her sister and, yes, her mother who had turned away from her in her grief at the death of Josh Hayes. Was it because of the child she was carrying? Or the hurt done to Emma of whom she had made a friend despite her lowly station in life? Well, whatever it was it had made her more compassionate, more willing to put her own feelings aside and stand loyally and protectively next to those who needed her. He wanted to speak to her, get to know her, he supposed he meant, for he felt she was becoming a woman he would not only love, but a woman he would *like*.

Perhaps later, when she had slept in her own bed and been fussed over by Emma and the other servants, they might talk, bring something – what? – out into the open and from it build, if not the conventional marriage a firm rock on which the child could survive. He asked for no more than that from her.

Her voice from the opposite seat was quiet, calm, tranquil and he looked up from the newspaper he had been pretending to read.

"You know, don't you?"

"Know . . . ?"

"Ben, don't. You and I are strangers but I think, hope, that we have always been honest with one another."

"You have not been honest with me, Kitty."

"About your child, you mean." He felt a thrill of anticipation race through him and his heart gave a leap of excitement in his chest, for she was acknowledging it and, even more wonderful, was saying she did not mind.

"Yes. I . . . saw you last week with Emma. I wanted to . . . ask you but I felt you wanted to choose your own time to tell me. You *were* going to tell me, weren't you?" He smiled wryly, raising his eyebrows.

She returned his smile. "I could hardly escape it, could I?"

"No, not really. When will it be? Have you seen a doctor?"

"No, not yet and I should think . . . about the end of January."

"You must see a doctor as soon as we . . ."

She stiffened at once and her face lost that dreaming air of contemplation.

"Don't, please. Don't start ordering me about, or trying to. I won't have it, Ben. This child is mine."

"And mine, Kitty. But I'm sorry, I'm just concerned. The last time . . ."

"I know, but this time I promise I will take care."

"You are . . . not unhappy about it?"

"No . . . no."

He wanted to reach out for her hand which lay in her lap. It seemed to him, to his amazement, that she wished her hand to be taken but his nerve gave up on him, for he had just now almost sent her back into the stubbornness, the mutinous obstinacy she had shown at the beginning of their marriage. Don't rush it. Don't bloody rush it, his thumping heart told him and so he sat, smiling facetiously, he thought, and was relieved when she smiled back.

She looked away then but in his heart and in hers, though they did not recognise it, was a little tremor of something neither of them knew how to name.

She dined in her sitting-room that night but she sent word down to her husband, if he should be there, she added hastily to Tansy, that she was tired and would see him tomorrow, to which he had replied, through Tansy, that he quite understood and would look forward to it.

"Well, what do you make of that?" Tansy asked them triumphantly when she told them of it in the kitchen. Messages to one another now, where before they both did as they pleased and not a word to anyone. And, she hardly dare say this for, by God, she didn't want to tempt the fates or anything like that but had any of them noticed that Mrs Maddox was . . . was putting on a bit of weight?

"And what's that supposed to mean?" Mrs Pembroke, who did not see as much of the mistress as some of the others, asked in a scathing voice, but Tansy would not be put off.

"What d'you think, Clarrie?" she begged the housemaid. "You see her about the place an' doesn't it seem to you that she's . . . well, settled down. For a start she's not dashin' about as madly as she used to. In fact all she does is sit with Emma and walk the damn dog."

"Well, there you are then," Mrs Pembroke answered. "Perhaps that's why she's putting on a bit of weight. You remember how mad she used to be, never still for a minute at a time and anyway, what I'd like to know is when . . . well, when it happened, because as far as I'm aware and I'm sure one of you would have noticed it and told me, the master and mistress haven't shared a bed since Adam was a lad."

"Not here they haven't," Tansy answered mysteriously, tapping her nose and tossing her head.

"What you saying, girl?" Mrs Pembroke narrowed her eyes and thrust forward her chin aggressively as though she'd not have gossip in her kitchen, and if Mrs Ullett was around and not ensconsed in her own sitting-room, all this chatter would soon be put an end to.

"I'm saying that on the night her pa died . . ."

"Yes?"

"Well, p'raps I'd better say no more."

"No, perhaps you'd better not . . ." But they all had a faraway look in their eyes as they moved about the kitchen finishing off the jobs that needed doing before they could get to their beds.

Tansy had the last word though.

"Well, what I'd like to know is where they've been for the past couple o' days."

32

Ben sank back into the depths of the cab and put his right hand to his forehead, taking in it the weight of his head which was pounding with the fierceness of his painful emotions. He thought it was perhaps the worst hour he had ever spent, not counting the time when Kitty had miscarried their first child. He had imagined it a dozen times and rehearsed the words, stupidly, he knew, for how could he plan for what Helen might say? But it had still not been said as he would have wanted it to be said. He had wanted to spare her as much pain as he could, take it from her, let her see that circumstances had forced his hand, but he had merely ended up looking, at least in his own eyes, a monster.

She was calm, her exquisite face the colour of pipe clay, only her eyes alive and revealing her agony. She had known, even before he began to speak, for it was almost a week – he who had almost been living with her – since he had seen her. In a way she reminded him of Kitty and he marvelled at the strength women seemed to gather about them when their lives were at their lowest point. She did not weep, nor even show the depth of what he knew she was suffering, except in her eyes which some fool had said were the windows of the soul, but perhaps it was true, for hers were tormented. She kept her lips rigidly together and he had waited for her to speak, to reply in some way to the devastation he had just heaped on her. Thank God she had not yet sold her house, he remembered saying to himself and was instantly contrite. He loved her, he could not deny that but she was not the woman he loved and though that sounded foolish and contrary, he himself knew what he meant.

At last she spoke. "I knew she loved you when we saw her at Aintree."

He stared at her incredulously. Knowing her as he did he had been aware that she would not create a scene, call him a bastard, beg him to stay or do any of the things a discarded woman has been known to do, but the words she spoke were the last he had expected to hear.

"I don't understand. She may be having my child but she does not love me, Helen. She never has."

"I saw her face when you weren't looking. No one was looking and when I turned she was watching you. She was jealous. She hated me . . ."

"No. No, that's not true, Helen." He had not called her "darling" or "dearest" since he arrived and not only did she notice it, but so did he.

She shrugged her shoulders and smiled a little. "Men are blind sometimes but a woman can see what is in another woman. She would not have let you . . . make love to her, which I presume you must have done to get her with child, if she had not loved you. It is yours, I suppose." She was not being cruel, just asking a question, for Kitty Maddox's life in the past had not been known for its moral probity.

"Yes, it's mine."

"How do you know?"

"I know . . . when it was conceived. And I know Kitty. She may have been wild, reckless, headstrong but she was always honest."

"So, not only does your Kitty love you, you love your Kitty."

"Helen, really, you do say the most curious things." He was aghast, he didn't know quite why. Was it at the idea that Kitty loved him, or that Helen knew he loved Kitty? God almighty, what a bloody mix-up life was. He had been prepared . . . should he say *resigned* to settling down with Helen, who was the sweetest-natured woman he had ever known and with whom his life would have been even-tenored, comfortable, with no storms, no arguments, no hot-headed statements that she would have her own way on this or that and . . . Dear God, where was his mind going? What was he thinking about this lovely woman to whom he had just dealt the worst, most cowardly blow a man can deliver to a woman. There was not another thing he could do, he knew that. The child must come first and Helen would understand that but, by God, it was difficult, and try as he might he could think of no way to soften what he was doing to her.

"Is there anything . . . ?"

"Of course not, Ben. You must, naturally, stay with the mother of your child. I shall go and spend a few weeks with my sister in Buxton."

"When you return may I call to see that . . ."

Her voice rose dangerously. "No. Dear God, no. I have loved you, Ben. I still love you, for it is not always possible to turn one's feelings on and off like a tap."

"Helen," he said wretchedly. "I must know that you are . . . all right. I cannot just cut you out of my life without a backward glance."

She softened. "You must; you must! Please go, Ben. You're a good man, a kind man, a decent man who—"

"Stop it, Helen. I'm none of those things."

"You just . . . love the woman you married?"

He bent his head. "Yes."

The cab drew up at the front door and he walked slowly up the steps to where Tansy bobbed and beamed and took his hat.

"The mistress is in . . . in the nursery, sir," her smile growing even broader, for by now it was official that Mrs Maddox was with child.

"Is she alone?"

"I believe so, sir. Emma is resting." She almost pulled a face, as children do when something amuses them, for who would have thought that a servant, the mistress's personal maid, should be treated as though she were a lady, a lady carrying her first child. Mrs Maddox fussed over her, making light of her own pregnancy, insisting that she rest, that Mrs Pembroke make her light, nourishing, inviting dishes to keep her strength up just as though Emma were not a countrywoman, strong and healthy and perfectly capable of bearing a child any day of the week. The pair of them had been up in what they were calling the nursery for the past week, ever since it had come to light that the mistress was also to have a child, directing painters and needle-women and scrubbing women, consulting books on colours and wallpapers, furniture, which was to be of plain, simple polished wood, layettes, toys, books, high chairs, cradles and even perambulators of which they would need two. In fact two of everything, for it seemed the mistress's child and the servant's child were to be brought up together, would you believe? They could scarcely manage it but knowing their mistress as they did by now, if she said it was so, it was so!

She was sitting on the window seat, her knees drawn up to her chest, her back against the frame and Henry lay against her, his eyes glazed with content as she rubbed his ears. She turned as he entered, evidently expecting someone else, for her eyes, which had been bright with dreams, became guarded. They had been polite with one another, pleasant even when the past was considered, during the past week or so, both of them doing their best to begin the process of making a home, a secure and happy home for their child but it was not easy. In his way he was grieving for Helen, not for *her* exactly but for what she was suffering and it would take him a long time to rid himself of the feeling that he had behaved badly.

He began at once, for if there was to be anything between them it must be truth.

"I have just come from Helen Bedford. I told her you were to have a child and that she and I . . . must part."

She made no movement. Her hand still continued to fondle the dog's ears but there was a kind of frozen inflexibility in her posture, though she had not moved, nor did she speak.

"You know who I mean?" Though he had not intended it to, his voice was as stiff as her back.

"Your mistress?" Her voice was light, cool, as though it really were of no importance to her.

"She was. Kitty, I must tell you—"

"You have no need to tell me anything, Ben. You have no need to give her up, if that's what you're saying. Your life is your own."

"Kitty, don't. Surely we are both to make an effort to give our child a normal happy childhood. A safe childhood with its mother and father in it, a conventional childhood with two loving parents. The child is not to blame for anything you and I have done."

She slowly relaxed, turning away to stare out of the window to the garden below where Wilf and his two lads were cutting the lawn. The window was open and she could smell the sharp, pleasant fragrance of the cuttings which George was carefully raking into tidy heaps. The second lad, she thought his name was Joey, was being allowed to cut the edges of the lawn, under Wilf's strict supervision, of course, and their voices drifted up to her, along with the scent of the smoke from Wilf's pipe, peaceful and calm, a perfect setting in which a child might be free to grow up in the security that was its right. Grow up loved and protected. The beds that surrounded the lawns and ran in a ribbon of colour down the drive to the front gates were so lovely, so vividly aflame they almost hurt the eye. Sweet William which would finish soon, she had been told by Wilf, a riot of vivid colour from pink, magenta, crimson, scarlet and white, standing beside dahlias, in the same rainbow shades, their pom-poms moving gently in the slight breeze. There were phlox swaying beside late delphiniums and when they had cut the lawn, she heard Wilf say, the lads could set to and hoe the beds.

"What do you wish me to say, Ben? That I agree with you, is that what you want? That I understand why you took a mistress and why you are now to give her up?" For a brief moment the lovely face that had gazed adoringly up into Ben's at the races flashed before her eyes and she winced. He saw it and moved a step or two towards her, wanting to touch her, take her hand, tell her that . . . what? That Helen was . . . Oh, Jesus, this was hard and going to be harder if they could not find some common ground on which to build their lives.

"She . . . loved you. I saw it when—"

Before he could stop himself he said, "Those were the very words she used."

She turned to him sharply. "What?" Her eyes were cold and expressionless and he knew that Helen had been wrong.

"I'm sorry, there was a misunderstanding but . . . well, I wanted you to know that she and I are . . . that I mean to . . ."

"Yes?"

"Be whatever you need me to be."

"I see." But in her heart she didn't. What *was* he saying? She knew he was doing his best to let her know that he would no longer be the . . . well, she supposed it could be called "man about town" that he had been while she had been gallivanting about with the Olivers. That they were to give the appearance of a "couple". Their baby must be born into what *looked* like a happy marriage and if she was willing to work at it so was he.

"Do you . . . will you . . . Can you agree that we might try?" He was awkward, she wondered why, but really, did it matter? She didn't even know how she felt about him giving up his mistress, since it was not for her that he was doing it but for the child.

She stood up and was surprised when he took her arm to help her. His hand was warm, firm and a ripple of something lovely moved through her. She felt her throat tighten with tears, which she seemed to shed easily these days for no reason at all, but she fought them down, keeping her voice cool, but pleasant.

"Thank you. Now I must go and see if Emma is awake. She seems to tire easily."

"You should rest more yourself, Kitty. Emma is not the only one to be carrying a child."

"I'm fine, Ben. Besides, Emma is further along than I am and her child was not conceived as ours was."

He felt his heart jump and bent to look into her face.

"What does that mean, Kitty? That though Emma was taken against her will, you weren't."

"You know perfectly well what it means," she answered huffily, flustered since it seemed she had said more than she meant to.

He did not press her though he would dearly have liked to continue the conversation. He sighed. "Very well. Now then, may we dine together this evening, if you're not too tired?"

"Let's wait and see, shall we?"

"Of course."

The days drifted by most pleasantly, as they both made the effort needed, not to bring about a reconciliation, which seemed an impossibility, but at least to live under the same roof in harmony. They dined together several nights a week, though Kitty continued to share Emma's evening meal on occasion. Strangely, they found a great deal to talk about. The newspapers and every prominent politician were demanding an expedition to Khartoum where Sir Henry Gordon was besieged and both of them were following the progress of events with keen interest. There was unrest in Britain and a demonstration had taken place in Hyde Park consisting of some thirty thousand artisans and labourers, who marched in orderly fashion and on entering the park demanded universal suffrage. Kitty questioned Ben on his views, for should men who owned no property have the vote and, more provocative still, did he consider women, some of whom were asking for it, should be included in this universal suffrage?

The servants who waited on them often reported back to the kitchen that the master and mistress were going at it ding-dong again but they were not overly concerned, for it was only about "them damn politicals" which both of them seemed to find extremely absorbing. At least they were sitting down together at the same table, though – and this was whispered where Mrs Ullett couldn't overhear – they were not yet sharing a bedroom.

Kitty and her mother exchanged cautious letters, in one of which Nancy conveyed to her without actually using the words, that Marguerite was not to suffer any long-lasting consequences from her ordeal.

"Thank God," Ben said, putting his hand to his forehead. "I would never have forgiven myself if she had a child. She is only a child herself and will get over what happened, but to bear that bastard's baby would have . . ."

She was strangely moved, wondering why this man seemed to feel such pain on others' behalf, like Marguerite, like her father and mother in the past, like Emma who would, she knew quite clearly, never again be the same cheerful young woman she once had been, and yet he showed no emotion, no feelings, nothing that could be called anything other than a father's concern for his unborn child, and nothing for her who was to bear that child.

"Ben, she is all right. You must not take it on yourself to . . . to bear everyone's burdens. She will marry. Oh, yes, Mother says that she is to sell the house in Lytham and find herself and the girls something in Alderley Edge. Apparently the prospects are better there for a good marriage for both of them. The servants at Lytham are not quite to be trusted, she thinks, since they knew something was up when Marguerite vanished and then you and I brought her back from wherever she had been. And then there is Sebastian. He is fourteen now and when he comes home in the school holidays Lytham will not really be convenient. Later, if he goes into the mill he will need a home close by, she says. Now promise me you won't go chasing about all over the place looking for a house for her. Surely Freddy could help her there? She will stay at Riverside while she looks about and you have enough to do with your business and with the mill, since in my opinion Freddy will never be any use. Really, sometimes I don't know . . ."

Ben looked up in amazement, then smiled. "Kitty, I do believe you are worried about me. Worried that I might be 'put upon' by your mother and the rest of your family."

"Don't be ridiculous, Ben. It's just that you have enough on your plate with . . ."

"With you," he answered gently, "and the family we are to start."

She reared up but he could see she was not really offended. "The family! God almighty, let's get this one born before you start talking about another." She was smiling, her eyes cast down and for an ecstatic moment he allowed himself to believe that perhaps, when the baby came, and she took a liking to it, there might be others. But she was so touchy he must move slowly, gently, allow her to become accustomed to this rather pleasant way of life they had taken up together.

The hot weather of the summer came to an end as August moved into September, and then to October. Though they still walked every day in the gardens and the woods Emma's body was so grotesquely swollen it was difficult to believe that she still had weeks to endure. She was more and more out of breath and Kitty worried about her. Her own health was superb and when Emma was reluctant to walk out in the autumn winds that came with November Ben began to take her place, striding out with Kitty, doing his best to make her slow down, since she herself was in her seventh month. The days were cold now but with bright sunshine which put pink poppies in the cheeks of his wife. The leaves were gone from the branches, spreading thickly on the ground, gold and brown and flame and she kicked them like a child, laughing at Henry's antics as he tried to chase ones that flew into the air. Only the oaks still had some foliage and were all shades of bronze and brown, and the hedges that bordered the lanes glowed with the golden tints of nut leaves. The delicious autumn scent of burning leaves filled the air as Wilf and George and Joey cleared up the garden, the two lads, as lads will, larking about until Wilf called them to order. Pale yellow fronds of bracken grew among the dark bramble leaves under the great trees and, as they jumped a small stream, Ben held out a hand to Kitty and when they arrived safely at the other side she let him keep it. A thrush was singing its head off in the branches of a big beech tree and she let herself believe she was beginning to be happy.

They were both smiling, saying little when they got back to the house and for a moment, Clarrie was to tell the others afterwards, she felt a wave of joy surge through her before she spoke to Mrs Maddox.

"Oh, madam . . . Emma is . . . Mrs Ullett's taken it upon herself to call the doctor." She looked in an embarrassed fashion at the master, then whispered hastily, "She's bleeding, madam and . . ."

Without removing her coat and woollen tam-o'-shanter, or her muddy boots, Kitty began to race for the stairs, going up them two at a time, her face suddenly ashen. Emma's child was not due for another month.

"Kitty, darling . . . take it easy. Don't run like that." Ben was behind her, ready to catch her should she fall, or indeed do, or be anything she might need, his whole being concentrated, not on Emma's child but on his own and the woman who was to bear it.

"The doctor's with her, madam," Clarrie shouted up the stairs after her, protocol thrown to the winds, "and Tansy's there," wishing to comfort, for there was nobody like Tansy in an emergency.

Ben stopped at the door of Emma's room, for childbirth, especially if it was someone else's child, was not for gentlemen. Now if it had been Kitty nothing on God's earth would have kept him out but when Kitty shut the door in his face he sighed and turned away, making his way downstairs again where Clarrie hung about, ready to be tearful.

"Fetch me a brandy, there's a good girl," he murmured. "I'll be in my study."

Emma's pains had begun at almost the moment Kitty and Ben had walked off along the path to the woodland, Tansy whispered to her mistress and she was not to worry, for Emma was a strong woman. Hot water was simmering in readiness for Kitty knew not what; the nurse who was to look after not only Emma but herself when her time came had been sent for; and the doctor seemed to have settled himself down to wait, saying to Mrs Maddox, and to Mrs Maddox's husband who hung about at the bedroom door, that as this was a first confinement it might be somewhat protracted. Yes, the pains were coming very quickly, and yes, he did not care for the bleeding but Mr Maddox was not to worry, wondering, as he comforted the man, why indeed Mr Maddox *should* worry.

"I insist that my wife comes out of there, Doctor."

"Mr Maddox, if you can get your wife out of there I should be eternally grateful, since a woman in her condition should not be witness to . . . to what the mother is suffering, but she takes no notice of me, sir. You are welcome to go in and demand she leaves. Don't worry, the . . . mother," since he had no idea what to call the labouring woman as she was not married, "will not notice. She is resting."

Emma was in labour for the whole of that day, the whole of the night, the next day and the next night which was not unusual, the doctor continued to maintain.

By the second morning Emma's pains were so rapid and so severe she could scarcely draw breath between them and Kitty, who looked like a scarecrow, gaunt and falling apart, her eyes sunken, begged the doctor to give her something to ease the pain.

"Mrs Maddox, this is one job that can't be done without a degree of pain."

"*A degree of pain*," she hissed. "She is in agony and I demand you give her something."

Emma lay for an hour or two in a drugged sleep, whimpering a little and even though Ben came to the bedside and, staring in horror at what his wife had become, did his best to lift her up and carry her from the room, she would not allow it, struggling frantically in his grasp.

"I must be here when she wakes," she whispered through dry lips.

"Darling, please, the doctor will tell you when that is. Come and lie down for a moment or two. Please, for God's sake, Kitty, come with me."

"Take your hands off me, Ben, unless you mean to

drag me and then I shall scream since Emma cannot hear me."

Emma's daughter was born an hour later and was at once put into Kitty's waiting arms though Doctor Croxley had expressly ordered her out of the room as the child was born.

"Take her away from here, Mr Maddox, and at once, or I shall not be responsible for my actions. This is not the place for her now." And with these words Ben Maddox was made aware that Emma, though her child would live, would not.

The baby who, when she lifted her long, fine lashes looked at Kitty with Tam Oliver's eyes, was placed in the arms of a nurse and whisked off to the nursery where a wet nurse was waiting, where a pretty bassinet was waiting, where everything a child might need, even a child born of royalty, was waiting for her. And in the room below it, Ben Maddox undressed his almost unconscious wife and then himself and wrapped them both in the warmth of her bed, leaving instructions that they were not to be disturbed until he rang. She slept for twelve hours in his arms while he agonised on how to tell her that Emma was dead, but when she awoke, finding herself in her husband's arms, she knew.

She began to weep, to jerk about in his grasp and under his hands he felt the strong movement of his own child as it squirmed in what seemed to be vast annoyance in her distended belly. Please God, let her be all right. Don't let her go the same way as Emma. Keep her safe and her child, he prayed, as he did his best to calm her. I couldn't bear it if I lost her, not now when it seems we are to find one another again. Please God . . . Please God, make them safe. Make *her* safe, for she is more to me than my own life. It seemed, for the moment, God listened but then Kitty's time had not yet come.

They buried Emma a week later and though they had not approved of her since most of them secretly believed it was not possible to rape a woman, that *they* would have put up more of a fight, they all went to her funeral. Mrs Maddox was inconsolable and you could see Mr Maddox was out of his mind, for might it not damage the health of his own child, not to mention Mrs Maddox? When they returned to the house the servants were not surprised when she went at once up to the nursery where, for the past week, she had spent most of her time nursing Emma Taylor's daughter

33

She sat for hours, the baby in her arms, and the only time they could get her to part with Emma's child was when she was passed to the wet nurse to be fed. Then she allowed herself to be led away to be bathed, changed, swallow the food that they put in front of her, which she did obediently though it was obvious she had no idea what she ate. She even, to their horror and to the master's too, they could all see that, insisted that the child sleep in her room. The cradle must be placed next to her bed and if she needed anyone she would ring her bell, she told them quietly and, remembering her waywardness in the past, they let her have her way.

She spoke little to anyone, even the master, except on the subject of the child and they could see that Mr Maddox was not only worried out of his mind at what it might be doing to her health and the health of the unborn child, but was becoming somewhat impatient. He hadn't been out of the house since the birth of the child, sending urgent notes and telegraphs every few hours to his place of business and to the mill in Manchester, receiving responses which he replied to, and Tim or John were run off their feet dashing here and there, to the post office, the master's place of business and even to the docks and the ships' captains with whom their master dealt.

He did his best, poor chap, spending time with Mrs Maddox in the nursery after sending the wet nurse away, and the nursery nurse employed to look after the child – who had done nothing but sit on her backside all day – or so Tansy reported. Well, what else was the poor woman to do, since Mrs Maddox wouldn't even let her bathe the infant?

Every time Tansy, who had been told by the master that she was to look after her mistress, came downstairs to the kitchens she shook her head sadly as the others clustered round her, begging for news of the mistress who seemed to have lost her mind.

"She'll not part with that bairn no matter what anyone says and her to have her own in a few weeks. She flies off the handle if anyone so much as suggests she lets that nurse see to the child and the master isn't going to put up with it much longer. I can see the signs."

She became thinner, fine-drawn. She did not weep and Tansy was of the opinion, telling the others so, that she'd be better if she did. It really was beyond understanding that a woman, a lady, should go into a decline over the death of her maid, but that was what was happening and if something wasn't done about it, and soon, she couldn't bear to think what was to become of them all, though they did not quite understand this last remark. The mistress needed all her strength to get through her own coming ordeal, she went on, and it was doing her no good sitting about fretting. She had always been such a live wire, causing them all no end of bother with her tantrums and headstrong ways but, by God, they wished they could get them back again, those stormy days.

To their vast relief it seemed the master thought so too. He strode into the nursery when the baby was ten days old and sent them all packing and as Tansy closed the door behind her she saw him squat down on his haunches at his wife's feet.

"Kitty, this won't do at all, you know. You cannot just sit here day after day nursing the infant. It's not good for you, nor, I'm sure, is it good for the child. You need to get out and take a walk, and so does she. Neither of you have been out of the house since Emma died and though I know you are grieving you must think of yourself and *our* child."

He waited and was rewarded by a slow lifting of Kitty's head from her deep contemplation of the baby. He waited again but Kitty said nothing and he tutted impatiently, for really, this was going too far; but at the same time his heart contracted in pain, a shared pain, for his love for this woman was deep and enduring.

She studied him for a moment as though not awfully sure who he was or what he wanted with her, then slowly bent her head, looking once more into the baby's face.

She was a lovely child, he couldn't deny that. She had her mother's colouring, a cap of dark flat curls about her neat head. Her cheeks were plump and pink, like a ripe peach, and her eyelashes were long, fine and the colour of charcoal, as were her delicately arched eyebrows. She had a newborn's blob of a nose above pursed and sucking rosy lips and her hands, which rested placidly outside the lacy shawl wrapped about her, were small, like starfish. As he watched one of them jerked convulsively, the fingers spreading against the wool, then she was still again, perfectly content, it seemed, to spend the rest of her baby days in the safe arms of Kitty Maddox.

It wouldn't do, of course, and Kitty must be made to see it.

He spoke directly into Kitty's face, bending his head, trying to look into her eyes.

"You can't go on like this, Kitty. You'll damage your own health if you do. Won't you come for a walk in the garden with me? We can talk. It's cold, there was sharp frost last night" – which of course, Kitty had not noticed – "so you must wrap up warm. See, give me the baby and I'll call the nurse. Tansy will help you and when you're dressed we'll collect Henry, who is pining for you, by the way, and walk down to the lake. I believe it is frozen, so Wilf told me, and the ducks are making a great fuss trying to skate. Come, darling, let me help you up."

Kitty looked up and something moved in her eyes and she wet her lips with her tongue as though she were about to speak.

"I can't."

"Of course you can. You're the strongest woman I ever knew and you know Emma wouldn't want to think of you brooding over her like this. She would want you to get on with your life . . . your child."

"And hers."

"I beg your pardon?" He frowned suddenly.

"Her child. She must have a life. Emma's was taken but this . . . I shall call her Emma."

"You can't give her a name, sweetheart." The caution he had always maintained up to the time of Emma's death was thrown to the wind and his natural need to call her the endearments that were in his heart for her slipped quite easily from between his lips.

"Why not . . . why not? She must have a name, Ben, and I think Emma would like it if we called her daughter after her."

"But her parents might want to call her something else. Not that it matters, I suppose, since she won't know the difference at her age. Come, darling, hand her to me and . . ."

The brain in Kitty Maddox's head which had lived in a fog of grief and guilt for the past ten days began to clear and the words Ben had spoken shone through that fog, bright and sharp, like a lamp being turned up in a darkened room. Her mind, her thoughts, which were not really thoughts at all, but small pictures, images flashing on and off, came to life and Ben's words with them.

Her arms closed protectively about the small body so that the baby began to wriggle in protest.

"Let me take her, Kitty. I'll put her in her crib."

"No, she must stay here with me. I shall be her mother now that Emma is gone."

"She will have a new mother, darling, one who will love her as much as Emma would have done, and a father, too, which she wouldn't have . . ."

"I don't understand. Please, what are you saying?"

"That she will be happy in her new home, happy and well loved."

"Don't you touch her, you bastard, and don't touch me." Her eyes, which had been a dull, flat blue, almost the colour of the sky at night, sprang to vivid sapphire as her understanding, and madness, grew. "Get out. Go on, get out or I swear I'll take your eyes from your head. How dare you. *How dare you.* If you are saying what I think you're saying, then let me tell you I shall never part with this child, ever. She is all that I have left of Emma and she will stay with me."

"Don't talk nonsense, Kitty." Ben's face was as hard as a rock and his mouth was inclined to snarl with temper, for how could she be so . . . so insane. She was to have a child herself soon and yet here she was telling him she was about to keep the illegitimate child of one of her servants, bring it up, presumably with *their* child; but before he could finish his train of thought and get to his feet she kicked out at him, her foot catching him in his genitals. He fell back on the floor, clutching at the agony, the fire that raced through him, his face contorted, not only with the worst pain a man can know but with an explosive rage. Why in hell was she so intent on keeping this child, the child of Emma Taylor and Tam Oliver? In the midst of his outraged manhood and furious anger, the thought meandered, small, dangerous, insidious, through his inflamed mind, like some worm that was eating at his flesh and he could not stand the jealous devastation. He did not know Tam Oliver, not personally, and had only seen him at a distance, at the races, and at other functions they had both attended, so was this child like him? Did she have a look of the Olivers with whom Kitty had been so friendly last year and the beginning of this? Did Emma's child bring back to Kitty the face of the man who had fathered her and if that was the case was that why she . . . ? Oh, God, he couldn't stand the thought. Was she . . . Did she . . . Somehow he lost the thread of what he was thinking, his mind was so stunned at something that hid there.

She had drawn right back in the chair, the infant, who was wailing in distress, clutched tightly to her breast and when he leaped to his feet, roaring at something he did not care to contemplate, she cowered away from him, her face like a skull, her terrified eyes sunk in dark circles, her cheekbones standing out in such a way they looked as though they might pierce her flesh.

She had no time to set herself, for she believed that Ben, even in his rage, would offer no harm to the child, so that when he reached out and wrenched the small body from her arms she was taken totally by surprise. The baby began to scream and so did she and on the landing where she loitered Tansy muttered that she was not having this and began to run towards the stairs that led to the nursery floor.

"Give her to me, Ben. Please, don't hurt her. She has done nothing, don't hurt her," Kitty shrieked, making a decent effort to control herself for the baby's sake. The baby hiccuped against Ben's shoulder, her face red with outrage and when Tansy burst into the room, her face as white as her freshly washed and ironed apron, neither of them noticed her, nor the two women who were at her back.

"I don't intend to hurt her, Kitty, nor you, though really I feel like . . . but that doesn't matter. I have found a decent home for the child. A couple who have no family, good people. I have had them carefully checked so there is no need for you to—"

"No, no. I won't let her go. I love her."

"Stop it, Kitty. She is not your child. She is to go to . . . her own people. The man is a master stonemason with a good position—"

"You unfeeling, evil, callous bastard. Dear God, I thought Tam Oliver was the lowest thing that ever crawled out from under a stone but I see I was wrong."

"So, we are getting to the true reason, are we, for this attachment you have formed for this child? *His* child. Well, perhaps when he hears that she is to go back to her own sort . . ."

For a moment her face took on an expression of total incomprehension. She frowned as though she were doing her best to unravel his words, make sense of them, then her face twisted with loathing, whether for him, or for Tam Oliver, she didn't know herself; she only knew she would make this man pay for what he was doing to her.

"Are you saying that there was something between me and Tam Oliver and that is why I want to keep his child?" Her voice was low now, cold and hating. "So it's jealousy that's driving you then." Though why Ben Maddox should be jealous was a mystery to her, for one had to love to be jealous and Ben certainly didn't love her or he would not be doing this cruel thing to her.

"Don't be absurd. Why do you always twist everything about. I have merely arranged for the child to return to her roots."

"Her roots!" Kitty's voice rose to a thin scream and the women at the door cowered back in horror. "You are saying that she is to be brought up as a working-class child since her mother came from the working classes. I can't believe this. Dear God, after all that happened to Emma you are simply to hand over her child to strangers."

"We are strangers to the infant so—"

"This could have been my child, Ben. If Tam Oliver had got me instead of Emma this would have been my child. It was me he wanted, not Emma, but she bore the consequences. Don't you think that gives me the right to bring up her daughter as though she were mine?"

"Oh, please, Mr Maddox," a voice from the doorway said tremulously though neither of them turned towards it. "Please, give me the bairn. Let me take her."

"No one is to take her and if they do it is over my dead body. Put her in her crib, Ben, and then get out. Get out of this room and out of my life. I cannot bear to see you again."

"Don't be absurd," he said again, though less forcefully. "You cannot be alone just now. The baby . . ."

"I can have this baby without your help, Ben Maddox, since I presume you are referring to *your* child. Or do you perhaps think that this is Tam Oliver's as well?"

"No. Good God, no."

"Give me Emma's child then, or hand her to Tansy. I shall leave here today."

"Sweet Jesus, I didn't mean . . ."

"I don't think you know what you mean, Ben. I don't think you know much about anything when it comes to your wife. I loved Emma as if she were my sister and I would no more think of sending her child off to live with strangers than I would my own child when it is born. But I find I cannot live here with you any more. I want some peace. I thought that . . . you and I were to . . ."

"We are, Kitty, but with our own child, not Emma's. We cannot bring up Emma's child with our own, can you not see that?"

"No, I'm afraid I can't." She moved forward and with infinite tenderness took the baby from his arms and he allowed it. He passed a hand across his face as though cobwebs of doubt, of fear, of something that terrified him, were drifting against his flesh, then moved like a marionette towards the door, his arms and legs jerking awkwardly. The three women stood aside for him.

"Pack my bags, Tansy, and the baby's and tell Tim I shall need the carriage."

"Yes, madam, but where . . ."

"You shall come with me, and the nurse." She smiled down into the face of the child. "And of course, so shall Emma Maddox. My mother is at Riverside House and Elm Cottage in Lytham has not, as yet, been sold. We shall go there. I'm sure my mother will not mind." Nor care, she thought, for when had Nancy Hayes ever cared what Kitty Maddox did.

She was herself again. She had thrown off the dark cloud of her grief, though she would always feel sorrow for Emma. She would do what she could for her dead friend in the only way she knew how and she would do it alone. She was alert, incisive as she gave orders to Tansy, to the wet nurse, to the nursery nurse who were to go with her.

The man who crouched in his study with the curtains half drawn heard her go. His face was impassive but inside him everything was breaking up, bleeding, draining the life out of him, for he could not contemplate a life without her in it.

His son was born three weeks later. Surprisingly, the first person Kitty saw after the birth, though her boy was no more than a few hours old, was her mother.

"Mother!" She sat up in her bed, much to the annoyance of the nurse who was employed to look after her for the three weeks she would spend there. Three weeks and not a foot to the floor and here was Mrs Maddox throwing herself about like a fool. The birth had been easy, even she had to admit that, just to herself, of course, since she must keep a sense of her own importance, and Mrs Maddox was already on the road to recovery, which was somewhat strange, for ladies of her sort were delicate creatures. She knew nothing of Kitty's antecedents, who had been peasants and weavers, good country stock, nor that her patient had inherited their strength.

"Yes, I thought I had better come and give you some support, though I doubt it is you who needs it. I have brought Ben with me and he is eager to see his son."

Kitty's face hardened but only for a moment, then she sighed.

"Mother, this is not your concern."

"Is it not? I think I am the only one who can speak with any authority on the subject. We had three illegitimate children in our family, four if you count the bastard who is, I hope, working like a convict in Australia, and I think we . . . I . . . managed it very well. Freddy, you, Ciara, and though Freddy and Ciara are not much to write home about, you turned out all right and I told Ben Maddox so."

"Mother!" Kitty could say no more in her amazement. Her mother, who had always seemed aloof and uncaring, taking up for her, praising her and as she marvelled at it something inside her softened and broke up, vanishing into the past. She held out her hand and her mother took it, kissing the back of it in the most extraordinary way. She shook herself briskly, then turned away to hide what might have been tears in her eyes.

"Now then, where is my grandson? My first grandchild. I just want to check him out to make sure he does not look like . . . his grandfather."

"And if he does?"

"He has you and Ben in him and that's good enough for me."

"What am I to do about Ben, Mother?" Kitty asked, beginning to believe she might enjoy this friendship her mother was offering her.

"Ben is not my concern, Kitty, but I think you must see him. And you must have your answer ready to the question he is going to ask you."

"Question? Answer?"

"Don't be silly, dear. Shall I send him up?"

He strode into the room with the imperious movement of a king bestowing a favour on a milkmaid.

"I have a son, I believe."

"You have and if you're to take that damned attitude then you can go to hell."

"Dear God, are we never to—" He clamped his lips together, standing, she could see it now, nervously in the centre of the room, his eyes straying to the cradle by the window.

"Well, I suppose you'd better have a look though he is still somewhat crumpled," she said casually.

He tiptoed across the room and peered uncertainly into the cradle and she watched him, watched his face turn from a worried speculation to a slow smile of recognition.

"My son . . ."

"Yes, I said so, didn't I?"

"Can I . . . ? Bloody hell, I have no need to ask, he is my son after all." He leaned forward into the cradle and picked up the sleeping child, studying his face with a smile of wonder, of love, of approval, of pride, then turned to her. "I can't see why you called him crumpled. He is quite the handsomest boy I have ever seen."

"And how many is that?"

"Well . . . I couldn't say."

"He has your eyes and ears."

"Poor little sod." But the fatuous smile remained.

She allowed it for several minutes, then, her voice quite without expression said, "Emma is doing well. You would hardly know her."

For a long moment his face looked bewildered, then he walked towards her, still holding his son in his arms.

"I must go and . . . renew our acquaintance."

"Thank you, Ben."

"I was unfeeling."

"Yes, you were but perhaps now . . ."

"There is no question of it. She is this chap's sister."

Nothing more was said for a few moments and she studied his face as he looked down into his son's.

"Why did you come, apart from the child?"

Carefully he laid the baby in his cradle then moved slowly across the room towards her, his face suddenly haggard.

"Can't you guess?"

"I must hear the words, Ben, and soon. We are . . ."

"I love you, Kitty. Do you love me?"

"Yes."

"That's good."

It seemed that neither of them knew what to do or say next. They had spent years hiding their love for one another, fighting, arguing, sometimes making love, sometimes making war and now, here they were at a place where both of them longed to be and both were tongue-tied.

"Would you have come back to me, with our son, or did you mean to keep him from me?"

She was shocked. "Oh, no, Ben, he is . . . he belongs to you as much as he does to me and I would not have kept him from you."

"You would have lived with me?"

"Aah, I don't know about that." Suddenly her throat was tight with tears and seeing her distress he sat down on the bed and took her hand.

"Even though . . . you loved me."

"If there was nothing . . . if you had nothing for me . . . I don't know."

"I have wanted to please you, cherish you, for as long

as I can remember. You didn't know that, did you? From that first time I saw you at the ball and you were tapping your foot impatiently since you wanted Freddy to notice you and—"

"Why did I not see you?"

"Because your eyes were full of Freddy. When he chose Ciara that was my chance and I seized it, thinking I would make you love me but . . . you went your own way, as always."

"Just as I always will, I suppose."

"I suppose so but . . . will you always do it within sight of me? I don't think I can manage without you, you see, and if you continue to look at me like that I shall have no option but to put my arms about you . . ."

"Please do."

Bemused and tremulous they put their arms about one another, both of them so unaccustomed to the pure joy of being in complete agreement it threatened to take control of them.

"If you had not just had a child and if I was in perfect working order, which I doubt after that kick you landed on my private parts I swear I would climb into bed with you and make you pregnant again."

"You could try." He could feel her smile of enchantment against his neck where she nuzzled her mouth. A sudden burst of sunshine seemed to fill the room and they pulled apart for a moment to look wonderingly into one another's face.

"The nurse would have a fit."

"To the devil with the nurse. Take off your things and

come lie with me. I'm afraid I cannot . . . accommodate you, my darling, not yet, but I would be glad of your arms about me for a while."

"You will take me as a true husband, then, Kitty Maddox?"

"I will."

"As lover, in due season," smiling down into her face, "and as friend."

"I will."

"You will trust me."

"I always have, Ben Maddox. I don't know why."

"Well, that seems a good enough start."

When the nurse came to tell Mr Maddox that really his wife needed her rest and might she suggest he leave her alone until morning, she found Mr and Mrs Maddox sleeping peacefully in one another's arms.